- Djuna: searching for her purpose in life and for love, she is overwhelmed by her new responsibilities

- Jean-Auguste: Djuna's husband and manager of her winery; his handsome courtliness hides cruelty and disloyalty

- Naravine: beautiful mixed-blood fashion model who loves not wisely but very well

- Joaquím Carlos: Djuna's grandfather; a man of tremendous appetites—for women, for wine, for great art

- Sylvie: Joaquím Carlos's Jewish wife, a woman drowning in the success she once hoped for

- Pascal: a poet; she was Joaquím Carlos's last great love, a love never consummated and all the stronger for it

"Richly textured . . . readers can admire the villas' vistas or smell the air. Robbins's knack for physical descriptions conveys the opium languor of Carlos's wife, the cuddly plumpness of baby Emlle, the skeletal haughtiness of Princess Mitya on her deathbed . . . like the contents of an elegant storage box, full of menus, maps, jotted notes, portraits, postcards, and family snapshots." —*Publishers Weekly*

"A tale of the rich and famous from the daughter of the late novelist Harold Robbins." —*Ann Arbor News*

"Continues [Harold Robbins's] tradition of chronicling the lives of the rich and famous. The major players here are beautiful, wealthy, [and] oversexed." —*Booklist*

"Robbins offers a story of beautiful people in some of the most visually exciting places on earth. Readers will be drawn to this young girl as she finds her place in the world. Add touches of romance, a winery, and the Nazis during World War II, and you have a novel that will appeal widely." —*Library Journal*

"A Paris romance in which Cinderella marries Prince Charming, only to find he's secretly the Beast." —*Kirkus Reviews*

"The story jumps back and forth between a painter in Paris in the 1930s, all very F. Scott Fitzgerald, and his modern-day granddaughter. Everyone is rich, everyone is beautiful. You'll like this." —*Cincinnati Enquirer, Florida Times-Union, Macon Telegraph*

ADRÉANA ROBBINS

PARIS
NEVER LEAVES YOU

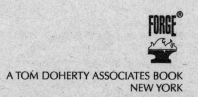

A TOM DOHERTY ASSOCIATES BOOK
NEW YORK

This is a work of fiction. All the characters and events portrayed in this book are either products of the author's imagination or are used fictitiously.

PARIS NEVER LEAVES YOU

Copyright © 1999 by Adréana Robbins

All rights reserved, including the right to reproduce this book, or portions thereof, in any form.

A Forge Book
Published by Tom Doherty Associates, LLC
175 Fifth Avenue
New York, NY 10010

www.tor.com

Forge® is a registered trademark of Tom Doherty Associates, LLC.

ISBN: 0-812-57078-2
Library of Congress Catalog Card Number: 99-21743

First edition: May 1999
First mass market edition: August 2000

Printed in the United States of America

0 9 8 7 6 5 4 3 2 1

For two outstanding men who continue to inspire me:

My father, Harold Robbins (1916–1997). His youthful, exuberant spirit and humor live on in his books and in my fondest memories.

My deepest gratitude is to my husband, Jeffrey. Thank you for sharing my dreams.

It is no accident that propels people like us to Paris. Paris is simply an artificial stage, a revolving stage that permits the spectator to glimpse all phases of the conflict. Of itself Paris is simply an obstetric instrument that tears the living embryo from the womb and puts it in the incubator.

—HENRY MILLER, *Tropic of Cancer*

If you are lucky enough to have lived in Paris as a young man, then wherever you go for the rest of your life, it stays with you, for Paris is a moveable feast.

—ERNEST HEMINGWAY, *A Moveable Feast*

ACKNOWLEDGMENTS

I am indebted to the following people: My parents, who wanted me to be born in France and follow them in their travels. My family and friends, who have been most supportive of my writing schedule. The partnership with my husband has been invaluable, as Jeffrey challenges me always to strive harder and find greater clarity, depth, and precision in my work. I appreciate the involvement over the years of my encouraging creative writing teachers: Holly Prado, William Relling, Jr., and Karen Dale Wolman, who was the first person to read and critique my entire manuscript.

I am also grateful for the generous help of the following people: Brenda Parr, Kim Wilson, Michael Giovanniello, Kris Garfield-Gendler, and Elauna Smith, for her knowledge of art and our mutual memories in Avignon. Gene Schwam, for introducing me to my dynamic agent. My agent, Frank Weimann, for his belief in this novel and for finding me Tom Doherty Associates. I am thankful to them for taking on a new writer and publishing this book. My deepest appreciation is for the assistance of a brilliant and inspiring editor, Melissa Ann Singer, whose talent and vision have helped shape and transform this novel. Lastly, I would like to thank the American College in Paris, Marymount College, U.C.L.A. research library and writers' extension, and the Beyond Baroque foundation.

PROLOGUE

It was a sweltering summer day on the Left Bank. The air was acrid and stale, leaving a thick layer of exhaust fumes that rose above the sidewalks and mixed in with the cigarette smoke from the lively outdoor cafés. It was impossible to breathe, or get anywhere on time during rush hour, except by foot or Métro. Briskly, Pascal Maron crossed boulevard Saint-Germain, shoving her lithe figure through the crowds by the Drugstore Publicis. Her nicotine fix was overdue, but this time she would have to forgo her craving. Every second mattered, as something was terribly wrong with her dearest friend and mentor, Joaquím Carlos Cortez.

He was almost forty years her senior. At one time, he had joined an elite group of talented artists and writers that first united in a Surrealist Manifesto before World War II. These men and women had discarded bourgeois restrictions in favor of the liberation of their creativity. Pascal admired his prolific artwork and eccentric lifestyle. His friendship allowed her a vicarious enjoyment. However, scandalous rumors prevailed about her mentor; the most shocking was that his sexual appetite had not waned in his later years, and was only satisfied by unfledged prostitutes, which he consumed as regularly as breakfast croissants.

They had been friends for twelve years. She thought she understood him. But a conversation they had earlier in the day perplexed and disturbed her. Pascal had phoned to tell him about an art opening, when he began babbling incoherently.

"The ravishing angels are dancing for me. Their flowing gowns and wings feel like a fresh breeze against my face. I can't see my beautiful goddesses, but I don't care. I'm blind and I don't care anymore," he had exclaimed, roaring with laughter.

Pascal had pressed her ear tightly to the receiver and heard him strike a match and inhale deeply. "*Merde!* I've set the cord on fire," he yelled.

"Are you all right?" she asked with concern.

"Why should that matter? I'm old."

"You're as old as you think. You've always been the most vivacious person I know."

"Give me more. Yes, that's what I want," he stammered.

"Who's with you? Are you working with models?" she asked.

"Maybe I am. Don't get jealous on me. I've been through that before. You know I can't stand it."

"I know, but I'm worried about you. I haven't seen you in weeks." She heard the clinking of glasses. "Are you drinking?"

"Yes, Bella. To live is to drink. To drink is to live, and the spirit of love is in my tainted blood, in my wine, in paint and in sin. *Santé,*" he said. Glasses chimed again.

"I'm not Bella."

"Djuna, I miss you. I've always missed you."

"Who is Djuna? I'm Pascal. You know that. I don't understand what you're saying."

"I'm tired of painting for bloody morons! I'm tired . . ."

Seconds later, the line was disconnected. She had phoned back and counted twenty rings, but he hadn't answered. Without a moment of hesitation, she grabbed her black leather purse and scurried down five flights of stairs. She sensed that time was of the essence. Plagued with fear and dread, her heart raced. She made no eye contact with passersby and hurried down the steps into the Métro station.

In less than thirty minutes, she arrived at her destination on avenue Foch. Dashing into an elegant apartment building, she was led by an attendant to a private elevator that took her to the penthouse. The elevator opened into a neoclassical foyer: a room dominated by a stained glass dome ceiling and Italian *pietra dura* floors of onyx and lapis lazuli. Accustomed to the extreme wealth, she ignored the opulent art and collectibles and entered the main living room. French doors that led to a circular balcony were closed, the shutters rolled down. The windows were usually open, as Joaquím Carlos liked to admire the view of the Champs-Elysées and the Arc de Triomphe.

"Where are you hiding?" Her voice echoed against the gilded cathedral ceilings. The room was dark, and while she rushed to open the shutters, she tripped over an empty bottle of Napoléon brandy.

"Zut!" she yelled. Once all the windows were open, the light made visible a horrific scene: canvases smeared with globs of oil paint were scattered on the floor, along with dozens of empty wine bottles, torn books, melted candles, wilted sunflowers, ashtrays, women's lingerie, and plates of half-eaten food. Never before had she seen his apartment in such chaos. Usually it was kept immaculate. She called to him again. This time her voice quavered.

"Carlos . . . Carlos?" She called him by his middle name, which he preferred. But again there was no response. Leaving the room, she passed by the telephone and noted the burned cord trailing from the dislodged receiver. Stealthily, she approached the master bedroom and found the door open.

"Mon Dieu!" she exclaimed.

Joaquím Carlos was sprawled on his canopy bed like a dead starfish, his arms and legs stretched in opposite directions. She screamed again, but this time only a faint squeal came out of her throat. Although she wanted to run to him, her knees buckled beneath her. Stumbling toward the bed, she collapsed by his side. His eyes were opaque and fixed on his mirrored ceiling. Joaquím Carlos's jaw hung open. The bed was a ghastly site. Blood and chocolate were imbedded in the sheets. And on the floor below him were half-filled bottles of Château Hélianthe d'Or, the wine bottled by his winery; tubes of smeared oil paints; empty turpentine cans; and a box of Lindt chocolates with only the crumpled wrappers left.

"This must be a joke. Wake up!" she shouted, grabbing his shoulders and shaking him with all her strength. His body remained rigid and cold.

"Did I do this to you? Am I to blame? I don't understand. Damn you!" Angrily, she grabbed a wine bottle and threw it across the room, shattering it; the remaining red vintage trickled down the gold satin wall fabric like blood from a gaping wound. Mascara-stained tears streamed down her face, soaking into his red paisley robe. More tears fell onto his pale cheeks. And, for the first time, she caressed his forehead with tenderness. Clasping his cold hand in hers, she kissed his stiff fingers and gingerly let his left hand fall back onto the burgundy velvet bedspread. His fingers brushed against a pile of papers. Looking more closely, she saw three envelopes. One was addressed to her; in desperate hope of a revelation, she tore it open. Enclosed was a cashier's check for two hundred thousand francs and a handwritten suicide note instructing her how to proceed with his funeral, making her the executor of his estate. She was tempted to open the other sealed envelopes, but resisted. The names of the addressees were Djuna Cortez and Princess Mitya Troubetzskoy. Underneath their envelopes she found a folder with a label identifying it as Joaquím Carlos's last will and testament.

To the side of these documents were three tall stacks of journals tied with a thin brown string; a note on top of them read, Property of Djuna Cortez. That name eluded her. Was she a wife he had never spoken of? A sister? Through the bedroom window, she could see the sky was darkening. It was getting late. Soon, she would have to call for help.

Carlos's physician arrived thirty minutes later. As he entered the main living room, Pascal was seated on a red velvet banquette by the entrance hall telephone. The doctor was a stout, husky man, whose build had always reminded her of a bulldog. His salt-and-pepper hair was disheveled from riding a Harley-Davidson through the streets of Paris. Pascal's body stiffened when she saw him approach; she refused to get up. The reality of the situation would be finalized with his confirmation. Like a queen ordering a servant, she pointed to the bedroom. He dutifully obeyed.

Exhausted, Pascal retreated to the library, where built-in bookshelves framed a white marble fireplace. The furniture was mostly nineteenth-century Spanish antiques made of bleached pine. This was her favorite room, and it had a stunning collection of art books. The library was brighter than the other rooms, more feminine, and feeling more relaxed within it, she reclined on the ecru muslin sofa, stretching her arms and legs like an indolent Persian house cat. For a second, she glanced at her reflection in a gilded mirror.

"Devastatingly beautiful," Carlos used to say, in his loud baritone voice, when she posed for him. In this room, they had shared numerous bottles of champagne and talked for hours about art and poetry. The artist's strong presence lingered. Instinctively, she glanced over her shoulder, expecting to find Carlos staring at her with his devouring eyes that ripped apart her secrets and pretenses. When her senses returned, she realized that it was the doctor standing in the doorway. His sullen face explained the situation.

"Of all people, he seemed immortal," she said solemnly.

The physician cleared his throat. "I know what you mean. I'm very sorry, mademoiselle. I think he meant to die like he had lived—a man of indulgences. He must have spent days consuming wine, chocolates, cognac, and God knows what else. By the end, he must have been delirious. It looks to me like he also drank turpentine. I believe this may have been the actual cause of death. However, an autopsy will have to be done to confirm. If I can recall correctly, in October he would have turned seventy."

"No, sixty-nine. I did find this," she said, handing him the suicide note.

"Again, I'm very sorry, mademoiselle."

"He was in good health. I don't understand why he would do this," she questioned.

"You knew him better than anyone."

"I know. But he loved painting and life, and never complained about anything. He was always brilliant and engaging."

"Would you like me to call the coroner?" the doctor asked.

"That will be helpful. Thank you. And I have to make funeral arrangements," she said, sighing. "I don't know where to begin."

"You're looking terribly pale, mademoiselle. If I may make a suggestion, you should get some rest first. Make the calls tomorrow. Can I give you a sedative?"

"No! I don't want drugs," she adamantly protested.

The doctor began scribbling on a prescription pad. "Then a homeopathic tea will help you. I recommend drinking the *fleur d'oranger* before bedtime," he said, as he tore off a piece of paper and handed it to her.

Pascal nodded, remaining as glacial and immobile as a Rodin sculpture. The coroner's attendants and the police arrived. An obscene image of death froze in Pascal's mind as she saw them abruptly carry away one of the most celebrated artists and lovers of France and Spain. A sheet was indiscriminately draped over the deceased, and Joaquím Carlos looked like an ape massacred by poachers with his arms hanging limply by his sides. She covered her mouth with her hands, holding her breath.

As an artist, his hands ruled his life. Even in death, they couldn't be contained. Once the body was gone, she rose from the sofa and walked onto the terrace. She was gasping for air and felt enshrouded in a dark veil of melancholy that was almost blinding. With his absence, a part of her began to atrophy, the person Carlos had awakened.

The gendarmes called her back to the library. She calmly answered their questions and then returned to the bedroom, collecting the will, stacks of journals and envelopes.

"I'll be upstairs if you need me," she said politely to the doctor and the police. "Otherwise, if there's nothing else you need to know, please let yourselves out."

Moving like a somnambulist, she entered the art studio. The garret was built under the roof and had the classic Paris charm, featuring a vaulted ceiling and polished hardwood floors. The room was sparsely furnished, except for an exquisitely veneered Queen Anne bureau and several matching walnut chairs. The rest of the space was scattered with oil paintings, easels, and art supplies. Immediately, she opened the balcony window to disperse the fumes of oils and turpentine. An artist she would never dare to become, but a poet and writer she was. Pulling a chair up to the desk, she opened several drawers. Once she found a blank piece of sketching paper and a pen, she began to compose a poem.

"You led me into the art world—your underworld."

All night, she continued to write and discard stanzas. Only through the power of the written word could she ease her pain and eventually heal. Ever since she was a young girl, writing had always given her solace. However, that night, serenity never came. Desperately, she yearned for a greater understanding of her friend. She read his will several times. While she did this, her fingers grazed the stack of his worn journals, and tempted as she was to read them, she obeyed his wishes, leaving them to whom they were willed. Money was never her intention in befriending the artist. Yet she felt jilted that he had chosen to give the bulk of his estate and most of his possessions to a woman he had never spoken of.

Where had she failed him? All these years, she thought they had understood one another. Perhaps she had just been arrogant in thinking she was special to him. He had told her many times that her mind had far surpassed most of the women he knew. Obviously, there were more women, lovers, and muses than she had been aware of. Pascal couldn't help but wonder if his journals held some of the answers to his beguiling and controversial nature, maybe even his possible reasons for suicide at a time when he could command the prices of his surrealistic paintings and run a profitable winery in Loire. But in the end, the mistresses, the ravishing models, and his friendships had all lost. Only one name now carried all the importance—Djuna Cortez. It didn't seem just. Did this woman even love him? When did she visit him? Would she even mourn his passing?

PART ONE

ONE

Djuna Cortez

Death and deception brought me to Paris at the beginning of September in 1985. Before I knew I would become an expatriate, I was enrolled in a French studies program at the American University in Avignon. I resided in a former convent named the Foyer des Jeunes. For a modest fee, the sisters opened their doors to traveling young women and students of all races and religions. The rules at 75 rue Joseph-Vernet were strict: no men allowed on the premises and a nightly curfew of midnight. But I found it a serene place to study with superb French cuisine.

I was given the luxury of my own room overlooking a gray pebbled garden courtyard. Every afternoon, following lunch, I would sit on my private balcony and smoke a cigarette as I watched the scenes unfold before me. Perhaps that was when my artistic eye began to develop. By midday, many of the women, while free on break, were languidly ensconced on white deck chairs. Between casual glances at their textbooks, they shared their leftover baguettes with hungry finches. The enormous maple leaves from the trees that lined the courtyard diffused the August Provençal sun and bathed the garden in speckled shadows and a spattering of light like floating dia-

monds. Strung between the trees were clotheslines heavy with
billowing linens. The air was humid and fragrant with lavender. At this time of the day, the town shut down for two
hours. However, it was impossible to rest, as next door was
the Calvet museum. Their gardens were teeming with peacocks. The birds suffered from the sultry temperatures, and
their agonizing cries and moans echoed through the courtyard.
In between the museum and the foyer courtyard was a private
residence occupied by a reclusive elderly nun, who had been
retired from most of her ecclesiastic duties. Also from my
balcony, I could see over our wall into the sister's brick and
cobblestone front yard. Every day after lunch, she crept out
of her house. Dressed in her calf-length black habit with dark
stockings and a flowing white headdress, in the full sun, she
would hunch over a sad rosebush well past its prime. Three
wilting roses became her primary preoccupation as she lov-
ingly gave the flowers a few drops of nourishment from a
silver coffeepot that substituted for a watering can. I studied
the lines on her time-ravaged face like a map to the past. She
must have lived through two wars. What wisdom did this quiet
nun have to share? Every gesture she made seemed like a
silent prayer. Anyone else would have abandoned those pathetic roses, but to her they were her blessed and preferred
companions. I spent several afternoons with a sketch pad, from
the respectful distance of my balcony, trying to make crude
studies of her face. Once, I tried to speak to her, but I was
told she kept a vow of silence.

Just like the cloistered nun, I had kept to myself in Avignon.
To help overcome my shyness, I decided to join a thespian
group. But, instead of unleashing my talent, I uncovered a
terrible stage fright. I preferred to rehearse Molière alone.
With a copy of *The Misanthrope*, I headed up the back roads
from the village into the hills, where in seclusion, by an abandoned fortress that loomed above the city, I played out all of
the roles. I was in search of an identity.

Creativity was in the summer air during the Festival of Arts.
There were hundreds of theater performances, dance recitals,
and concerts. At night, place de l'Horloge was illuminated in
white and orange lights, and the square was teeming with
painters, potters, jewelry designers, sculptors, street perform-

ers, and fortune tellers. Anyone who hoped to profit from their talent was there.

After I abandoned my drama group, I attempted ballet. To get to the class, I had to cross the busy place de l'Horloge and walk along rue des Marchands. It took fifteen minutes to traverse the many narrow cobblestone streets and alleys to find the school that was hidden away in an upstairs loft. But that venture also proved unsuccessful, when during the second session, a wispy ballerina made her grand debut. She glided into the class with two elegant greyhounds who were as trim about the waist as their mistress. The dogs were tethered by gold leashes which she tied to the ballet bar. When she danced, the entire class and even the dogs watched her. She transformed into a gazelle as she leaped in the air. Then she sailed through space and her legs became wings. When she finally touched the ground, she was as light as a falling feather. Even though I'm five feet eight and I've been athletic all my life, compared to this ballerina, I felt foolish and clumsy. To achieve such fluidity in ballet at twenty years of age would be impossible. The longer she performed, the more my confidence waned. It was pointless to return to the class, as I hated being an amateur.

For my remaining time in Avignon I focused on reading French authors and conjugating verbs to perfect my use of the language. That summer, I was supposed to find a raison d'etre, a lover, or both, before I was to turn twenty-one. I was afraid of becoming one of the sister's wilted flowers. Somehow, I needed to feel close to where my life began, here in Provence. That was where my parents were happy. But that was long before I could remember, before the American dream had taken them for a wild ride to its unmerciful end. Let it be said that I am not a product of divorce. It is much more complicated than that, for what I can only describe is we were all bloody victims of war. There are the scars of our generation— mine particularly had left me empty and yearning for deeper meaning.

By the end of the summer, I was pressured to return to college in California. It was too soon for me to leave, as I felt torn apart by two different cultures—separate nationalities. Uncertain of where I belonged, I came to France hoping that

I could fuse these fragments of a divided self. Life seemed simpler in France. The burdens of rules, morals, and obligations were back in America, with my father. Extremes of behavior were accepted more readily than they were in the States. The French have always had a more permissive attitude than Americans. Taboos appear less prevalent in France. Nude sunbathing is acceptable. And lovers embrace passionately in public. The ambiance is most liberating, especially within this cherished city of Roman footprints, Avignon. And during the summer Festival of Arts, even social pariahs found refuge and acceptance. Some stayed hidden behind sequined masks, while others were more visible.

I had an encounter with a rather eccentric person, a Gypsy performer, who was respected by the locals. Her ritual was to appear during sundown at the café across from the Palais des Papes. When I first approached her, she was as hideous as any character described in a Voltaire novel: her face was marred by hairy moles and her bulbous nose was covered in gin blossoms. Planting herself in a chair, she slammed a large wooden clog onto the table, spilling out a few coins. The waiter recognized her, bowed, and returned with a silver pot of tea. Although one might think that all she could inspire was revulsion, she commanded the attention of the entire square with her a cappella performances of arias from well-known operas. Her most outstanding performance came from *Madame Butterfly*. When you looked at this woman in her late middle years, a mass of corpulent flesh, ratted hair, and soiled clothing, she was indeed frightening, but her voice was as refined as the divas who commanded three hundred dollars per ticket. Stunned tourists would pass by and leave her generous donations.

I had been listening to her every night for a week when she began making eye contact with me. After her performance, one night, she motioned for me to sit at her table. She slid aside the shoe containing that evening's donations to make room for another place setting.

"Would you like a reading? I'll only charge you ten francs," she trilled.

She already knew I was curious about my future. And without acknowledging my answer, she called the waiter over with a snap of her dirty fingers and ordered more tea.

"Do you want to know about love?" she asked.

Before I could respond, she continued, "We Gypsies have many talents. I tell you everything I see, *d'accord.*"

"*D'accord,*" I answered and sat down.

She graciously poured me a steaming cup of jasmine tea. I was instructed not to add milk or sugar. After the steam had settled, she told me to sip it slowly. When I finished the tea, she grabbed the cup and carefully studied the dispersed leaves. She nodded her head several times before beginning her psychic oration.

"You will meet a dark and handsome man. A beautiful man. I also see that love is not the only thing you're seeking. Are you searching for a talent?"

She caught me off guard. Swallowing hard, I didn't answer.

Her black eyes were fierce with the conviction of her words. "Yes, I see that clearly. Don't give up. You'll find it. However, you mustn't let yourself be fooled."

"What do you mean exactly?"

"Beware! You're cursed and uniquely blessed. This is dangerous! There will be battles of good and evil. I don't know which will win. For one hundred francs I could do a cleansing for you."

"No, thank you. That won't be necessary." I stood up to leave.

"I see you living in Paris. Be careful," she warned, shoving the shoe at me. I dropped in a ten-franc coin. Immediately, she whisked the shoe away and left, limping across the square with one shoe on her left foot, as she cradled the money shoe in her arms like an infant. Her silhouette vanished down a dark stairwell of the palais. I was tempted to follow her. Instead, I gazed out at the Rhône river and lit a Rothman cigarette. My thoughts focused on the harsh reality of returning home, rather than on her false premonition, as I was scheduled to leave the following week. I couldn't bear the thought of going.

As it turned out, the Gypsy was as talented in her divinations as she was with her singing. The following day, after the reading, I received a telegram demanding I attend a funeral in Paris. In the contents of this brief telegram was my first revelation that a part of my family's past had been concealed from me. I was confronted with the death of a relative, whose existence I had never been aware of. It didn't take long for me to make new arrangements and reschedule my flight.

The City of Light awaited me. The year I spent in Paris I was to discover a place far removed from the self-sacrificing nuns—a city of art and sin. I experienced Paris not through my mind, but through an awakening of the senses, allowing me to discover hidden desires. I became aware of a city filled with mutable colors, rich textures, contagious moods, intoxicating powers, diaphanous and distorted faces, masks of comedy and tragedy.

Paris captured my heart, imprinting my memory like a first romantic kiss. To prevent getting crushed under its spell, the city demanded confidence, arrogance, or at least an attitude. It was time for me to abandon a diffident self, even if it was in pretense. In Paris one could reach as high as the Eiffel Tower; I had no limitations, except for my own anger, which was ignited along with my passion the moment I set foot along the Champs-Elysées.

TWO

I came to Paris naive, open, untouched, and as transparent as a glass palette. My journey first began with the color white. At the Gare de Lyon, I arrived wearing a white lace summer dress. White was for my innocence and for the ghosts that had left me a legacy to uncover.

Inevitably, like a chameleon, I began to acquire colors as I tried to blend in with my new surroundings. Shortly after I arrived, I telephoned a friend's brother. She was a kind girl from the *foyer* in Avignon. I assumed her brother, Gilles, would also be hospitable.

We arranged to meet at the Grille d'Honneur—a gilded gate at the entrance of the Bagatelle gardens. He seemed to be the dark and silent type. Without speaking, we strolled along a gravel path toward the rose gardens. Against the rules, he gallantly picked me a bud. The tips of the flower's petals looked dipped in sherry and the rest in rich butter. The elderly nun in Avignon would have adored caring for this sweet-smelling rose. Gilles reminded me of the French actor Alain Delon with large, deep-set blue eyes, black hair, a complexion that maintained a Paris winter paleness, and a slight, but sturdy build. Although he seemed about ten years my senior, I couldn't help but wonder if he were the man the Gypsy had spoken of.

We rested under a gazebo and watched squirrels chasing their mates. Monarch butterflies and dragonflies with sparkling sapphire wings glided over the Japanese mirror lake. The air was limpid and temperate, making the sun exceptionally bright, but the warmth of summer was quickly dissipating. In the animal kingdom, mating was simple. For me, relationships had always been complicated. Yet, I wanted to believe that if I could understand the depths of the human heart, and the complexities of love, I would then transform into the person I needed to become. Unless I could do this, I would be trapped in the past, in the years of turbulent adolescence, and the timidity of a young girl. Only a man could help me, and only then would I cross the threshold into adulthood and maturity. I knew I would meet him in Paris. Was Gilles the one? During our blissful promenade, we were lured to the park café by the aromas of coffee and fresh pastries. Gilles offered to buy me whatever I wanted. After we sat down at a table, peacocks entertained us by displaying their feathers like enormous Japanese fans. Emerald circles glowed on the birds' tails like third eyes. Our interlude was witnessed by hundreds of glances. But the most discerning looks came from my perception. Would Gilles be able to see beyond my superficial charm?

This day was unlike any other. My world, my already unstable foundation was collapsing. What I had thought was truth was indeed fiction. Growing up, I had been told that the family on my father's side had died in World War II. In one day, I learned that this had been a lie. Pulling the crumpled telegram from my pocket, I read it again as Gilles ordered our coffee, and dessert.

Djuna Cortez:

Your presence has been requested to attend the funeral of Joaquím Carlos Cortez. Montmartre Cemetery: 14 hours, September 2, 1985. It is urgent that you attend and meet with me, as your financial interest is involved.

Sincerely,

Pascal E. Maron

We remained silent until the waiter returned with our coffees and two slices of apple tart. Gilles's intense blue eyes and the contrast of his dark hair were pleasant to look at. However, shivers traveled through my spine. I was becoming fearful and anxious. I felt like a broken porcelain doll that had been glued back together by a collector who couldn't discard her.

"What was that you were reading?" he asked.

I quickly stuffed the telegram in my purse and pulled out a folded map of Paris.

"It was just an address. Where is Montmartre from here?" I asked, unfolding my map on our table.

"It's quite a ways from this park. See it's at the top of the map," he said, pointing with his index finger. "There's the Sacré-Coeur; Montmartre overlooks all of Paris."

"I can't wait to go. Didn't Toulouse-Lautrec have a studio there?"

"I believe he did. But I don't follow art much and museums make me tired. I prefer science and computers."

"Have you seen the "Mona Lisa"? What about Monet's murals of waterlilies?" I asked.

"I'll take you if you want me to."

I was about to tell him my reason for coming to Paris, when Gilles's eyes caught sight of the bare legs of a young woman passing by.

He paused for a few minutes and then said, "I'm sorry, what were we discussing?"

"It wasn't important," I answered meekly.

With his attention still diverted, he continued talking. "Since you like art you should see the park's sculpture of the sphinx. We'll walk over later." He took hold of my hand and added, "I'm pleased you called me. I hope you'll stay with me. I'd be happy to show you around. If you like parks, you should also see the Luxembourg. I could keep you busy for weeks just showing you the parks in Paris. How much time do you have here?"

"I'm not sure. It's very kind of you to make yourself available," I answered.

"It's nothing," he replied. The froth from his cappuccino clung to his upper lip to form a foamy white milk mustache. In order not to laugh, I diverted my attention from him as I admired the verdant stateliness of the park.

Suddenly, he leaned over and boldly kissed my lips. I was terribly offended by his forwardness, but was afraid to show it.

"I know you'll find other ways of repaying me," he said suggestively. Then he winked at me.

I had wanted to take my hand and instantly wipe away his slobbery kiss, as children do when they're cajoled by adults. Laughing nervously, I stood up and excused myself. That moment, I had a sensation of observing the two of us from the viewpoint of a third person at a nearby table. We were complete opposites. I was dressed in my long white dress. And he wore a black conservative suit. But it was never my intention for our friendship to progress this quickly. I washed my mouth in the W.C. Looking in the mirror, I stared at my own reflection. Friends often told me I was striking in appearance. Is this what he saw? Or was it my choice in clothing that had made him think I would be easy. My delicate shoulders were exposed in the latest fashion craze inspired by the singer Sade. Also, I wore long hooped earrings that dangled from my ears and my dark hair fell wildly like a lion's mane to the middle of my back. For years now, I had never bothered with makeup. My large golden-green eyes stood out on their own. Maybe he had assumptions about American women. I couldn't guess. But I only wished I was now covered from head to toe in a dark cape.

Returning to the table, I tried to hide my irritation with him and gave him a compromising smile. Nervously, I crossed my arms and legs before me, and began swinging my calf. My ankle tapped the table leg. All I could do was hope the incident would be forgotten. However, he didn't get the message that I was not welcoming his advances. He placed his hand on my bare shoulder and said, "We have a lot to discover together."

The prospect of being alone in Paris now seemed more appealing than staying with him a second longer.

"I must go," I abruptly announced.

As I stood up to leave the park, Gilles forcefully grabbed my arm, clenching it so tightly that my circulation stopped. At the same time, I sensed him undressing me with his eyes. Trying to break free, I pulled away, but my arm locked, twisting my shoulder blade. My long dress twirled like an umbrella.

"Please let go. You're hurting me," I pleaded.

"You're nothing but a tease. *Arrête de bouder!* No, please, come on, don't be mad. I'm sorry. I couldn't help myself; you're *magnifique*. You've told me nothing about yourself. My sister told me more than you have."

"I know. I'm sorry. But I can't stay with you after all. There is someone else I should attend to."

"Is it another man?" he asked, finally letting go of my arm.

"Yes, it is."

"I see," he said sorrowfully.

That answer seemed to be all that was needed to set me free. What he didn't know was that the answer I gave was partially true, except that there were three men on my mind: the unknown man that I would soon meet, and he certainly wasn't Gilles. Then my father, whom I would soon have to contend with. However, foremost on my mind was the dead relative. Since the funeral was a day away, I would have some time to try to find out more information about this man. As I walked away, Gilles sat motionless, surrounded by vacant tables. On one table a crumbled baguette and an empty bottle of red wine with two half-filled glasses remained. Obviously the setting had been romantic for another couple. Finches had already begun to feast on the leftover crumbs. This would have made an interesting ending in a French film, just before the credits begin to role. I had wanted to tell Gilles that I found him rude and boorish. Being confrontational was difficult for me as I was afraid of hurting people's feelings. It was a relief to know that I had stored my luggage in a locker at the train station. I could leave the park and never have to see Gilles again.

When I returned to the busy streets, I found myself in the middle of an open-air crafts market that had been set up outside the gates of the Bagatelle gardens. African men from the Ivory Coast beckoned me to purchase their handmade trinkets. Rows of black boxes were set out on the sidewalk, containing mostly simple beadwork jewelry and some pieces in silver and forbidden ivory. I felt a pathos for the men, as they tried to make a living, pleading in their melodic French accents, for anyone to look into their secret boxes. I smiled at them in acknowledgement. Then they chased me calling out, "Mademoiselle, mademoiselle," as they began pulling stuffed animals from their pockets. Brown, white, black, teddy bears of every color, the toys seemed to tumble forth endlessly from within the folds of the peddlers' caftans, as if in a magician's act. The men continued to pursue me until I crossed to the next avenue. The dangers of making eye contact had become evident.

The weather began to change: thick clusters of charcoal clouds concealed the blue sky. Cars raced down avenue Foch, and a jarring cacophony of horns blasted. At the pace I was walking, it didn't take that long for me to reach the expansive avenue des Champs-Elysées. The street burst forth with kaleidoscopic colors: flags, banners, cinema advertisements, neon signs, boutiques, American fast food chains, exchange booths, and banks. As I darted through the herds of people rushing into the Métro, newspaper kiosks and booksellers began closing; brasseries folded back their awnings. The city was preparing for a summer storm—a quiet moment of ablution. It seemed natural to gravitate inside a smoky café and listen to others complain about the temperamental weather.

The first thing I did before ordering was go to the back of the café where there was a public telephone. Locking myself in the glass booth, I placed a collect call to my father in Los Angeles. He knew immediately where I was calling from, as he had informed Pascal Maron where to find me. He was furious that I had gone to Paris without asking his permission. He was also livid that I would be attending the funeral. Even though our relationship had always been formal and on delicate ground, I couldn't hold back my questions.

"Who was Joaquím Carlos Cortez? Why didn't you ever tell me about him?" I asked politely.

"You'll find out soon enough. That bastard doesn't deserve any recognition," he answered bitterly.

"Since he was a relation of ours, it's only fair that I should have known about him," I insisted, trying to hide the hurt in my voice.

"Don't tell me what's fair! If you can't respect my reasons, then I don't give a damn what becomes of you. Do whatever you want. If you want to know about that bastard you're on your own," he chided. Then he hung up on me. For several minutes I listened to the empty dial tone and the long distance static and crackling. I was absolutely stunned by his tirade. He never asked when I would be returning home, or if I was going to finish my last year of college. I couldn't believe that this relative had caused such vehemence in my father. And he left me no options but to ponder the kind of fury he would have to feel to treat me that way. Anger, like laughter, was contagious. The cycle was continuing, as I had the same kind of outrage and blinding resentments over having been denied the knowledge of this person. To some people, this wouldn't have mattered much. But I had always longed for a nurturing and close family, something I never had. My father's brutal words kept replaying in my mind and bore through me again. Something had finally severed between us; it seemed beyond repair.

Feebly, I left the phone booth. I was bleeding from invisible wounds; it felt as if my body had been mercilessly whipped by a tyrannical landowner during the times of slavery. My father hated when I disagreed with him. Yet, once again, I was asserting my willfulness, which I always had plenty of. I had allowed him to select my schools, always Catholic and female, except for college. But we fought about my interests. He never approved of my major and would have preferred that I studied Japanese and international business, and not spend my time trying to understand Stendhal or Proust.

This was a much-needed separation for me. But I felt completely alone in the world; my father was the only relation I had left. Throughout my life, I had always felt like a rootless tree, that was why I had studied French literature, a language I knew was the key to my past and to a fascinating culture. I felt I never belonged anywhere; I was always an outsider.

It didn't seem to matter, as I hid in a corner booth, taking on the role of an astute, yet detached observer. This was my first time in a Paris café. Unemployed men sat for hours at the bar and complained about the *chômage*. They reeked of endless packs of unfiltered Gitane cigarettes and from the strong, but sweet licorice smell of pastis. From what I could understand, they had a bleak outlook of Paris, since they mostly complained about their unemployment. Nevertheless, I found the aroma of pastis to be particularly inviting. I ordered a glass of the murky green liquid and a carafe of water. As I sipped the refreshing apéritif, it felt natural for me to light up. Every patron in the café puffed away as if cigarettes were a mysterious cure for boredom; in their idle pensiveness, hidden in their deep inhalations of warm smoke, the French bore centuries of adversity with a proud detachment. I felt as though I should be writing, like Hemingway, and yet I had nothing to say. Instead, I opened my second pack of Rothmans reds. I preferred smoking English cigarettes. French cigarettes were too strong and American ones lacked flavor.

My awkwardness was cured when I joined in with the smoking. As the sky darkened outside, the red tips of cigarettes glowed like clusters of fireflies; smoke rings floated in the air as they were expelled from sensuously pursed red Chanel lips. The women in the café were adorned in perfectly tied silk scarfs and expensive clothing. Style, taste, and beauty secrets were carried on from one generation to the next, from mother to daughter. That was another aspect of the culture that I lacked and envied.

I was intrigued by the Parisian café society, by what seemed to be a natural immunity from harm. The pleasures of the moment were what mattered, to be able to observe others, as you furtively admired a stranger, an eye for an eye, and ultimately one viewed the person beside them like a magnificent painting in the Louvre. It was a crime to rush a meal, a drink, or a glance. Every minute was savored, and the mood around me was indulgent, languid, hedonistic, and extremely contagious. I had spent forty francs on the pastis and it was well worth it. My drink became an elixir, gently lifting away my burdens. I envisioned my problems rising above the Arc de Triomphe and flying over the Eiffel Tower like an orgy of angels in a Chagall painting. If one drink could do this, what would another do?

In the bar mirror, I noticed a young man seated behind me. He was wearing a blue-and-white horizontal-striped shirt and sailor's cap. I smiled at him and he winked back. After I took my last sip of pastis, he boldly walked over to my table.

"Puis-je vous offrir un autre coup, mademoiselle?"

"Non, merci," I refused. I really was past my limit. Plus, he seemed overly eager, anxious and frail. He told me he was the captain of a *bâteau mouche* and also asked if I would join him that night on his dinner cruise, where he promised me a good time and all the frog legs I wanted to eat. I tried to hide my laughter (there was nothing more distasteful I could have imagined eating), as I politely turned him down. Anyway, he certainly wasn't my type. And I had little intention of pursuing him. All the fun was in the flirtation, and that only lasted a few seconds.

When I left the café the sun had burst through the clouds and a rainbow had formed over the golden obelisk of place de la Concorde, arcing toward the pont de la Concorde and the pont Alexandre III. The city was pristine and baptized after the celestial downpour. Lighthearted and pleasantly intoxicated, I wandered along the quai des Tuileries, beside the Seine. The air smelled of fresh rain, new beginnings. With my map as a guide, I headed in the direction of the Sorbonne and crossed over the pont des Arts. Everything seemed so close on paper, but always proved to be exhaustively further. I stopped by Notre Dame de France and ogled the Gothic church with its infamous lunging stone gargoyles. At a newspaper kiosk, I stopped and asked for directions to the Sorbonne. It wasn't far, but I decided to take a taxi. When I arrived, I found a cluster of academic bookshops and a campus that blended in with the venerable neighborhood. There were no gates or guards, and I was able to explore the long hallways unfettered. In the university library, I inquired if they had the obituaries that ran this last week in the local papers. The librarian was extremely energetic and vivacious, a contrast to any bookish stereotypes. It didn't take long for me to find several obituaries on Joaquím Carlos Cortez. Once I saw the photographs of him, there was no mistaking our family resemblance. He had the same black hair and thick eyebrows as my father and I, and his eyes looked hauntingly familiar, alluring and temperamental. My hands began trembling. This was too much information all at once, and I was still a bit tipsy from the pastis. I tried to read the articles, but I found myself staring more at the photographs. My mind was consumed with curiosity. At the same time, I was bowled over by the reality of his fame. I had vaguely known of him. *Le Monde* said that Cortez was most famous for his Surrealist inspired nudes. *France Soir* said he was known as a "degenerate" painter who often worked in Paris cafés. All of the obituaries noted that he owned a winery and had had numerous affairs with women, mostly his beautiful models. Lastly, all the papers confirmed he was survived by his only son, Emile, my father.

After I left the library, I tried to buy a sandwich in a nearby brasserie, but my credit card failed to work. When I called Visa, they confirmed what I had feared. My father had canceled my account and was trying to force my hand. But I refused to give in to him by slavishly begging for his forgiveness.

I found myself wandering aimlessly in the streets. I continued walking down boulevard Saint-Michel, where in the distance, I saw the Panthéon looming ahead like a beguiling citadel. The buzz from the pastis had worn off, and the carefree demeanor of a tourist had dissipated with it. Hungry, thirsty, and exhausted, I drifted into the Luxembourg gardens.

Once inside the park, I found a shady section and rested beside the Medici fountain. I closed my eyes and tried to stretch my legs in the method I had learned in ballet class. This seemed to relax my mood a bit, so I started to go through the entire exercise. The green chair became a ballet bar. In the middle of the routine, a band of vagabonds began to gather around me. For a short time, they politely and quietly watched my limited pliés and port de bras. I was beginning to feel a bit self-conscious. A man stepped ahead of the group and set a shopping bag on a chair. He wore a moth-eaten blue cardigan three sizes too large for his slight frame. On his head was a black knit cap, and around his neck hung a weather-worn mandolin.

"This is our section," he insisted. His accent was thick with a dialect unfamiliar to me, so that it took me a minute before I realized what he had said.

"Then by all means I'll move," I answered.

My first reaction was to run away from them and leave the park. But I gave them their corner. The only chairs left were two facing them, so I sat there. Another bum joined the group.

He was balancing a flat cardboard carton in the palm of one hand. A small terrier mix followed behind him.

"I got lucky," he said. "Generosity abounds."

The homeless gathered around him while he opened the top of the box, setting it on a chair. Slices of pizza were passed around to eagerly awaiting hands. These odd characters were not a manifestation of a rebellious youth culture, like what had transpired in the sixties, but a random collection of a dozen people, ranging in age from their late teens to their late sixties, who didn't fit in anywhere else. Meanwhile, these vagrants shared their loneliness and their lunacy with each other. There was safety in numbers, in their mutual vulnerabilities, in their humility, and most of all, from surrendering their materialistic desires. They accepted their impoverished fate, taking what was offered to them, which must have given them a certain independence from society.

I, on the other hand, couldn't be content with meager offerings. There was so much I wanted out of life and had so many aspirations. My problem was I didn't know where to focus. My mind was forever wandering and I was easily bored. I remained in the park and observed the bums' vivid faces. While viewing them, I tried to keep my eyes free of judgment, only wondering what had led all of them to this path in life. Were they just victims of unfortunate circumstances? Could this happen to anyone? Especially someone without a family. I contemplated giving each one some change, but I really didn't know where the money for my next meal would be coming from. It was cruel of me to hope the telegram was accurate and that there would be financial interest in this for me.

My primary objective was to stay in Paris; and I made a resolution that I would do almost anything to make this happen, except live in the parks. Even if no money were to come out of this experience, there were many things I could do. For one, I could become an au pair and look after wealthy people's children. That shouldn't be too challenging. Children always liked me, babies especially liked to engage my attention. The people that would hire me would be a nice French family. I would dine with them every evening to a five-course meal. And they would allow me two days off per week, so I could go sightseeing. Then one afternoon, at the top of the Eiffel Tower, I would meet a handsome diplomat, who spoke seven languages and could recite sections of Dante's *Divine Comedy* to me in fluent Italian.

The bums won my attention again. One old woman who wore her pewter hair piled high into a chignon sat down in the chair next to me. She had a fading elegance about her and carried herself with importance. She reminded me of a wilting tulip; her petals would soon fall away from her completely. I wondered what her story was and noticed that with every few bites of pizza, she removed a partially chewed bit from her mouth and stuffed it into her pocket. Taking notice of my curiosity, she informally explained that she was sharing her portion with Monet. I was taken aback, thinking she must be schizophrenic, when the twittery brown head of a squirrel popped out from her coat pocket. Little Monet, it would seem, had become accustomed to a very human junk food diet. Then she complained to me that her meal was missing the complement of a bottle of fine Chianti. Politely, she asked if I would give her some change so that she could have some. I couldn't say no and reached into my purse to hand her a five-franc coin. She cursied for me and held on to what may have been an invisible skirt and affirmed, "You're a very fine girl. Bless you, dear child."

Suddenly all of the bums wanted to befriend me. The man who had first spoken to me introduced himself as Mouche. He sat down next to me and began to strum a mandolin, and in a respectable tenor sang a peculiar song about a lost sea goddess, a creature part woman and part dolphin with sea-green hair, whom he met on the coast of Marseille. One night they made passionate love and then she dove into the ocean and vanished, never to be found again. One day, he planned to return and hoped to find her again. Only she could lead him to the treasures of sunken galleons. Mouche sang with such innocent sweetness, that in this setting it seemed like a lullaby for this slumber party of society's castoffs. Most of the attendants were beginning to drink from their private stashes and were too tired to applaud him. When he finished, I was the only one he looked at for a reaction.

"That was wonderful," I said with sincere enthusiasm. "You have such a beautiful voice!"

"*Merci.* It is a gift I have that I try not to abuse. However, I must sing for my suppers. I can only hope that my voice will last, so I won't have to starve."

Again, I felt compelled to give him some money. I could hear my father's practical and rational voice in my head, telling me to never give in to beggars. It was not the time for me to be generous, but I couldn't help myself. The mandolin player left his chair and settled in for a nap beside the fountain. Another man came forward and smiled as he sat down next to me. I grinned, knowing that it was his turn to try to impress me. He introduced himself as Pierrot *le fou*. All I could do was hope that he was wasn't completely insane. Pierrot had dirty blond hair, a frail build, and seemed to be in his midtwenties. When he spoke he had the boisterous energy of a court jester. His hands never stopped moving.

"Why do you choose to live in a park? Isn't there more you could do?" I asked.

"I have my work cut out for me here," he said.

He confessed to me that he didn't frequent other parks, even if he was able to find better food elsewhere. He preferred to remain in the Luxembourg gardens because it was near the Panthéon. He pointed to the view we had of the Panthéon framed between a cluster of chestnut trees and a sculpture of Mercury; a fingernail moon floated in the sky above the neoclassical dome edifice.

"It certainly is inspiring!" I exclaimed.

"I like it when you can see the moon during the day. But you should see the park at night, especially when the moon is full," he declared seriously.

"I think I understand why you like it here," I admitted.

"Do you?"

He jumped up to his feet and leaned toward me. "Do Victor Hugo and Voltaire speak to you too?"

"I wish they did, but no," I answered somberly.

"How sad. I'm sorry for you. They have fascinating comments and observations." He reached into his torn corduroy pocket, lit a broken cigarette, and offered me a drag.

"No, thank you. I have my own cigarettes."

Pierrot closed his eyes and extended his hands with his palms facing upwards like a yogi.

"*Silence!*" he commanded. "They're speaking now."

The few transients who were babbling near to us quieted; those snoring in a drunken stupor also respected Pierrot's channeling.

"They tell me you don't belong in this park. They see you living far away from this dirty city in a Gothic château. And you will see many moons from exotic places."

"That would be nice," I said.

He turned his head away and bashfully stared down at his torn shoes. Again, I reached into my purse and pulled out another five-franc coin. Pierrot bowed and returned to the group. I waved to the bums as I left the park. I had thought about asking them about hotels, but decided that may have been offensive. Instead, I placed my trust in waiters and bartenders, and stopped at the first café outside the Luxembourg gardens.

"How much money do you want to spend?" a waiter curtly asked, as he was collecting some dishes.

Turning away a moment, I quickly looked inside my wallet and saw only fifty francs left.

"Never mind. Thank you anyway," I answered.

The waiter shrugged his shoulders and then gave his attention to someone else.

To save money, I took the Métro to the Gare de Lyon station. The pace was frenetic in the maze of the hazardous railways and tunnels. People hastily darted around like laboratory rats and seemed just as capable of violence as rodents in these dank cramped quarters. A darker and angrier civilization existed beneath the city where desperate retailers from foreign countries sold clothing, jewelry, food, shoes, bric-a-brac, and children's toys. At one change, when I walked through a busy tunnel, a man darted in front of me and exposed himself while screaming out a flurry of obscenities. People walked past and ignored him, as if it was an everyday occurrence. But I felt trapped in a catacomb of despair. With all the events of the last twenty-four hours, this triggered an outpouring of tears. Alone in this immense city, I sobbed uncontrollably on the train. No one expressed concern, not even the mother and child sitting next to me. The Métro doors automatically opened and closed. All faces started to look alike as they passed through, some were smiling, others frowning. As in any large metropolis, indifference had also become automatic. Lost faces had to be common, as were tears. The lonely journey in diminished light was transitory, as there was always an exit. I just had to find the right one. It took me a while to arrive at my destination. Since I had been weeping, I had missed the stop to change trains. Fortunately, the information clerk redirected me and I found my way to the train station and retrieved my belongings.

On my way out, I noticed a modest hotel beside the station. I knew it had to be cheap, as it didn't have any star ratings and the guests could probably never sleep with the trains coming and going at all hours of the night. The rooms cost only forty-five francs. I was shown to a room the size of my closet back home with only a single bed and a sink. The shower and toilet were down the hall and were shared with the entire floor. When I went to wash my hands, several roaches were resting in the sink. My tolerance for frugal accommodations was pressed to the limit. Without a second thought, I left the hotel, politely telling them I wouldn't be needing a place to stay after all, instead of the truth; that their rooms were completely unacceptable.

Since my arrival in Paris, I had been looking forward to being more independent, especially since I no longer had any restrictions set upon me. Alas, the day was unfolding into a major disappointment. Again, I found myself in a public telephone on the verge of calling my father. However, much to my surprise, I didn't dial his number. Instead, I phoned information for Pascal E. Maron's listing. After two rings, someone answered.

"Could I please speak to Pascal Maron?" I politely asked.

"Yes, speaking," a woman replied with reservation in her voice.

"I'm not sure if I have the right Pascal Maron." My voice trembled. "I am responding to a telegram Monsieur Pascal Maron sent me."

"There isn't any monsieur. It was me that sent it. You must be Djuna Cortez."

"Yes," I said swallowing back tears. I needed a shoulder to cry on. But I quickly regained my composure.

"Are you in Paris? Are you okay?" she asked with sudden concern. Her voice grew deeper and warmer.

"I'm here. But I haven't found a place to stay yet."

"That's no problem. I can make a hotel reservation for you. Is there any area that you particularly like?"

"I do like the Sorbonne and Saint-Germain-des-Prés."

"The Latin Quarter is one of the liveliest sections. That's where I live. There are many hotels I can recommend. However, on short notice it may be difficult. Can you call me back in about fifteen minutes? I should have something by then," she said confidently.

My luck soon began to change. Pascal made a reservation for me and directed me to a hotel in the seventh arrondissement. Later that evening, I checked into a quaint hotel on the rue Saint-Dominique. The hotel was about a fifteen-minute walk to Saint-Germain-des-Prés. And every room in the hotel was identified as a French Impressionist, not a number. Rousseau was the name of my suite, which had a decorative motif of forest-green colors like the paradisiacal gardens the painter liked to depict. The bright and airy Rousseau room was on the top floor, situated under the angular roof with a private bathroom. And every window had a magnificient view. From the bathroom, I could see the plush Champs de Mars gardens and duck lake. And from the bedroom was the Eiffel Tower. It was easy to forget that my fate in Paris was still unknown. Meanwhile, residing in this inspiring setting, I could rest and dream.

THREE

The following afternoon, a black Mercedes-Benz equipped with a uniformed chauffeur collected me and drove me to the Montmartre cemetery. I gazed out my window with fascination and intrigue as the car passed elegant boutiques along the rue Saint-Honoré. Fashion: couture, elegance, style, the collections, prêt-a-porter, it all happened in this beguiling city. Along the way we passed the Opéra and the Madeleine. Every second my eyes feasted on the magnificent architecture. I clung tightly to my crumpled Ponchet Plan Net map, knowing *Montmartre* was further north and we still had a ways to go. The traffic stopped completely along the boulevard des Italians. Soon we were climbing along the narrow, winding streets of Clichy. I hoped to see every section in Paris. Would that be possible? My heart began pounding when I noticed the white domes of Sacré-Coeur. Unfortunately, we didn't approach the basilica. Instead, we turned on rue de Maistre, until the car slowed down before the cemetery. Immediately, the chauffeur opened my door and helped me out of the car. Gathering my courage, I slowly entered the grounds. Many of the mausoleums and tombstones were exquisite marble sculptures and were works of art in themselves. Some of the most renowned people of Paris were interred beneath me: Degas, Zola, Stendhal, and Nijinsky, to name a few. The ancient soil was rich in inspiration. I thought of Pierrot, and wondered if he could truly communicate with the dead; he would have one hell of a conversation here.

A service was taking place at the north end of the graveyard. Gingerly, I walked across the grounds, respectfully avoiding stepping on any of the plaques, where photographs of the deceased were set beside their names. When I approached the crowd of mourners, I kept back a distance. What if this was the wrong funeral? The entire cemetery wasn't visible, but I saw no evidence of any other ceremony. A line of attractive female pallbearers carried a mahogany casket that was covered in white flowers. Each woman wore a long, flowing crimson silk dress that looked like a burst of flames in the wind. One could tell that they labored under the weight of their burden, the difficulty enhanced by the precarious balance of their red stiletto-heeled shoes. Suddenly, the coffin dropped and skidded down a small embankment. Nervous laughter and rude comments erupted from the spectators. The pallbearers ignored the sarcastic remarks, and with the aid of two cemetery attendants, they confidently picked up the coffin, carried it a few more yards, and set it in place beside the grave site. I couldn't help but stare at a life-size white marble sculpture that stood at the head of the grave next to the coffin. It was of a reclining young woman; a long flowing cloak was draped loosely around her. I studied her angelic face, looking for something familiar, some resemblance. The inscription beneath the statue indicated that her name was Sylvie Cortez, beloved wife and mother.

A woman emerged from the crowd. She wore a wide-brim black hat with a dark veil that covered her face. It was difficult to make out her features, but she appeared to be a person who defied her age. Photographers frantically snapped pictures and flashes lit up the scene. She blinked several times, faced the gathering, and began speaking in a low gravelly voice.

"This is a most tragic day for all of us. I have lost my most loyal friend. Few of you knew him the way I did, but I'm not here to tell you about my grief. Many of you knew Joaquím Carlos as an artist whom you admired, for others he was a great teacher. It is true that he invented his own standard of morals and I respected him for that. He walked the tightrope between genius and insanity. And his essence was fathomless. But Joaquím Carlos will have to remain an enigma to us, so let his art become his spirit. Let his art live on."

It appeared there was more she wanted to say, but her hands began trembling. Seconds after, she burst into tears and left the podium. Another woman eased her way through the crowd. She was much younger and elegantly dressed in a black linen pants suit. Her dark hair was worn in a short raven bob. My eyes focused on her hand-painted violet silk tie. It was a man's tie with Cubist images of flutes and violins. Confidently, the second speaker took command of the microphone.

"I wrote this poem after his death. I suppose you don't truly appreciate someone until they're gone. There is still much more I need to say, but this will have to suffice." She wiped a tear from her eye and unfolded a piece of paper.

"The art world
  Multiple reflections of sad music
  An old man's love became
  his life and identity
  Monstrous ideas flirted with his subconscious
  that he was half a person
  In paint he found his other self
  a demon
  he claimed

  Like Hades
  he became king of subterranean desires
  secret carnal treasures
  and screaming kaleidoscopic colors
  The underworld

  The right eye is now the mouth
  the mouth is now the left eye
  Babies strolled by him and barked
  dogs cried tears
  He couldn't stop seeing
  the sad music

"He is in his resting place. I will miss him," she said reflectively. She removed a long-stemmed red rose from the podium and after kissing the bud, she then gently set it on top of the casket. As she stepped back, several beautiful women moved forward and threw themselves on top of the coffin, sobbing like young war widows. I eased my way to the front of the congregation. Before me was the gaping hole with heaps of dirt and earth haphazardly strewn, set beside it was a shovel clinging to the ground. Looking into the cold earth, all I saw was suffocating darkness. My imagination took over; I began to visualize the corpses decaying in the soil, coffin after coffin, bones, worms, rotting flesh. Overcome by sudden nausea, I bolted to the gates and tried to remain as far away from the open grave as possible, yet still retaining some visibility. Several people gave me scathing glances for leaving. The distance temporarily eased my queasiness and leaning against one of the black iron spokes, I continued to watch the mourners pay their last respects. The scent of cigarette smoke drifted past me, and I turned to find the source. A man several feet behind me was smoking. Glancing in my direction, he smiled. His skin tone was café au lait, his eyes were hazel, and he had short light-brown hair. It was difficult to discern his age, but I guessed him to be in his forties.

He was dressed in a white cotton turtleneck and casual tan slacks. Then he withdrew a pack of Rothmans from his pocket and tapped the package several times on the palm of his hand.

"Would you like one?" he offered, moving closer to me.

"Thank you. I happen to smoke the same brand," I said, taking one between my fingers.

He tried to light my cigarette, but every time the wind blew out the flame from his lighter.

"Come a bit closer," he suggested, cupping the lighter with his hands. Finally, he lit my Rothman by holding his cigarette between his delicately shaped lips, so that the burning tip of his cigarette collided with mine. From the distance of the gate, we smoked and watched the remaining service. The coffin was lowered into the ground and each mourner tossed in a rose.

"You must also get sick from funerals. It always happens to me. Was he someone close to you?" he asked.

"Not really," I answered vaguely.

"I was one of his students," he announced.

"What was he like?" I asked with interest.

"You didn't know him?"

"I knew him, but I was curious how he was, as a teacher I mean."

"Were you one of his women?"

"Yes," I answered. I wanted to make my answer simple, as the truth was far too complicated to expose.

"Joaquím Carlos was a true perfectionist and didn't believe in helping his students. He made one suffer to create. But it was well worth the torment. He's been my role model ever since. But I'll never be able to paint the way he did. Have I properly introduced myself?" he asked.

"I don't think so."

Extending his arm, he took my hand and politely pressed his lips against my knuckles. I giggled as his cold nose touched my skin.

"Bernard-Louis Valencourt. The pleasure is all mine. I must confess you're absolutely stunning. I would love for you to model for me sometime."

I tried to stop myself from blushing. *"Enchanté,"* I answered.

He reached into his pocket and handed me a black business card with gold lettering. "I teach at the Beaux-Arts. It was nice meeting you. I'm sorry it was under such grave circumstances. Please pardon the pun. Stop by and visit me sometime. I always need models. I regret I must leave now."

I watched him saunter down the cobblestone street toward Sacré-Coeur. Bernard hadn't asked for my name. What did it matter? I probably wouldn't see him again. Looking back at the grave site, I saw that the funeral had ended and a swarm of people were flooding toward the gates. I stepped aside to let them pass by. At the end of the procession, I recognized the woman with the enormous black hat and veil. Quickly, almost abruptly, she patted a pallbearer on the shoulder to comfort her, and then stepped aside to approach me.

"Who are you?" she asked harshly.

"Djuna Cortez," I answered, extending my hand, which she did not take.

"I should have known that he would leave everything to a

neophyte. I'm Princess Mitya Troubetzskoy," she loudly announced, while directing her voice for the photographers and journalists to hear. Cameras flashed at us.

The princess sported a conservative black Chanel suit with a neckline dripping in pearls. A large Art Deco marcasite brooch was pinned on her left shoulder. Every item of jewelry that she wore was a statement of her affluence. Her bold personality was intimidating.

"That was a moving speech," I commented nervously. Then I realized how hypocritical that must have sounded, since I had never met the deceased.

"It should be. I'm not an idiot. I was once one of the top chapeau designers in all of Paris."

"How interesting!" I sincerely remarked.

She didn't seem to care about my response. I glanced again at her hat. It was a creation that reminded me of one I had seen in a Greta Garbo film. The hat was worn askew, and Princess Mitya's well-preserved face was complimented by the design. However, I didn't doubt her allure was maintained, at least in part, by the finest plastic surgeons. Her eyes were an electric blue, and when she looked at me, they seemed filled with rancor. We kept staring at each other in silence, until another woman, the second speaker at the funeral, walked over to us. Her skin was as pale as creme fraîche. It was evident that she also had a panache for fashion. And with her tall and lanky figure, she might also been a fashion designer or a model.

"This is Djuna Cortez," Mitya told her.

She extended her hand to me; her clasp was ethereal.

"Pascal E. Marón. I see you made it here fine. How do you like your accommodations?" she asked.

"The hotel is very charming. Thank you."

Pascal's voice was several octaves deeper than on the phone and had a rich butterscotch sound.

"Where's the reception?" Mitya nonchalantly inquired.

"I decided not to have one," Pascal answered.

"Why? I don't understand you! Carlos would have wanted all of us to have a big fête. He would have wanted all of us to drink and have a marvelous time and live it up the way we used to during the thirties," Mitya protested.

"Perhaps. But funerals aren't a time to celebrate for me. And that wasn't the Carlos I knew. He was also a very private person. I felt that the funeral would be enough. Anyway, most of the people who came, I don't think even knew him personally. And I certainly didn't want a bunch of strangers trapsing through his apartment. May I suggest the three of us have lunch instead?" Pascal asked.

"I suppose so," Mitya answered with obvious irritation.

Pascal turned to me and said, "He left me important instructions, and as the executor I'm obliged to explain everything to you. You're certainly the type Carlos loved to paint."

"Except for her clothes, so obviously American," Mitya sardonically remarked.

I had forgotten what I was wearing. Feeling terribly self-conscious, I gazed down at my simple black cotton dress, knit sweater, and espadrilles. I had thought my clothes were fine, until Mitya's comment. Then I took notice that to them fashion and clothing were a statement of their individuality and prestige and went with the image they wanted to project. One of the main reasons I had never paid close attention to clothes or makeup was because of the restrictions in the girls' schools I attended. Even later in college, my father was so strict that if I ever wore lipstick, he would have a fit, telling me that I looked like a harlot.

"Please, Mitya, let's try to be civil for once," Pascal reprimanded her.

Three black Mercedes-Benzes pulled up. Each chauffeur jumped out and held open the rear passenger doors. I was instructed by Pascal to enter my car alone. Then each of us entered our separate vehicles. My driver followed the others down the hill and through the winding streets into the center of Paris, retracing our previous route. I was so anxious about what Pascal would have to say to me that I didn't take much notice of my surroundings. It must have been quite a distance from Montmartre before the car circled around place Vendôme and pulled up before the Ritz Hotel.

The women didn't speak to each other or to me as we walked up the red-carpeted entrance and in single file ventured through the gilded revolving doors. I had to catch my breath as I took in some of the opulence of the lobby: wall tapestries, a spiral stairwell covered with ornate carpeting, exotic flower arrangements presented on antique French furniture, and rooms that were vast and airy with vaulted ceilings and glazed doors. I followed the women down a long carpeted corridor, where rows of window cases displayed designer jewelry and clothing.

We passed the formal dining room and entered the more informal Espadon restaurant. Mitya and I were seated on a burgundy-rose velvet banquette, and Pascal sat on a pine carved chair opposite us. The interior of the room was made to appear as if we were in a garden. The ceiling had a trompe l'oeil effect of sky and clouds. A palm tree towered behind our banquette, and even the brocade draperies didn't detract from the natural allure, where carved doors opened to a court-yard adorned with bamboo and ficus trees, topiaries, white trellis, and hanging plants. From where we sat, Mitya and I could watch the guests dining on the patio under white canvas umbrellas. Set before us, on the table, was a bowl of crisp bread rolls, a menu that had a watercolor painting of place Vendôme with the famous bronze column, and an arrangement of pink roses. Everything was so perfect—the folded linens, sparkling crystal, silver cutlery, and china that appeared never to have been used before—that I didn't want to touch anything. A waiter dressed in a white coat arrived and ruined the table by removing the napkins and placing them on our laps.

"Would you care for some wine? Here is the list," he offered us.

"You must be old enough to drink. Are you having wine?" Mitya asked me.

"No, thank you," I answered.

"You're not one of those young recovering booze hounds like her," Mitya asked, as she pointed her finger at Pascal, "are you?"

Pascal gently reprimanded her. "Mitya, please don't be rude. This isn't the time."

"There's no time like the present," Mitya gleefully teased. "I'll have a Stoli straight up, no ice," she instructed the waiter. Then she pulled out an ornate cigarette holder and a pack of Camel Lights from her purse.

Pascal ordered a large bottle of Evian water. And I asked for a pastis.

"My, you have bourgeois taste," Mitya commented, between drags of her cigarette.

"We need to discuss business," Pascal said sternly, clearing her throat. "In the will, Carlos wanted you to have almost everything, which includes his properties and all of his bank accounts."

"But he left me his furniture and antiques in the Paris apartment," Mitya interjected.

"Yes. They're worth a lot of money. But he left me the furniture in the library, a nineteenth-century Spanish vanity mirror, muslin sofa, and screen," Pascal went on.

"Yes, yes. I know. And he left you his books. I don't want those dusty things," Mitya said irritably to Pascal.

I was absolutely stunned at the enormity of the inheritance. My drink arrived and instead of taking a delicate sip, I took a rather large gulp. Then I became completely embarrassed. I didn't know what had come over me. Also, I couldn't hide my dissatisfaction. What had tasted fine as an aperitif the day before was now startlingly unpleasant. Mitya noticed me purse my lips and cough.

"Is there something wrong?" she asked with a smile of amusement on her red lips.

"I don't care for this drink after all. I'm sorry."

The princess snapped her fingers, calling the waiter over.

"I don't need to make a fuss. It's really not important. I'll just have water," I said, rather humiliated that I had brought all of this attention upon myself.

"Bring her a kir royale," Mitya said. "I used to drink those when I was your age. Well, then again, maybe not. Anyway, I think you'll like it."

Pascal continued, "I'm aware Carlos had a son, Emile."

"He's my father," I added.

"I see. It all makes sense now. Your father was very cold on the phone. He wouldn't answer any of my questions. All he told me was where to contact you in Avignon. He seemed extremely bitter. I'm concerned he may contest the will."

"I don't think he'll do that," I answered.

"Why do you say that?" Pascal asked.

"He never told me about Joaquím Carlos and refused to tell me why. We're not on speaking terms now. However, I think his anger is directed mostly at me. And I doubt very much he'll demand any money from the father whom he claimed was dead all these years. Anyway, he is financially stable."

"So you never met Carlos?" Mitya asked.

"No," I answered. "My father is probably more upset that he can't shelter me anymore from his deception. I feel terrible that Joaquím Carlos and I never met. I'm at quite a loss for words. It's hard to believe that he would leave all of this to me."

"It certainly is shocking!" Mitya exclaimed.

"I'm sorry I'm taking all of this away from both of you," I said.

"Your grandfather also left you the responsibilities for the winery and château in Loire. You will have your hands full," Pascal informed.

The princess added, "That annoying staff keeps calling me and demanding money. He didn't leave me the château. I told them to wait for you. At least now they'll be off my back."

"I'm sorry for both of your losses, really I am. He must have been a fascinating man," I concluded.

"That he was," Pascal agreed.

Mitya nodded her head.

"If I may ask, how did he pass away? The newspapers didn't say. Was he very ill? I do hope this isn't the wrong question of me to ask."

Mitya's eye began to twitch and her hands shook.

"We've been trying to keep this private. Do you want to answer, or should I?" Pascal said with alarm in her voice.

"He killed himself," Mitya curtly replied.

The waiter returned and handed me another drink and recommended the *plat du jour*: a fresh duck and goat cheese salad on frisé lettuce. I couldn't speak and felt completely awkward. Mitya ordered for me. I sat dumbfounded, staring blankly into my kir royale, as I began to shred the paper cocktail napkin set under my glass.

"We'll have two specials," Mitya informed the waiter.

Pascal ordered an appetizer of roast duck liver pâté with

truffles and then a quail-breast salad with green peppercorns for her entrée.

"I take it this is your first time in Paris," Pascal commented.

Mitya answered for me. "I was younger than you when I first came to Paris. The prince and I used to rendezvous in this hotel. At that time, Paris was swarming with fascinating men. The lovers I've had, each one—"

Pascal abruptly interrupted her. "We're not here to listen to you rant on about your scandalous affairs."

Then Pascal whispered to me, "That's her favorite topic of conversation and she can go on until the moon rises."

"I heard that. I may be old, but I'm not deaf," Mitya said angrily.

"Not yet!" Pascal quipped and returned the conversation to business. When Pascal's appetizer arrived, I became ravenous and wished I had ordered the same dish. I found myself staring covetously at Pascal's plate. She barely ate, taking only a few bites and then setting her knife and fork down.

Pascal carefully explained, "There's something few people knew about Carlos, as he hid this from almost everyone. But you should be made aware of—"

Mitya interrupted. "What did he hide? Why should she have this information? I was his oldest friend."

"I know that, Mitya," Pascal diplomatically confirmed. "However, it is Djuna that he wanted to have control of his journals."

"Oh, that. I knew he wrote. But it's mostly nonsense, isn't it? The journals aren't worth anything, are they?" Mitya asked.

"I think they will be quite valuable," Pascal answered.

"What about the art collection? Don't tell me he gave all of his paintings to her and those of the other artists as well," Mitya said.

"Yes. Everything," Pascal confirmed.

"She doesn't deserve them," Mitya said, mumbling under her breath.

As the ladies continued to bicker, I wanted to hide under the table. All I could think about were his writings. This information interested me the most. Perhaps now I could learn about my family history.

"Where are the journals?" I asked politely.

"I put them in the art studio," Pascal answered as she reached into her purse and handed me a silver Cartier key chain full of keys. At the same time, she handed me a manila envelope. Once her hands were free of responsibilities, she lit a thin brown cigar that playfully dangled between her slender, well-manicured red fingernails. There was dead silence among the three of us. I began to fidget with the keys, until I got up enough courage to ask, "How did you both come to know my grandfather?"

Mitya sighed pensively and answered first. "We go back a long way. Before Hitler's occupation. Back then we knew how to have a gay time. Things have changed so much. I can't even use that word in the same fashion."

Mitya glared intentionally at Pascal and continued. "Those were the days; the City of Light will never be as enchanting as those wanton nights in Montparnasse, where I first met Carlos."

"And you?" I asked Pascal.

"She was his whore," Mitya sneered.

Pascal stood up and shouted, "That's enough! I won't endure your rudeness any longer."

Mitya glanced at her watch and tossed her cloth napkin on the table. "Then I will go. Ta ta, au revoir. I'll let *you* be tour guide."

"It was nice meeting you," I stammered.

"Ha!" Princess Mitya rebuffed and abruptly left the room.

"Try not to take her personally," Pascal confided.

"It's hard not to. Did I say something wrong?" I asked.

"You did nothing. Her impudence is uncalled for. I think she was in love with him. The loss has been traumatic for all of us. She resents me, and it's much worse since you've arrived."

"Was she one of his mistresses?" I asked.

"It's possible. He did love many women. They were very close."

"Were you also one?" I asked.

Pascal guffawed and replied, "I'm not going to answer that."

It was foolish of me to ask such an impertinent question. My face flushed in embarrassment. Pascal had made an effort to make me feel comfortable; therefore, I would not have expected her to withhold any answer. However, I learned my lesson and apologized. Nervously, I reached for the envelope and then clumsily dropped it on the floor. Pascal reached down and picked it up for me.

"Thank you. I'm *maladroit* sometimes, as they say in French," I confessed.

"It's nothing," she said, extinguishing her cigarillo. She glanced at the bill and said, "I assume you don't have much money."

"I don't."

"I guess this will have to be on me until you get your inheritance."

"Thank you. How long do think that will take?" I asked.

"I'm not certain. Tomorrow you'll need to sign some documents and I'll take you by all the banks."

As we walked out, Pascal gave me a brief tour of the hotel, explaining to me some of the famous writers and royalty that had stayed at the Ritz. Suites were named after them. Included in the hotel were a cooking school, gym, several bars, a nightclub, and an indoor pool with piped-in music that could be heard underwater.

"You could stay here if you wanted to," Pascal offered.

"I'd rather be less extravagant," I said.

"You're pragmatic. I respect that," she answered.

I had a feeling Pascal was really thinking, I wonder how long that will last with her.

She led me outside the hotel to the busy rue de Rivoli, and quickly pointed out the Louvre and the Tuileries facing us. Pascal walked with a determined pace, which was the prevailing attitude for Parisians. Then without a moment's notice, she stepped off the curb, stared into the oncoming traffic, and authoritatively raised her right hand.

"The cars were only hired for the funeral," she explained. A taxi came to a screeching halt and we climbed in. Pascal gave the driver the address and the car began to traverse the congested rotary. In the car, she told me that she hoped I would honor Joaquím Carlos's wishes. I promised to do my best. When the taxi reached avenue Foch, she announced, "We're almost there."

The car pulled up to an elegant five-story building with a

gray pitched roof. It was more stately then I could have imagined of a Parisian apartment. She pointed to the top floor, just below the pinnacle of the roof. Three circular windows, resembling portholes, peered out above a French window with a wrought-iron balcony. The floor beneath had a curving stone terrace.

"Carlos's apartment is on the top two floors. This is one of my favorite Second Empire buildings in Paris," she noted.

"Yes, of course," I answered, trying to hide my ignorance.

Once we got out of the taxi, we walked through an exterior courtyard; on the right was a fountain of Venus rising out of the half shell. The white stone façade of the building was decorated with bas-reliefs and friezes of mythological deities.

"Avenue Foch is one the finest streets in Paris. The *bois* is across the street," Pascal kindly informed me.

A doorman wearing a top hat and white gloves opened the front door and politely instructed us to wait in the lobby. The entrance hall looked like an elegant parlor with an immense oak fireplace and plush blue silk sofas. Facing the seating area was a library, and beside the bookshelves was a glass window that overlooked another courtyard and garden.

The doorman bowed and said, "I'm sorry to keep you ladies waiting. Since his passing, we have been mobbed with reporters, and our instructions are not to let anyone up."

Pascal answered, "I know, but this is his granddaughter. It's her place now. I called the management about her and the cleaning service."

He glanced at a black notebook. "Oh, yes. The cleaning service came yesterday. This must be Djuna Cortez."

"Yes," I answered.

"Do you have any documentation to prove this?" he asked. I handed him my passport.

"That will be fine. I'm sorry for the confusion. Then he bowed and left me to follow Pascal.

We entered a private elevator that took us to the penthouse. The doors opened into a colossol foyer with a stained glass dome ceiling.

"This magnificent place belongs to me!" I exclaimed.

"You're most fortunate," Pascal said dryly.

With every step, the apartment became more impressive. A

circular terrace decorated with lemon and orange trees in Italian ceramic pots surrounded the penthouse. There was a panoramic view of the city and the *bois*. Unlike at the Ritz Hotel, Pascal wasn't compelled to give me a tour. Taking my own initiative, I left her in the foyer and explored each room, taking notice of the crown moldings, trompe l'oeil walls, fresco panels, marble columns, and gilded accents. The bathrooms had the finest Italian marble, tile, and hand-painted porcelin. It felt as if I had entered a Venetian palace, several centuries ago. The furniture was ornate: burgandy velvet sofas and draperies, gold chintz pillows, onyx candelabras, dark cherrywood commodes, and gilded chandiers. The only modern accent was my grandfather's taste in art. Hanging in the most exquisite museum frames, I recognized some of the works of Bonnard, Matisse, Dalí, Picasso, Léger, Soutine, and Modigliani.

Pascal followed behind me as I found my way to a library with walls of polished wood paneling and built-in bookcases. Moving to the limestone and marble fireplace mantel, I noticed a black-and-white photograph of a group of friends in a café. Turning to Pascal, I said, "That must be Joaquím Carlos."

Yes, that's him, clowning around in the middle of all those women," she affirmed, pointing to the artist in the center of the group.

"He must have been quite a ladies' man. Isn't that Mitya next to him?" I asked.

Pascal refused to look again at the picture. "Probably. I'll let you look around some more. If you don't mind, I'll be sorting through these bookshelves."

"What's upstairs?" I asked.

"The art studio."

"Do you mind if I go explore?"

"It's your place. You can do whatever you like," she said dryly.

I climbed the marble stairs and opened the door to the studio. The distinct smell of oil paints and turpentine fumes engulfed the room. The stuffiness of the room was eased after I opened the balcony door. This was the peak of the roof Pascal had pointed out. The wrought-iron balcony was secured at the highest level of the building, allowing a view of the glistening silver rooftops of Paris and some well-known landmarks. I could clearly identify the Eiffel Tower, the Champs de Mars, and the Trocadéro.

Inside the bright studio were stacks of paintings piled against a wall. My hands began to tremble with excitement as I sorted through a pile of canvases. An inscription on the back of one painting first caught my attention.

"To my darling, Isabella. A woman of ardent passions." Turning the painting over, I saw it was a portrait. The model lay suggestively on a white lace bed, and outlining her voluptuous nude body were scattered red poppies. She was exceptionally beautiful, with glistening raven hair cascading to her narrow waist; a necklace of gold peso coins decorated her pale neck. Long hooped earrings dangled from her ears, and delicate gold bangles covered her arms. Joaquím Carlos captured the details of etchings on the bracelets and the faces of the coins. His vibrant colors were impressive; the crimson flowers matched her full ruby lips. A deep violet macaw perched on her left shoulder and a pale pink cockatoo was captured in flight above the bed. I recognized the view from the art studio, except the sky was enhanced by a distinctive shade of pale mauve.

The second painting was of two women draped in ancient Egyptian clothing. Both were kneeling at opposite ends of an emerald lagoon. The right arm of each model was stretched out to touch the other, but the water separated them. Their placid reflections were perfectly mirrored in the calm surface of the lake. One of the models had raven hair and smooth ebony skin. The other woman looked like an albino with platinum-colored curls and a pale opalescent complexion that appeared almost translucent. Behind the blond woman was a desert landscape with golden sand dunes. The sky was salmon colored, and next to the blonde was a red cobra coiled to strike. Behind the dark woman was a forest and an indigo sky. A bald eagle was perched on her shoulder. The inscription on the back of the canvas read, *"The Forest and the Desert.* They will never meet or mend my heart."

Another enormous canvas was painted in the style of a Cubist collage. There were images of a jazz club: a black saxophone player, with red musical clefs spewing out of his instrument like volcanic sparks. In the crowded club were smoke-covered faces, embracing lovers, a seductive diva dressed in a clinging red sheath dress, swingers, and loners glued to the bar, brandy glasses held to their lips. When I studied the painting more closely, I saw a blindfolded man holding a paintbrush in the corner of the club. It may have been the artist. As I stepped back from the canvas, the total concept of the painting took form: the scenes occurred within Adolph Hitler's profile.

The painting left me breathless. Exploring more of the studio, I found a glass palette and jars of oils. When I touched the palette, light portrait pink and ivory black marked the tip of my finger. Inspired by the impact of his artwork and immersed in this creative environment, I felt bold enough to open the envelope Pascal had given me.

Inside I found a letter and a copy of his will.

AUGUST 1985
Dearest Djuna,

I hope you are a free-spirited woman with a mind of your own, as you are named after a very talented American writer and artist who lived in Paris.

I have so much to tell you. It is a tragedy we will never meet, as I've spent a lifetime being misunderstood. You never knew me, so you cannot loathe me like your father does. I can only hope that if we had met, you would have treated me differently. Therefore, I leave my estate in your cherished hands.

My apartment in Paris belongs to you, as does the winery, the art collection, my paintings, and the château in Loire. I have also left you the journals I began when I moved to Paris and became an expatriate. The journals are numbered. Begin with the first one and do not read them out of sequence.

My words are entrusted to your care in the selection of a publisher, and only you will earn the profits. Death gives me the liberty to speak truthfully.

*When you read my work you will be the same age as
when my life began in this splendid city. I only ask that
you be open-minded. I doubt your father told you anything about me, so what you are about to read is un-
adulterated nonfiction. I hope you will never have anyone
alter my words. There is nothing I loathe more than censorship and forced morality.*

*You are my last hope for the Cortez family, so please
don't let me be forgotten, not even by your father. I hope
your life abounds with vitality, passion, and color.*

Vive l'art et l'amour,
Joaquím Carlos Cortez

After setting down the letter, I caressed the tip of a bleached
pig-hair paintbrush and reached for an empty canvas. First, I
dipped the brush into a can of Quinacridone red, the deepest
shade of crimson I could find. I painted a few words to Joaquím Carlos in the form of a haiku poem:

Surrealist, lover,
and revolutionary.
What do you mean to me?

Then I found a fountain pen and I responded to his letter.

Dear Joaquím Carlos,

*Were you a revolutionary? I guess that maybe you were
as you struggled to give birth to your immense creativity.
How I wish I had something to fight for, a cause to express. So much time has passed between our worlds, so
many social issues have already been challenged: equal
rights, abortion, and civil rights. It is said that you belonged to a "lost generation." Yet, you were so prolific.
I am the one who is lost. My struggle is in this age of
anxiety, and it seems such a banal and selfish battle compared to what you must have experienced. I'm afraid that*

*twenty years from now I'll be asking myself the same
questions: Who am I? What do I want in life?*

*I feel as if I'm dangling from a hot air balloon at a high
altitude; the wind is pulling me down; I can't see the
ground and I need someone's hand to tether me. A man
perhaps. I want to feel whole instead of empty. Will Paris
inspire me?*

*The view from this balcony is captivating; I would also
like to paint, but equal to that impulse is the thought of
jumping off, falling, asserting my existential rights and
joining you in death. Why did you take your life? What
is freedom? Are we ever happy? Is freedom close to madness?*

Djuna

After I wrote the letter, I folded it into an airplane, as children do in grade school, and stepped onto the balcony. There
I watched the paper plane glide and then crash toward the
street. A hint of autumn was in the night air. Shivering, I
returned to the studio and opened a journal. As I began to
read, I forgot about my anguish. I forgot about Pascal downstairs. Several hours could have passed. All I could feel was
Joaquím Carlos's struggles, his desires.

FOUR

Goddesses, Wine, Dead Artists & Chocolate
The Journals of Joaquím Carlos Cortez

PARIS, APRIL 1936

Every day in Paris is a mystery and tomorrow never brings recognition. I ponder my sanity within this lifestyle and wait for the day when my art will be in demand. It is four in the morning and this is my third week of insomnia. Lately, the moment my head hits the pillow I become revived; my heart flutters as fast as the feet of a flamenco dancer. Sleeping is almost impossible. Forces beyond my control take over. The monster of loneliness and darkness croons. I am savage—uncontainable.

I rush to my easel and stare at a blank canvas. Inspiration is all I need, a model, flesh. A soul. For mine is lost—damned. But I don't care, so I run down to the boulevard du Montparnasse. The night air is thick with tobacco and exotic perfumes. New Orleans jazz blasts from a nearby cabaret; a plethora of foreign languages are being spoken by boisterous patrons of outdoor cafés. I am fascinated with the desperate side of life, the debase and sacrilegious. Under the street lamps, hovering like moths, are an assortment of whores. Our hungers join in a glance, as they wait to be freed before the rising sun. My empty palette can only be satiated by these ladies of the night.

They notice me eyeing them like a famished wolf and begin

their charade. One girl flashes her ample bosoms, while another shows me her upper thigh and leather garter. Like a tray of petit fours, I can't select only one. All the *dames* look rich in experience and lascivious charms. My famine needs them all, until one woman sinks her claws into my neck and I become her prey.

The hunt changes when she enters my studio. Her eyes see only francs. I control her with oils and pastels and spell out the rules. She strips. Even though I am about to explode, my trained perspective redeems me. Inspired, I study every vein and tendon, every patch of her anatomy. Instantly, without a preliminary sketch, the color of her eyes and the sheen of her hair appear in paint. A mesmeric and bemusing world bursts forth as I proceed to paint her. Our eyes rarely engage, yet she understands, I am the master and she the slave. And with each glance, I invade her, infiltrating beyond her thoughts, her vulnerability, and her nudity. I see what she is afraid of disclosing to me, all her fears and sorrows. Rarely do I inquire into a prostitute's life, as I already hear her tragic voice. With this gift of clairvoyance, when I encounter sadness I paint her skin a translucent blue. A woman of pure carnality, I paint purple and the hair on her body scarlet. Animals can represent their temperaments, so I may paint birds or reptiles beside them.

Putas and I share an elusive angst. Nothing about ourselves remains sacred. Only colors soothe us. Nightly, she applies her mask of war paint and camouflages her sorrows, as she hopes to allure the deviant. If I could give a harlot wings, I would let her fly away from the bondage of this earth to a plane without morals. I wish the same liberation for my art. These women, like myself, have restless and insatiable souls. As anarchists, we thrive in our damnation.

There are times when I don't need live models. But when I can't sleep, I'm deprived of my most valuable source of inspiration: dreams. I've painted my memories of home in rich Spanish landscapes. A golden Roman aqueduct in a dandelion field, a colosseum in Tarragona overlooking the azure sea, the charming stone villages and balconies with flower pots, the red fertile mountains of Montserrat, and lastly, a portrait of my dear Tia Rosa waiting by the edge of the port, her long black dress floating with the gusts of wind. Alas, my paintings of my country haven't sold. Are they rejecting my nationality, my existence?

Some think I'm insane for leaving my affluent family. What few understand is we have different blood; theirs runs cold, mine boils. When I was thirteen years of age, on the day of my confirmation, I met Rosa. She was standing outside the Gothic cathedral of Barcelona and called me over. At first I was afraid of this stranger. But her soft brown eyes seemed kind and sympathetic. She handed me a paintbrush and a letter. Everyday thereafter, I found a way to see her again. Through her, I learned that my blood father was a handsome bull fighter and my mother was a stunning peasant girl who caught his attention while he was in a ring. He wooed her during the slaying of a savage bull. Their romance for him was a passing exploit; and my mother was quickly discarded like his dead cows.

Like a trained fighter, I have a predatory nature. Sometimes, I can treat women as conquests. Yet I also want to believe that I have the sensitivity and idealism of my mother—a young woman who wanted to trust her matador's adorations and promises of devotion. However, the fate of my conception and the mystery of her complicated womb led to her demise. My life for hers. Can I merit the sacrifice?

My adoptive parents are aristocratic and conservative, grooming me to become a diplomat. Before art school, I studied languages and politics. With them I felt more needed than loved, an object, a possession to be displayed instead of a person. That was why I rebelled. Our passions differed. Eventually they gave up trying to influence me. Painting in Paris was my dream and their ultimate disappointment in me. My philosophies have never been understood, except by Rosa.

PARIS, APRIL 1936

I am grateful that my style continues to evolve. I've begun studying in the best atelier with a Beaux Arts professor. Fauvism's candy colors and suffused images are vanishing; bolder colors and sharper angles find their way to my canvas, as I'm discovering the world of automatism and the importance of dreams.

Almost every night, I am haunted by a recurring nightmare. I'm inside the cathedral of Notre-Dame, kneeling before a white marble sculpture of Death claiming a young man. Death is an enormous faceless person wearing a long dark cape. A distraught widow is crying over the body of her young lover. Then I begin to hear the sobs of the woman. Their eyes blink. Colors appear and stone turns into moving flesh. Death leaps up and grabs hold of my arms. He is stronger than I am, stronger than an ox. Effortlessly, he drags me into a confessional. Inside the dark booth I can't see him. I call out for help and he stabs me with a sword.

I wake just before dying. And for the rest of the day, I'm terrified of sculptures and cathedrals. The pain of a dagger leaves my ribs aching and my body weak. Drops of blood have stained my pillow.

There are many methods for interpreting dreams. But I don't want to be analyzed. I've found that surrealistic painting is the best form of expression for these night visions. As a result, I've joined a group of Surrealists, spending hours freely discussing our ideas and techniques. Art is as important to me as having air to breathe. Miró suffered a nervous breakdown when he denied his love of painting. This is why I've begun to write about my life and career, so I can't deceive myself.

PARIS, APRIL 1936

I earned a few francs in Montmartre last week. Tourists can't buy enough paintings of the Sacré-Coeur and Notre-Dame, and I can paint a set of five oils in one day. Since my nightmares, I refuse to enter any church. Therefore, I never pray, not even when I make the rounds of the galleries and show them my latest creations. The words from the art dealers all sound alike. "You have talent, but we're looking for something else."

Time is my enemy, or perhaps it's a fickle public. Nonetheless, I cling to my dream that one day my work will be wanted. Colors never betray me.

I'm sitting alone at a corner booth inside the Café Deux Magots. I write in my journal while I wait for my poet friend, Marcel Tourrain, to join me for dinner. I try to ignore the noise: clanking silverware and plates, the waiters hurried footsteps, laughter, voices.

Marcel arrives and we split a *plat du jour*. Marcel is poorer than I am and also comes from an affluent background. His parents stopped supporting him when he dropped out of medical school. Marcel has a pretty face that is more beautiful than some of the whores I've painted. He proudly proclaims that you have to be tortured to be a great artist. Most of Marcel's problems come from his affairs with women.

"I'm in love. I highly recommend it," Marcel orates.

"This could be terrible for your poetry. When you're happy, you never write," I tell him.

"I know. But don't you want to hear about her?" he asks.

"Go on then. Who is she? When did you meet her?"

"We met last night. She's the most beautiful creature I've ever seen," he says dreamily.

"Really? So, when can I meet her?"

"You can't touch her!" he protests.

"I didn't ask to fuck her. I just want to see her, now that you have my curiosity going. Tell me who she is? This could be dangerous. You're already getting jealous."

Marcel opens a blue pack of Gitanes and orders a carafe of Merlot. "We're making the rounds at the Sphinx and the Jockey tonight after we've exhausted our discussions on art, philosophy, and politics. Fifi will be there. Why don't you join us?"

"I'll go, but only if I don't have to discuss politics. You know how I hate that."

"You're making a big mistake, Carlos. Unless you take a political stance your life will flounder."

"I know. That's what you always say."

Our Surrealist group is a mixture of artists, most are Communists like Marcel. However, these photographers, poets, writers, and philosophers believe in the sanctity of one's freedom of expression. All of them are producing the most astounding work. Paris is an inspiration to all of us. The streets sizzle in Montparnasse on Saturday nights. Later in the evening, Marcel introduces me to his girl, Fifi de la Villette. She's a stripper who looks as sweet as a farm girl and thinks she's an intellectual because she reads Nietzsche. She performs at the Jockey before the famous Kiki de Montparnasse. I find Fifi's moves to be stiff and haughty. She's too thin for my taste. I prefer Kiki. I'd love to find a model like her who'd create such controversy. Kiki stopped posing for other artists after Man Ray grabbed her. It's rumored that she doesn't wear undergarments.

By three in the morning we're all starving again and head for the Café du Dôme. Marcel pokes me in the arm and points to the table next to ours. A stunning blonde is eyeing me. She's seated between two men who are wearing tuxedos with matching black silk top hats. The men are dressed identically, even their white bow ties match. I feel completely underdressed in comparison with my two-piece brown wool suit, bell-bottom trousers, and checkered tweed cap.

"Go over and introduce yourself. I think she likes you," Marcel tells me.

I walk over to their table and bow before them, tipping my cap.

"Joaquím Carlos Cortez, but please call me by my middle name, Carlos. You are certainly one of the most elegant ladies in Montparnasse. I would be honored to paint you sometime."

"Did anyone ever tell you that you look like Rudolph Valentino," the blonde says to me.

"Yes. I've been told that before," I answer.

"Carlos, please join us for a drink," she commands.

When I pull up a chair, a glass of Dom Perignon is instantly filled for me. The golden bubbles are quick to go to my head.

"I'm Princess Mitya Troubetzskoy. And these are my dearest friends Patrick Louvat and Felix Colombiere."

"I'm pleased to meet you," I say to the men.

"I know almost everyone who frequents the Dome. Why

haven't I seen your handsome face before?" she asks boldly.

I couldn't help but stare at her elaborate white skull hat decorated with ermine fur and ostrich feathers. The princess is wearing a cream satin evening gown gathered in a corsage that accentuates an ample cleavage, bare shoulders and arms. Ropes of pearls are tied around her delicate neck. Her makeup is dramatic—violet and mauve eye shadows with perfectly lined full lips in magenta.

Another man comes to the table and shouts, "Mitya, darling, it's been ages. How is the dear prince?"

The princess excuses herself and begins her table hopping. She carries herself like royalty, a touch of arrogance and innocence. Nothing about her is understated. As she moves, the long dress flows within the satin folds. Her feet look like they don't touch the ground; instead she appears to be floating on a cloud.

I am left with the two men. Patrick says, "Princess Mitya would like to invite you to a soirée tomorrow evening. She is celebrating the success of her first hat collection."

"Why does she want to invite me?"

"She likes to surround herself only with beautiful and talented people. We will see you tomorrow at the Tour d'Argent at eight o'clock," Felix explains.

"Thank you, I'd be delighted to attend."

I get up to leave and Princess Mitya yanks on my jacket sleeve.

"I hope to see you tomorrow," she says with a faint Slavic accent. I bow graciously and kiss her hand. Her pale skin is soft and smells like violets.

I return to Marcel's table. They're all laughing at me.

"She's got her eye on you for her next victim. Be careful of women with power and money. They're like black widows. You'll never know when they'll bite," Paul, a writer for *Humanité* says.

"She certainly has a swelled head," Marcel says.

"She designs hats after all. I heard she has two husbands," Fifi comments.

"I wouldn't be surprised if she had three, but I don't know why men fall all over her. She doesn't hold a candle to you," Marcel says to Fifi.

We stuff ourselves with apple crepes and fresh croissants and sip bowls of sweet *café crémes*. As we finish our meal, the sky is beginning to brighten to shades of tangerine and dusty rose. I pull out a notebook and pastels and sketch my friends. When I'm finished, I give the sketches to Fifi and she buys me a pack of Gitanes. The three of us share the pack during a brief taxi ride. I get out first. Rue Palantine, where I live, is dormant, except for the fluttering of feathers and the cooing noises of the pigeons awakening in the porticoes of the church of Saint-Sulpice.

I enter the Tour d'Argent in a white single-breasted dinner jacket that I borrowed from Marcel, along with all the accessories: a black silk cummerbund, white collar shirt, silk handkerchief, black bow tie and cuff links in the shape of a painter's palette. Even though I'm a gregarious person, I become mute in a room of strangers. Most of the people know one another and converse freely while hors d'oeuvres are being served. The party is silenced when Princess Mitya makes her formal entrance with her dandified men: Felix holding her right hand and Patrick her left.

The princess is wearing a long pleated gold lamé skirt and bolero jacket. A rose hat and veiling covers a small part of her coiffure. Tonight she looks wise, more mature; yet there are moments when she resembles a petulant child. She quickly discards her escorts and walks in my direction.

"I'm thrilled you came," she says to me.

Before I can answer, she takes hold of my hand and begins introducing me to a group of celebrities. She politely refers to them as Monsieur or Madame Poiret, Cocteau, Chanel, Gide, Genet, Piaf, and Hemingway.

At dinner I am seated at a table with a Hollywood producer and several French cinema actors, the most famous being Jean Gabin and Charles Boyer. Mitya is at another table with the fashion designers. Everyone feasts on quail eggs, caviar, salmon mousse, a vegetable terrine, beef en croûte, spinach souffle, and *pommes de terre au gratin* with truffles. For dessert there are a variety of cheeses, fruit tarts, chocolate eclairs, and flan. Just as people are finishing with their coffee, the lights in the restaurant go out. We hear a drum roll and whispering voices. Nobody knows what is going to happen. Then a spotlight shines on a stage, where the enticing and statuesque entertainer, Josephine Baker, dressed in a feathery pink costume, begins to sing for everyone with her high-pitched bird-like voice. While she's performing, Princess Mitya pulls me out of my chair, leading me to a secluded area of the restaurant, facing the terrace. Street lights are flickering and reflecting on the Seine like New Year's Eve streamers.

"I just wanted a moment alone with you," she says.

"I can't believe all the famous people here," I say, "Why did you invite me? I'm nobody."

"That may change. I want you to do my portrait. Will you paint me?" she asks sweetly.

"I'd be honored, but you don't even know my work."

"It doesn't matter. Bring your portfolio to my place tomorrow. Let's say around noon. Don't come any earlier, and be prepared to start work immediately if I like what I see."

"I wish I could paint you here with this colorful background of people."

"I always look beautiful. You'll soon find that out," she answers smugly. She heads for the swinging doors to an adjoining room. Then she stops for a moment, turns her head around like a coy fox and approvingly scans my physique with her eyes. "I see something grand in you. When I have this feeling about a person, I'm never wrong," she says fervently.

Djuna Cortez

PARIS, SEPTEMBER 1985

I spent the following week signing documents and visiting the banks on place Vendôme with Pascal. She arranged for me to be given three credit cards so that I could have access to money before everything was settled with the estate. When I moved to the Hôtel de l'Academie, I didn't want to become a nuisance to Pascal or force her to become a tour guide, so I left her alone.

The Hôtel de l'Academie was another quaint lodging situated in the heart of the Latin Quarter on rue Saint-Pères. Unlike my other hotel, they didn't put a time limit on my stay. I could have moved into the apartment, except Mitya had cleared out all of the furniture. Anyway, I didn't feel lonely staying in a hotel. There were lots of people around. It also gave me some time to get acquainted with my surroundings and slowly purchase the furniture I would need.

Every morning I would have breakfast in a different café, when suddenly, out of nowhere, a street market would begin setting up and swarms of active shoppers would come flooding in. From my outdoor table, I would watch these energetic people, both young and old, as they filled up baskets full of fresh produce and flowers. I would wonder what type of life did they have in this alluring, yet aloof city. I felt so indulgent in comparison, as I sat with my French-pressed coffee, basket of croissants, and pack of cigarettes, eating and smoking, and trying not to feel so alone and conspicuous. However, most of the time my thoughts would drift away from the street, to the past, as the aroma of coffee always reminded me of my father.

As a child, I loathed the bitter taste of my father's strong brew. In college, it grew on me, as I drank cups of espresso to cram for exams. My father took his coffee black and even drank it when it turned cold. I had to fill my cup with cream and add several sugars. I thought it would be easy to forget him and our argument. Money would soon grant me independence. And I would be free to live my life without his restrictions and biased opinions.

Emile liked to malign everything European. He gave up his French citizenship when he met my mother, Josephine Flynn, his lady of liberty. With a burning torch, Josephine guided him to the promised land of America, where he had many careless adventures. The first was enlisting in the army during the Vietnam War. Having a gift for languages allowed Emile to quickly climb ranks and earn new titles. All he told me was that he became a personnel and communications director. I assumed he had managed to stay out of combat. But he never spoke about his experiences. On the surface my father appeared hard and stoic, yet I always sensed a hidden fragility. It was out of my respect and honor for him that I never dared to challenge his introspectiveness. I was hesitant to assert myself, afraid of my questions and that his warrior nature would turn on me. It was as much my fault as his that I knew so little about Emile's childhood. I had wanted to ask how his parents died, but I imagined such horrific details about their tragic ending, that I didn't want to burden or force Emile to relive them. All I knew was that he had spent some of his life in Spain, France, and Switzerland, leaving him fluent in several languages. Emile's enthusiasm came in obliterating his past, living for the moment, and embracing everything American: anti-Communism, Cadillacs, hamburgers, milk shakes, Winston cigarettes, and rock and roll. More than anything else, the Vietnam War gave Emile's volatile nature an excuse to fight. Even when he returned, he continued to be ready for a battle; he was always guarded, except when he was ultimately defeated by love.

I wonder how my father lured Josephine, as they had such different temperaments. My mother was completely distraught when Emile left for Vietnam. Since he could no longer control her, a disgust for the American government became her primary focus. Josephine protested against the war by running across university campuses and screaming at the top of her lungs. She continued publicly to demonstrate until she was arrested. After that incident, she began to have difficulty coping with the responsibility of being a mother, so we moved in with my grandmother, who had a Spanish-style home in Beverly Hills. But nothing really changed. We closed ourselves off in our large rooms. And Mother was still distraught, as we were reminded of the war every moment we turned on the television and saw the red, white, and blue–striped caskets solemnly carried off planes. With this sadness, I went to school and resented that everyday I was forced to cross my hand over my heart and sing to the same flag that I thought would eventually kill my father. What I didn't expect, however, was that my country would save my father and that my mother would end up missing instead.

Josephine came from an Anglo-Saxon lineage that could be traced back to the first pilgrims. All I can remember of her is that the years my father was gone, she threw herself into music lessons and sang all day. She also watched soap operas, carried around romance novels, and ignored everyone around her. My grandmother also read a great deal, but it was always from the same formidable book. She had every version of the Old and New Testament and gave all her friends Bibles for their birthdays and Christmas. Grandmother often spent her afternoons lunching at the Assistance League with other pampered ladies. She would return with gifts and clothes for all of us, including my absent father, and even purchased several business suits for him that had belonged to Neil Armstrong. Sundays, she spent all morning and afternoon in church. Grandmother's parents had manufactured pianos, leaving her financially secure so that she need never worry about money. The only anxiety she had ever experienced in her life was caused by her gambling and cheating husband. He spent his days at the race track, losing pieces of their fortune. It was more of a relief to her when he passed away. I was too young to remember him.

The three of us suffered in our own ways from the absence of my father. I had nightmares of the innocent children dying in Vietnam and was forced to repeatedly witness my father's death. My mother and I never spoke of our fears. I never told her that my grandmother terrified me the most. In order to discipline me to her liking, Grandmother would show me pictures in her illustrated Bible of the devil—a red serpent creature was perched on a rock with hoofed feet like a goat, a monkey's tail, and the face of man with beady rodent eyes and a pointed goatee. Thanks to her, I had many terrifying nightmares which were timed with all of the publicity that surrounded the release of the *Exorcist* movie. Years later, I saw the film on cable television. The girl in the film was not much older than myself. I became terrified of the dark, of demons possessing me, which made it difficult to fall asleep without the light on.

Around us was a time of accelerated growth and social changes. We celebrated the man on the moon, and to the horror of Grandmother, my mother burned her bras, sang to the soundtrack of the Broadway Musical *Hair*, wore shiny thigh-high white boots with psychedelic miniskirts, and read books on women's liberation. Mother refused to set foot in a kitchen or stir a sauce and smoked cigarettes that were manufactured and marketed only for the female gender.

We didn't prepare ourselves for my father's return, only his demise. The year he came back, our lives went haywire. He brought back with him his own invisible demons and nightmares. That was the beginning of our tortured seventies. One night when I had awakened to get a glass of milk, I found my father hunched over the breakfast table. The small flame of a candle lit the kitchen. He was clenching a crumbled note in his hand, books were scattered on one corner of the table, and he sobbed into a bowl of Rice Krispies. I had never heard him cry before; he wept like an injured school boy. I tried to comfort him. But he wouldn't let me touch him. That day, he changed forever, and became a rock of coarse salt, solid and impenetrable. Drowning in his private pain, he pushed me away for good.

Mother left us. Where she had gone was a mystery. I was embarrassed at school. My father was humiliated at work. Nevertheless, we carried on. He made money for his clients in the stock market and worked day and night. I was occupied with school and busied myself with lessons: horseback riding, tennis, piano, karate, ice skating, and swimming. Everyday after school, and on the weekends, I was involved with a different activity. And like my father, I never stopped to let myself feel the pain of loss.

I have only one picture of my mother. Emile threw out the rest. In the picture, taken on their honeymoon in Paris, she stood on the deck of a *bateau mouche*, leaning against the back of the railing. A controlled smile was on her face. Was she happy? Her shoulder-length golden hair was loose and wild from the wind. Josephine had satin-smooth skin that was as pure and white as refined sugar. Her absence decayed our lives.

Grandmother developed cancer after Mother left and had to have chemotherapy treatments. This caused her to lose her lush mane of white hair. She wanted only me to wash the patches of hair that remained on her head with baby shampoo. Every time I see Johnson's baby shampoo, I think of her, and feel a tinge of guilt for treating her badly and not being able to love her. I had resented her for replacing the maternal role. When she lay on her sick bed, she asked only for me to keep her company. We would sit together on her bed and watch

The Lawrence Welk Show and *Hee Haw*. I was never more bored. In her own way, she felt sorry for me that my mother was gone and my father was oblivious to the needs of his child. She must have pitied my father, too, as she left him her house. When grandmother became sicker, she stopped talking about the devil and spoke of guardian angels. She said an angel was in the room with us and would look after me when she passed on.

The flea market was ending. Vendors were packing away their kiosks as I left the café. I headed in the direction of my hotel and stopped before the Faculté de Medicine, which was across the street. Looking up at the medical school, I noticed the building's stone edifice with detailed reliefs of the Hippocratic oath and ancient healing methods. Exorcism was among them, depicted by a collapsed young woman who was being held up by two men; one of the men had an amphibious body. In the vicinity of the school were antique shops, booksellers, stylish boutiques, and art galleries. In one rare bookshop, I purchased an illustrated early edition of *Les Dames aux Camelia*, the tragic love story of a Parisian courtesan and a writer. The salesman asked for two thousand francs. I was clueless as to whether that was a good price, but I didn't really care. And without even converting the exchange in my head, I automatically handed him a new credit card. Once I signed the receipt, he then carefully wrapped my book in brown paper. Most stores had the same etiquette, even with trivial items. All I could guess was that most shop owners didn't mind taking the extra time that was needed for a client. For the rest of the afternoon, I strolled around the quarter and stopped at Les Deux Magots for lunch. They seated me in a secluded section of the patio hidden behind a row of ficus trees. From that private spot, I admired the green awning with bright gold lettering and watched a variety of people enter and leave the café. Languidly, I nibbled on a *croque-monsieur* and sipped a *citron pressé*; I didn't have a care in the world. Liveried waiters called me "Mademoiselle" and served me with pristine white gloves. To occupy more of my time, I surrendered to a world not my own, as I read for companionship, devouring more of Joaquím Carlos's journals.

The next few weeks, the enchantment of the city and its museums became my primary companion. One of the first sights I explored was the Jardin des Tuileries, the gardens surrounding the Louvre. Several museums were in walking distance of the park. First, I entered the l'Orangerie. Cézanne's painting *Boat and Bathers* caught my eye. The softness of his brush strokes added a gracefulness to the nude bathers and captured their movements like a ballet. My mood quickly changed from dejection to exhilaration as I proceeded into other galleries. Renoir's talent for refractions of light and Van Gogh's flagrant sensitivity, conveyed through his bold oils and distorted angles, fascinated me.

In a downstairs gallery, I found Monet's paintings of water lilies covering the entire gallery's walls, from floor to ceiling. Complete serenity came over me, as I gazed into the shifting currents of the blue-green pond, imagining ambrosial fragrances bursting forth from the lilies and an aria of croaking frogs.

After touring the Jeu de Paume, I headed toward the Louvre. In the park, I passed through a smaller arch of Triumph. A mass of construction and scaffolding was obstructing the entrance of the Louvre, (I was told they were building a pyramid,) so I had to walk further and enter through a side entrance. By the time I got there, only two hours were left before closing. I rushed through the rooms to get to the Mona Lisa. As I approached the painting, a huddle of Japanese tourists were gathered around the portrait. When I finally was able to cut in, I was shocked to find out that all the hype was about a tiny oil painting, smaller than the book I had purchased. My knowledge of art was certainly limited. I had expected it to be enormous. The disappointment was also in finding the Mona Lisa protected by glass, which reflected forbidden camera flashes and made it impossible to get a closer view. Hurriedly, I passed through the rooms of Greek and Roman sculptures, until I found the Winged Victory of Samothrace. The colossal stone statue of a headless woman with seraphim wings stood at the top of a marble staircase, beneath a glass dome ceiling. At any moment, it seemed possible for her to take flight. Overwhelmed by the dazzling eight-foot-tall Winged Victory, I became motionless. What had happened to her head and arms? Who had shattered this magnificent goddess into pieces? Unfortunately, the room next door closed before I could see the Venus de Milo. I begged the attendants, but they refused to let me pass.

After several weeks of visiting museums, I thought I would be sick of art, instead I found myself spending more time in Joaquím Carlos's art studio. The faces of his models began to look more familiar, some I swore he had described in his journals. Then one evening—I think it was approaching midnight—I was overcome by an urge to paint. It was only when I was in the art studio that I didn't feel like a trespasser in this apartment. The loft was my favorite place in the apartment; I would have been content if that was all I had inherited, as I could see myself living as a bohemian in this studio, even eating on the floor, and giving up nights of sleep, such as tonight, when the rain tap-danced on the roof shingles. Calmly, I picked up a tube of oil paint and began squeezing globs onto a glass palette. Then more vigorously I added varied textures. Within minutes, colors bombarded me: vermilion, the nun's wilting floribundas, the silent war that was erupting inside me, a rage calmed by Cabernet wine; chartreuse, glasses filled with absinthe, emeralds, my sorrowful eyes, the Seine, pistachio ice cream, envy, greed, and dollars. Amber was lust, Van Gogh's *Sunflowers*, and cognac sifters. Black was Beluga caviar and my shadow side that terrified me. The palette I had created was extremely colorful and thick with my grandfather's lush oils. I played with my brush strokes like a twelve-year-old. Eight years ago, my father had displayed an aloofness to my artwork and discarded a painting I had made for him. My mother wasn't around then. After that heartache, I had lost interest in art. This time, I vowed only to be painting for myself. The challenge was transforming raw emotions and vivid colors into images. I didn't know where to begin.

FIVE

PARIS, APRIL 1936

I arrive at noon at Mitya's gigantic suite in the Hôtel George V. Felix placidly answers the door and is wearing another expensive black tuxedo. Patrick is also dressed for a formal occasion and is seated at the bar. Both men look like matching bookends. Their sycophantic eyes are callow, while their blood is fueled by champagne. The men toast to each other. Then, without asking me, Felix hands me a glass of Moët. I politely accept, but don't drink it. I must keep my senses clear.

Mitya quietly drifts into the room. Her azure eyes are sparkling. She is luminous, resplendent. Everyone turns to admire her in a teal Chinese silk pants suit with five strands of black pearls.

"I'm thrilled you came," she says, as she gracefully ensconces herself in a satin divan with miniscule gold bees sewn into the lavish fabric and overstuffed pillows.

"It's an honor to be here," I tell her, as I open the case and kneel on the floor beside her feet.

"Show me your work," she orders, while authoritatively reaching for my portfolio.

Turning the work upside down for her, I explain my first pastel. "This is my *Tia* Rosa."

In the drawing Rosa is leaning against the stone lighthouse at the opening of the Barcelona harbor. Her black clothes and long silver hair are disheveled from the wind. A thick pewter crucifix hangs around her neck.

"I tried to capture the woeful expression on her face. You see, Rosa could foresee the approaching storm and the loss of lives. It was always a very sad time for the wives of fishermen."

"I like the sketch. She looks like an interesting woman."

"She was. She passed away last year."

"You must miss her."

"Very much."

"I'm sorry."

I go on to show her the next charcoal. "I'll probably turn this one into an oil. Coco has lovely auburn hair, pale translucent skin, and Rubenesque curves. She posed very well for someone with little experience in modeling."

"So, you know her," Mitya comments.

"Yes."

"How will you paint me?" Mitya asks jealously.

"I can paint you in any style you like," I boast.

"You're the artist. You must choose."

She rings a silver bell and orders the men out of the room. They don't seem to mind as they're engrossed in their own conversation.

"I'll be right back. Get your materials ready," she commands.

While she's gone, I open an ivory cigarette box and chain-smoke to pass the time. I don't see her return.

"Paint me here and light my fire," she says coyly holding up a cigarette. A gold lamé tunic covers her body. Before I can say a word, she has prostrated herself on a tiger-skin rug, resting her elbow on the animal's head.

"Who's the hunter?" I ask.

"Me," she answers.

"I don't believe you."

"Believe what you like," she replies indifferently.

I bend down and light her Camel cigarette, which dangles from a sapphire and diamond–jeweled holder.

"I prefer American cigarettes to French ones," she adds, "but my tastes are different as far as men go."

"What kind of men do you like?"

"Spanish ones," she teases.

I smile at the compliment. "I need to adjust your pose," I explain.

"Do as you wish. I'm your model, your clay. Mold me."

Kneeling beside her, I run my fingers through her hair to loosen her perfect coiffure of gold shingles. Next, I angle her on her right side, allowing her head to rest in her right hand. The tiger's face is next to hers as she's propped up by her elbow; one knee is bent. She takes it upon herself to drop some of the fabric and expose her smooth white shoulders. When I return to my easel, she has exposed her breasts and part of her abdomen. Every part of her anatomy is flawless: her breasts are full, rounded, and firm, her nipples are small and pink. Her stomach is flat and her waist is defined. Her navel smiles inwardly. And her long masterful legs are as developed and as lithe as a ballerina. But what intrigues me the most are her feet.

"You're mysterious. I find that appealing in a man," she muses.

"I've never been told that before. I usually feel like an open book. It's you who seems to have many secrets."

"I love men and life. Is that a crime?" she asks.

"Not at all. Passion is a virtue in my opinion."

"I just adore your thinking. How charming you are!"

As I study her enormous blue eyes, she stops speaking and her emotions become mine. This disturbs me, as I want to expel my intuition and become captivated by her mystique. Instead, I'm faced with seeing her cunning narcissism.

Patrick enters the room and announces a visitor.

"I'm sorry to interrupt, but Mademoiselle Sylvie insists on seeing you today. I told her you're busy, but she won't leave."

"Send her in," Mitya instructs without moving from her pose.

An elegant woman enters. She is wearing a tailored gray chalk-striped suit. Padded shoulders accentuate her belted narrow waist, a straight skirt her long legs. She walks with the sophistication of wealth and refined breeding. I could easily see her posed on the pages of the latest fashion magazines.

"I'm sorry to be bothering you. I know you weren't expecting me, Princess Mitya, but I've got the bill from your dinner party. Were you satisfied with the wines?" the woman asks.

Mitya doesn't move or flinch, nor does she make any effort to hide her nudity. "As you can see, I'm in the middle of a session. But if the artist doesn't mind, you can stay. Would she be an interruption?" Mitya asks me.

"I don't mind if you discuss business, as long as you don't move," I answer. "I certainly would never turn away an alluring woman."

"Let me introduce you. Sylvie Goldstein, this is my new friend Joaquím Carlos Cortez. He prefers to be called Carlos."

"That's a shame. I prefer Joaquím," Sylvie voices.

"Sylvie, please sit down and make yourself comfortable. You can ask him if he enjoyed your wines. He was a guest at my soirée."

Sylvie turns to me and asks me the same question.

"The wines were fit for Bacchus. I'm just very sorry you weren't there to experience such a memorable evening," I answer.

"Well, there you have it then," Mitya says.

"I'm sorry I was unable to make it. I had a business engagement," Sylvie explains, removing her leather gloves.

I knew then that she was lying. Her eyes told me the truth, more than I needed to know.

"This lady is a brilliant business woman and consults on wines for parties. She even has her own winery," Mitya says.

Sylvie walks over to a mirrored bar and fixes herself a gin and tonic. "Mitya, please don't flatter me in front of strangers. It's embarrassing."

Sylvie's fashionably short waved hair is light brown with a hint of auburn. Her almond eyes have a wild feline stare. I can tell that she can be ferocious as well as fragile, and she has been terribly hurt. Yet unlike Mitya, she cannot hide her wounds. Once again, I focus on Princesss Mitya, letting her dominate my canvas.

In Mitya's portrait, I paint a snake coiled around her arm, because Mitya reminds me of an anaconda. She slithers through precarious situations, but her venom isn't poisonous. However, her urges are primal, and often she acts without remorse.

"Let me have five more cases of Château Helianthe d'Or ready for my next fête," Mitya orders.

"When do you need them by?" Sylvie asks.

"Next week will be fine," the princess answers.

"How does the portrait look?" Mitya asks her.

Sylvie walks behind me and peaks over my shoulder.

"It's remarkable. What an imagination this man has!"

Mitya is aching to move. "Tell me what you see. I must know. How do I look?"

"Well, he's painted antlers on your head with pearls wrapped around them. It's fascinating. Don't worry, you look beautiful. Where did you find him?"

"I know how to spot a genius; and he's gorgeous too, n'est-ce pas?" Mitya proudly says, as she plays with the pearls around her neck.

Sylvie blushes and looks down at her pointed shoes. My eyes follow her. Her gray leather shoes look new. I wish she'd remove them. Feet can disclose so much about a woman's character. I imagine that Sylvie has fragile delicate toes that reveal her innocent, childlike nature. Mitya's feet are well arched and wide; her toes are painted devil-red, and her heels are rough and calloused. This tells me she loves openly and is unrestrained sexually, but she's sometimes rough and domineering. My fragile heart would never sustain her impetuousness.

The women agree on a price for the bill and then chat about mutual friends. I lose track of time. Mitya begins to whine and complain. "Every part of my body has fallen asleep. I can't keep this pose much longer."

"I'm sorry. I shouldn't exhaust you any more. You've been an exceptional model. We can stop," I tell her.

Mitya sighs in relief and moves slowly, stretching and yawning. When she has covered herself with her tunic, she eases over to the painting. She nods her head and applauds approvingly. "Splendid! I adore it. Surrealism is so much in vogue. I can't wait for you to finish so I can show all my friends at my next party. A moment such as this is a cause for a celebration. Darlings, will you join me out for a drink? We've got great talent to celebrate and I'm not just talking about myself for a change. What do you say, Sylvie, will you join me?"

"Yes, if you insist," Sylvie answers.

"I insist. Let me also include my men. You are coming, aren't you, Carlos?"

"I'd be happy to," I answer.

The princess rushes down the hall and calls first for Patrick and then Felix.

"Are you intrigued by Princess Mitya?" Sylvie asks me.

"Who isn't? Does she really have two husbands?"

She whispers to me, "She may even have more. And I couldn't even begin to count her lovers. Aren't you one?"

"Me? Oh, no. She's much too wild for my taste," I answer.

"It's hard to believe she's barely twenty and has the design world under her spell," Sylvie gossips.

"That's not possible. I thought she was much older than me."

"She has a remarkable maturity and confidence about her," Sylvie concludes.

"How does she have time for all those men?" I ask.

"That is part of her mystery."

We are distracted by a loud female scream, coming from one of the bedrooms. Before we have time to investigate, Mitya returns with Patrick scampering behind her. He's wrapped in a white sheet like a toga.

"I see you've lost interest in me completely. You never even bothered to check on the portrait, and instead I find you fucking Felix. How dare you betray me! How long has this been going on?"

"I never wanted to hurt you. I worship you. You know that," Patrick says, falling to his knees and begging her forgiveness.

"You're pathetic. I don't believe you. You're only after my money."

"I want to stay with you," he pleads.

"You disgust me," Mitya says turning her head.

"I never meant to hurt you, Mitya," Patrick says, "I want to be with you. I'll do anything you want."

"Get out. I want both of you out of my sight. I won't tolerate this kind of behavior and disloyalty," Mitya screams irately.

" 'Do as I say and not as I do.' We're not the one who is married," Patrick snaps back.

"Get out!" Mitya yells.

I whisper to Sylvie, "What does the prince have to say about all this?"

Sylvie shrugs her shoulders. "I don't know. Who knows where he is? I understand he is much older. Obviously he doesn't mind what she does."

Mitya is enjoying showing off the drama of her tantrum. Patrick dashes for the bedroom like a disobedient dog. Mitya excuses herself. Twenty minutes later, Felix and Patrick return with packed suitcases. I find the scene quite amusing and nothing like I've ever witnessed. Sylvie and I snicker at each other as the men storm out of the apartment and doors slam.

Mitya returns in a short amount of time. She is composed and vivacious again. Her hair is pinned up with decorative amber hair combs and her face is freshly powdered; her lips are crimson and moist. She is stunningly dressed in a black crêpe de Chine sheath with a low-cut back. Black satin gloves reach her elbows and diamond jewelry decorates her fingers, earlobes, wrists, and neck. The incident has been forgotten; Mitya is ready to conquer Paris again and the world of seduction.

"How do I look?" she asks us.

"You look spectacular," Sylvie says.

"I have to agree," I add.

"I want to give you something," Mitya tells Sylvie, handing her a silver beaded cloche hat.

"The hat looks made for you," I comment.

Sylvie tries on the hat. Her heart-shaped face is complimented by the design that falls over her ears.

"I made it with you in mind," Mitya says proudly.

"I don't know what to say. I'm very touched," Sylvie says, looking into the bar mirror.

"How long did it take to sew all those beads?" I ask.

"About a month. Before we go, I want Carlos to come with me," the princess says.

I'm dreading what she's going to do. Mitya takes me by the

hand and leads me into the pink satin master bedroom.

"Wait here," she orders.

She returns with hangers full of men's clothing, the finest of silks and fabrics. "These belong to the prince. Pick a suit, any one you want. You can keep it. I think you're about the same size."

"It's very kind of you, but, I couldn't possibly."

"I want you too. This is a special night. You need to look rich and successful, not like a starving artist. Please don't worry about my husband. Believe me, he won't even notice the suit missing. And I can always blame it on an absent-minded valet."

"I suppose I like this suit," I say, pointing to double-breasted jacket with a black silk lapel.

"I was hoping you would choose that one. Here's a top hat and walking stick to go with it."

Both women compliment me on my costume change.

"You look dashing," Sylvie says.

Just as we leave the suite, Sylvie takes hold of my left arm and Mitya my right. The evening seems surreal, as the same day last week, I was eating sardines and day-old bread. To-night, I'm feeling like an actor in a Noel Coward play that I don't want to end.

A tan-and-white Rolls-Royce Phantom II coupé is waiting for us outside the hotel. The three of us squeeze in. Mitya leans over and whispers instructions to Sylvie, who is behind the wheel.

"Where are we going?" I ask.

"Don't worry, darling. It's someplace exciting. I have it all arranged," Mitya answers with a coy smile.

The car circles around place Vendôme and then we pull up in front of the Ritz Hotel. A mob scene has gathered outside. There are ogling spectators standing on the sidewalk, nosy journalists asking questions, and elegantly dressed people waiting in line to get into the hotel.

"This is a complete zoo," Sylvie says wearily. "What is going on here?"

"Just be patient. You'll soon find out," Mitya answers confidently.

One of the doormen recognizes Mitya and we are ushered

inside. As we enter the lobby, Mitya grabs hold of both our hands and leads us around a long corridor, taking us to the Cambon bar. People are shouting, laughing, and applauding as we enter the lounge. I've never been in a more boisterous atmosphere, except on New Year's Eve. We are seated on a leather banquette, before an Art Deco panel which reminds me of Tamara de Lempicka's work. Mitya plants herself between Sylvie and me. From this seat we have a complete view of the smoky bar, which is mostly packed with sophisticated ladies buying their own drinks, downing one after another.

"Order whatever you like, darlings," Mitya instructs. "Tonight will be an evening none of us will ever want to forget."

I order a stinger, Mitya orders a rye and ginger highball, and Sylvie has a dry martini.

When our drinks arrive, Mitya raises her glass and toasts, "To loyal friends, art aficionados, and to the importance of women!"

"I'll toast to that," I say, raising my glass.

The crowd applauds again, as a female jazz trio enters. The women are dressed in men's trousers and tails, with gold sequined bow ties. We watch them set up beside the bar.

"What is the occasion?" I ask.

"The Cambon bar has finally agreed to open its doors to women. Now everyone in the city wants to come," Mitya answers.

After we finish our drinks, we move to the formal restaurant. The room is crowded with the celebrants of this historic event. Silver platters of cold lobsters, mussels, clams, oysters, and crabs are set on each table. We are seated and immediately a bottle of Ritz champagne arrives along with the platters of seafood and an iced jar of caviar.

"I come here often, and they know exactly what I like, Mitya says. "Sylvie, please order a selection of wines for us."

Sylvie calls the waiter over and places her request.

"I can't tell you how thrilled I am about my portrait," Mitya tells me. "I'm going to hang it up in the foyer for everyone to admire. I would love another one for my boudoir. Sylvie, you should have your portrait done. It's truly liberating."

Wine bottles arrive in silver buckets and are set next to me. A waiter pours our glasses, asking me to taste the red first and then the white. I nod that they are fine, but turn to Sylvie for her approval. She then tastes both wines and confirms, "Everything is excellent." ·

"Sylvie, you must have Carlos paint you," Mitya says jovially.

"Oh, I don't know if I could model," Sylvie answers. "The thought of being still for hours sounds tortuous. I don't even like to get manicures. I'm much too fidgety."

I glance at Sylvie's hands, her nails are nervously bitten. She has thin pianist fingers and with them, she begins to peal off a wine label. Mitya is oblivious as she opens an opal cigarette case, placing it in the center of the table for all of us to share.

"What do you do with the labels?" I inquire.

"When they dry, I write notes on the back."

"What do you write about?" I ask.

"I describe the food, the wine, and the conversation that took place, or anything about the evening that leaves an impression on me. I like to have fond memories."

"It's a great idea," Mitya chimes in.

"There's an art to removing the labels and keeping them intact. You just have to dip the bottle a few times in ice water. Then let them dry on the table," Sylvie explains, illustrating the technique, first with a Sancerre bottle and then a Château La Fitte. "Most of the time the labels come off intact."

"You should make a book," I suggest.

"I save them in a tin box. I have a vast collection."

"She's so modest; I can't stand it. She has labels from around the world!" Mitya adds.

"I would love to see them sometime," I comment.

"When are you going to do Sylvie's portrait?" Mitya asks me.

"It's up to her. It would be a great tragedy for the sake of art if Sylvie never poses. A painting will always preserve a woman's beauty," I answer.

Mitya gasps and whispers to me, "Go easy on the champagne and bullshit, Carlos."

Sylvie pretends she doesn't hear my last remark. Mitya interjects: "I wanted him, but he will have to pick one of us to chase. I'm trying to avoid another ménage à trois." ·

Sylvie smiles astutely. Her eyes are sagacious, as she bites into her appetizer of coquille Saint-Jacques and then peels off the Ritz champagne label.

"How often do you see Prince Troubetzskoy?" I ask Mitya.

"He never bothers me when I'm working on a collection. We try to meet in the earlier part of the summer. He's a wonderful man. You should meet him."

Sylvie changes the subject. "Did you always want to be an artist?" she asks me.

"Either that or an undertaker."

"What an odd combination," Mitya comments.

"Not really. When I was a kid, I hoped to draw like Da Vinci, so I'd visit the local mortician and he'd let me sketch the corpses. In exchange, I would paint faces before their funerals. He liked my makeup and allowed me to come and go as I pleased. I worked there until I was punished by my parents."

"Why were you punished?" Sylvie asks with concern.

"They found out that I wasn't going to school. I was then sent away to a Catholic boarding school until I was eighteen."

"Did you stop painting?" Mitya asks.

"Not at all. I continued painting and was awarded a scholarship to an art academy in Barcelona, which I attended against my parents wishes."

"You must be a very strong person. Parental rejection is extremely difficult to overcome," Sylvie voices reflectively.

A man walks over to our table. Mitya introduces him. "I'd like you to meet René Vouchon. He's an art dealer. René, you've met Sylvie before. This is Joaquím Carlos. He's doing my portrait. I think you should see it."

"Enchanté," Vouchon remarks gaily.

René Vouchon has a kind fleshy face and a thin handlebar mustache that is twisted on the ends with wax, curving upwards. He combs his hair back with brilliantine and like myself maintains a short haircut. He is slight of build and appears to be exceedingly charming to women. His clothes are chosen with taste and an eye for rich fabrics. Vouchon bows to Mitya and then turns to me to listen attentively.

"I still have finishing touches to make on Mitya's portrait.

As you know, it's hard to transport oils. In a week, the painting could be viewed at Mitya's place."

Mitya continues to boast about my work. Then just before leaving our table, René gives me his business card and invites me to drop by his gallery and show him my work.

"René is honest. I do hope you'll take him up on his offer. He could make something happen for you," Mitya says.

I interject, "I appreciate the introduction. And I will visit him. But I'm afraid I must go now. I have to clean an art studio before midnight."

"Will you turn into a pumpkin if you're late?" Mitya jokes.

"A man who keeps his promises. What do you think about that, Mitya?" Sylvie asks.

"He does seem respectable. That's why I took to him," Mitya answers. "It's all right with me if you want him. I've been noticing the eyes you two are making at each other. I refuse to fight over a man, as if I don't already have my hands full. Anyway, I think he's made his decision."

Mitya politely excuses herself from the table.

"I'm hoping for a night alone with you. Do I stand a chance?" I boldly ask Sylvie.

"I could dine with you tomorrow," Sylvie replies.

My hands begin sweating. I'm in over my head; I can't afford to invite Sylvie out for a meal. It would be rude of me to take her to one of the *cantines* that feed starving artists.

Sylvie apologizes. "I just remembered tomorrow evening will be a bit difficult for me. Next week would be better. Let's meet for coffee in Montparnasse on Saturday around three in the afternoon. Here's my number. Call me next Friday to confirm and we'll decide which café."

"That would be perfect. You must have read my mind," I answer.

Mitya returns to the table, quietly places a cigarette in her holder, and raises her gloved hand to signal the waiter for the check. Money comes spilling out of her purse. Without a trace of modesty, she hands me several hundred francs and says, "For my portrait and the next one." She turns to Sylvie and gives her a thick wad of bills. "The wines were excellent as always. We should let this man go."

I stand up to leave. "This has been an evening I will never

forget," I say. "Thank you both for your delightful company
and Mitya for your generosity." Bowing to them, I kiss both
their hands and leave the dining room. Once I'm outside the
Ritz Hotel, I have to run to catch the last Métro to Montmartre.
I don't have time to change. The painter I apprentice under is
completely intolerant if I'm late. God knows what he'll think
of me when I show up in this tailored suit. He'll probably
think I'm rich and dismiss me on the spot.

Djuna Cortez

PARIS, SEPTEMBER 1985

From morning until night, art was all I could think about. I
finally decided that before even moving into the apartment, I
would enroll in an oil painting class.

The last day of September, I entered the enormous paved
cobblestone arcade to the École des Beaux-Arts. The architecture was impressive. A Corinthian column was centered in the
courtyard and friezes of columns covered the Renaissance
building's façade, along with flower boxes with red and white
azaleas that decorated wrought-iron balconies. Life-size sculptures of Greek deities were set beneath tall arched windows.
A sculpture of Zeus was comically dressed with a red bikini
bottom instead of a fig leaf. As I strolled around the campus,
students were languidly seated on a stone ledge that ran the
length of the building. At the end of one exterior corridor was
a shrine made of marble, bronze, and gold leaf. A woman
sculpted in white marble was reaching up toward a bronze
bust. The word *Patrie* was engraved in gold at the top of the
sculpture. I shuddered as it translated to homeland and birth-
place. Was this a message for me? Perhaps some divine intervention was guiding my path in France.

Inside the school were faux-finished walls and paneled en-
gravings. There also were lush frescoes, chandeliers, Sienna
marble columns, and Italian stone floors.

On exhibit were two canvases painted by students. The
work was modern and created in an abstract expression of red,
yellow, and green swirls that reminded me of a Kandinsky. I
wandered through the studios. In one room, I found a cluster

of life-size papier-mâché sculptures. They were humorous caricatures of contorted bodies with large bottoms. One sculpture caught my attention. The body was bent over and titled in French, *Le Péter*.

I wandered in and out of empty studios. Most of the spaces had large sky lights, tall windows, and second-story lofts. A student directed me to Bernard's class, where I found a bright pavilion room that was also used as a theater. The roof was made of iron and glass; natural light beamed down on a nude model with jet-black hair and pale skin. In order to remain unnoticed, I quietly climbed up a back stairwell to the balcony.

"May I help you?" a voice startled me. I turned and saw Bernard standing in the stairwell behind me. His voice was cold and reserved until he recognized me.

"We met at the funeral. My name is Djuna Cortez."

"Oh, yes. It's good to see you again. I didn't think you'd come. Are you here to model?" he politely asked.

"Not exactly. I would like to paint."

"I see," he said indifferently.

"I had no idea you taught in such a prestigious academy. Do you think I could observe your class? I don't want to bother you."

"If you would like, you could join my next session. It's private and not part of the school's enrollment. Have you ever painted before?"

"Not really," I answered bashfully.

"Sometimes that's better. Then you won't have bad habits to break. The next class begins in an hour. There are some beginners. Everyone is at their own level. Now, excuse me, I must return to my students."

After an hour passed, the pavilion room emptied and I walked downstairs. The model was also gone. Bernard and I were alone. He gave me a seat, setting me up with an easel, a sketching pad, and a box of charcoals.

"All you have to do is let the model inspire you," he said.

"You can't expect me to sketch a live model! I've never done that before," I exclaimed.

"You must try. I don't coddle my students. Art is about taking risks," he answered.

On the hour, an influx of students arrived and assembled

themselves into their seats, beside easels. Shifting nervously in my seat, my heart fluttered. As I held a charcoal, my hands began to tremble, making smudges on the paper. Already, I felt useless. This was a mistake. But it was too late to back out without looking like a fool. The other students seemed relaxed and prepared when Bernard began his lecture. He stood in the center of the class and began saying, "I want all of you to first empty your minds of everything you have ever learned about the word limitation. Imagine yourself being five years old again, fearless, bold. With the eyes of an inquisitive child, I want you to put charcoal, oils, or pastels to paper. Try to cease your critical thinking.

"I have a special model for us this afternoon. She's worked for magazine photographers and not just ateliers, so it's a great privilege to have her. But first I want to mention that I'm pleased to see some new faces. We learn through other artists. Artists need honest criticism. We'll begin this semester by studying Les Nabis, a style also known as Intimisme. And during your free time, I want you to frequent as many museums as you can and study the works of Bonnard, Gauguin, and Vuillard. I expect a ten-page paper on each artist. As painters in this class, I want you to strive for impressionism *dans la vie quotidienne.* In your everyday life, I want you to make observations, putting them into a sketchbook. By the end of this session, we'll begin to explore Expressionism and Surrealism: the works of Van Gogh, Soutine, Modigliani, Chagall, Dali, and Picasso. For those of you who are beginners, I don't expect you to be proficient in oil painting. What I prefer is that every week you fill up a sketch pad and hand it in to me. Now, help me welcome our model."

Bernard opened a side door. A model of African descent sashayed into the room. She stood over six feet, and tied around her lithe body was a turquoise, white, and gold sarong. Blue-black hair cascaded in curls past her shoulders. Bernard continued speaking. "By studying with me, I hope to raise your level of passion and intensity for color. Don't just look at the surface, as beautiful as she may be, but try to look beyond the circumference of the model. Tell me what she's feeling. Delve into your own psyche. Challenge your apprehensions and break through your fears. This is the place to release inhibitions and forget everything you've ever been taught."

The model sat down on a tall wood stool in the center of the room. Bernard signaled for her to stand up and drop her wrap to the floor. Her ebony skin was the texture of velvet. She stood with her arms to her sides, one foot flexed in front of her. Black kohl and lime shadow outlined her dark animated eyes like the portraits of Egyptian queens. Her gaze was focused at the far end of the room, never making eye contact with the students. She had an aquiline nose, pomaceous cheekbones, and pouting bronze lips. Her body had the strength of an athlete and reminded me of the Winged Victory. As I sketched her, I drew wings around her shoulders. What was most compelling about her was a mischievous smile that reminded me of the Mona Lisa. She was serious, but also amused, yet removed from reality. Her smile was impossible to capture. I gave my best efforts to the sketch, but was frustrated with the outcome. A student winked at me as he acknowledged my work. His oil painting was almost flawless. He even captured the light that reflected off the model's skin and hair.

"You must be patient and practice every day," he whispered.

"How do you develop patience?" I asked.

"You fall in love with the process. I've been painting since I was four. I'm Rudi Lasalle, by the way."

Rudi was in his early twenties. He had long disheveled strawberry-blond hair and a goatee. It didn't take long to see that he possessed a striking resemblance to Van Gogh, which he seemed to know and exploit. A straw hat rested on the left side of his easel.

Bernard interrupted us. "Stop talking! You'll have time for that when we break. For those of you who want to, you can join me at the Café Voltaire after class. Then we can talk forever, but in class we must concentrate. I want to see you work!" The teacher turned to Rudi and said, "You have to change her smile. What's that mess you did? It's all wrong. Do it over."

I would have died if he had said that to me. I would have run out of the class completely distraught, never to return again. Fortunately, Bernard glanced quickly at my work and smiled approvingly. I was spared any judgement, at least for the time being.

When the class ended, a few students remained behind. I also stayed. Once we left the school, the instructor guided a talkative group along the quai Malaquais to the Café Voltaire, which overlooked the Seine. This was evidently part of a routine, because the waiter recognized Bernard and quickly gathered a few tables together, so all of us could sit together outside.

"Where are you from, mademoiselle?" I asked the model with the aloof smile.

"Please, call me Naravine. I was born in Somalia, but my parents moved to London when I was ten. What about you? Aren't you from the States?"

"Yes. However, I was born in France."

"You've only just moved to Paris. Isn't that right?" Bernard asked.

"Yes. Did I tell you that?"

Bernard addressed the group: "Let me commend all of you for your work today, especially Naravine. It was most generous of her to keep her appointment. She just got back from a safari. You must still be terribly jet-lagged."

"I'm always jet-lagged," Naravine conceded.

"How was Kenya?" Bernard asked her.

Naravine smiled. She had everyone's attention. "Most of the time I was working. I had a photo shoot off the Gulf of Guinea, where I made love with a voodoo shaman in Keta. He lived in an enormous cave where we drank splendid potions. I brought back some of his special healing blends. I also befriended a zoologist and witnessed the birth of an elephant. The zoologist gave me a baby spider monkey."

She opened her purse and showed us a picture of her pet and a stash of shiny amber bottles.

"Where's your monkey?" a student asked.

"She was confiscated at the airport." Naravine shed a tear. Bernard wrapped his arm around her. "There, there. It can't be that bad."

"Titiwa was so cute," she said wiping away her quick tears.

"I'm very sorry about your monkey. Can you get another one?" I asked.

The model crossed her legs and held up a fresh cigarette. Bernard promptly lit it for her. She inhaled deeply, and while expelling smoke, she said, "I'm a fatalist. It's better I don't have any pets. I've been unsuccessful with cats; I must have bad feline karma. Since I travel so much, I'm better off without an animal."

Bernard joked, "You can never be accused of having a monkey on your back."

"What an adventurous life you lead! Wherever you go, excitement follows," Rudi said with admiration.

Bernard whispered something in Naravine's ear. She glanced at me and then turned to him, giving him a disapproving look. Then without speaking, Naravine got up from the table and walked inside the café.

"What are your plans for the rest of the evening?" Rudi asked me.

Before I could answer, Naravine returned and everyone's attention was focused on her. Her hair was now pinned up, which exposed more of her perfect facial bone structure.

Bernard leaned forward and said to me, "You should let Naravine show you around Paris. She knows where all the best shopping is."

Naravine didn't answer. Her expression became more distant and reserved.

"I certainly don't want to impose myself on anyone," I said. "It may take me some time. But eventually I'll find my way around this city and stop getting lost in the Métro. I really don't mind. It's been fun discovering new areas."

"I'd be happy to show you around," Rudi said enthusiastically.

"Rudi, you have a lot of work to do. Don't neglect your exams," Bernard warned.

"You're right. But it's my fault for going out with my teacher. How much fun can I expect to have?"

Naravine stood up, handed me her card, and said to me in a rather formal tone, "Call me next week and we'll arrange something. I'll be free by then."

I hesitantly thanked her. After she left, more students departed, until only Bernard and Rudi remained.

Sundown was approaching, so we moved to an indoor table. Bernard sat between Rudi and me like an overprotective chaperone. I ordered a Kir royale. The men had second rounds of a *demi pression*.

"You should probably eat something. I'm going to have a paté sandwich. Will you have one?" Rudi asked.

"Yes, that sounds good," I answered.

"Bernard?"

"No, thank you, nothing for me," Bernard said pensively.

"Is something wrong?" Rudi asked.

"No," Bernard answered, shaking himself out of his trance, "I'm just tired. It's my own damn fault. I live too much for the moment. I'm on my own bizarre schedule, sleeping when I shouldn't, waking when it's dark, eating when restaurants are empty, rising early on Sundays, and sleeping late on Monday mornings."

"I'd like to live like that. You live by your own rules," Rudi commented. "One day, I hope to be like you."

Bernard placed his hand over his mouth, "Bah, I'm a sad spectacle. If I had a choice, I'd never be an artist."

"What would you do?" I asked incredulously.

"One becomes an artist out of compulsion. Art chooses you. Then you live at the mercy of your creativity. I worship inspiration; I'm a whore for it and will do anything to feel it. Students who tell me they want to be artists, I tell them to commit only if they're completely miserable doing everything else. They have to tell me that they *must* create or they'd rather die!"

"That's quite extreme," I observed.

"It appears you have some imagination. I can tell that from your first sketch. Give yourself a few months to see how you transform. In the meantime, absorb everything, drink in life, and pay attention to colors. But let me ask you this first question. Do you believe black is better than white?" Bernard asked in a serious manner.

"I don't quite understand."

"All right. Do you prefer the color white to black?"

"You've still confused me. I like all colors. I don't have a preference for one or the other. All are important to painting. Anyway black, white, and green are my favorite colors to wear," I answered.

"Good enough. Think about this. Do you think character equals fate?" Bernard asked me.

"With some people that may be true. But I would hate to think that people deserve their misfortunes. Children don't deserve hunger, abuse, or the cruelties of war. Therefore, character cannot equal fate," I replied.

"You have to know that the French love philosophy. So, let me continue on the subject. Do you believe in God?" Rudi asked.

"I don't believe in a punishing one. I think all humans have a divine nature," I answered.

"You're idealistic. That's good for an artist. I'm looking forward to working with you. It's time for me to leave. Here's my class schedule and fees. I'll see you next Wednesday," Bernard said. He poked his finger at Rudi's shoulder. "And I want to see you in good shape tomorrow for your exam."

"Oui, oui. D'accord," Rudi answered.

Bernard stood up and shook my hand. "It was nice seeing you again, Djuna," he said warmly.

Rudi angled his chair and put his feet up on the empty chair between us. "He's a terrific teacher. I've learned a great deal from him. If you don't mind me being honest, I think he's attracted to you."

"I don't think so. He's far too old for me, and I'd never get involved with a teacher," I protested.

"Maybe you don't like the color black?"

"I don't have a problem with that. He's just not my type."

"What about me?"

I avoided his question and took several bites of my sandwich.

"You didn't answer me," Rudi repeated.

"I'd like to be friends. For now, I only want to sit at this table until I see the sunrise. Then it will be my twenty-first birthday. I was born at five in the morning."

"Are you sure you want to spend your birthday in this dingy café?" he asked.

"Positive."

Hours passed. We continued talking and had the café to ourselves.

"Do you know what color the Seine becomes at dawn?" I asked.

"I haven't a clue. Let's find out. It sounds like you're serious about becoming a painter," he remarked.

"Frankly, I'm not really sure of what I want. The artist's mind fascinates and intimidates me. An exquisite painting makes me feel alive and grateful to be able to witness it. My grandfather had a gift of moving people through his vivid oil paintings. There's so much for me to learn before I could ever get to that point."

"You need to give yourself time."

"That's another problem I have. I'm not very patient," I confessed.

"It is terribly hard and almost impossible to make a living as an artist. I take it your grandfather made a living at his art. Have I heard of him?"

"You may have. Joaquím Carlos Cortez."

"Oh, yes. His work was very good. I'm also studying graphic design so I can work as an illustrator or as a designer's assistant. I can't rely on painting alone," he admitted.

"You're fortunate that you have a direction. One of my fears is of wasting my life and ending up like a discarded bouquet of flowers found in an alley by a street bum. They could have been beautiful roses, but the buds wilted before their prime. The petals never opened and their sweet fragrance soured."

"It sounds like the beginning of a short story. Do you write?" Rudi asked.

"I wrote a macabre play when I was ten. It was about a royal family and everyone killed each other. That was before I read Shakespeare's *Richard III*. I don't know if I have enough imagination to write fiction."

Rudi leaned back again in his chair. "Why don't you try? Tell me a story. I can't afford a television. And I don't get out much to see films. I don't care if your story is true or fictitious."

"It's my birthday and you're asking me to entertain you?"

"Why not? I'll sketch for you. Let's challenge ourselves."

"I've never been asked do anything like this. But I like challenges. Give me a minute," I said.

"Tell me a poèm. Start with an image. I like the discarded flowers; I see them clearly. They're red roses."

"Yes," I said closing my eyes. "I see them too!" I exclaimed. "There lived a man, a vagabond—"

"Yes. Yes. Go on. I bet you do have a good imagination," he interrupted.

"His home was in an alley behind the rue Saint-Jacques. One night he found a discarded bouquet of crimson roses next to his favorite trash bin. The trash bin belonged mostly to a créperie that had the best leftovers in the Latin Quarter. He nibbled on a few strawberries with *chantilly* and picked up the bouquet as he finished a half-eaten waffle. It didn't take long before he drifted off to sleep beside the trash bin, the bouquet cradled in his arms like a purring kitten. The roses made him dream of love, romance, and clandestine lovers. Shall I continue?"

"You've peaked my interest. Please go on."

"The following evening he stood outside a restaurant watching a beautiful woman. Her name was Céline. He could see her clearly through the glass window. She sat in an elegant brasserie that overlooked Notre-Dame. He imagined what her life was like and why she was there, alone. It was going to be a special night for Céline, as it was her twenty-first birthday. Tonight was most exciting for her since she was going to celebrate it with Gaston. For her special rendezvous, she wore a new red dress and she paid careful attention to what she wore underneath: white lace garters, a satin bra and matching undergarments, as she knew Gaston appreciated her taste in expensive lingerie."

"You're too much! Is this going to be porno?" Rudi asked. "I don't think I can take this."

"Is it bad?"

"No, no, it's interesting. Go on."

"An hour passed, and with owllike precision, she gazed out the window. A deluge was coming down. Water droplets shone under the street lamps like liquid mercury; pools of water carried reflections from the streets, reflections of her somber face. Tapping the pavement, the falling rain droned in her head like rhythmic drums, almost hypnotizing her. Another hour lapsed. She shifted positions on the red velvet cushions. Her silky legs were crossed at the knee. Nervously, she was swinging one leg. Perhaps her watch was wrong. She stared at it several times and disturbed the waiter for the exact time. On her third kir and her tenth Gitane, she began to worry. It was impossible for her to reach Gaston by phone."

"Why?" Rudi asked.

"I will explain. The restaurant began emptying; clients stared at Céline as if she was an impostor. An immigrant worker in a white apron pulled out a mop and began to wash the floors with ammonia. Meanwhile, Céline stoically remained in her booth. The worker patiently cleaned around her shaking feet. Any moment, her handsome lover would arrive.

"The bum staggered into the restaurant. The workers seemed too tired to stop him. He knew his stench made Céline cringe, but he moved toward her and tossed a fresh bouquet of red roses and a card onto her white linen tablecloth. The swaying bum was simply following orders. Orders that would reward him with a best friend, his own bottle of port.

"Céline's heart fluttered. Was Gaston hiding behind the corner, waiting to surprise her with a ring? Was he in a limousine that would dash them off to the Riviera? She opened the sealed white card. Her heart sank in her chest as she read the note.

I'm sorry for ever dragging you into this mess. I can't leave my wife like I had promised. We have to call this off. You deserve better than what I can give you, than what I am.

Please forgive me.

Gaston

"Céline burst into tears. Forgetting to pay her check, she bolted out of the restaurant. Frantic, she searched the dark alley for Gaston. Where did he go? Would Gaston admit his mistake and take her back? Swaying under a streep lamp, the bum watched the dejected woman. It was cold outside. She had left her cape inside the brasserie. He saw the outline of her breasts in her scant dress. Cars raced along rue Saint-Jacques, wheels hissing and splattering dirty water. Céline ran through the dark alley, discarding the bouquet of roses in a trash bin. As she kept running, pain was strangling her heart; rain was soaking her clothes. The fog was dense, inhibiting her visibility. A sudden flash of yellow lights, a moment of blindness, and then panic, Céline froze like a frightened deer on the highway. Her body hit the street with a loud thud—flesh against stone. A white Renault came to a screeching halt; tires reeked of burning rubber. Gaston got out of the car. There was morbid silence as he looked down at his dead mistress.

"Ambulance sirens hurt the bum's ears. He winced. He had never liked to gawk at accidents, as they happened frequently. And he was always the first witness. The bum walked away with his fingers plugging his ears. Loyally, he returned to his favorite trash bin and found a bottle of Courvoisier and emptied the last remaining drops. Delicately, he picked up the discarded bouquet. The fresh roses smelled better than the blood spilling into the gutter. Then he curled up beside the bin and dreamed of finding more roses that would feel like a woman's breasts against his cold dry lips."

Rudi swallowed several times and took a sip of beer. "It's film noir, but I like it. Did you plan it that way?"

"No. I just made it up."

He pulled out a sketch pad from a soft brown leather backpack. "How did you come up with all of that?"

"It was simple. The very first sentence felt almost dictated to me."

"Here, you should write it all down," he said, handing me some paper and a pencil.

"I couldn't. It just wouldn't be the same. The moment is gone." I refused, pushing his sketch pad away.

Rudi lit another cigarette and said, "Well, if I were you I'd keep writing. It was quite entertaining."

"Thank you. But I want to tell true stories, have my own experiences. I don't want to have to lock myself up in a room with a typewriter or computer and have to make something up for it to be exciting. Adventures happen in this city everyday. One can breathe in the history from the streets. Do you know that tomorrow I haven't a clue what I'm going to do? I may go to Parc Monceau, or the Rodin museum, or just take a walk and browse the shops in Les Halles. I don't have any obligations. Anything could happen tomorrow. It's complete freedom. Does this make me a bad person?" I asked.

"I think you're a spirited person. Your life is certainly enviable to someone like me who has nothing but responsibilities. It does sound nice. I wish I had that kind of freedom. I was supposed to work in a restaurant tonight, clean the floors and dishes. Maybe I would have met Céline. There are probably thousands of pitiable women like her in this city. Love. Love. Oh, the perils of love, I think it's a disease one should avoid." He reached for the sketch pad and began sketching my profile. "Do you know you're an interesting study?"

I rested my head on my fists and enthusiastically asked, "What makes me interesting?"

"I can't quite put my finger on it. *Tu séduis;* you're the type of woman who could seduce any man in the room, yet you're completely oblivious. I suspect you're also kindhearted, but I know you're indifferent to me, so I won't force myself on you. Anyhow, it's better I stay away from attractive women. They're terribly dangerous for me."

"Why? Have you been hurt?"

"I'm not one to wallow in my mistakes. This has been a most interesting evening. I've completely lost track of time."

"It's five-thirty," I remarked, glancing at my watch.

"Happy birthday! I'm surprised they didn't shut down the café."

"I gave them a generous tip."

"Tip? Don't you know that's included!"

"I wasn't sure. I wanted to make a good impression."

"On a waiter? That's ridiculous. How much did you give him?"

"I can't give away all my secrets." I specifically hid the fact I had tipped three times the bill. My lavish tipping gave me an immediate sense of importance.

"It's getting close to sunrise," he said eagerly.

We packed up our belongings and left the café. Rudi followed me outside. The street was empty as we crossed to the quai Voltaire. Finding our way to an empty bench, we sat side by side, near the edge of the shimmering onyx river, gazing at the Seine, which became our mirror, our voyeur and crystal ball, telling us that the moment called for lovers, but there was nothing between us except camaraderie. I didn't know exactly what role I had fulfilled for Rudi, or what he was searching for. However, the purpose of our encounter soon became clear. That morning belonged to artists, or writers, or poets; our desire to create beauty lay before us, as we sat in homage to the river. For a Zen moment, breathlessly, we witnessed the sunrise, as all of Paris was splashed in an incandescence of rose. The bridges, buildings, cars, and trees appeared ethereal, softened like the faces in old photographs. A bâteau mouche sliced the water, leaving behind a wake and rippling tides of the most spectacular colors, transforming the Seine like a mood stone into fuchsia, aubergine, sepia, and then tangerine. And for our grand finale, the water gleamed a shade of fire gold.

"That certainly was worth waiting for; it seemed like our own private screening," Rudi said fervently.

"I'd like to remember it forever," I affirmed.

"I've enjoyed spending time with you, Djuna. Go paint the town red. I'll see you in class. And happy birthday!"

He stood up and waved an imaginary paintbrush in the air.

"Thank you for waiting with me. It's been very nice meeting you," I said, extending my hand. He grabbed me by the shoulders and flamboyantly kissed me on both sides of the cheek. "In France, this is how we say good-bye to friends," he explained cheerfully.

It was light enough for me to walk home. After we parted, I headed down rue du Bac and stopped in another café to have a continental breakfast of croissants, Brie, and grapes. That morning, I was intrigued and fascinated by the many colors of Paris; flashing in my mind like postcards were the places and sights I had thus far witnessed. Every day the novelty of my surroundings became more pronounced as I observed cultural differences between the Americans and the French.

In France, bread symbolizes a craft, a life force, and a culinary staple. On display in storefront bakeries were hundreds of assortments of breads in all sizes, colors, and shapes to choose from. Men, women, and children always seem triumphant when they walk home from work or school with a baguette or two tucked safely under their arms. However, it's the canines of Paris that represent a laissez-faire attitude and a love of hedonism that is shared by their masters. Pampered dogs sit like welcomed guests on café chairs. And all sorts of breeds dine out in restaurants. Butchers even list outside their shops the fresh meats ground especially for pets. On one occasion, I overheard two women at a café discussing birth control pills for their energetic bitches. The dogs mark the city; yet without them it would not be as decadent or as endearing.

I stopped at my apartment and rushed to the art studio. Daylight flooded in through the balcony window. Immediately I set up an easel and began sketching the reliefs of angels blowing trumpets on the Arc de Triomphe. I sketched the muscular back and arms of the gargantuan stone man in the Trocadéro, along with the fountains spurting jets of water into the air, appearing to reach the top of the Eiffel Tower. In one corner of the paper, I drew the waiters serving patrons at the Café de Flore and the Deux Magots. Even a chain-smoking old man with a derby hat appeared. Every time I passed the ivy-laced church of Saint-Germain-des-Prés, he was planted on a bench in the garden. He always seemed deep in thought as he sucked on a cigarette butt. Another day I saw him in the Luxembourg gardens. The vagabonds were an inveterate part of the landmark just like the fat pigeons that flocked around discarded pieces of bread or perched on the heads of illustrious statues. My throat felt dry. I was thirsty, but couldn't break away from drawing. All of that afternoon I remained in the studio, until I filled up an entire sketchbook.

PART TWO
WINE AND LOVERS

SIX

Goddesses, Wine, Dead Artists & Chocolate
The Journals of Joaquím Carlos Cortez

PARIS, MAY 1936

Sylvie and I are sitting outside the Closerie de Lilas, sipping icy Pernods. Montparnasse is crowded with the celebrations of spring: girls carrying bouquets of sweet lily of the valley, flower vendors displaying rows of magenta, fuchsia, and purple tulips, fat strawberries bursting with juice in every *coupe* of ice cream, and strolling lovers dressed in white hold up spinning tricolor parasols as street musicians play to them. The screams and laughter of children can be heard from a nearby park, along with the bells of a carousel. It is the beginning of rejuvenation, birth, sweet-blooming fragrances that cling to the air, wild bird calls, and my silent yearnings.

Sylvie is dressed for the occasion in a wide-brim trilby hat and an écru pencil-thin skirt and an aquamarine tunic top. Her taste in clothes is simple, classic, with a subtle elegance. She doesn't know what I had to go through to dress for our meeting. I sold five paintings of Paris scenery and a watch to buy a pair of gray flannel slacks, a black polo shirt, a Basque beret, and a gabardine sport jacket.

"Can you believe Mitya wants to be submerged in a bath filled with champagne for her next portrait?" I tell Sylvie.

"She's quite a wild card. I think if anyone were to read

about her, they wouldn't believe she's real. By the way, I saw the finished portrait. It's wonderful. Has René seen it yet?"

"I don't know. I haven't stopped by his gallery. But maybe I will after I do your portrait."

"What makes you think I will succumb?"

Raising one eyebrow, I say, "I can be very persuasive."

Sylvie smiles and watches the people. I offer her a cigarette. Holding up her hand, she politely refuses. "No, I only smoke a pipe. This is my first day off in years. I must admit, I have a lot to learn from you. You seem like you know how to enjoy life. Is that true?" she asks.

"It's been a struggle to have a good meal, but I appreciate everything so much more. You see I could never settle for a regular job. I'm Dionysian in temperament; I love the mystery of not knowing what tomorrow will bring. What about you? What do you live for? What compels you to work when most women are happy to be married and raise children?"

Sylvie rests her chin in her hand, carefully pondering her answer. "I have a reputation to maintain."

"I have a reputation, too," I say, as I stroke her soft hand. We laugh.

"I like to be in control of my future. That's not to say I don't want children. I love them. But when my family died, many responsibilities were given to me. It would have been different if my brother were still alive. You see, I had to take over a man's profession," she confides.

"How long has it been since you lost your family?"

She pauses with her hands pressed together like a praying monk. "Ten years. But it seems like yesterday."

"Were you very close?"

"Yes. We traveled everywhere. My parents took me around the world."

"How did you lose them?"

"My father took the wrong turn off the Grande Cornishe on his way back from Monte Carlo. I had declined to go on that trip."

"That must have been devastating for you. I'm very sorry."

"My entire family was in the car, including my only brother. I thought I would never recover. I miss my brother a great deal. We were only two years apart in age. The hard part is that there's nobody to help me or even to reminisce with."

"I thought I was the only person who was alone," I answer.

"There are many lonely people in Paris."

Changing the subject, I ask, "Would you like to see my atelier?"

"I'd love to."

In less than fifteen minutes we arrive at my studio. I'm relieved my roommate is working and we can be alone. Paintings of nudes line the floor where I sleep and work. She enters my room without speaking.

"I often paint prostitutes," I boldly declare.

"So I gather." She stops before each painting, carefully examining each canvas without speaking. Feeling her scrutinizing glances, I want to jump into her thoughts, run away, hide. Before I can stand a moment longer, she breaks the silence.

"I especially like this one."

"The poor girl sold herself to a drunken brute so she could buy a baguette, a bottle of wine, and a slice of Camembert."

"Did she sell herself to you?" Sylvie cautiously, but daringly asks.

"No, I only painted her." Pointing out more oils, I continue: "When I noticed the girl she was standing under a stone archway, near Pigalle. Her dress was torn; she was sobbing, and her only friend was a black stray cat wrapped around her legs."

"She looks like her entire world has crumbled. I want to know her story. I feel sorry for her," Sylvie says.

"That's exactly what I want you to see."

"Why do you paint prostitutes?"

"Because they're the vermin of our sexuality, the sinners and the temptresses who have lost their way and taken the dark and forbidden path. For me, these ladies embody depravity and pain beneath their blatant wiles. They are the ultimate victims. From a café, I can watch one stand on a street corner for hours, and I have at least five studies. Does this bother you?"

"I don't know what to think. I've been a bit sheltered. I was not brought up to try to understand these types of women or to feel any compassion for them."

She glances at my nightstand and picks up a copy of *Tropic of Cancer* by Henry Miller.

"That book was banned in the United States because of its pornographic content. He also has a fascination for unseemly women," I tell her.

She moves away from the book and studies my paintings again. "What artists have influenced you the most? Whom do you admire, or is that the same question?" she asks.

"Admiration and influence are similar. Often there are influences an artist is not necessarily aware of. However, I do love Rubens's lush mythological paintings. I also admire El Greco, but dislike Goya's faces and his mocking tone. I adore Ingres and da Vinci. As for my contemporaries, there will always be one Picasso, Miró, and Dali. I know them all quite well. All of us have our own distinctive style and flair. We borrow from one another. Soutine taught me a great deal about brushstrokes. Delvaux, De Chirico, and I do share the most common themes and images. However, when I paint a portrait, I like to accentuate some Classicism, like the work of Lord Frederick Leighton. At the same time, I try to give my paintings the mood of our current fashions; the work of women painters such as Tamara de Lempicka and Marie Laurencin do this. It is a shame there are so few women artists. A woman's perspective is important. You would be a better judge to tell about my work than I."

"I'm not an expert by any means. But I find it fascinating that you express yourself in this medium. I envy you. I'm not artistic at all."

"It's not a choice. I must paint. Life is precious. I feel this way at twenty, when most maybe feel the same way at thirty, forty or fifty. I race against time and hope I don't die before I get discovered. That is, if my work merits any recognition."

"It has to, because I can't stop staring into the faces of these provocative women. I want to know more about their lives. What has led them to temptation? You're provoking my sensibilities for them," she says, walking around the room and discovering another book from the floor.

"Are you an avid reader?" she asks.

"I like poetry, especially, Baudelaire and Rimbaud. And I like mysticism, the supernatural, and Greek mythology; I enjoy stories about deities. What do you like to read?"

"Flaubert, Stendhal, Shakespeare, Zola, and Proust are some

of my favorites. But I do enjoy poetry. In fact, there's a reading going on this afternoon in the Luxembourg gardens. Would you like to attend it with me?" she asks.

"Yes. I would like that."

"Good. Then you have to answer one question."

"What question is that?"

"Does it bother you that I'm older than you?"

"How much older are you?"

Sylvie laughs and waives a reprimanding finger at me.

"A smart woman never reveals her age. If you can accept that, I'll condone your paintings of whores."

"That's an easy compromise with someone as lovely as you. Let's go."

As we leave my street, Sylvie walks in smooth strides. Her feet barely touch the cobblestones. I admire her long slender legs, revealed through the slit in her skirt, and her rose-painted toenails, visible in open silver sandals. Her body seems weightless. I want to carry her, lift her to the sky, but I refrain. I must wait, as she needs to be treated differently than the other women I've known. Aristocratically bred, she's accustomed to codes of behavior that elude me. I'm probably not of her echelon, as I sometimes lack refinement due to my impulsive nature. In many ways, Sylvie reminds me of my father, the politician—she can be aloof one moment and charming the next. It's not that she's two-faced, only preoccupied with her mercurial thoughts. But I'm determined to prove myself worthy of this intelligent woman's affections.

A gathering of people form around the fountain de Médicis. I recognize Marcel and several other Bohemian poets. Sylvie and I find an empty bench under the laurels. Marcel stands up and walks into the center of the circle. The crowd cheers him and he begins to read. "The title of my poem is 'Diamonds for Breakfast'." He clears his throat and begins to recite:

"Voyeurs pay to look at you.
Glistening, nude—bound,

You arouse them beyond mercy,
Dancing away dreams.

Beyond a gossamer of sleaze,
I see your gilded soul.
A fallen goddess,
Who belongs in a marble palace,
Protected by sentries.

Let me serve you diamonds for breakfast,
Opals and amethysts for lunch,
And emeralds for a bedtime feast.
Drown every centimeter of your physique
in champagne kisses.
Beg you not to leave me,
Again

Trembling in this empty bed,
Your Mona Lisa smile gone.
You only belong
to salivating strangers,
and their devouring eyes."

After Marcel finishes his poem, an angry man stands up and says before the crowd, "That's enough about sex and dirty love. I want to hear about war. We must kill the Fascists. Spain is red." Marcel allows the man to take his place. The man is heavyset and short, contrasting with Marcel's tall and refined good looks. He begins to lecture us. "You should all be ashamed of yourselves indulging in love, when a country will soon bleed to death."

Sylvie elbows me and whispers, "Is this upsetting you?"

"Yes," I answer.

"Do you want to say something?" she asks.

I stand up and say, "I don't care for Fascism either. But I thought this was a poetry reading, not a political demonstration. People express their opinions in poetry, be it about war or love. However, the greatest virtue in man will always be love. That is what gives him the control to forgive and surrender to his enemy, looking at him with eyes of compassion, and never giving in to violence!"

The angry man is silenced. Sylvie smiles at me adoringly and asks, Do you still want to stay?"

"Let's get out of here," I answer.

We head toward the Panthéon, running through the gardens like rambunctious children, and hail a taxi on boulevard Saint-Michel.

Place de Trocadéro awaits us. Sylvie and I walk around the fountains and admire the gigantic statues of nudes sculpted to project an ideal of anatomical beauty. Walking along the edge of the fountains, she carefully tries to balance herself. Daringly, I pick her up, swinging her in a circle. Then, gently, I set her down. We find ourselves in the Champs de Mars beneath the Eiffel Tower and gaze upwards at the metal edifice like awestruck tourists. Her body is trembling.

"Are you afraid?" I ask.

"Yes. I hate heights."

"Come on." I goad her up the stairwell. "Don't look down," I shout.

"That's easy for you to say."

She clings to my waist and follows behind me. When we reach the top, the panorama of Paris is impressive and forboding.

"This is the most beautiful place," I say. A wind begins to kick up. Sylvie is trembling again and I hold her tightly.

"Don't be afraid," I tell her.

A hint of light casts down on her face like a spotlight.

"You are going to be some painting! Can I paint you in Versailles tomorrow?" I ask.

"No," she answers.

"Why not?" I ask meekly.

"I have to work. But I'm free next Sunday."

"Then next Sunday will be the day," I answer with glee.

After a languid dinner on a bâteau mouche, I escort her to her apartment behind the Trocadéro gardens. She allows me to kiss her. More than that, I want to hold her, but I'm afraid of

crushing her. Kissing again, our mouths open to drink in our
enticement. After a long embrace, I tell her with my lips that
she's the only woman I can cherish. Desire clouds our eyes,
dulls our perceptions, gently intoxicating us. It becomes painful to separate when she closes the door. I wave. She opens
the door again and blows me a kiss.

"*Adieu, adieu,*" she says. As the door finally closes, I'm ill
without her. We belong together. What can I do? My emotions
are out of control. Only she can satiate the void that has returned to strangle me.

I ride the Métro home. It's still early by nightlife standards.
The clubs are just starting to open. As I exit the train, I'm
feeling whimsical, impudent. I make an appearance at the Café
de la Marie, which is packed with a rambunctious crowd.

My roommate Guy tends bar and always gives me free
drinks. Before I can order, a woman comes up from behind
me and covers my eyes with her hands. A lock of her soft
auburn hair falls over my face, and with one sniff of her cheap,
gaudy perfume, I know I'm in trouble.

"Christ!" I shout.

"Guess who?" the woman precociously asks.

"The devil in disguise," I retort.

"Yes," she says and wiggles before me like a fish out of
water.

"I see you're out on the prowl," I observe.

"That's my job, *idiot.* I must always have my eyes open for
a good catch. Why haven't I seen you in a while? Where have
you been hiding?" she asks.

"I've been working and trying to stay out of trouble."

"That's too bad. *Tu m'ennuie déjà.*" She jumps on my lap
and rubs her large peasant breasts into my neck. "But you're
so *adorable,* Carlos. It doesn't matter that you're a prick."

"You should be able to leave me alone, Coco, since you
think I'm so boring! I'm not up to playing games. And I don't
want a model tonight."

"I love it when you play rough. I have something in my
pocket for you," she teases.

"Cool it, Coco," Guy says. "*Mon pot* wants to be left alone.
I, on the other hand, could use some warming up tonight and
these crisp bills in my pocket need some creasing."

"I'll drink to that," I reply. Guy pours me a snifter of Armagnac and we share a toast.

"To the splendor of whores," Guy shouts.

Coco interrupts, "I feel like modeling tonight. Carlos here told me I was the best he ever had." She begins to pose with her hands resting on her rounded hips.

"Carlos, you give all the women the best lines. How do you do it?" Guy asks.

"Did you see the painting he did of me?" Coco interrupts again before I can respond.

"I did, and you look fabulous, *Cocotte*. I may not paint, but I have other remarkable talents," Guy teases.

"Don't you want me tonight for a little inspiration?" Coco beckons me.

"Leave him alone. Can't you tell the man's in love?" Guy says firmly.

"Is this true?" she questions.

I nod.

Guy leans over the bar and asks, "What's the new *dame* like?"

"She's full of class. And I don't want a fucking whore tonight," I tell Coco.

"What right do you have to insult me?" she retorts.

"I have every right when I pay," I answer.

Coco slaps my face and yells, "You mean *brute!*"

The entire downstairs of the café turns to look at us. I smile in embarrassment. Coco loves the attention of the crowd and begins to milk it for all it's worth. She chides, "Well, so now you're too good for a simple girl like me. You've found a high-class bitch and you dump me. You told me I was beautiful and gifted. You have no right to degrade me."

The patrons began to jeer me. *"Cochon! Lache!"* they yell to my face.

Coco slaps me again and continues her *théâtre.* "I gave you everything I could. You stole my heart," she weeps loudly.

I laugh and stand up. "I'm out of here."

Guy asks, "So, what do you have that drives all the models *folles* for you? What's your secret?"

"It's nothing to do with me. It's the cadmium that makes them crazy," I answer, winking at my friend.

"Than I better start painting," Guy replies.

I throw an olive at him. Coco waits for her next match. I touch her painted face and say, "You're a real beauty. There's nobody quite like you, Coco. I'd love to see you naked again and cover you in paint, but I'm exhausted."

She whispers in my ear, "This is against my ethics, but you can have me *gratuit* tonight. What do you say?"

"If the offer still holds, I'll take you up on it another time."

She starts yelling again. "You piece of *merde,* worm, snake, flea bag!"

I walk away from the café and she continues to assail me. When I reach the fountain, I can still hear her shrill *"Salaud!"*

Guy catches up to me by the fountain. He's laughing hysterically. "You should see the drinks people are buying her. You'd think she was a great *vedette.* I only have a minute, but tell me about this rich bitch you're going out with." he inquires.

"Please don't call her a bitch. She's not like the tramps around here."

"Well, excuse me. Since when have you cleaned up your misogyny?" he asks sarcastically.

"If I ever bring her by the apartment, I want you on your best behavior. Is that understood?" I seriously affirm.

"Oui, monsieur. She must be something!"

"That she is. *Bonne nuit,* Guy. I'll be asleep when you come home, so try to be quiet."

"I will. Carlos, I need the rent by noon tomorrow. I want to pay on time this month."

"Pas de probleme," I answer.

Guy walks back to the bar. I sigh for a moment. He doesn't have a clue that I'd just spent all the money I earned on my evening out with Sylvie. Tomorrow will be a day of fasting, a day for building strength of character. I open my tattered leather wallet, only a franc is left. The coin falls on the ground, bouncing on the stones. I need money, fast, because I'm feeling as desperate as a whore. Picking up the silver coin, I make a serious wish, and toss it into the fountain of Saint-Sulpice. Hundreds of thousands of wishes have been made here. Perhaps as much as ten wishes every hour. How many actually come true? It was time to turn in, close my door on Paris; on the nightlife. It was also time for a journal entry before falling asleep. I knew if I didn't write, I would begin to doubt my dreams.

Djuna Cortez

PARIS, OCTOBER 1985

It was surprising to receive a phone call the following week from the art model, Naravine, who invited me out to lunch. I think if she hadn't called, I probably wouldn't have contacted her. I was usually timid about phoning new people. Yet, I must have mentioned in conversation where I was staying, as she reached me at the hotel.

We arranged to meet at noon in the Marais district. I arrived fifteen minutes late, because on my way there I had to stop and purchase the latest copy of *Paris-Match*. I despise delays and hate waiting for others, especially when I have nothing to read. I'd rather be prepared. When I've been stranded alone in a restaurant, I've memorized the ingredients on ketchup, mustard, and mayonnaise bottles and even the patent on silverware. People might consider me rude for my tardiness. That may be true, but I do always apologize profusely. Part of this unmerciful habit comes from my upbringing. Being late at the dinner table was my rebellion against my father who maintained his military discipline regarding time, adhering to the second. It seems disruptive, if not sadistic to force oneself to wake at precisely the same hour no matter the quality of sleep. Even on the weekends, my father wakes at sunrise to partake in a series of vigorous exercises. Even though I try to forget him, the way I was raised, my habits and fears follow me like a distorted shadow. How did my father so effectively vanquish his memories? I'm beginning to find that enviable.

Naravine was waiting for me at place des Vosges dressed in a florescent orange raincoat, a matching dress, oversized Elton John sunglasses and thigh-high white leather boots. She was an anachronism from the sixties, as she leaned against a stone pillar, looking posed for a photo shoot.

"I'm sorry I'm late," I said regretfully.

"No problem. I'm usually late myself. I know how it goes.

Did you get lost in the Métro?" she said impatiently.

"No. I took a cab. It's my fault."

"It's all right. I'm just hungry. Are you ready for lunch?" she asked.

"Yes."

"There are lots of good places in this square." We began walking around the classical brick and stone arcade, where symmetrical houses encircled us. On the ground level were restaurants and shops. And the second story appeared to be private apartments with pitched roofs and garret windows. Searching for the perfect meal, Naravine and I carefully read each outdoor menu.

"What do you think of this restaurant? Have you eaten here before? I asked.

"The menu looks good. All the restaurants around here are decent. Let's just hurry up and order. I'm absolutely famished," Naravine said, as she quickly enthroned herself in a chair. Sitting down after her, I inhaled deeply. Autumn was approaching; the air was crisper. That afternoon, the sun was shining brightly, unobstructed by clouds or haze.

"It must be exciting to be new to Paris," Naravine asked.

I cleared my throat and answered. "This city is overwhelming. There's so much to see. I've never been to this area before."

"It's one of the oldest sections," she answered. "How are you enjoying the art class?"

"Bernard has thrown me in with the sharks. It's quite a challenge, but I'm learning."

The waiter arrived with a strained smile and plopped down two menus.

"What do you recommend today?" I asked him.

"Everything is good," he answered impatiently. "I'll come back."

"Du pain, s'il vous plaît," Naravine shouted to him. Naravine ranted on, "Some of these waiters can be so damn haughty. I must apologize if I seem a bit impatient," she said, leaning over to me. "You see I haven't been able to eat all day. I had a lingerie shoot at five this morning; and I had to skip dinner last night so my stomach would be flatter." She began rummaging through her Gucci purse. "Damn it. Fuck.

Shit. Christ! I'm out. Excuse me while I go inside and get some fags."

"Get what?" I asked perplexedly.

Naravine laughed. "Americans rarely understand when I say that."

Naravine pranced coquettishly inside the restaurant, swaying her hips and moving like she must have done on the Paris runways. In her eyes, it was as if an invisible audience was watching her; and she was anticipating them at any moment to break out in applause. Returning with a sealed pack of Merits, she gracefully sat back down and pulled a gold and tortoise shell Dunhill lighter from her purse. Somehow, she had forgotten to offer me one. As she inhaled and leaned back in her chair, all the anxiety of the day evaporated from her stunning face. Smiling serenely, she removed a piece of tobacco from her tongue and confidently flicked the brown speck onto the ground with an orange fingernail. "So, tell me what happened after I left Café Voltaire," Naravine asked. "That was quite an exciting predicament you were in. Both men seemed desirous of you. Did they put up a duel?"

"It was all perfectly innocent. We had an engaging conversation. Nothing else."

"You must be naïve when it comes to men. I know Bernard, and nothing is innocent with him. He hasn't shown interest in anyone since his wife died."

"How awful! When did she die?"

"About three years ago. Life can be tragic," she said for a moment in a mock French accent. "It has been hard for him, cruel." She continued, "Anyway, there's much more uplifting things to talk about. This city calls to be experienced by lovers. Have you met anyone who tickles your fancy?"

I shook my head and studied the pedestrians wandering in the square. Most appeared to be tourists.

"Have you ever been in love?" Naravine probed further.

"I haven't. I do hope it will happen for me soon. What about you? Are you in love?" I asked.

Naravine's right eye twitched. At the same time, her mouth curled, giving her a crooked smile.

"You don't have to answer. I didn't mean to pry into your personal life. Really, I'm sorry," I said apologetically.

"That's okay. I don't mind. If you're a romantic that's fine and wonderful for you. Your exploration should be encouraged. Personally, I don't care to drown myself in sentimentality. *Il faut que je m'amuse.* I must have fun. For me, variety is the spice of life. I'll be turning, well, I'm not going to reveal my age, but I don't get the jobs I used to. Designers want anorexic prepubescent girls. I don't dwell on it. I want to enjoy life while I still can, before I have to commit myself to one man. Unless of course, he owns a yacht and a Lear jet," she mused, while puffing her chest out like an autocratic turkey. The waiter returned to take our order.

"I'll have the *Lapin à la Provençal.* What are you ordering?" Naravine asked me.

"The salad *Niçoise* and a *citron pressé,*" I told the waiter.

"Luv, you need to loosen up. Shall we order some wine? You're in France, relax and enjoy a two-hour lunch; it comes with the territory. Meals are the one thing the French never rush. Sex too." Naravine leaned over the table and whispered: "Keep your eyes open for some alluring men."

I tried to hide my blushing cheeks with my napkin.

"I've embarrassed you. You must be a virgin," she said ruefully.

"Do you always say what's on your mind?" I asked.

"Always. It's a compulsion."

Naravine possessed a remarkable self-assurance. Her rich British accent was refined enough to belong in the better circles of society; only occasionally did she sound cockney, but that seemed to be more a part of her jocular humor. She was sometimes brash and always savvy, yet she retained a childish quality that was charming, playful and spontaneous. I didn't know whether to admire or rebuke her insouciant manner.

"You were saying you only want to have fun. How do you make that possible?" I asked.

Naravine reached for the basket of bread and selected a few slices of white baguette. Meticulously, she removed the dough from the bread and rolled it into tiny balls, which she set aside in an ashtray. After that ritual was finished, she gobbled up the remaining crusts.

"I don't eat the soft parts; they're bad for the hips," Naravine protested and poured me a glass of rosé. "Luv, you really need to get *décontractée*. To Paris," she said, raising her glass.

I lifted my full glass to meet hers. "Yes, and to new friends," I added.

"It's important to cherish every moment," she said with her famous polished smile.

"How did you meet Bernard?" I casually asked.

"I first became friends with his wife. I model for him whenever I'm in Paris, because I feel so badly about the loss of poor Ange. Solange was her full name."

"How did she die?"

Naravine crossed her legs and took another bite of crust.

"Ange could have had the fashion world at her feet. Her beauty fit her name. She had the face and hair of a Botticelli painting, with skin pale like porcelain, and a stunning mane of strawberry blond hair. The camera adored her and so did the top designers. But Ange loved to party, champagne and cocaine. I mean the girl was *sauvage,* really wild. In order to keep her happy, Bernard had to take her to the finest clubs almost every night, where they partied with an elite crowd who spent the summers in Saint Tropez and Marbella. The exposure was also good for Bernard. He even had several art shows that sold out."

The food arrived and we began eating.

"How long were they married?"

"I think it was about five years, until her tragic death. Ange fell onto the Grenelle station Métro rails."

"My God! That's horrible, like *Anna Karenina.* I can't imagine anything more tragic for him."

"I don't think she did it intentionally. She was probably stoned. But Bernard has never been quite the same since," Naravine said, taking several bites of her food. "You know, life in Paris is mysterious. You can change living here. I don't know how it will happen for you, as everyone's experience is different. Can you feel an intoxicating sensuality in the air?"

"Yes, I think so."

"A certain mood comes over me when I'm in this city." Naravine lifted up her glass and shrugged her shoulders. "Then again, it may simply be the delicious wine. Are you ready to go shopping?"

"I've been so busy visiting the museums that I haven't had a chance yet. That would be great."

"What's your budget?" Naravine asked.

"I don't have to worry about that."

"No budget, even better! How difficult it must be to be *poivre.*"

"You mean *pauvre*, not pepper," I corrected her.

"A little spice never hurt anyone, luv."

After lunch we stopped in every antique and furniture store that tempted us. I purchased an Indonesian teak armoire, a Biedermeier credenza, and a Louis XIV writing desk.

"I'll take this and that and this too," I kept saying, as storekeepers followed me around their shops. *"Oui*, mademoiselle. *Oui. Oui,"* they repeated with exuberent grins.

"I like your motto. Spend. Spend. Spend. It's funny. You didn't strike me as an impulsive person," Naravine commented.

"I'm usually not. I've never done anything like this before. Then again, I've never had to furnish an apartment."

"I think this city is already affecting you."

Naravine showed me her favorite haute couture boutiques. She strutted into each store as though a red carpet should be pulled out for her. In one shop, when she walked up to the counter to pay for several items, the salesgirl turned her back and continued with a telephone conversation. Infuriated, Naravine slammed her clothes on the counter, walked up to the girl, looked her boldly in the face, and flashed a gold American Express card.

"It's too bad that you have better things to do than earn money. I wanted to buy these. *Tant pis,"* Naravine said bitterly and marched out of the store.

"Come on, Djuna, let's get away from that cold bitch. God, I hate it when they think they're too good to serve you."

Naravine was doted over in the next boutique and consequently she selected five silk blouses, a dress, and several belts. Her eyes sparkled when she finished the purchase. In another dress shop, I bought several outfits: Valentino and Dior black crêpe dresses, a white cocktail dress, a green velvet evening dress, and a pair of black slingback pumps. Naravine convinced me to wear one of the black dresses.

"Don't change. Let's go somewhere special tonight," she gleefully suggested.

"Where do you want to go?"

"I don't know. But you deserve to have a wonderful time. Let's see if we can meet some eligible men."

Naravine changed into her new fitted backless white dress and purchased a thousand-franc pair of shoes to match. She also didn't restrain herself in a luggage store.

"Are you planning a trip?" I asked.

"When I get a break, I want to go to Venice."

"How nice."

"Have you ever been?"

"No. I would love to go."

"Why don't you visit me? I usually stay in a delightful villa and there's plenty of room."

"Oh, I don't know. I'm going to be busy with my art class."

"I'd enjoy having a companion. I'm sure you can make up the classes. Venice might even inspire you." Naravine picked up another suitcase and caressed the smooth black and brown leather. "This is a gorgeous design. Do you think I'm making a mistake? Should I buy Fendi instead?" she asked me.

"The Vuitton suits you. It's dramatic," I answered.

"You should buy the Fendi."

"Oh, I don't know. It's quite expensive."

"So is everything. Come on. I'm sure you want to travel in style. If you can afford it, flaunt it," Naravine coaxed.

By the time we left the store, I had purchased a set of Fendi luggage, three handbags, and a wallet.

"My driver will come and pick everything up for us, so we won't have to lug anything around. I suggest we go back to the square. Can you believe we've been shopping for four hours? No wonder I'm famished again. Shopping always makes me ravenous."

"It didn't seem that long," I answered.

A chauffeur dressed in a navy uniform and cap arrived at the front door of the boutique and collected the shopping bags and luggage. We watched as he piled everything into a gold convertible Mercedes. When the car drove off, we returned to the place des Vosges.

"You must excuse me for a moment," Naravine said as she

vanished inside a café. As soon as she left, I became fair game to the hungry sidewalk artists. One terribly thin young man approached me and offered to sketch my portrait. He looked tired and hungry. Feeling sorry for him, I gave into his request and climbed onto a tall folding director's chair. A long period of scrutiny ensued. Faced with the emptiness of waiting, modeling made me nervous and uncomfortable. Naravine obviously felt differently, but I didn't like being stared at. It was already too late to decline. To occupy myself, I pulled out the magazine from my purse. As I turned the pages, I was faced with a far greater dilemma than exercising patience by being still. On the sixth page was my picture taken at the funeral and a story about me. My heart began to race, stop, and then start up again, skipping beats. To most people, seeing their picture in a magazine had to be a thrill. I suppose it was, but I quickly shoved the *Paris-Match* into my purse. It would be impossible to explain to Naravine my situation. I was embarrassed. Nothing I was given had I accomplished on my own merits, nor could I divulge that I often dined and slept with books, that sometimes ten books covered one side of my bed where a lover should be. Naravine must have found me dull, but was too polite to say. The fast and glamorous life Naravine led was alluring. Perhaps I could get used to it, except I felt like an imposter in Joaquím Carlos enormous apartment.

Naravine returned to watch the artist. "You see that restaurant over there?" she said, pointing her finger at an arched window.

"Don't move your head," the artist ordered.

"I can't look right now."

"The restaurant, l'Ambroisie, is one of the finest in the area. That's where we're going tonight."

"Do you know when you'll finish?" Naravine asked the painter.

"It's finished when it's finished. Great art can't be rushed. Think of the Sistine Chapel," the artist sarcastically replied.

"Hopefully it won't take that long! We're going to have a wonderful time tonight. I just know it. The two of us will cause a sensation," Naravine asserted energetically.

"Finished," the artist quickly announced.

"Already?" I asked.

The artist stepped away from his easel and proudly smiled. Naravine studied the pastel, as I eagerly hopped off the chair.

"It's quite good. He's captured you well."

"Do you like it?" the artist asked me in English.

I didn't care for the drawing. He had exaggerated my features in a style that mimicked, but couldn't compare with Modigliani. My eyes appeared dimorphic, my face elongated and hard. When the artist asked me again for my opinion, I pretended to be pleased and paid him his asking price.

After he left, Naravine reached into her purse and pulled out a bottle of perfume. "Before we go inside the restaurant, I want you to smell something divine," she said, dabbing some perfume on the inside of my wrist.

As I inhaled the fragrance, I commented, "It's sweet like gardenias and honeysuckle. What is it?"

"Paris. It just came out. I knew it would smell perfect on you. Now, go on and dab some between your breasts."

"Naravine! I can't do that in public," I exclaimed.

"God, girl, you really need to loosen up," she reprimanded me and pulled out another bottle of perfume, splashing some between her cleavage. She confessed, "For me, it's a night of Poison. I feel dangerous."

Her fragrance was also floral, but the aroma of ginger, musk, and other exotic spices dominated.

I followed Naravine into the elegantly decorated white marble foyer of the restaurant. Before we could enter the main dining room, a hostess glared disdainfully at us.

"We would like a table, please," I asked.

"They're all reserved," the woman curtly replied, scanning her eyes up and down Naravine's dress. I turned to leave, but Naravine wouldn't budge. Taking Naravine's hand, I whispered, "Maybe we should go."

"We would like a table," Naravine repeated. This time our request fell upon deaf ears. The woman opened her reservation book and avoided making eye contact with us.

"I refuse to be treated this way," Naravine whispered to me.

"What can we do?" I asked.

"I have an idea," Naravine said and reached into her large purse to pull out a slim navy Concorde notebook. Naravine said loudly to me, "I'm just going to have to write in my travel article that this place refused to let people of color in. They'll have a field day with this back at *The Sun*."

Naravine moved forward, peering into the dining room. Tables were set with freshly pressed white linens, flickering candles, and floral arrangements.

"Maybe we could have a drink at the bar?" Naravine asked politely. The woman studied our attire again. A man came over and nodded his head at the hostess. Following his instructions, she reluctantly led us to the bar. "Come this way then," she said abruptly.

Naravine triumphantly propped herself comfortably into a chair.

"You would think you have to be royalty to get into this place. I wanted to say to that old bat that we don't have lice, but I refrained," Naravine ventilated.

"I don't think we'll ever be in her good graces, but hopefully you can tell her before we leave," I suggested.

Naravine ordered two glasses of Muscatel for us.

"Why was that woman so rude?" I asked.

"She's a *vache*. Obviously she doesn't like dark-skinned people and must think that single women don't have money. I'll never know the reason, but I often get treated that way, not that I tolerate it. Josephine Baker left America and came to France to get away from discrimination. It goes to show you, even in the eighties, society can be fickle. It's obvious they prefer their own kind."

"I can't imagine what that would feel like. But she didn't seem to like me either."

Naravine elbowed me and pointed to a pair of well-dressed men who had just entered the restaurant. "Take a look at those two hors d'oeuvres. They're whetting my appetite."

The men walked toward the bar. Naravine gave them her acclaimed cover-girl smile and the men approached.

"Can we buy your next drink?" the blond man asked Naravine.

Naravine batted her long eyelashes, crossed her long bare legs, and flirtatiously replied in her heavily accented French: *"Non, mais on est disponible pour diner avec vous."*

The men chuckled and sat down on either side of us.

"We speak English. I'm Xavier Chéreau and this is my

friend Jean-Auguste de Briard, the shorter man said.

Naravine jubilantly introduced us.

"She didn't mean to offend you by inviting ourselves to dinner. She's just frank and speaks her mind," I told the men.

"We like that," Xavier said.

The men were in their midtwenties. The taller man, Jean-Auguste, sat next to me. He was well over six feet with a mane of coal-black hair and bright blue eyes. Tanned and athletically built, he towered over the pale, attenuated Xavier. Both men were dressed in expensive Italian suits with colorful silk ties.

"Do you come here often?" Jean-Auguste asked me.

"This is my first time."

"We would be honored if you two beautiful ladies would keep us company for dinner," Xavier offered.

"We certainly don't want to impose," I answered.

"She's terribly diplomatic. It's very kind of you both to invite us. On that premise, we graciously accept to dine in your company," Naravine answered for me.

When their table was ready, we were led to a private room by the same hostess. Naravine made a point of gloating before her like the peacocks did to the pigeons in the Bagatelle gardens.

"This is one of our finest table. It's a pleasure to serve you again," the hostess said, bowing to Jean-Auguste.

The sommelier arrived and pulled two chairs out for Naravine and I. "It's always a pleasure to serve you again, Monsieur de Briard. Here's our wine list," he politely offered.

Jean-Auguste spent several minutes carefully reading the inventory and then passed it to Xavier.

"I would like a bottle of Bourgueil Domaine des Ragueniéres, a bottle of Pouilly-Fumé Jean-Claude Dagueneau, and a bottle of Vouvray Domaine Huët," Jean-Auguste ordered.

The wine waiter bowed and left with his order.

"Where are you from?" Xavier asked me.

"I'm from California and Naravine is from England, but we were both born in different countries."

"California must be a beautiful place. I've been wanting to go. Americans really know how to live. Isn't this true?" Jean-Auguste asked me.

"I did live in a beautiful setting, but like everything else, the grass is always greener. To me the French have a joie de vivre and a finer quality of life," I answered.

"How long do you plan to stay in Paris?" Xavier asked.

"I hope rather indefinitely, since I've just moved here," I told them.

"That's adventurous of you," Jean-Auguste commented and leaned forward to study my expression.

"Do you come here often?" Naravine asked the men.

"When I come into the city, I make a point of dining here," Jean-Auguste replied formally.

"And I feel fortunate that he invites me," Xavier jovially added.

"Where do you live?" I asked Jean-Auguste.

"In the Loire Valley. Xavier lives in town. I hate Paris and only come in for business. Xavier and I work together. He's my accountant."

"What do you ladies like do in town?" Xavier asked. His eyes were widening with curiosity.

"Shop, for one," Naravine quickly remarked. Naravine and I burst into laughter. She continued, "The two us bought out some boutiques today. It was jolly good fun."

"Besides shopping. Do you both work?" Jean-Auguste asked in a serious tone.

I stopped laughing and answered, "I'm studying art and Naravine is a professional model."

"You're both in the right city for that," Xavier answered.

The sommelier returned and displayed three bottles of wine to Jean-Auguste. He read the labels and approved of each one. All of our attention was then focused on the sommelier who removed the corks and first poured a taste of Pouilly-Fumé in a glass for Jean-Auguste. Swirling the wine in his glass, Jean-Auguste delicately sipped, swallowed, then nodded to the wine waiter, who poured our glasses. This ritual continued, until Jean-Auguste had tasted all three wines.

"What do you think of the bouquets?" Jean-Auguste asked Xavier.

Xavier tasted from all of his glasses. "The Fumé is elegant and dry. The Bourgueil is rich and supple. And the Vouvray is just perfect."

"How do you like the wines?" Jean-Auguste asked me.

"They're all delicious, but I'm not a connoisseur. I'm ashamed that my father is French and I'm so uncultured when it comes to wine."

"I didn't think you were completely American. Does your father live in California?" Jean-Auguste asked.

"Yes," I answered.

"They have some excellent wines there." Jean-Auguste commented.

"What do you think of the wine choices?" Xavier asked Naravine.

"I taste a hint of raspberries in the red. It's full bodied—rich. I've never tasted such excellent vintages," Naravine answered approvingly.

"I'm impressed with your palette. That's precisely what the *vigneron* wants you to capture. Everyone, please order what tempts you. I recommend the roast veal chop or the duck. Does everyone like caviar?" Jean-Auguste asked.

"Oh, yes. Are you men celebrating a special occasion?" Naravine asked eagerly.

"Only our success," Jean-Auguste said, and raised his glass to toast.

"Santé," Xavier said.

"What type of business are you in?" Naravine asked the men.

"It must be obvious. Jean-Auguste is a *négociant* and owns his own château," Xavier said.

A hot appetizer served in an eggshell arrived. I had never before tasted a more delicate and sumptuous flavor of caviar and scrambled eggs blended with crème fraîche.

Naravine and Xavier lit cigarettes between courses and chatted together. Jean-Auguste's attention was focused on me. He had a mysterious, dark, and brooding intensity to his features; chiseled cheekbones and a ski jump nose gave a distinguished regal masculinity to his face. There was not a detail left unattended to in his appearance: his clothes were neatly pressed, his leather shoes polished, and his fingernails were even and clean.

"So, tell me, *poulette*. I like dangerous things. Motorcycles and skydiving. How about you?" Xavier asked Naravine.

"Just looking at me is dangerous. To quote the words of Mick Jagger, "If you play with me, you're playing with fire," Naravine answered coyly.

"You're certainly not modest," Xavier replied.

"I can't afford to be," Naravine answered haughtily.

"The lady knows what she likes!" Xavier exclaimed to Jean-Auguste.

The meal became a Bacchanalian feast. Jean-Auguste and I had the veal chop in a wild mushroom and Burgundy sauce with a side of lavender-tipped asparagus. Xavier and Naravine had roast duck, with a tangerine, lime, and plum sauce. After finishing our salads and cheeses, Jean-Auguste said, "You must save room for dessert."

"Please, no," Naravine cried out.

"Give it some time. You won't regret it," Jean-Auguste said, ordering a chocolate and Grand Marnier soufflé.

"I do love chocolate," I confessed.

"I do too," Jean-Auguste affirmed.

"Do you enjoy your work?" I asked him.

"*Passionné*. I can work fifteen hours and never tire. I'm proud of what I do; I love good wine and for generations my family has produced some of the finest vintages in France." He poured me another glass of Pouilly-Fumé.

"I'm already over my limit," I timidly confessed.

"Do you limit yourself with everything?" Jean-Auguste flirtatiously asked.

"There are some things I don't limit," I said giggling.

Jean-Auguste smiled and reached for my hand. I felt my cheeks flush and my heart flutter.

"You seem so delicate, but I can tell you've had many challenges in your life."

"How would you know?" I asked skeptically.

"I know people. I have excellent instincts. I'm certain you will discover more of your talents in France. You belong here. I have a feeling you will find something spectacular, even more than what you've imagined," Jean-Auguste remarked.

"Why is it that you speak with such insight? You can't be that much older than me."

"I'm twenty-seven. You're a special person, that I can also tell. What's that on the floor?" he asked.

"A pastel," I answered.

"Did you paint it? May I see it?" Jean-Auguste asked, as he reached for the sketch.

"No. I mean, you can see it. I didn't paint it."

"It reminds me of a Léger. Don't you agree, Xavier?" Jean-Auguste asked.

"Yes, but also Modigliani," Xavier said.

"That's what I thought," I confirmed.

After dinner, the four of us walked around the place des Vosges.

Naravine was twirling and spinning herself in a circle.

"I love this night," she kept repeating.

Taking hold of Xavier's hand, she said, "Let's go dancing. I want to let loose."

"We'll all go together," Xavier answered.

Jean-Auguste interrupted, "I can't. I'm afraid I have to leave for London early in the morning." Moments later, a row of street lamps extinguished. I grabbed Jean-Auguste's strong shoulder and he stoically helped guide me down a step.

"That's a remarkable sign. This has been an electrically charged meeting," Xavier commented.

Jean-Auguste turned to me and said, "I really don't want to leave. I find you *ravissant*. I must invite both of you to the *fête de vin* at my château."

"Jean-Auguste's Renaissance costume party is an event you shouldn't miss," Xavier remarked.

Naravine said, "We hope to attend. Thank you again for such a smashing evening."

"Don't forget the party. It may be in a few more months, depending on the vines. Give me your addresses and I'll send you both invitations," Xavier suggested. Naravine handed her card to Xavier. "You can send them both to me and I'll give one to Djuna."

Jean-Auguste asked, "Could I have that sketch of you? I don't want to forget you and our special encounter."

"It's the least I can give you, to thank you for your generosity," I said, as I handed him the drawing. He reached for my hand and kissed it.

Xavier suggested the three of us go to a club, but I politely declined. Naravine left in one taxi with Xavier, and Jean-Auguste and I shared another cab. I was dropped off first. Before I exited the car, Jean-Auguste said, "Please visit me in Loire. I would really like to see you again."

"I'd like that too. Perhaps you'll also call me the next time you come to Paris," I suggested.

"Then it's not good-bye," he said.

I stepped out of the car and said, "No, it's *à bientôt.*"

He waived to me as he closed the taxi door.

Later that night, as I tried to fall asleep, the memory of Jean-Auguste's face was rapidly fading. How long would it take before I'd completely forget him? The thought of not seeing him again disturbed me. I expected that night to dream about him, but Princess Mitya appeared instead.

In the dream, I was transported back in time to the thirties in Paris. Standing before me, looking youthful and entrancing was Princess Mitya, dressed in the fashion of the day: a fitted black suit, a white silk ruffled blouse, and a black cloche-hat decorated with a diamond hat pin in the shape of a dragonfly. We were alone in her apartment. The portrait Joaquím Carlos painted of her with deer antlers was displayed above the fireplace. On the floor beside the dancing flames was the tiger skin rug that Mitya had posed on. The princess was standing by the mirrored bar, reflecting around her were hundreds of images of her stately elegance, refractions of platinum-blond hair, sparkling jewelry, her animated eyes. Taking center stage, she spoke clearly, without her usual affectation and said in a kind, comforting voice, "This is the most important time in your life. Your twenties are your most impressionable years. I've completely transformed since I've lived in Paris. I will never be the same. For the better or for the worse, the same can happen to you. In this city you can learn about history, beauty, art, romance. I knew countless men. All were fascinating. But it's not only about the men. You'll see. Let yourself discover. Pay attention. Keep your eyes wide open, even when the light may be blinding. Listen to the artists, to the poets, to Joaquím Carlos. Try to understand their visions. Muses are everywhere. Listen. Listen to your heart. But don't be afraid to sometimes cover your ears, your mouth, your curious eyes, and be silent. The answers are there. *Vive l'art et l'amour!*"

SEVEN

Goddesses, Wine, Dead Artists & Chocolate
The Journals of Joaquím Carlos Cortez

I sleep for only four hours, but revive myself to meet Sylvie by noon. She's waiting outside her apartment with her chauffeur-driven Rolls-Royce. Once again, she's ravishing in a flowing white silk dress covered in enormous poppies, flowers that look open, blowing softly in a breeze, as the material of the dress gracefully folds and flows behind her in a long train. Sylvie reminds me of a swan gliding on a lake, especially with her long slender neck. She floats toward me and says, "Today will be my treat. I don't want you to worry about anything."

"But a man should wine and dine a woman," I protest.

"Yes. But you're a struggling artist."

"I'm still an honorable gentleman."

She gives me her hand and says. "Then I'll let you take me out. Did you bring your paints?"

"I would never forget them." I point to a turquoise plastic case that is already set on the car's running board.

After a long drive, we arrive at the entrance of Versailles, a dense emerald-green forest. As we pass the Petit Trianon, Sylvie rushes out of the car before I can get out.

"I must walk. I need air," she insists.

Carrying a blanket and picnic basket in one arm and the

back of her long dress in the other, she leads the way to the manicured gardens. I'm several paces behind her, lugging the art supplies. It takes a while, but we do reach the Orangerie, a still pond shrouded by orange trees. Once we're there, she unfolds a blanket and gestures for me to rest beside her. Miraculously, we are completely alone; only the faces of whimsical clay and stone grotesques decorating flower pots can see us. Sylvie unpacks the basket and serves me a plate of *chacuteries*.

"What sort of pâté is this?" I ask.

"Probably goose liver."

"Do you have any dietary restrictions?" she asks.

"If I was born hundreds of years ago I would have. My ancestors in Spain were Jewish and were forced to convert," I say.

"What is your religion now?" she asks.

"Atheist."

"Are you ever going to paint me or not?" she asks.

I begin pulling out my palette. Then I observe the grounds and try to match the garden's colors with my oils.

"Can you imagine what it must have been like living here? Did you ever dream of being a princess?" I ask.

"I think every girl dreams of being a princess. What about you?"

"Did I ever dream of being a princess?" I curtsy for her. "Can you imagine me a princess?"

She bellows, "You're outrageous. When I'm here I always think about Marie Antoinette and imagine what it must have been like when the citizens stormed the Bastille. You have more experience with nobility than I do. What do think of your Spanish aristocracy?"

"Many Spaniards speculate that King Alfonso XIII's days are numbered. I don't know what to think. But I do know there are many advantages of royalty, including a castle in every city in Spain. I've always wanted my own *castillo.*"

Sylvie answers, "I hear the poverty in Spain is demoralizing. Spain used to be such a prosperous country. Like the French Revolution, I'm afraid history will repeat itself like what that man said in the park."

"You're probably right," I concede.

"Nevertheless, you must never give up hope for a peaceful resolution or even a château," she says.

"Why? You don't happen to have a castle I can borrow do you?" I ask in jest.

"As a matter of fact, I do."

"Dios mio! You are the most luscious woman I've ever known. What did I do to merit your companionship?"

"Please, Carlos, don't put me on such a high pedestal. I could easily disappoint you. If war breaks out in Spain will you go back?"

"Are you kidding? That would be completely foolish. I value my life too much to risk it for my country."

Returning to my canvas, I study her, as she rests wistfully on her elbows, her legs stretched in front of her. I say fetchingly, "I wish you could remove all your clothes, but then you'd have so many suitors, I'd have to fight them off."

Sylvie's lips curl flirtatiously. She reaches into the picnic basket and pulls out a Chinese jade pipe.

"I thought you were teasing when you said you smoked a pipe."

She tosses her chestnut hair to one side and raises the pipe to her lips; I rush to light the center of the pipe for her.

"You look different when you work," she comments between puffs, "a more serious side to you comes out. What are you thinking about?"

"I'm wondering if I'll be able to capture you, on canvas that is." As I focus on her configuration, I refuse to make her an expressionistic statement. This painting demands the flair of Toulouse-Lautrec and Degas. In order to capture the portrait's background, I need my colors to be as vibrant as a Rousseau, as the most challenging aspect is capturing the model. I want to switch off my feelings; instead an outpouring of intuition floods my paintbrush. Hidden from most people is Sylvie's anguish and despair, manifesting in an insidious melancholia and timidity. Outwardly she appears confident, but she's conflicted and craves companionship. Most men she judges too harshly. With me it's different. Somehow, she respects the ardor in my heart. I have a calming influence on her, allowing her a reprieve from her tormenting thoughts.

Dark menacing clouds start to encumber my light, subtle

shadows vanish. I set my brushes down and genuflect beside her. Leaning toward her, I kiss her lips. Our mouths part, and with our tongues, we find the caverns of our sensuality. She tells me of her suppressed desires, her need for union. It seems possible to vanish within her. Both of us exist in a void, a separateness, until this lust begins to chisel away at our rough edges. I nibble at her neck, and through her dress, caress her breasts. As I roll on top of her, it begins to rain. Thunder detonates. Screams echo through the gardens, as people emerge from secluded areas of the park, running for shelter. We're soon drenched.

"I don't know what it is about you, but I can't have enough of you," she says breathlessly.

After packing up our belongings, we make a mad dash to the car. The driver rescues us. Inside the Rolls, Sylvie leans her pretty head against my shoulder and falls asleep. Gazing out the car window, I think about the deluge and how rain puts me in a reflective mood. When it rains in Paris, which can be often, the city becomes disguised in a shade of mercurial silver, a hazy drunken mist, tangos of hail, and a slate veil of aloofness that is almost as impossible to penetrate as the cold stare of a prostitute when she receives her final payment. This beguiling city that I've exiled myself to oscillates between the yin and yang, masculine and feminine. Paris can be simultaneously cold and explosive. Yet I hope never to grow tired of the precipitations, the ablutions; where once again, when the sun appears, the city returns to its remarkable incandescence.

The driver pulls up to Sylvie's apartment. She wakes as the car slows down. "Please come in and dry off," she offers.

As we enter a luxurious Art Deco–style apartment, a Burmese cat greets us by the front door. Sylvie scoops up the purring cat in her arms and says, "This is my precious Bijou. She actually thinks she's a dog."

I pet the young feline's brown sable fur, remarking that Bijou's eyes are the same emerald color as Sylvie's.

"You have a beautiful place," I say, looking around the ornate apartment.

"Thank you."

Sylvie disappears into the kitchen. The cat follows at her

feet. I pace the room until she returns with a silver tray and teapot, setting it down on a coffee table.

"I don't want us to catch cold, so I prepared a special infusion," she explains.

"That's very nice of you."

She sits next to me on a gold satin banquette and pours me a cup of tea. Steam clouds her eyes. "I hope you like it. It's an Indian *chai* blend. On one of my trips to Bombay I fell in love with this tea and spice bazaar. I have the tea sent to me every month. May I add milk and sugar?" she asks.

"Please. I like it sweet." I allow her to prepare my hot beverage, and I watch her delicately stir the cup, the spoon chiming against her floral Limoges china. As I sip the tea, cloves and exotic spices dance on my tongue, leaving a pleasant tingling sensation in my mouth, giving me a boost of energy.

"What was your impression of India?" I ask.

"It's the land of contrasts—a heaven and a hell, the sacred and the profane. As an artist, I'm sure you'd enjoy painting the enchanting women in their vibrant silk saris, the religious bathers in the Ganges, and the gardens lush with exotic birds, fragrant blossoms, and wild monkeys."

"I love birds. It sounds extraordinary."

"It can be. I enjoyed their festivals, especially, the one called Holi where people douse themselves in vibrantly colored powders and dyes. It's a mystical place, but nevertheless, foreboding. Especially when you witness sick children left to perish on the streets."

"I would like to go, but I'm not certain I could take the destitution. I'm really quite sensitive," I confess.

"I like that about you. You're not afraid to show your feelings," she says, clearing her throat. "What places have you traveled to that have left an impression on you?"

"I haven't traveled very far. But I'm wild about Madrid."

"Yes, I adore that city too," she enthusiastically states. "I love strolling through the Prado, the Buen Retiro Park and the Crystal Palace."

I fervently add, "Those are my favorite places. I've sat for hours studying how light refracts off the Crystal Palace. I've sketched almost every pond, fountain, and statue in the park. I couldn't paint for two months after visiting the Prado. The

sad thing is I'll always be an amateur painter compared to
Rubens, El Greco, and Goya."

"Does this remind you of anyone?" she asks, prostrating
herself on the banquette and then lounging on her side, with
her back facing me.

"Yes! Ingres. You're calling for an odalisque painting."

Without my asking, she slowly begins to remove her dress.
Her shoulders are perfectly shaped. Her skin is milky white
with a hue of apricot. I'm speechless as she removes her pink
silk lingerie. Her body differs from the trollops I'm used to.
She's unblemished, virginal. My eyes follow the lines from
the back of her neck, to the indentation of her waistline, the
curve of her slim hips, her round buttocks, and long sleek legs.
I'm weakening. Instead of painting her, I gather her up in my
arms and carry her to her boudoir. The walls in the room are
covered in padded amber silks with a matching bedspread.
Still lifes hang on the walls. I recognize an original Bonnard
and a La Tour oil. As I set Sylvie down on a bed covered in
satin and chintz pillows, she gestures for me to lie beside her.
Without speaking, she removes my clothes. Naked, I lean over
her, balancing my weight on my shoulders and hands. Immediately she wraps her legs around me like a package. I kiss
her breasts, which are shaped like Anjou pears. My flesh
scorches; I hope she'll allow me to burst inside her, evanesce.
Stroking her lean thighs, I remove her stockings. Her legs are
as smooth as the silk that adorns them. I begin kissing the
bottom of one foot, moving up to her ankle and then kneecap.
Her feet speak to me, telling me her nature is benevolent and
romantic. My lips move up her velvety thighs, and with my
fingertips, I part her moist fleece, caressing her softest cavern
with my tongue. She responds in soft moans, as her hands
explore the arch of my chest and shoulders. Then our palms
interlock. I pin her arms down above her head. Leaning over
her, and looking into her eyes, I notice she's trembling. Desperately, I need to find the source of her drowning tropical
warmth, lose myself in the core of her. Utilizing all my restraint and self-control, I pull away, instead of delving inside
her.

"We don't have to go on. I don't want you to be afraid," I
whisper softly.

She begins to whimper. "I never wanted anybody more than I want you now, but I'm tarnished. You shouldn't have me."

"We don't have to rush into anything. I think you're perfect. There's plenty of time to get to know each other better."

"Just hold me," she cries out. "Don't let go."

"Sylvie, please confide in me. Tell me how you were hurt," I plead.

"I was *violer,* raped."

"I know how you feel," I tell her.

"That is sweet of you, but how would you know?"

I move her gently and together we sit up in the bed.

"Please tell me what happened to you," I plead.

"About a decade ago, I used to be a bit wild, sort of a flapper, as many young women were. I enjoyed parties and dancing. It was my twentieth birthday party. It was a lovely gathering, but it will always be ruined by what took place later that night."

"What happened?" I asked.

"I had thought all the guests had left. I was getting ready to go to bed, and one of the male guests was waiting for me in my bathroom. The rooms are so vast in the château that nobody heard my screams for help. I've never wanted to throw or attend another party since. Now you must understand why I don't go to many social events."

"Yes. I'm so very sorry. I do know how helpless you must have felt," I answer.

"How would you know how I feel? Often, I wish I was born a man. That way I wouldn't have to live in fear. I hate not being able to go to a park alone."

"Fear exists for everyone. We were all children once. Children are vulnerable."

"I don't quite understand what you mean."

"Since I've moved to Paris I've been haunted by this violent dream. Seeing you this way brings back my pain. The dream has been wanting me to face up to the fact that my innocence was robbed from me at the age of fourteen. For me, it happened in a boys' school run by priests. I was Father Pedro's favorite. In the mornings we climbed to the top of the church tower to ring the bells. Usually, we would rush back down to help prepare breakfast. One morning, Father Pedro told me not to leave. He said, 'I need to speak frankly with you. It is evident that you're becoming a man and a handsome one, too. I know you admire my dedication to this church and pious life, but I don't want you to become like me. I implore you not to.'

" 'I don't understand.' I said to him. 'This is not in accordance to what you've been teaching us.'

" 'I know, Joaquím Carlos, but I must confess that the pleasures of the body do not leave when you become a priest. Have you ever experienced the pleasures of the flesh?' he asked me."

"What happened after that?" Sylvie asks.

"I wanted to leave, but I was also curious. He had never spoken to me that way before. Falling to his knees, he began weeping and said, 'I will never be able to love a woman, or feel her softness.' Then he reached up and touched my cheek. 'But you can.' He pulled some photographs out of his pocket. They were of seminude women posed in scant lingerie. Some of them were fanning themselves with large ostrich feathers. The photographs aroused me and he was aware of it.

" 'This will be our secret. We will be best friends and I will protect you if you ever need help,' he said."

"What happened after that?" Sylvie asks.

"That was when my descent into purgatory began. It began with Father Pedro, and then I no longer cared about being good and going to heaven. I knew I would be going straight to hell."

"How long did this go on?"

"For an entire summer, he took me to brothels and allowed me to sleep with fallen women of all ages. Sometimes, I really wanted nothing to do with the women, so I began sketching them. That's when my fascination with these lost women began. Father Pedro wanted me to have the pleasures of the flesh, never to let go."

"How completely atrocious! Why didn't you go home, or at least stay away from him?"

"Father Pedro's opinion of me was important. I wanted to please him. I've never told anyone this before. I had avoided thinking about it until I felt your anguish. I had to tell you. We're not that different. Do I revolt you?" I ask.

"Not at all. I respect you more for telling me. Have you been blaming yourself all this time?"

"I think so."

"Then we do feel the same powerlessness. Don't let what happened to you ruin your chances for love. You're not a bad person. You deserve more than prostitues," she says, kissing my lips. "You said you were an atheist. Is this really true?"

"Absolutely. If God exists, I want to be the first one to kill the hypocritical bastard."

"I don't think you should blame God. It wasn't God who wronged you."

"Perhaps not. But he certainly didn't save me."

Djuna Cortez

LOIRE, OCTOBER 1985

It was early autumn when I visited the antiquated villages of Loire. Artistic inspiration could be found in the charm of taking a long walk and discovering a secret passageway. Then I would be wandering in another direction, having found a subject to paint: the hidden staircases decorated in fallen brown, gold, and orange leaves, an elderly widow, dressed in classic noir, climbing the hundreds of narrow stone steps, and cradling under her arm a straw basket, the contents of her purchases open to view: a bottle of local red wine, a loaf of *pain de champagne,* a head of lettuce, a Camembert, a small pumpkin, some pâté, and a few Granny Smith apples. Following her were several cats. It was true that the agile felines ruled the villages and roamed about freely like the rumors of famous ghosts. In Chinon, history recounts Joan of Arc coming to the town and warning the people of future distress. As if in compensation for her brutal treatment, the region now has an abundance of soothsayers.

When I arrived at the Château Hélianthe d'Or, I had expected to find an abandoned fortress in a state of disrepair. However, when the car reached the top of the mile-long curving driveway, much to my surprise, a grandiose medieval château surrounded by overgrown lilac trees and blooming hydrangea in clusters of China blue and violet awaited me.

The aged white stone château had four corner turrets of gray slate, pointed arches, porticos of all sizes, and windows, some of delicate stained glass. The longer the château had remained standing, the more impressive it had become. Centuries had only added to its character. Before I could get out of the car, the caretakers ran out of the château to greet me.

"Bonjour, mademoiselle. *C'est notre honneur,"* the couple said in unison. They were in their mid sixties and engraved on their smiling faces were the trials and tribulations of a lifetime of servitude.

"I'm Mionne and this is my husband, Jacques. We're so happy to finally meet you," the woman said.

Mionne was a heavyset woman with pale legs that were marred by varicose veins. She wore a plain blue smock dress and her hair was short and tinted flaming red. Jacques was almost the opposite of her, tall, slim, and timid. I later learned that they had endured wartime starvation and were now compensating for it by eating the freshest fruits, vegetables, meats, butter, and eggs that were available.

As the first order of business, Mionne drove me to the hills above the château, where I was given a tour. The vineyards were quiet, except for the birds. On occasion a squawking crow would sound off. I asked Mionne to stop the car and I got out. I approached a vine and picked a red grape.

"No, mademoiselle. Don't eat it," Mionne warned.

I didn't listen. As I bit into the grape, a rancid taste burst onto my tongue, making it impossible to swallow. I tried to hide my dissatisfaction. Then looking more closely at the vines, I saw that all the grapes were spoiled, row after row.

"Are all the grapes sour?" I asked Mionne.

She shrugged her shoulders and answered. "It is a pity. *Millerandange.* We did everything we could. But our annual harvest has been destroyed from crop failure. We've had too much rain. The odds were against this crop. Please try not to be upset. Let me show you around the winery."

I followed her down a graveled path that led to the winery. My presence didn't inhibit Mionne. She sang boisterously as she walked while keys jingled in her large pockets. Her voice grew louder as we approached the solid oak front door of the winery. Before she inserted a key into the front lock, I screamed, causing Mionne to drop her set of keys. A gray mouse had scurried beside my feet. Mionne noticed what had happened and broke out laughing.

"That tiny mouse won't harm you, or even a fly. It's sort of cute. We have some outdoor cats that usually take care of that problem. But, they must be on diets."

The smell of dampness and oak barrels greeted us as we entered the winery. Mionne showed me the *érafoir*—the large wood fermenting vats that gave off a dank and musty fragrance. Inside the main room, heaps of empty glass bottles and unused corks were piled on a table.

"When do you think you'll be making wine again?" I asked.

Mionne shrugged her shoulders. "If we're lucky maybe next year's crop will be better. But I really don't know."

"What is all the money you requested for?" I asked.

"It's a tremendous amount of work maintaining the vineyards with pruning, fertilizing, pesticides, and watering. We have to hire several families to help out during the busier months. There is also the château's maintenance. Your grandfather stopped paying us last year. We've only had a small savings to live on. I'm sorry about your loss. But it has been difficult for us too."

We moved closer to a storage area of wine racks that was built into the limestone wall. Mionne removed a bottle from the shelf and carefully dusted it off with her dress.

"This was a good year. It won several awards. I think this was when your grandfather began putting his paintings on the labels. We have few of these bottles left. They're quite expensive. Take it and have it later with your *repas.*"

"What year is the bottle?" I asked.

Mionne handed me the bottle and smiled. "Nineteen sixty-four."

"That was the year I was born."

"What a coincidence! You were born in a very lucky year. But that's obvious." Mionne chuckled.

"Where did my grandfather paint when he was here?"

"He painted in the winery, in one of these rooms, except when the sun was shining. Then he was always in the vineyards with his portable paints and easel. Do you paint?"

"I'm learning."

"Interesting. I must go and prepare lunch. What time would you like to eat?" she asked.

"It doesn't matter. Whenever it's ready. I'll stay here a little while longer," I said.

Mionne left the winery. I followed her outside and she drove away in a gray Peugeot truck that backfired down the hill. Walking again through the vineyards, I shielded my eyes from the glaring sun. Above the winery were more hills with what would be sunflowers in the summer months. Where I stood afforded a view of the dense forest, the Vienne river, cow pastures, and the shimmering terra cotta and blue-gray roof-tops of the nearby village. Amid all this beauty, I suddenly felt stricken with grief, its source unknown.

The interior of the château was equally solemn. There were enormous rooms with black-and-white tiled floors, weeping crystal chandeliers, French antiques, and hand-painted ceil-ings. Sheets covered the furniture, making the place feel sterile and cold. Every room craved mirth.

Mionne called me to lunch. The dining room was sur-rounded by open French windows that overlooked a coy pond set under a weeping willow tree. Further in the distance was a black-bottomed pool and a calla lily garden. After Mionne finished serving, I invited her to join me. She accepted without hesitation.

"I hope you'll be happy in Loire. We grew up in the country and thrive here. Your grandfather always enjoyed visiting, but still loved city life. When it got too quiet for him, he'd invite all these flashy types to stay. Do you know a lot of people?" she asked.

"I don't. I only know one person in Loire."

"You're a good quiet girl. I knew it." She turned her head and sighed in relief. "Do you want to know what your future here will bring? Some say I'm gifted with these cards," she said, tapping her front dress pocket. "I could read them for you."

"Clairvoyants are a popular thing in France," I commented.

Whipping out a deck of playing cards and a pair of reading

glasses from her pocket, she shuffled with the technical flair of a Las Vegas blackjack dealer. As she dealt the cards, she pondered their meaning like a complex tarot.

"I do this for all the young women in the village. They come to me when they have men troubles."

"I don't have any problems," I said indignantly.

"You're a beautiful girl. Why should you? It is important that you've come to live in France. I can tell you love our country. The souls know you belong here."

"Souls?" I questioned.

"Your ancestors," she continued. "You will make nice friends and find a husband."

"Husband?"

"He will be extremely handsome and tall. He'll love you deeply and you will have one child, a beautiful blond baby boy. You will be happy in Loire."

I humored Mionne with a polite "Thank you."

For a moment her eyes fixed on the queen of spades. She sighed, "The cards told me when I was to meet Jacques. But I never had a chance to have children. I was pregnant once, six months along," she said mournfully.

"What happened?" I asked.

"There were complications. I was carrying twins."

"I'm very sorry."

"We're happy with our daughter, Mimi. You'll have to meet her."

"Then you do have a child."

Jacques burst out of the kitchen. "I can't find any coffee. Where's the coffee?" he asked impatiently. Taking notice of the table, he reprimanded his wife. "No, not those cards again. Why couldn't you leave mademoiselle alone?"

"It's fine. I asked her to," I remarked.

Mionne nodded, quickly collected the cards, and left for the kitchen. While I was finishing dessert, a dog began whimpering. Loud and rapid gunfire echoed outside, rattling the windows. Startled, I tipped over my wine glass, spilling the red vintage over a fresh white tablecloth. The gunfire continued as I ran into the kitchen.

"What's going on outside?" I asked.

Mionne was crouched on the kitchen floor cradling a frightened black and tan German shepherd. *"Povre Mimi, chérie,"* Mionne hummed to her dog.

She chuckled. "It's nothing. Mimi hates it too. It's just Jacques protecting us from *les bêtes sauvages."*

"What wild beasts?"

"You're in the country. Predators are everywhere. Now that Mimi is in season, the wolves have come scratching at our door. That's why the cats are missing. But don't worry, dear, Jacques will protect us. My husband may be quiet and reserved, but he can be fierce when he hunts."

I had thought life would be simpler and more restful in the country, but all night howling wolves circled the château. I lay awake worrying about how little I knew about winemaking and the overwhelming responsibility of running such a large property.

The following morning, I visited the local library and tried to read up on wineries. Then, on the spur of the moment, I contacted Jean-Auguste. We met two hours later at a café in town. It was a surprise to me that I arrived early. Just as I sat down, I noticed something balancing on a trash bin. My curiosity led me to see what it was, finding a partially burned book, with damaged corners but clear and legible pages. The book was *The Art Spirit*, by Robert Henri.

This felt like a divine message sent just for me. The book was all about art and painting techniques. Absorbed in my reading, I didn't notice Jean-Auguste when he arrived.

"Excuse me," he said.

When I looked up from the book, Jean-Auguste was standing with two tethered dogs.

"You're not alone," I playfully commented.

"I hope you don't mind that I brought some friends. They needed exercise."

"No, not at all. I love dogs."

"My mother breeds Italian greyhounds," he explained, "I'm trying to teach them how to walk on a leash. She loves to spoil them."

"They look like they're doing quite well. What are their names?"

"Napoléon and Josephine."

"How clever," I said, my voice dropping an octave.

He sat down and asked with concern, "What's wrong?"

"Nothing. That was my mother's name."

"Napoléon?" he joked.

"No. But that certainly would be unique."

"Please forgive me. I didn't mean to upset you," he said. The small dogs stood on their hind legs and placed their slim front paws on my knees. "What brings you to Loire?" he asked. "I didn't expect to see you so soon. Although, I had hoped you would come visit."

"Actually, I have a place here."

"Why didn't you tell me that before?"

"I didn't want to sound ostentatious."

"You don't seem that way at all. Are you still in art school?"

"Yes. But, I've been a bit distracted lately. I have a lot on my mind."

"Is there anything I can help with?"

"Maybe. I hate to ask you a favor. I was wondering if you might give me some tips about vineyards and winemaking."

"Certainly. But why do you ask?"

"My grandfather left me his vineyards and winery. I've been told the vines are dying. I don't know what to do."

"Where's the winery?"

"Just across the Vienne. I hope it won't take up too much of your time."

"I could never leave a beautiful lady in distress. It would be a privilege to help you out."

"I don't want to impose."

"What was your grandfather's name?"

"Joaquím Carlos Cortez."

He clapped his hands together and said, "It's such a small world. My mother was acquainted with him. We were very sorry to hear of his passing. He's been absent from the château a long time. We were wondering what would happen to the property. I assumed it would become a hotel. I can't believe this! *C'est beau la vie.* You should have told me earlier. My mother introduced us once. I don't think I was older than twelve. He must have loved you very much."

"I don't know," I answered vaguely.

"We always saw him in the cheese shop. He enjoyed doing his own shopping. *Maman* and I were astounded at what he purchased. He would leave with dozens of varieties of cheeses, an entire basketful. What was your impression of him? Were you very close?"

"It's a long story. But I'm interested in hearing more of your impressions."

"My mother could tell you more. You'll have to meet her sometime. Do you have any brothers or sisters to share the responsibility of such a large property?" Jean-Auguste asked.

"No. I'm all alone."

"I'm also an only child, and believe me, I understand the burden of that responsibility. You're very sweet," he said, touching my hand. I bashfully turned my head.

"Would you like another coffee?" he asked.

I nodded.

"Did you grow up here?" I asked.

"Born and raised. I wouldn't change my childhood for the world. This is an enchanting place. I want my children to run in these woods and have the same nostalgic memories of nature. If I'm ever depressed, I can recall these fond remembrances and my problems fade away."

"Do you get depressed often?" I asked.

"Almost never. I'm fortunate about that, because I live in this beautiful setting."

"It's quite remarkable that you appreciate everything, as most people are always dreaming of better places and jobs."

"France is the best country in the world. We care about our children—the future of our nation. Children should be able to breathe clean air and play freely. I especially hate seeing schools fenced in by barbed wire and concrete." Without saying another word, a seriousness came over his face. Silently, he drank his coffee. He had an appealing intensity of emotion and depth, which indicated to me that he was a person of strong moral convictions. "Please have dinner with me tonight," he said.

"Why don't you come see the vineyards and dine at my place? You'll be my first guest," I offered.

"How can I decline?" He then looked down at his clothing. "You'll have to give me some time to change."

"You look fine to me," I said. I thought he looked rather good in blue jeans, a white turtleneck, and a black leather jacket.

"I couldn't possibly show up like this."

"There's nobody there but me and a few servants," I answered. "It wouldn't matter."

"I know. Why don't you give me about an hour. Then I'll meet you at your place around four."

"That's fine. Do you know how to get there?"

"Yes. No problem."

When I returned to the château, butterflies began to whirl in my stomach. What was I doing? We would be alone in the evening. What would we talk about? What if he then decided that I was too dull? I was becoming rather fond of him. This was already going beyond my control. What did he think of me? It was too soon to tell if he liked me. But when I saw him standing downstairs, dressed in a tailored navy-blue suit as he patiently waited by the bottom of the staircase, for a moment I had to stop and gather my senses. He looked like a cosmopolitan hero out of a Fitzgerald novel. It would be a test, a challenge, to try not to show my emotions, how much I was beginning to like him, and wanted him to feel the same way.

"I'd love a tour of the grounds before it gets dark," he asked.

I led him outside. The birch, pine, and chestnut trees surrounding some of the property had turned various shades of gold and red. As I guided him up the steep hill to the vineyards, our footsteps crunched on scattered autumn leaves. From time to time, a wild rabbit would run out from behind a bush, scurrying fast, and then hiding again if it noticed us. When we approached the vines, I watched him prune a few leaves with a Swiss army knife, lifting one translucent lime-green leaf toward the waning sunlight. As he did this, minuscule veins shone a hint of glazed amber that looked brushed on by an artist. I also watched him carefully dig into the dirt, smear soil into his fingertips, smell and taste the damp earth.

"What have you concluded?" I asked.

"Do you think we're alone?"

"There's a nest of blue jays in that tree," I commented.

"They can be vicious and territorial. I'd prefer to stay away from them," he affirmed.

"Except for the birds, we're alone, unless someone is hiding in the tool shed."

"Your crops are being destroyed. This soil is terribly malnourished. Unfavorable weather conditions could be blamed, possibly some neglect as well. Pesticides have not been applied properly. I don't know when these vines were last grafted. You have an irrigation system, but it doesn't seem to be working. This is the richest limestone soil in Loire," he said, handing me a clump of wet earth. "I will have it tested. But, in my opinion, I see no reason why Cabernet Franc grapes can't thrive here."

"What should I do?" I said.

"Producing wine is a serious business. The owner has to be present to supervise, or at least he or she has to hire experts. You have splendid old vines. I'm certain with the right expertise you could have a prolific winery."

"Thank you for your opinion. I do appreciate it. But, I came here to explore the country and surroundings, to travel and paint. I don't want all these responsibilities. Maybe I should just sell this property."

"Can I make a suggestion?"

"Certainly."

"I'll look after your vines and supervise your staff for you. If your vines respond to my treatment, you could have a crop by next spring."

"I couldn't ask you to do this without paying you."

"I don't want you to pay me anything, only the expenses of the supplies. If you produce a crop than we'll split the profits fifty-fifty. If nothing happens, then you won't owe me anything. Does that sound fair to you?"

"Is there a guarantee that I'll make a profit? I asked.

"There are always risks. I understand how this can be overwhelming for someone so young. But I'm here to help you. Take advantage of me," he said.

"You've already lifted a burden off my shoulders. I can't thank you enough."

"Have courage and be patient. This may take some financial investment and time, but the results are well worth it. There is no better satisfaction than seeing your wine being enjoyed throughout Europe. I've worked hard, and my Bourgueil is now savored in the United States, Canada, and Great Britain. I receive invitations from all over the world. There are few businesses that would allow me to travel and be outdoors everyday. I would hate to have to go to the same office day after day. Every day is different in the vineyards. It may take time to earn a profit, but it can happen," he said encouragingly.

"It's beautiful here. However, I can't see myself spending my life worrying about sour grapes. This isn't what I had in mind."

"Then let me do the worrying for you and take on your burdens."

We returned inside and I excused myself to clean up and change before dinner. I put on a long forest-green velvet dress, with a scooped neckline and pleats that ran down to the bottom of the scalloped skirt. Once we were seated at the dining room table, Mionne began serving a culinary feast of appetizing local dishes. Jean-Auguste couldn't take his eyes off of me. To set us more at ease, I insisted he taste the wine first, giving me his honest opinion. "This is an excellent red with a fine texture and fullness. I would only add some more ripe blackberries to give it a fruitier flavor," he suggested.

"I don't know if I should let you do all this work," I pondered.

"I want to help. How long do you plan on staying in Loire?" he asked.

"I leave in a few days. My plan is to come up mostly on weekends. Have you ever lived away from here?" I asked.

"I spent some time studying English in Oxford."

"How did you like England?"

"There were some parts that I enjoyed more that others. London is an exciting city. I do go back quite often. But I was terribly unhappy and homesick living away from Loire. And the weather was dreadful in England, worse than Paris. Do you miss your family?" he inquired.

"Not really. We aren't very close. Everything changed when

we lost my mother. My father has since remarried three times. Each wife gets younger and more demanding."

"I'm sorry."

"It's okay. My father and I have many differences. It's better that I live in another country."

"I lost my father when I was fifteen. I was fortunate to have grown up with an attentive mother. She was always waiting for me when I came home from school and had my *goûter* ready. I loved being a kid and hated growing up. It must have been different for you."

"It was. I couldn't wait to grow up. Childhood felt like a jail term."

"Evidently, whatever upbringing you had was beneficial. You're *charmante*," he observed.

"You are old-fashioned. But don't get me wrong, I like it," I said.

"I'm a bit traditional. I would have liked to have lived in the days of chivalry when people courted one another and there was an art to romance."

"You're also fortunate that you enjoy your work so much."

"I couldn't be happier," he added jovially.

"I'm envious. I would like to become completely absorbed like you are. I hate this empty feeling I have, that something is missing. Yet I don't know what it is. I feel undeserving of all this lavishness. It would be nice to acquire something on my own. However, I couldn't tell you what exactly I want that to be."

"You should be grateful that money gives you plenty of leisure time. I'm sure you'll find what you're searching for." He glanced at his silver Rolex watch. "Speaking of time, I have a full day tomorrow. I'll be back around noon tomorrow, so I can study the vines in the day and run a few tests. Is that good for you?"

"Yes, that will be fine."

"You've been a very gracious hostess," he said standing up. "Thank you for dinner." Then he kissed me on both cheeks. His touch was confident, soothing, exhilarating.

EIGHT

Goddesses, Wine, Dead Artists & Chocolate
The Journals of Joaquím Carlos Cortez

I am in the majestic square of Saint-Sulpice, hearing the fluttering of wings, the cooing of pigeons, the gushing stone lion fountain, and the ringing church bells. It's late and the *librairies*, frame shops, and *tabacs* are closing. Workers are returning home for their cathartic evening meal. I dine alone at the Café de la Marie in the boisterous Latin Quarter, which reminds me of the Bario Gotico in Barcelona. A *croque-madame, frittes*, and *une demi-blonde* fill me up. My journal and sketch pad are my dinner companions; the pigeons are my audience. As I read to these fatuous creatures, they become my sycophants, with black trusting eyes, eyes that only crave gentleness, compassion, and crumbs. "If only women were this simple," I joke to a hungry bird.

It's twilight, my favorite time, when day and night melt in opalescent hues, light is liquid, soft, like the foam on my beer, it evaporates and transforms. The mood around me becomes indolent as the evening crowd infiltrates the café: tourists, harlots, sailors, poets, writers, students, and artists. I am one of millions of aspiring painters in this city. There are so many of us, that art has become a mediocrity. Yet, this evening I feel exalted. I must paint all night. But first, I must find more subjects, different faces and stories. Coco sees me and struts over to my table. I try to hide behind a newspaper, but it's too late.

"I'm sorry about the other night. I don't know what came over me. Will you buy me a drink?" she asks.

"Whatever you want, *belle fille,*" I answer.

She calls to the waiter. "I want a carafe of your finest rouge. And I'll also have what's he's eating."

I pull out my sketch pad and draw her leaning over the small round table. She looks adorable in a simple blue frock, matching beret and red scarf. The carafe of red wine catches her seductive reflection as she rests her elbows on the marble top; her voluminous bosoms are spilling out of her low-cut dress. This evening the harshness of street life is lifted from her young face. Posing makes her feel important, more than a whore, as she nibbles on a green olive, and tells me she'll charge me only half price tonight, a *spécialité de la maison.*

Women are my muses, and like birds, I am compelled to feed and protect them. My inexorable fate lies with these goddesses. Coco is brazen like Venus. Mitya is strong like Athena. And Sylvie is endearing and fragile like Persephone. If they knew better, they would run away from me, for I am the ultimate warrior: destroyer, ravager, exploiter. My ego revolts against fidelity.

Coco becomes jealous when a Gypsy girl wrapped in a knitted green shawl stops at our table. I am kind to the nymph, who can't be more than fourteen. She's beginning her night's work and displays a bouquet of red roses to sell to the romantic. Ironically, in this Gypsy girl's world, love, like flowers, are luxuries. Her inbred face is like a puma's, feral and wild. I watch her pounce on each man as she travels to the tables. These street urchin girls are all trained in pathos, in mimicking the same chastised expressions, with worn dejected deep-set eyes, pouting lips; yet hidden beneath their self-pity are sharpened claws. Claws that could tear any man apart.

Mitya and Sylvie approach the café. Somehow I must have sensed that I would be seeing them. Now I must try to ingratiate all three muses. Which goddess will win tonight? Mitya sees me and begins frantically waving. "We thought we'd find you here," she says, approaching my table.

"It's nice to see you both," I say, as I introduce Coco to them. Coco smiles arrogantly, crosses her arms before her chest, and refuses to speak, preferring to brood.

"Please join us," I offer to Sylvie and Mitya, pulling out more chairs.

The women settle in their chairs and order drinks.

"Can I see your sketches?" Sylvie asks. I hand them to her. Mitya leans over to me and says, "Carlos, darling, I want you to visit me in Antibes this summer. I met this adorable rich baron and we're going to have a big party in July for my birthday. I was born on the fourth, you know, so we'll also celebrate American Independence Day. You must come. Sylvie, I want you there too."

"I don't know, Mitya. I'm not one for big parties," Sylvie replies.

Coco is being ignored by the women, until Mitya says, "You look familiar, mademoiselle. Have we met before?"

"We've seen sketches of you. Haven't we?" Sylvie asked.

Before Coco can answer, Mitya adds, "René saw the portrait you did of me. He's very excited about your work. You really should visit his gallery. He's looking for new artists. I wouldn't let this go again. He's very serious."

"I knew you could do it," Sylvie says, grabbing hold of my arm. "Have you finished my portrait?" she asks.

"Yes, it's drying."

"I'd love to see it," Mitya says clinging to my other arm.

"You can all come over to my place," I tell the women, before they get any more jealous.

"I'd love to go, but I'm meeting the baron later," Mitya says and excuses herself to leave the café. Coco and Sylvie remain. Coco is studying me as she smokes, and haughtily leans back in her chair. I excuse myself for a moment and run inside the bar.

"I'm in a predicament," I tell Guy. "Look over there, Sylvie's here and Coco refuses to leave. What do I do? I don't want to piss Coco off and have her cause one of her scenes again. That would embarrass me terribly and I could lose Sylvie."

"You may have to let them have a cat fight. You lucky

bastard. I'll see if I can take off. No wait! There's Marcel. Invite him and have him swoon over Coco."

I call Marcel over. "Can you do me a favor?" I quickly explain and he joins the table and introduces himself to the women. He bows, gallantly kisses both their hands, and says, "I'm charmed to meet you lovely ladies."

In a group, we stroll across the square to my apartment. Guy sends over several bottles of booze with some of Marcel's friends. Lucien plays the saxophone for us. There is dancing and laughter. Marcel recites a tortured love poem and makes a sincere play for Coco. Fortunately, Coco becomes calm and placid with the help of Armagnac and Marcel's charm. In the dark and smoky room, I notice Sylvie's glittering silver hat and her alert eyes watching me. My concentration fades in and out of multiple conversations; voices become silent; all I hear is my frantically beating heart. It seems ridiculous to let Sylvie leave with the other guests. I whisper to her, "Please stay with me tonight." She gives me her hand and I lead her into my bedroom. After closing the door, I embrace her and say, "I don't know why you feel so good, taste so good, and smell so good in my arms. I can't let go of you. It's beyond my control."

"You don't have to," she pleads.

There's a knock at the door. "We're all leaving," Marcel says. Finally, Sylvie and I are completely alone. Paint fumes are making our heads spin faster then the drinks. I open all the windows and gusts of wind billow the sheer curtains and Sylvie's dress. The air is cool, but our lust is an inferno. She removes her dress. We tumble onto my bed. Her miraculous body frees under me, her nectar soothes and envelops me and carries me away to unexplored places. Her cheeks are flushing the same color as the ripe peaches in a Bonnard painting.

"Don't move. Let me open to you," she says.

Losing myself within her, I am transported to the places Sylvie has spoken of: the south of France, where I imagine an artist's window, a view of palm, sycamore, and cypress trees. Every nerve in my body is awakening, every cell vibrant. She moans; I explode. *"Dios Mio!"* I scream.

"I love you," she says tearfully.

I feel purified, absolved of sins. A sense of weightlessness is about me. Jubilantly, I stroll to the bathroom. I have never felt this way after sex with other women and it terrifies me. Looking in the mirror, my serene eyes tell me our union has captured a rare innocence. She evokes a tenderness in me that I never knew existed. And unlike my last prostitute, who demanded to be treated badly and spanked, Sylvie deserves the worship of a goddess.

This love is viciously ardent. Can I sustain it? Will it make me complacent? Is love a weakness or a strength? My art demands *angoisse*. Sylvié trusts me, but will I destroy her? Betray her? There is little I can offer her. I am almost penniless and I've cavorted with whores. How can she care for such an undeserving person? Rage whirls within me. How did I become fucked up? Perhaps it's the blood of a matador that makes me incapable of loving a woman. My penis is a deadly sword.

LOIRE, JUNE 1936

I'm writing this from a magnificent château in the Loire Valley. Sylvie and I haven't wanted to be apart. This morning I had a tour of her winery, while she explained the process of winemaking to me. It's dangerously quiet in the country. The telephone never rings and her servants never speak, unless asked a direct question. All week I've been doing studies of grape leaves. Thus far, I'm not tiring of their incongruous shapes and colors. In some of the sketches, I'll place Roman ruins in the background. I'm also creating several portraits of Sylvie, who's becoming a wonderful model. I would be content never leaving here. Rarely do we listen to the radio or read newspapers, as we make our own music, write our own adventures. Daily, the most wonderful food and spectacular wines are presented to us. At night, after making love, we fall asleep to sonorous crickets and frogs. Every moment that I spend with this woman is fascinating. Sylvie is buying my paintings of Loire and has already bought several of her portraits. I want to offer them to her as gifts, but she refuses. I've been thinking about Van Gogh in Arles and Bonnard in Le Cannet—artists who painted the French countryside. I'm also a different painter and person in this lush setting. The sky, sun, and soil absorb me, as the ailments of humanity are hidden from view.

CAP D'ANTIBES, JULY 1936

Mitya waits for us in the garden of the Hôtel du Cap, where tables are set up overlooking a coastline framed with pine, olive, and almond trees. A slight breeze rustles the trees, making the air as clear as the champagne, which is as abundant as the glamorous women. Birds are singing and the idle rich flitter about from their lounge chairs to their luncheon tables. Mitya proudly introduces her German baron. Lobster and Dom Perignon are amply served for lunch. Sylvie is wearing her long white poppy dress that exposes her swanlike neck and midback. Every moment I can, I try to kiss her lips. She smells of salt water and L'Heure Bleu by Guerlin.

I pull out my pastels and begin capturing my surroundings. René Vouchon finds me and says, "Your portrait of Mitya is dazzling, sensational if I must say. You've got what it takes. I hate Dada. Every artist wants to give me their kitchen sink or some old fucking tire and call it art. I hate that crap, but you have style. You have the flair of Gauguin's colors mixed with your Latin blood and Surrealist's imagination. I must see more of your work. How's your painting going?"

"Right now I'm painting landscapes and portraits of Sylvie. It seems to be going well. Would you care to go for a walk?" I ask, standing up. Vouchon follows me into the garden.

"I'm anxious to see more of your work. When are you returning to Paris?" he asks.

"I'd be happy never to return."

"You devil. Be careful. You're getting spoiled. She's indulging you," Vouchon teases, poking me in the ribs.

"It's true. I'm completely enchanted. I couldn't be happier."

"She's quite a find, beautiful and rich. You'd be a fool not to marry her. But don't become lazy. I've seen that happen to many talented artists. They lose touch with their suffering. Maybe you should go back to Spain and paint images of the war. It's atrocious what's happening in your country. How do you feel about it?"

"Completely helpless. My people are slaughtering each

other, Spaniard against Spaniard, brother against brother. It's an abomination. But I'm not going back there, never!"

Vouchon adds, "Some say it's a matter of time and it will happen here too. War is contagious. Hitler scares me a lot more than Franco."

"I'm not afraid of Hitler. Nothing can harm France."

"You sound just like a Frenchman. Since you've been away, you should see the commotion going on in Paris. People are leaving to volunteer in Spain. There are massive protests. As a Spaniard, you should paint about this situation. I'd especially be interested in your reactions. I understand that Picasso and Miró have begun some paintings on the tragedy. Don't you still have family in Spain?"

"I do."

"When you get settled back in Paris, I want to invite you to lunch. But, don't forget I want to see a collection of oil paintings. Do you have enough for a show?" he asked.

"I could have a series to show you by next month. This is a good incentive for me. Now, let's get back to the party. My champagne glass is getting empty," I tell him.

We have dessert in the gardens. Mitya blows out some candles that are on top of a towering glazed caramel profiterole cake. She and her new friend, Baron Fritz von Slausen, hand us plates, heaping with whipped cream and chocolate sauce.

"We thought we would find you mourning the loss of your husband, and here you are, as gay as ever," Sylvie says to Mitya.

I whisper to Sylvie, "Which husband are you talking about?"

"The prince of course."

"He died?"

"Yes. It was sudden, in his sleep."

"I can't keep up. I didn't know."

Mitya says, "I'm not one to mourn, darling. All that crying is a waste of time. I will always love the prince, but Fritz has changed my life. We're leaving tomorrow for the Greek isles on his yacht. Maybe the two of you would like to come along?"

"I have to paint," I answer.

"Why can't we go for a week?" Sylvie asks.

I whisper in her ear what I had promised to René.

I take Sylvie aside and ask, "How much do you know about this baron?"

"He's kind and rich. That's all I care to know. And Mitya is ecstatic."

"It was very generous of you to invite us. But I will have to decline," I inform them.

The baron says, "There'll be other times, my friend. Once you're my guest, you'll always be invited." He passes me a cigar and takes me aside. "I love Spain. What a tragedy for your poor country. Some people have told me they think you're a gigolo. I want you to know that I don't listen to gossip, my friend. You seem like a fine man to me. Can you keep a secret?" he asks.

"I'll try my best."

"I adore Mitya. She's a fantastic girl. I never thought I could care about a gal who works and has her own money. She couldn't care less about my fortune. Have you ever been rejected, my friend?"

"All the time."

"By women."

I shook my head. "Never."

"How can I win her heart? You know her. I want to marry her. This morning, before all of you arrived, I asked her to marry me. She said she loves me and wants to be devoted, but told me she'll never marry again. I don't understand."

"Her independence is part of her charm. You'll never be able to predict Mitya's behavior. She thrives on mystery. Give her her freedom and I'm sure your love will last an eternity. Mitya is a woman with tremendous integrity. Don't try to change her."

"I only hope in time she'll change her mind," the baron notes.

"That's always a woman's prerogative. Thank you again for inviting us," I add.

"It's my pleasure. I must go. My mistress is calling. I think I like the way that sounds," he says in jest.

The baron and Mitya leave their guests and board a small speedboat that drives them to an enormous Italian yacht. A part of me wants to go, regrets my decision, the truth being I don't feel adequate in their social circles. I'm afraid to tell Sylvie that, especially since I can't support her financially.

Once the guests have left, I insist on strolling through the hotel gardens to the forest of pines. The mistral has suddenly started blowing hard, nearly levitating us off the ground. I grab hold of Sylvie with one arm and with the other clasp onto a tree branch.

"I hope our happiness continues. These weeks have been sublime. You make me feel needed," Sylvie intones.

"I do need you."

"What if I'm not enough?" she asks.

"You're wonderful. How can you say that? I just feel that it's not fair that you have to pay for everything. It makes me feel like a gigolo. I have to make my own money. I don't want things to change; they're perfect. But, I must work more diligently, every day from now on."

"You're not going back to Spain are you?"

"No."

She lets go of me. Crossing her arms in front of her chest, she asks, "Are you leaving me?"

"No. Never!" I unfold her arms and rub the furrow out of her pretty brow. "Please don't wrinkle that precious face. It mars your beauty. You'll look like an old woman before your time."

"Will you still love me when I'm old?"

"I'll be old too."

"You'll always be younger," she sadly proclaims.

"Age isn't important."

"Are you going back to Paris?" she questions.

"Yes. I have to concentrate on creating more paintings. I told René I would do a series on Spain in a month."

"That seems like a lot of work. Do you think you can manage?"

"I'll have to try and hope that he'll like my work once its completed. My art is like having another lover. I must give everything I have to the work, alone, without distractions. It probably isn't fair to you. I know. I'm very sorry."

"I don't think I have a choice in this matter if I want to be with you. But I can't go back to Paris. The winery needs my attention. I've neglected its supervision. The wines were important to my family. I must honor that. Besides, my needs are different now. I don't want hectic city living anymore."

"Why not?"

"Loire is the perfect place for children."

"What children?" I ask. She places her hands over her abdomen.

My jaw falls open. I'm afraid that from this point onward, I'll say everything wrong. She's already reacting to my stupefaction and has begun to bite her fingernails. Again, I rub the wrinkle out of the middle of her brow.

"Are you not pleased?" she asks meekly.

"I don't know what to say. I never planned on children. I can hardly support myself."

"I want this child, Joaquím Carlos. I'm past thirty. Society had cast me out as an old maid, until I met you. I don't expect you to understand how I feel, but it's empowering to feel a new life growing inside me—a life full of promise."

I drop to my knees and take her soft hand in mine.

"Then marry me, sweet Sylvie. I implore you."

"Do you mean that? Do you want this child?"

"Of course I do. We'll marry tomorrow, today, tonight, as soon as we can! I won't let our child be born out of wedlock."

The next morning, we board a train to Avignon, the ancient city of popes. It's my first time in Provence, and recalling again my artist predecessor, Van Gogh, I'm elated to see other villages in France.

We couldn't have planned for a more serendipitous outdoor ceremony. Just before sunset, we marry as traveling circus performers in bright fuchsia, orange, and red costumes form an audience around us. When we kiss, they clap and cheer. Acrobats perform somersaults. Children bang tambourines and fly colorful kites. A mime dances with Sylvie, to the music of an organ grinder. Along with the organ grinder, a swaying monkey is nipping at a bottle of Pernod. We dance and dance, as a hot summer moon rises over the pont d'Avignon and the sun begins to hide itself on the opposite end of the bridge. During that moment, when the heavens are divided, split between a flaming crimson sky and a cool slate horizon, during this exact moment, second, in my peripheral vision, I notice a shadowy apparition edging toward us. As it saunters closer, I see a gargantuan black animal, what appears to be a hybrid between a dog and a panther. The beast lunges toward us, its mouth hanging open, baring rows of sharp fangs. Instinctively, I grab Sylvie, seconds before the creature tries to maul her. Sylvie and I begin running for shelter and lose the animal through the winding cobblestone streets of Avignon. I can't tell her what I'm feeling, or divulge my terror. Nor, can I admit to her that this wild beast is a harbinger of evil, a demon that will always be chasing us.

We spend a few days in Avignon. On our last day, Sylvie arranges for us to take a hot-air balloon trip. We bring box lunches and jump into the basket below a yellow, red, and orange balloon. As we sail into the air, the town below resembles a minuscule architectural model with the Rhône shimmering beneath us like a basin of absinthe.

"I want to take you to Egypt and paint you on a boat gliding across the Nile. You'll look more sumptuous than Cleopatra," I muse.

Sailing toward the countryside, Sylvie points to a clearing and indicates that she wants to descend. We land in a pine forest beside a Roman aqueduct. "That's the pont du Gard!" she exclaims. Once we are out of the balloon, the pilot shouts, "I will come back in a few hours to collect you." We watch the colorful balloon sail away.

Before us is the aqueduct which is based on the same archetype of a ruin I had seen in Tarragona, Spain. Rome is eternal and present in these lofty arches that frame the cobalt sky, clouds, and trees. While Sylvie unpacks our belongings, I walk to the aqueduct. Standing before it, I'm completely mesmerized by the architecture. The honey colored sandstone is soft, crumbling in my fingertips like flecks of shimmering goldleaf. Its strength eludes me; it has remained intact since Caesar's reign of power. Looking away from the structure, I gaze at my sleeping lover; her magnificent body lies nude, encircled by wild rosemary, daisies, and lavender. I want to stay with her, spend more languid days in Provence, rejoicing in our affection, but the longer I'm away from painting, the more anxious I become. I must leave tonight for Paris. Already I feel smothered, trapped. Have I made an enormous mistake? I've only just found my wings. I'm an owl, a wild, nocturnal bird of prey with a six-foot wingspan, who must fly toward the sycamores in the stillness of night, guided only by the soft glow of the moon. But now I've been captured. Next to me, in the metal cage, is Sylvie: a docile white dove, that I can so easily devour.

Sylvie wakes from her nap. "Come relax with me," she suggests. Placing a blanket on the ground, she encourages me to sunbathe with her. I remove my clothes and lounge beside her. We are completely alone, except for the sounds of our own breathing, a pearling stream, singing crickets, pollinating bees, and screeching cicadas. Sylvie stands up and dips her toes into the cool water.

"It's completely refreshing," she says splashing me.

"I'm going to make you pay for that," I playfully warn, jumping in after her.

"My God! Look at you. Your skin is turning black from the sun. Who have I married?" she asks teasingly. "But don't worry, I like it. You look beautiful."

While we are splashing each other like mischievous children, I suddenly say in a serious tone, "You know I'll miss you when I go back to Paris." She pulls me toward her and voraciously kisses my lips, which are drenched in fresh water. Silently, she smooths my wet hair back with her hands and cups her palms around my face, studying me intently. When I need to read into a woman, it never happens. What is she thinking? Is she trying to understand me. Have I crushed her hopes by leaving? Should I give in and stay? Sylvie's hands drop to her sides. Taking advantage of the moment, I scoop her up in my arms and carry her under the aqueduct, where our passion quickly ignites. In the shade, beneath the ancient Roman stones, we desperately and daringly make love. During that exhilarating instant, I can't help but dread our future separation. The thought of being without her drives me insane with longing, intensifying her soothing and tortuous touch.

Suddenly, I need her more, because I know I must leave; it's impossible to completely satiate our desires.

We part that evening at the bustling train station. Commotion surrounds us, as travelers are frantically rushing and darting in haphazard directions, while lovers tearfully part and re-unite—a few ecstatic wives or fiancées shouting screams of elation. There are train whistles sounding off, valets carting first-class luggage, barking dogs, crying children, departure and arrival announcements, and shrieking brakes. We are standing silently, frozen by the depot, watching my train pull in. Sylvie is clinging so tightly to my hand that I can feel its circulation stop.

"This is not what a honeymoon is supposed to be like," she says sorrowfully.

"I know. But believe me the honeymoon will never end. This is just the beginning," I explain.

"It's the beginning of your career. I'll just have to sacrifice my selfish needs, as I know you'll make me proud."

"What will you do when I'm gone?" I ask.

"There's little choice for me. I'll be tending to the winery and preparing for this baby."

"Make sure to eat properly. You're eating for two now," I preach.

"I will," she says, fighting back tears.

When I step up to the first ledge of the train, she follows me and daringly stuffs a thick envelope into my front trouser pocket. The train engine starts up, wheels begin to churn, and a whistle blows. Before I can grab the envelope, she meets my level on the platform, rushing to get in our last tender kiss. Seconds matter; they are all we have to savor and taste our combustion, our fueled lust. The conductor separates our embrace, forcing Sylvie to step back on the concrete platform. Slowly, the train pulls away, leaving her shrouded in a cloud of steam and smoke. I wave. This time I can feel her tears choking me. It becomes too painful to look at her.

Venturing inside the train, I find my seat and close my eyes. I rest a moment, until the doors to my compartment open. A pinched-faced crone waddles in. After watching her a moment, I notice she has as much appeal as a diseased pigeon. Nevertheless, I smile out of politeness. But instead of returning a cordial exchange, or a grin, she sneers, while also giving me a disapproving pig's grunt that comes out of her flared nostrils. In order to distract myself from her ghastly demeanor, I open the window and stick my head out. I will miss Avignon, as I watch the town slowly disappearing, becoming flashes of trees and pastures—like smudges of chartreuse and sepia oils on my palette.

Later on, I try to sleep, but stabbing me in the hip is the fat envelope. Once I remove it, I'm compelled to take a quick peak. As I do this, the train tips to one side, scattering hundreds of francs across the floor. The sour-faced bitch across from me looks appalled and disgusted. I'm completely embarrassed as I drop to the floor to collect the bills. Did this woman witness our transaction? While I'm crawling on my hands and knees, I can't help but question if I've become like the ladies of the night whom I've exploited, fucking for francs. Perhaps I'm as cheap as they are, belonging among the soiled lot. Would I love Sylvie the same if she were poor? Will I still love her next year? What about ten years from now? I loathe myself for depending on her wealth. Men shouldn't be taken care of by their wives. However, I must realize that with her encouragement and financial assistance, I'm finally given a chance. Thus far, a handful of people I know believe in my art work. What a tremendous relief it is that all I have to do this month is paint. Night and day I can work. For now, and hopefully never again, will I have to worry about my next meal, my rent, or spend hours cleaning art studios.

Finally, I close my eyes again, and coalesce with the speed and rocking sensation of the train, as I imagine my unobstructed owl wings, waiting to disengage. When I wake, it'll be nighttime in Paris.

NINE

Djuna Cortez

I had just moved in and settled into the apartment in Paris when Jean-Auguste asked me to join him for a few days in London. The opportunity was too appealing to pass up, even if it meant missing art class for the week. Almost immediately, I began packing my suitcases and reserved a flight to Heathrow Airport.

I arrived early on a misty Tuesday morning. Jean-Auguste so graciously collected me at the airport, greeting me at the terminal with a bouquet of pink roses. Then he led me to a hired black Bentley with a liveried chauffeur. Already having been in the city a week on business, he was in need of some diversion, which included me, a bottle of Dom Perignon champagne (which he had resting in a bucket of ice on the floor of the car), and the stimulating effects of South American cocaine.

As soon as we settled into the backseat of the Bentley, he rolled up the dark window separating us from the driver, and withdrew a vial of cocaine from his navy blazer. I tried to appear nonchalant, like I had witnessed this type of indulgence before. But my eyes must have widened in astonishment.

Holding up the glass vial he said, "This powder is really

pure. It's flown in from Columbia. Once you try it, this day will flow like magic. And you'll find reserves of energy to stay out all night." He inhaled a spoonful and then handed it to me. "I'm so pleased you're here. There's so much I want to show you. Take some. Don't be afraid. In moderate amounts it's perfectly safe: even Sigmund Freud used the drug."

I suppose there are first times for everything, for me that included recreational drugs. But more than anything else, I wanted to please and impress him, hoping that he would think that I was as sophisticated as he was. Trying to hide my trepidation, I took the gold spoon and quickly inhaled.

In a matter of seconds, my whirlwind tour began. Soon I was feeling more awake and alive than if I had slept ten hours and consumed four cups of strong coffee. My mind felt clearer, more alert, and my body was aching to get out of the car, walk, run even. Rolling down the rear window and inhaling deeply, I cleared my sinuses of the temporary burning sensation. The air quickly became animated and smelled of a cool moist rain and the spicy aromas of exotic curries wafting in from a suburb saturated with Indian restaurants.

When we arrived in London, we met a cornucopia of garish contrasts—a beguiling and dualistic metropolis. At first, sandwiched between two buses, the Bentley was unable to move. Our Pakistani chauffeur ran out of the car, threw his hands up in the air, and yelled to the torpid bus driver in front of him, "Get moving you stupid sod!"

I too wanted to get out and scream, "Move, move, move." I didn't want to remain still.

"Can we get out of the car and walk?" I asked Jean-Auguste.

"Just be patient. The traffic jam won't last much longer," he said.

The car took off again. As we were driving, Jean-Auguste pointed out some magnificent sights: Big Ben, Westminster Abbey, Trafalgar Square, Piccadilly Circus, the changing of the guards at Buckingham Palace, and the Tower of London with its bloody history, where young heirs to the throne had died. London appeared to be a town of social refinement, as well as rebellion. We saw elegantly dressed couples walking in Kensington Gardens and coming out of Chelsea's million-dollar townhouses, which contrasted greatly with the punked-out Soho girls with magenta, florescent green, and flaming-orange spiked mohawks.

The tone of London went far beyond its gray skies and the dull clothing of conservative Parliament workers. London was fiery, effervescent, and flamboyant—bold, brash, and ruthless from past to present. From what I had thus far gathered, if London were to claim a gender, it would be either a transvestite or Lady Macbeth. In my opinion, London's primary color remains the deepest shade of crimson, characterized by its double-decker buses, fire-engine-red telephone booths, and the cardinal-colored uniforms of the palace guards.

When we first got out of the car, we admired the flowers in Kensington Gardens. At another stop, we saw the lavish tiaras of the crown jewels. The romantic mood quickly dissipated when we entered the Chamber of Horrors in Madame Toussaud's wax museum. After that experience, we needed to distract ourselves from all the tortures and brutality we had seen (the scenes from the plague were most distressing.) So, we stopped for a civilized afternoon tea at the Dorchester Hotel.

A pianist played Chopin as we entered the elegant Victorian tearoom. We sat among gossiping high society ladies who delicately sipped their Darjeeling blends with their pinkies raised and talked about growing orchids, designing their Ascot hats, and the latest divorce scandal. The service was impeccable, allowing us to copiously fill our bone china plates with a wide selection of scones, Devonshire cream, petit fours, and finger sandwiches.

Jean-Auguste whispered to me, "What would these ladies think if they saw me pull out this vial?"

"Please don't do that," I pleaded.

"High society here is all about breeding, that includes horses as well as people. Personally, I find it all too restrictive. But don't worry. I won't do anything shocking. How are you feeling?" he asked.

"I'm fine. Very good, as a matter of fact," I replied.

After tea, our next visit was Harrod's department store, where tourists browsed, the royals and the elite shopped, and haughty billionaire Arab men released their harems of docile wives. Jean-Auguste sat in a chair outside the changing room while I modeled designer clothes and furs. Since the change in my financial situation, I could have purchased everything myself. However, he insisted on indulging me, and urged me to keep a low-cut maroon velvet evening gown. As a result of his generosity, I left the clothing department with three dresses and two mink coats.

"Incroyable! Or, as they say in London, you look smashing," he exclaimed while quickly glancing at his watch. "Let's find you a pair of shoes to go with that adorable dress you have on." He pronounced "adorable" the French way. "I'll leave you to do that. Meet me at the Chanel makeup counter in a quarter of an hour. And please don't change." Handing me two hundred pounds, he continued, "I don't want you to worry about anything. Take this money for your shoes and accessories."

After I had found shoes, I browsed through the Food Halls of gourmet and imported foods, finding a vast international selection of provisions and condiments, ranging from American Pop Tarts to imported Norwegian smoked salmon and Russian caviar.

Once I arrived at the Chanel counter, an attractive woman with a deep baritone voice greeted me.

"I've been expecting you, Luv. I'm April. Why don't you sit up here and let me make you glamorous for your fellow," she said exuberantly, patting the cushion of the chair.

April stood over six feet and had perfectly coiffed auburn hair, mimicking the bouffant pageboy Jackie Kennedy had when she was First Lady. Everything she wore was classic Chanel: a fuchsia suit, heavy gold and pearl necklaces with matching bracelets and earrings. In addition, April's individuality was displayed through her makeup, showing off her wide-set amber eyes, which were heavily painted like a 1930s screen idol. Her complexion was flawless, a perfect peaches and cream, which also gave her an advantage for selling skin care products.

"We girls have our beauty secrets," she cooed. "Mascara and lipstick can mesmerize men. Don't be afraid to use more of them. First, I'm going to properly clean your skin."

I quickly retorted, "I usually don't wear much makeup."

"Don't worry, luv, I'll give you a natural look. You're in good hands with April. If you want I'll teach you how to apply all of this. It just takes some practice."

She pulled out some charts and began coloring in on a blank face the shadows she was starting to use on me.

"You'll need a set of good brushes. It's a lot like painting. How long are you in London for, luv?"

"We're visiting from Paris and plan to be here for a few days."

"How lovely. Oh, I just adore Paris. Your handsome Frenchman must be divine in bed. You're ever so lucky," she said while handing me a hand mirror. Her forwardness was a bit offensive. Nonetheless, I chose to ignore her last comment. For ten minutes, April's husky hands flitted rapidly as she dipped her brushes into eye shadows, plucked a few of my stray eyebrow hairs, blended foundation with sponges, painted and outlined my eyes with pencils, and smoothed on rouges.

Jean-Auguste soon arrived dressed in a black tuxedo with a black satin cummerbund and matching bow tie. The suit looked tailored for him; even his cuff links were designed in the shape of wine bottles.

April gasped and placed her right hand between her ample breasts. "Crikey! I mean, my goodness, aren't you lucky to have such a dashing chap."

"You look absolutely wonderful," Jean-Auguste said, handing me a blue velvet box.

"What's this?" I asked.

As I opened the box, April gasped again. "Oh, it's so beautiful. Diamonds!" she screamed.

"Do you like it? It came from a 1920s estate collection," he said.

"It's exquisite. It looks Art Deco. You must have spent a fortune. I don't know what to say. But, thank you," I answered.

"Let me help you put it on." He fastened the bracelet around my left wrist, brushing his hands against the inside of my arm. Just the sensation of his touch was enough to raise my blood pressure—and, so it seemed, April's, too.

"This lipstick is the perfect color for you, luv, it matches your gorgeous dress," April commented.

"I want her to have everything you're applying," Jean-Auguste ordered.

"Yes, sir, I'll have it all prepared for your sweet lady. Now, run along. We girls need a little more time and privacy. She'll be ready in about fifteen minutes," April said, winking at him.

April then whispered to me, "You should never let your *bonne homme* see you putting on makeup. Don't ever give away your secrets. You know what I mean," she said, handing me an eyelash curler.

"I think so."

April added, "Between us girls, don't be afraid to clamp down on it. That a girl. See, look at those big eyes you now have."

Jean-Auguste appeared again in half an hour. April shouted, "Violá. I studied French too, but not so thoroughly as you," she said to me. "She's all yours," she told him, "and here's your little *facture*. You can take it up to the V.A.T. counter." April curtsied and said graciously, "It was a pleasure serving you both. Please come visit me again."

Jean-Auguste pointed to the bottles of perfume decorating a glass cabinet. "Throw in a bottle of Cristalle and Number 5. The largest sizes you have," he ordered.

"Absolutely, sir," April said in a flurry.

Dressed in his Italian tuxedo, Jean-Auguste looked as if he could grace the pages of *GQ* magazine. Unlike me, who was often self-conscious and felt like I was parading around in borrowed clothes. It was different with Jean-Auguste, as he possessed a commanding nobility while he walked, leaving the heads of lonely hard-working women to furtively turn and admire him.

Our next destination was again a mystery. The Bentley took off and he instructed the driver, "Just follow the itinerary."

We arrived at Mr. Chow's restaurant, which was packed with a dynamic theater-going crowd. Upon entering, the maître d'hôtel bowed to us, confirmed the reservation, and sat us upstairs near an Andy Warhol portrait of Mr. Chow. Warhol's paintings were perfectly suited for the postmodern, upbeat dining atmosphere. Jazz was playing in the background, but the music was muted by gregarious conversations and laughter. Glancing at the other tables, I recognized a few celebrities. Kathleen Turner was sitting next to us and David Bowie was nearby.

"We don't have a lot of time. Do you mind if I order for us?" he asked.

"Not at all. Warhol must get free Chinese food when he comes to London," I said.

"He probably does. Your makeup looks wonderful. Transsexuals must know all the best tricks."

"That can't be!"

"Of course April was. Besides, you should wear more makeup. It's very becoming on you," he said.

Our palates were tantalized with each delicately prepared dish. I was surprised that Jean-Auguste ordered saki on the rocks and then plum wine. He explained that the drinks had to compliment the food. In his opinion, a rich Bordeaux would not become Asian cuisine, especially with the tangy flavors of ginger, peanut, and cilantro. To save time, he recommended we refrain from ordering dessert.

Again, I followed him out of the boisterous restaurant. Although, in London, they spoke my mother tongue, the city was completely foreign to me; and I would have felt lost without a guide. With magisterial flair, he instructed the driver to take us to the Barbican.

Given our limited time, we rushed inside the theater, bypassing a large crowd that had gathered outside. Once inside, we were guided to our seats in the forth row center. The lights dimmed just as we sat down, and the orchestra began to play. At the same time, stoplights beamed down on a revolving stage with a cast dressed in torn-peasant clothing. The actors' rich operatic voices reverberated throughout the theater, as they began to perform the opening of *Les Misérables*. Song after song exposed the profound sadness of Victor Hugo's prerevolutionary France. The music was as compelling as it was tragic. When young Cosette sang in her sweet soprano voice, there was hardly a dry eye in the theater. Silent tears ran down my cheeks, ruining all my new makeup.

At intermission most of the audience flowed out to the cocktail lounges located inside the Barbican, one on each level of the theater. Every person we saw standing by the bar was patting their puffy eyes with tissue and blowing their noses as they consumed three-layer Belgian chocolate cake, along with cups of strong coffee. As a result of all this melodrama, Jean-Auguste and I also gravitated to the sugar and caffeine for solace.

When we returned to our seats for the final act, I felt a deep veneration toward the French culture, intensifying my respect for Jean-Auguste profoundly. The performance gave me a greater appreciation for his country's suffering and triumphs. By the end of the performance, the spectators must have felt the same way, and gave the cast a standing ovation.

We left the play feeling exhausted and drained, as if we had also experienced a war. At last, we could rest. Our final destination was the luxurious Savoy Hotel. As we approached the entrance of the lobby, the staff recognized Jean-Auguste and rushed to take our luggage and shopping bags. Jean-Auguste seemed thrilled to be treated with such importance. Instead of retiring immediately to bed, we entered the American Bar and Grill for a nightcap.

The bar was a complete contrast to the stuffiness of afternoon tea and the grim atmosphere of the play. A group of obnoxious salesmen from a real estate convention were glued to the bar as they drank brimming mugs of ale. They didn't care how loud they laughed or who could overhear their crude jokes. We kept to ourselves and retreated to a secluded corner table.

"The bar is famous for their martinis. Would you care for one?" he asked me.

"I'd rather have a cognac."

"Fine choice. Me, too."

"The play reinforced my fascination with your culture and history," I said, "How do you feel about it?"

"I can't even imagine living during those drastic times," he lamented.

"Is there any part of history you would like to have lived in?" I asked.

"I do love Greece and its ancient philosophy and logic. It would have to be the times of Socrates and Aristotle. I did get my baccalaureate in philosophy and mathematics. What about you? What time would you liked to have lived?"

"For me it would be the Jazz Age, the days of Hemingway and Fitzgerald during the thirties. I would have liked to have stayed here and been a fly on the wall."

"Those writers frequented this hotel," he noted.

"I know. They're some of my favorites," I said enthusiastically, as I pulled out a fresh pack of Rothmans. This was one of the first times I had smoked around him, and doing this made me a bit nervous.

"I didn't know you—"

I interrupted, "Smoked."

"Yes. I like to when the mood strikes me, sitting in a bar late at night, or talking about writers, a prelude to . . . whatever. Does it bother you?"

He rushed to light my cigarette with a match.

"Not at all. Enjoy yourself," he remarked.

"Have you ever smoked?"

"Cigarettes? Never. I've had a wonderful time. I don't know how to thank you for joining me on such short notice," he said tenderly.

"I'm the one that should be thanking you. You've been overly generous. This has been an incredible experience, that I will never forget."

"Shall we retire to our room?" he said, extending his hand.

"Yes," I said.

He led me to our deluxe suite. Giving me a tour of our suite, Jean-Auguste continued to be gallant and formal. My suitcase was placed in a separate bedroom. By that point, I would not have minded sharing a room with him. When he kissed me good night, I could tell he was refraining from touching my lips. Gingerly, he closed the door between us, separating our bedrooms. I had wanted to ask him if he had brought a lover here before.

Alone, in my room, the tragic suffering of the characters in the play continued to haunt me. Often, I ignored beggars by the Métro stations, even since my afternoon in the Luxembourg gardens, where destitute strangers had befriended me. Would I become as insensitive to the needs of the indigent as the aristocrats had? Would I become hardened? Unlike Jean-

Auguste, I lacked French pride and self-worth. I hoped that by living in France, eventually, I would feel connected to a dynamic past. I needed to belong somewhere.

For an hour, I wept as I stared out the window at the misty Thames. Fog was beginning to settle around Waterloo Bridge. I lit another cigarette. Did my smoking repulse him? In a way, I liked the challenge he was proposing, letting me slowly uncover the affection and desire disguised behind his reserved and composed exterior. I admired his confidence, which I wanted to possess myself. Was he hiding a history of suffering? Like a sculptor, I wanted to chisel away at his protection that sometimes appeared as cold and hard as a slab of marble. However, underneath his shyness, I sensed a fragile vulnerability combined with inner strength. Unlike my college attractions that quickly ignited and then fizzled out, hopefully Jean-Auguste and I would endure. There was a purity about him that attracted my passion.

I was startled by the obnoxious noise of the telephone. Its ring was different from those in America: two sharp rings in one tone.

"*C'est moi.* Are you comfortable?" Jean-Auguste asked, pronouncing again "comfortable" in French.

"Fine."

"*Je t'embrasse* and sweet dreams. I want you to know that I respect you tremendously," he said, hanging up the phone.

That night, I couldn't have cared less about formalities and protocol. It surprised me that he did, when I also knew he had an independent streak. Yet, more than anything else, I just wanted to be held and comforted, taken out of my perpetual isolation. However, I couldn't tell him that I was upset and fearful of the future. I was ashamed of my emotions. It was better not to complain. Perhaps I was better suited to be someone's mistress rather than a wife. That way I would never have to fully disclose who I really was to someone. We could just pretend, play out different roles. How many famous torrid affairs had taken place in this extravagant Victorian suite? Who benefited more—the wife or the mistress?

Goddesses, Wine, Dead Artists & Chocolate

The Journals of Joaquím Carlos Cortez

PARIS, SEPTEMBER 1936

From this point onward, my life is not my own. I'm forced to think about a living creature other than myself. For my unborn child, I feel only pathos. Fatherhood is already burdening me, terrifying me. I don't want to be a man, nor do I envy being a woman. I want my libertinage back and I long to reclaim my frivolity.

Sylvie is changing with the passing months, most visibly her sleek body. The perfection she once had is altering. This distresses me. The curve of her waistline has vanished. She's become round, corpulent. Sylvie claims that Paris makes her ill; the noise bothers her. All the time now she prefers to stay in Loire. I try to visit her every other weekend. When I sleep alone, I do miss her lips, which sometimes taste like *cassis sorbet* and other times like fresh raspberries. When we kiss, I am still intoxicated. I want to whisper in her ear, "Be my whore, my slave." But I can no longer touch or speak to her amorously. With these changes, she's become inviolate, my precious object and possession.

PARIS, DECEMBER 1936

The gaiety of Paris is gradually fading. In the cafés, conversations are dominated by the war in Spain. Every morning, in the paper, I read about merciless killings: nuns who were raped, priests who were savagely tortured, and the hundreds of deaths of innocent children. I should be there fighting and standing for a position. But I refuse to become a soldier and bring about change through violence.

I meet Marcel at le Dôme. He's been emotionally devastated since he found Fifi in bed with another man and another girl. Since the incident, he's been quoting Camus and Sartre, writing broken-hearted love poems, and dreaming of existential suicide. I'm not worried about him. It's all part of his artistic drama, like he professes to want to join the crusades and fight in Spain.

"You're a fucking fool to want to fight a war that's not even yours," I tell him.

"For once, I'll have a real purpose. It won't matter there that I can't publish or pay my damned rent," he answers.

"I can lend you money. Luck has been in my favor. I showed René Vouchon more of my work and he wants to represent me. He's already advanced me some cash."

"I'll get by. What are you painting these days?" Marcel asks.

"Mostly nudes. I've also added a Spanish theme, reflections of my country."

"Sounds interesting. Isn't that your dealer?" Marcel points to a man approaching our table.

"Yes, that's him."

I introduce them.

René tells me, "Carlos, I have great news. I've sold some of your work to be included in a Surrealist exhibition at the Jeu de Paumme. Still that's a ways off. Before that, I want you to have a group show next week, just to get your name out. I want more paintings before the show, as much as you can produce."

"That's incredible!" I exclaim.

"You're going to have to work much harder and stop hanging around cafés," René says firmly.

PARIS, FEBRUARY 1937

After one sold-out show, I have become a success. My art is recognized throughout Paris. My name is in all the papers. My head is spinning; my ears are ringing all the time, along with the telephone. There is little time left for friends—or sleep, for that matter. As I cross the rue de Rivoli to the place de la Concorde, a flag catches my attention. A young woman is standing at the corner waving a gigantic Spanish flag that is snapping in the wind. I can't help but do a double take of the girl. Her long raven tresses flow to her slim waist. As I move closer, I notice her intense coal-black eyes. Her voice is sharp and high-pitched as she shouts, "Milk for the children. Please give money for the innocent children of Spain."

She doesn't look a day older than eighteen. When I approach, she says, "I'm raising money to be sent to Spain. Will you help the children?"

"Where are you from?" I ask.

"Barcelona."

"Me too."

I pull a twenty-franc bill from my pocket.

"I think I know who you are," she answers.

I reply, "But I don't know you. Can I buy you a drink?"

She accepts and quickly packs up her belongings. After following me to the nearest brasserie, her eyes widen when she sees the busy waiters serving platters of food. I recognize her desperate glances as a symptom of hunger and offer her lunch.

"How long have you been in Paris?" I ask.

"Almost two years. I've been studying political science and French at the Sorbonne."

"What a wonderful education you must be having. Why go back to Spain now?"

"I have to fight the Fascists. Don't you hate them?"

"Yes. But I hate war even more. Violence begets violence."

"Are you a royalist?" she asks.

"No. I refuse to take sides. I'm a pacifist like Gandhi. I admire his beliefs in nonviolence and equality."

"It sounds like an excuse to be a coward," she mocks.

"Watch it, *muchacha!* Don't bite the hand that feeds you."

"I'm sorry. I'm cursed with a sharp tongue and temper. My mother always said it would be the death of me."

"Don't negate yourself. You're obviously blessed with a mesmerizing beauty."

"That can also get me into trouble."

"Has it?" I eagerly inquire.

She tosses her mane of hair to one side and answers flirtatiously, "I'm not saying that it has, but it could."

"I'm sure it could. Even so, if you're smart, you'll listen to me. I can help you make more money."

"My you have an inflated ego! Why should I listen to you? Just what are you implying," she asks, with an edge to her voice.

"Not what you're thinking."

She raises her chin and says, "I should tell you right now,

I don't respect artists. They're immature and completely self-indulgent. Anyway, modern art rarely moves me."

"That's a pity, especially in this city. How did I find such a ravishing, intelligent girl *sans goût?*"

"I do have taste. Anyway, you didn't find me. We met by chance."

"Then, I assume, you don't believe in fate—destiny," I say.

"But I do believe in fate," she answers emphatically.

"When are you leaving for Spain?" I ask.

"I'm not sure. I need to raise more money before I go."

"Do you plan on returning to Paris once your mission is over?"

"I haven't thought much about it."

"Could you look up my family in Barcelona?"

"I will if you allow me to have dessert," she says feebly.

"My poor *muchacha*, you're starving. When was the last time you ate?"

She has too much pride to answer my question and instead replies, "The money I have been receiving from Spain has been delayed. It's been difficult getting by."

"How are you getting there?" I ask.

"My comrades have it all arranged," she answers.

"You're a Communist!"

"Yes. Do you have a problem with that?"

"No, not at all. Many of my friends are."

"Then I'd like to meet your friends."

"Most of them are painters and poets, you know."

She smiles as she sips her coffee. "I think I'm beginning to change my mind about artists. Obviously, you have a lot to teach me."

"Then I have something to propose. Our goals aren't that different; we both believe in fairness and, it seems, in candor. I'm sure you'll agree that if women had more political influence, we would have less war. I'll help your campaign; and in exchange, you'll model for me. Does that sound appealing?"

She finishes a rich Napoleon, stands up, and says, "I'm Isabella Martinez. My friends call me Bella. Are you ready for me now, monsieur?"

"Joaquím Carlos. Carlos is fine," I said.

Isabella enters my studio on rue Palatine. Inside, she gently sets down her flag and pamphlets and makes a quick study of the room.

"Before I model for you, may I take a bath?" she asks politely.

"That's an unusual request. But of course you may. Please make yourself comfortable."

While she's in the bathroom, I telephone Sylvie.

"My last show was again a big success. I only wish you could have been there. I sold everything," I tell her.

"I always knew you would succeed. I'm glad I bought my portraits when you painted them. They would have been gone by now. How do you let go of your work?" she asks.

"Sometimes it does bother me. I suppose the thrill of the sale then takes over."

"I'm proud of you. When are you coming to Loire?" she asks.

"Soon. It's been *une folie* around here. I haven't stopped working."

"Good. That's what you're supposed to be doing. I miss you desperately," she confesses.

"I know."

"I've got a contract with René," I continue. "He's buying my next series before they're painted. I'll be on permanent display in his gallery. Can you believe it?"

"I can. That's wonderful."

"It's all because of you, my angel. How's everything in the country?"

"Wonderful for winter. The snow is beautiful. I bought a goat and some chickens. Now, every morning, I have fresh eggs and milk. It's delightful here. I can't wait for our baby to be born."

"How are you feeling?"

"Tired. I'd really like you to be here. When are you coming?"

"I'll be there in a few days. I promise." Then I let slip, "I found a new model."

"That's good. Then I demand you come tomorrow," she teases. However, there's a hint of seriousness in her tone of voice.

"I'll try to be there soon."

"I love you," she says.

"I do too. I must go," I reply, hanging up the phone.

The nymph emerges from the bathroom bundled in a towel; her hair is soaking wet.

"You better dry off first. I don't want you getting sick, nor do I want to paint you looking waterlogged."

I retrieve another towel and light the fireplace. She sits down on a chair and begins shaking her damp hair.

"It's nice being clean again," she tells me, while vigorously rubbing the towel around her head and ears.

Isabella reminds me of an abandoned child. I want to help comb her hair. Instead, I try to remain detached.

"My roommate kicked me out," she explains.

"Why?"

"She got fed up with me not paying the bills."

"I remember what that was like."

"I haven't been able to find work."

"You're a model now, and if you're good, I'll refer you to other artists."

Excitedly, she moves the chair by the bright window.

"I'll do whatever you want, señor, anything you want."

I open the window, letting the cold air and crisp sunlight in. Then I move my easel closer to her and begin mixing oils.

"Do you paint many models?"

"I have," I answer without looking at her.

"How do I compare?"

When I glance at her again, I see that she's trembling. "Every woman is different; each one is equally interesting. But I can't tell you anything until you remove that towel. Are you cold with the window open?" I ask.

"Freezing. It seems strange posing without clothes," she says, clinging to the towel.

"Are you ashamed of your body?" I propose.

"No. I just never thought about doing this before."

"You're young and beautiful. There's nothing to be concerned about," I clarify, closing the window.

"I was taught not to exude pride, or indulge in pleasurable pursuits. Would this be considered vulgar?" she asks.

"Vulgarity is a matter of opinion. I don't view anatomy or art that way. What do you think?"

"I'm not sure. My life has changed since I've read Marx and Engels. I gave up on confession," she confides.

"Did you have a lot to confess?"

"Maybe." She bashfully looks down at the floor.

"I know you're idealistic, but that's good. You have a bright future ahead of you," I tell her.

Her black eyes are filled with ardor as she exclaims, "We could have a better world!"

"I agree. It's certainly worth trying for."

"What do you believe in? You're young like me. What do you hope for?" she asks.

I walk over to her and reach for her towel. Clenching the towel in her hands, she refuses to let it go. Backing up, I watch her, and wait a few moments. Her fingers open; gently she lets the towel drop to the floor. Without her layers of winter clothes, her body is skinny and undeveloped, a mere shell of a girl, a waif, a lost sparrow. Watching her shiver, I want to comfort her. Instead, I walk over to my phonograph and put on a tango record. Her foot starts tapping to the music. I resume our conversation, hoping to set her at ease.

"Peace. That's what I truly believe in," I answer.

"What about love?"

"What about it?" I question dryly.

"Do you believe in it?"

"Absolutely. However there are many variations on the theme, like the love of one's country. Caring for another person is a private matter. There shouldn't be one belief on how a person's emotions should respond. Every heart is different. Marriage is an institution to which I've regretfully conformed. Still, I feel it's wrong to set requirements on love. Enough of me! I think I know what *you* adore."

"What?" she asks curiously.

"Animals, music, and theater," I answer.

"What type of animals?"

"All animals, especially domestic ones—like birds, cats, and dogs. Am I right?"

"Yes. Back home, I collected birds. I don't know how you can know all that."

"Tell me what sort of music you like?" I ask.

"Perhaps you can answer for me. I love Stravinsky, Ravel, Moszkowski, and traditional Spanish rhythms."

"Can you dance the flamenco?"

"Absolutely!"

"You must dance for me sometime."

Finally, the tension from her muscles begin to leave her body. As I paint the nude, I set in the background the Gothic cathedral of Barcelona, bursting with flames. Isabella is lying seductively on the cathedral steps, loyally holding up her precious flag and tin cup, in order to collect for the orphans of Spain. A bloodred tear runs down her cheek. For hours, I paint, while visions come flooding through me: the wars of the past, present, and future, my longings and regrets, along with hers.

We stop around ten in the evening. She is tired, but refrains from complaining when she sees the money. Once she is dressed I tell her, "I must do a series of you. You're an inspiration. You provoke all kinds of imagery. I don't want to stop seeing you. I'll pay you every day this week to continue modeling."

"I'd like that," she answers.

"Now you're coming to dinner with me," I instruct.

We dine in a quaint bistro at the place de Tertre in Montmartre. Whenever I'm in Montmartre, I wonder why I'm not living here, nestled in the hills, high above the city, where I can spit on everyone below, if I want to. Her appetite is voracious, as she heartily devours a grilled *entrecôte* and *pommes frites*, mopping up the remaining sauce with bread. This pleases me. She needs more meat on her frail bones. All night, I entertain her with stories of painters who have lived in Montmartre. I don't expect her to care, but she listens. We don't bring up any personal subjects until she asks: "How long have you been married?"

"We tied the knot in July of last year. I have a baby on the way."

Her face pales, and the vitality in her eyes vanishes. She gulps down her glass of Burgundy and demands to leave.

Inside the taxi, she refuses to converse with me. Speaking only to the driver she says, "Take me to the youth hostel next to the Hôtel Dieu."

When we arrive, she says, "You can go now."

I protest, "Just confirm that they have a vacancy. I don't want to leave you stranded."

I follow her to the door. "Men aren't allowed inside," she haughtily declares.

When she enters the building, I hold the taxi and wait in the street while I smoke a Gitane. She returns and says, "It's completely full."

I toss my cigarette into the gutter. "Get in," I say, "this is ridiculous. I have plenty of room. I'm taking you back to my studio where you can stay *gratuit.*"

"I can call a comrade. I'm sure someone will put me up."

"It's late. You can have my bed. Believe me you'll sleep like a queen."

She asks, "What do you really want from me? I can't get in the way of new family, a baby."

I reply, "I just need you for inspiration. You'll be a great model."

She nods her head in acceptance and enters the taxi. Why have I brought this temptation upon myself? The challenge and excitement of a seduction are weakening me. That night, I tuck her safely into my bed, covering her with soft blankets. When I return to check on her, she's asleep on her back. Her face has the innocence of a saint. A kiss calls to be placed on her virgin lips. My heart pounds rapidly as I imagine defiling her and teaching this inexperienced girl about the arts of debauchery. Instead, I quietly close the door. Adrenaline is pumping through my veins, awakening me to the empty silence of the early morning. Only painting can redeem and console me. With satisfaction, I finish a second canvas around five in the morning.

I wake that afternoon to the aroma of fresh roasted coffee and buttery croissants. Isabella had gone to the flea market and purchased an appetizing *petit déjeuner*. A table is set for two, and decorating it is a milk jug with a bunch of fresh violets.

Sweetly she asks, "Are you hungry? It's past noon."

"Starved. How did you pay for all this?"

"With the money you gave me."

I pull out my wallet and give her more cash. "Save your money and take this. I insist."

"How do you like your coffee?" she asks.

"White, with sugar. This is so thoughtful. Thank you."

After serving me breakfast, she agrees to model. Once more, she provokes my palette, senses, imagination, and morality. As the paintbrush guides my hand, its soft bristles become my weapon, coat of armor, giving me courage to speak through oils. Her fragile appearance is an illusion, part of the mask she wears. She cannot fool me, as I see that within her is the strength of a legion of soldiers, combined with a profound gentleness. It is tragic that only violence lies ahead for her. Yet, she feels more alive, and is more vivacious then most, because she believes that her work will make a difference. I worry that her optimism, and the radiance that shines through her, will become destroyed by the harrowing truth and sin of the Spanish civil war. Hence, the only way I can be comforted is to see through Isabella's noble eyes, which tear me apart with nostalgia. In the end, what will matter most? Since I can only give of myself to this paintbrush—my invisible sword. Will my art forsake me, become a traitor, as it only wants glory, not sanctity or peace?

TEN

Djuna Cortez

After my trip to London, I spent a few days in Loire with Jean-Auguste and then returned to Paris, resuming my art class at the École des Beaux-Arts. However, during the time I had been away, I had missed out on learning some important painting techniques. Rudi offered to lend me his notes, so this didn't bother me as much as how the atmosphere of the class had changed. For one, Bernard had completely lost interest in my work and would pass by my easel, never stopping to look or make a comment. In fact, he refused even to speak to me, making me feel invisible. And every time the class ended, I was excluded from joining the other students at the Café Voltaire.

This presented me with a situation I was unprepared to confront. I thought perhaps the reason for Bernard's coldness was that he lacked the heart to tell me my work was mediocre, if not terrible. Nevertheless, it was clear that I was no longer welcome. Every morning I began my day by dreading my art class. Finally, I telephoned Naravine and invited her to dinner. I thought maybe she might have some insight into Bernard's behavior. However, she was unavailable for the next few weeks, claiming that her work schedule had increased. Much to my disappointment, there was also an irritable tone in her voice.

So, for the time being, I spent my days in solitude, Paris itself becoming my educator. It was thrilling to witness the pont Neuf's transformation, as the artist Christo wrapped the entire bridge in rope and white canvas. From early morning to late at night, I would stare at the bridge; its colors altering, from white to lemon yellow, depending upon the intensity of the sun. In one of the galleries, along the rue Saint-Honoré, I found a painting of Christo's bridge. Copying what I saw, I tried several times to paint the pont Neuf. However, feeling futile about my work, I eventually tossed the canvas into the Seine.

For an entire month, I continued to familiarize myself with a wide variety of art museums. Often, I would bring Joaquím Carlos's journals with me to the Beaubourg, the French people's nickname for the Georges Pompidou Center. Inside the modern art galleries, I would read an entry while I viewed the work of other Surrealists and Expressionists. If I loved a particular painting or sculpture, I would simply return several days in a row, until every detail of that chef d'oeuvre was completely etched in my memory. I would accomplish this by closing my eyes, forcing myself to recall the work of art, and when I did, there was nothing separating me from the masterpiece. In that moment, we shared the same space, an object and a person. I couldn't help but think that the object was valued so much more than my existence ever would be.

Jean-Auguste would send me postcards from his winery. In his brief notes, he would tell me how much he missed me and longed for my return to Loire. Without false modesty, he claimed my vines were profiting from his attention and I could, too.

Meanwhile, I owned my time and I thought that time was synonymous with money, and money was freedom. Petty amusements occupied some of my days, like ordering alone in a café and sometimes sounding fluent, which made others treat me like a native. Once, I even fooled an elderly man, who thought I was from Alsace. He had to have been a bit deaf.

More than anything else, I was enjoying a rebellion against rules and restrictions. There were few, if any, demands placed on me, only those I chose to acquire, until I ran into Pascal Maron, one morning, at the Café de Flore.

"I've been meaning to call you," she said, recognizing me in a booth.

"Would you care to join me?" I asked her.

"I'd love to," she said, sitting down across from me.

Pascal pulled out a pack of cigarillos and ordered a *café crème*. "So, tell me, how've you been? How's Paris been treating you?" she asked.

"I've been fine. How about you? What have you been up to?" I politely inquired.

"I've just finished writing a novel. Finally, it's getting published. I'm utterly exhausted. Thank God, I'm leaving for Saint-Tropez tomorrow. I can't wait to get some rest and enjoy some warmer weather. Are you very busy right now with the winery? Are you working on anything else?" she asked.

"Not really. A friend is helping me with the winery. It's been such a relief. I don't have to worry so much. You could say my time is pretty much my own. Why?"

"Perhaps I could ask you a small favor. Are you going to be in the city for a while?" she asked.

"I think so."

"You see, Mitya is quite ill. Two weeks ago, she called me in terrible pain. She couldn't breathe. To make a long story short, I rushed her to the hospital."

"I'm sorry to hear that. How's she doing?"

"Not well. It's serious. They still haven't released her. I never imagined this would happen, but she's come to depend on my visits. I feel very sorry for her. All of her friends have passed away. And she's never had children. It would make me feel better to know that someone will be checking in on her while I'm away. I'm terribly sorry about putting all of this on you. Do you mind?" she asked, as she lit her cigarillo.

I shifted my weight in the booth and reached for my cigarettes. "I don't really know her. I guess I could stop by," I answered hesitantly.

In truth, I was ashamed of telling Pascal that it would be awkward visiting a woman who had made her disdain for me quite clear the moment we met.

"She's really not that bad once you get to know her. She

came around for me. I'm sure she will for you too," Pascal tried to reassure me.

"How long will you be gone for?" I asked.

"About a month. I'll be renting an apartment overlooking the entire port of Saint-Tropez. If you can visit her, I would really appreciate it. I know it's a lot to ask. This would have meant a great deal to Carlos."

"I didn't know Carlos," I said with a sudden force in my voice that surprised me, as well as her.

For a moment the friendly expression on her face changed to one of deep reflection and angst. Her thoughts turned inward; she stopped speaking and making eye contact with me. Silently, she inhaled deeply on her thin brown cigar and then exhaled in one long puff of smoke.

"I really miss him. He was such an inspiring person," she lamented. "I'm sorry you never had a chance to meet. Do what you like. Here's the address of the hospital." She scribbled the location on a napkin and looked at her watch. "It's getting late. I have to get back home to pack. Oh, by the way, have you tried to publish the journals?"

"Not yet. I'm determined to read every word before sending them out."

"Let me know when you're finished. My editor is interested. She may be able to help you. It's really been nice seeing you again. I'm sorry I haven't called you before. I promise I'll be in touch when I get back. In case of an emergency, here's my number in Saint-Tropez," she said, as she quickly jotted the information on the napkin.

"I've been meaning to ask you about the spelling of your name. It's masculine. Isn't that atypical?"

She cleared her throat and explained cheerfully, "I hope so. You see, I hate limitations placed on my gender. In France our language does that. For a while, I thought men seemed to have more freedom. Now, I think we're all limited by time and space. I won't get into existential philosophy with you. However, this is my way of bending the rules. I'm not one of those people who think my culture is superior. In fact, I'm always in search of another place or country to call home. I never want to become set in my ways."

"I understand."

"If I may briefly address your question, I can't alter the French language, except with my name; it's my mark of individuality, without drastically changing my name to something like Paul. Also, I like the fact that I may fool my readers into thinking I'm a man. Years ago, I copied George Sand's style, dressing in men's clothes and joining an all-male writer's group. At the time, I found it amusing and beneficial to my creativity. Fortunately, it was just a phase. I don't mean to be rude. I'd like to stay here talking with you. You're really charming. We've hardly had a chance to spend any time together. But I must go home and prepare for my trip. It was nice seeing you again. I do hope you'll continue to enjoy your time in Paris. I can't promise I'll write, but I'll call you when I get back." She stood up, kissed me on both cheeks, and then dashed out of the café.

After Pascal left, I picked up the napkin she had written on, and while rubbing it several times between my fingers, repeatedly read the address of the hospital. My memory would not let me forget how stern and abrupt Mitya had been on the day of the funeral. However, it was time for me to do an unselfish act, set my hurt feelings aside, and imagine myself in Princess Mitya's current situation, sick and abandoned. A visit from someone could be all that was needed to pick up her spirits. I should be able to swallow some of my pride. After all, Pascal had done so, as Mitya had been reprehensible to her during our lunch. There had to be a way to the old woman's heart. Maybe I would tell Mitya that I was enjoying reading about her daring and extravagant life in the thirties. Then I could get her to open up and tell me some stories about her affairs and the times she had spent with Joaquím Carlos.

When I left the café, I was almost looking forward to the visit. On my way, I purchased a bouquet of irises and a get-well card. The taxi ride went quickly, letting me out before another historic building that looked more like museum than a hospital. However, once I was inside the dank and musty halls of Hôpital Salpêtrière, all I could smell was sickness masked under the gauze of antiseptics and ammonia cleaning solvents. A nun directed me to Mitya's room. Finding a closed door, I hesitated for several moments before knocking.

"Quoi? Qui est lá?" a raspy voice responded. Carefully, I

entered an oppressive room with cracked stone walls. As I looked around, I saw the room was bereft of flowers and cards. At first, I barely recognized the princess. A crucifix hung above her balding head. She reminded me of a condor, as illness had robbed her of all decoration. There were oxygen tubes in her nose and tubes running through her arms and wrists. Her sagging flesh was covered in purple and black bruises with blistered and bleeding legions.

"Who the fuck are you?" she squawked.

"Pascal asked me to visit you. I'm Djuna Cortez. We met not too long ago."

"I don't want visitors. What I need is a nurse. Are you a nurse? Are you here to nurse me?" she shouted angrily.

"No. But I came to see how you're doing," I said, while gently setting down the flowers.

"Why should you give a shit?"

"You were a good friend to my grandfather."

"Where's Pascal? I want Pascal," she demanded.

"She's in Saint-Tropez."

"What? Where's Pascal?"

"She's not able to be here right now. She asked me to come in her place," I patiently explained, as my voice shook.

The princess stuck her chin out and framed her swollen face with her bruised and shriveled hands. "Do you see this face?" she said, "take a good look, because I won't be around long. This is a death face. A death face! Can't you see I'm dying? So leave me alone!"

Terrified and stunned by her sudden outburst, I backed up toward the door, as she continued yelling, "This is a death face!"

"I only came to see if I could help," I said feebly.

Mitya mockingly replied, "What do you know about helping the sick? Are you a nurse?"

"No. I'm sorry you're not feeling well," I answered softly.

"Get the fuck out of my room. I don't need vultures. Leave me alone!"

The nurse entered and placed a tray of roast beef, cabbage, and scalloped potatoes on Mitya's lap. The princess picked up the fork and disdainfully poked at the meat, until the roast slid off the plate and onto the floor.

"I'm not hungry. My stomach has been upset for weeks and I have diarrhea. How am I supposed to eat this *merde* you serve?"

"Do you have some bouillon you could give her?" I asked the nurse.

"This is what's on the menu for dinner this evening. She'll eat what's given to her. This isn't room service in a fancy hotel," the nurse sarcastically replied.

Mitya stared contemptuously at her plate and said, "I can't eat this. They want to kill me. What do they care? It's one less bed for them to worry about."

I followed the nurse outside.

"Excuse me, but I think it would be better for her if she could have some bouillon and maybe a fruit compote, since she's complaining of an upset stomach and diarrhea."

"When they get to be her age, they always complain about something," the nurse retorted.

"I understand. But, could you please get her some soup?"

"I have to page the doctor if she wants something different to eat."

"How long will that take?" I asked.

As we were standing in the hall, another nurse entered the princess' room. "Get me a cigarette and a Stoli on the rocks!" Princess Mitya ordered. The nurse immediately bolted out of the room, raising her hands up in the air. "I've never seen anyone with emphysema shout like that. She must be getting better."

"How long will it take to get her some soup?" I asked the nurse again.

"I don't know. The doctors are very busy. She's not our only patient you know," the first nurse answered curtly.

When I returned to the room, Mitya had fallen asleep; her frail body was curled into a fetal position. She looked like a feeble chick that had just hatched. Snoring loudly, her exhalations resounded like loud, desperate sighs. There was little point in disturbing her. Before leaving, I gently removed the tray from beside her bed and placed it on a table. Then I set the irises in a glass of water and exited the room.

Even when I had returned to my apartment, it was impossible to forget Mitya and that afternoon. A sour feeling formed in the pit of my stomach. It was painful to see her dignity robbed. In the end, Princess Mitya's glamorous life mattered to no one. Without realizing it, I had grown attached to this femme fatale whom I was reading about. I wondered what my grandfather would have done. Would she have been pleased to see him? What had turned her so bitter? Was it me? I only hoped that she would find a kinder, gentler place in the hereafter. That was if heaven existed, and if she belonged there.

I was hesitant to return the preceding day to check on the princess, as I feared a repeat of the following incident. A week had gone by before I got up enough courage to visit her again. When I knocked on the hospital door, a sweet voice replied, *"Oui, entrer."* Enthusiastically, I burst into the room. Another elderly woman was sitting up in Mitya's bed. Unlike the princess, this woman had a kind face and a sweet smile.

"How can I help you?" she asked.

"I'm looking for Princess Mitya. Do you know where I can find her?"

A nurse entered and said blankly, "Didn't you know? She died last week."

"Oh, I wasn't aware. I'm very sorry for disturbing you. I won't bother you anymore," I said to the bed-ridden woman.

"It's fine, dear. I'm sorry about your grandmother. Are you feeling all right?" she asked.

I nodded and quietly left the room.

Later that afternoon, I called Pascal in Saint-Tropez. It seemed she had already been notified. After I hung up the phone, I vowed to turn over a new leaf, set more goals, and get healthier. I changed into a sweatsuit, put on a pair of running shoes, and threw a package of cigarettes into the trash, before I began a jog in the Bois de Boulogne. Hopefully, the exercise would clear my thoughts and eliminate my distilled sorrow. After the hospital visit, my mood was discolored; like an ink blot, somberness was beginning to seep into all of my pores. I was feeling severed from human contact. Negative internal voices, their guttural, almost subverbal recriminations told me I was destined to abandon a child like my mother had. But a part of me wanted one day to start my own family, as there was nothing worse than dying alone like Princess Mitya.

I had to jog longer to feel relaxed. My breath was slightly compromised from smoking, but my body felt light and agile. All the walking I had been doing had helped my fitness level. This allowed me to go further than I had planned. I ran out of the park and headed down avenue Foch. My intuition told me to return home, but I continued on, passing my apartment building. I forced myself to persevere through the tightening and burning in my calves. After an hour, the discomfort dissipated. Finally, my stride broke loose, almost like a bird's first flight. When I reached the energetic Champs-Elysées with its unique touch of American commercialism mixed in with French style, I felt a tremendous sense of accomplishment. Continuing on with my run, with each droplet of perspiration, I could feel my negative thoughts and toxins melting away. As I jogged past sidewalk cafés, older men gave me disgruntled looks. Athletic women were uncommon running about the city. It seemed I was defying a certain ideal of femininity. But I didn't care about their reproachful glances, as soon, I would get to a place of serenity and obtain the ultimate runner's nirvana.

Suddenly, I heard a loud bang, and the impact from what would later be identified as an explosion, catapulted several bodies against me, shoving me into a lamppost. I felt my fear of dying and my powerlessness to prevent it. The pavement trembled beneath me as the loud rumble of a second explosion resonated from inside an expensive shopping mall. I began shaking uncontrollably as glass shattered and particles flew toward me: shrapnel, concrete, nails, and severed limbs. A chilling bitter silence came after the explosion ended. The shock of the attack left everyone stupefied, until reality returned with a vengeance, leaving behind a blood-soaked wake of victims. All that was heard on the once-cheerful Champs-Elysées were now the tormented wails and agonizing moans of the injured. Fortunately, I had been buried underneath several bodies that acted as a human shield. Laying near me was a hysterical mother cradling her blood-soaked infant, who had a slashed throat. As I pried my way through the immobile bodies, traffic came to a screeching halt. Astonished gasps came from the spectators; several cars rear-ended each other.

Within ten minutes, ambulance and police sirens approached with their flashing red-and-white lights. My ears started to ring, the mayhem intensifying my distress. Paramedics quickly arrived, carrying empty stretchers. Following them were truck loads of intrusive newsmen and pushy photographers, who shoved their way through the crowds to photograph the battered and deceased. A microphone was shoved in my face, as one reporter said, "This is the third bombing this week. This time on the Champs-Elysées. We can guess they could be related to the same terrorist group. A violent message has been sent here."

The reporter continued to talk above my voice. I wanted to get away from him and the invasive camera, but I couldn't move. The carnage was unconceivable, body after unidentifiable body was being carried away. Stunned survivors with waxen faces stumbled out of the rubble. The air smelled of charred flesh and harsh black smoke. Ash floated in the wind, clinging to clothing, eyeglasses, and camera lenses. It was all a blur as to what I said when I was interviewed. My left arm was beginning to throb. I could hardly hear myself speak as the pain was intensifying. Shortly thereafter, I began to lose consciousness.

Goddesses, Wine, Dead Artists and Chocolate

The Journals of Joaquím Carlos Cortez

PARIS, MARCH 1937

I have lost track of time. My days and nights flow into one illusory state while I paint, living my dreams and my unconscious. Beauty enraptures me. War terrorizes me. I exploit both. Each week I churn out four paintings, sacrificing diversions and sleep. Loyally, the young model has remained. Now that I have some money of my own, I give most of it to her.

To thank me, she gets up early every morning and does our *marché*, bringing back fresh fruits, flowers, pastries, cheeses, eggs and other sumptuous treats. After breakfast, to capture the softest and clearest light, we begin working. I was just about to begin a painting session, when we were distracted by a loud knocking at the door. Startled, Isabella grabs a red silk kimono and covers herself.

"Who's there?" I ask.

Seconds before I can get to the door, the doorknob turns; I had forgotten to lock it. The door swings open and Sylvie marches in wearing an aigrette hat and a full-length chinchilla coat. Following her is a maidservant and a nanny holding a bundled infant. Perusing the room, her eyes flash at Isabella, and then Sylvie stops and glares at me with her hands resting on her matronly hips.

"I should never have condoned this. How could I have expected you to leave this beauty?" With a snap of her fingers, she summons the nanny holding the infant.

"Here is your son, Emile Valentino. He was born on Valentine's Day."

The nurse pulls back the ivory blanket, exposing the baby's cherubic face with plump rosy cheeks and round, alert dark-blue eyes. Taking in each other, he studies me as much as I do him; we are both perplexed and fascinated.

"He's so cute," I say, touching his tiny hands and counting all of his fingers and toes. "I can't believe how perfect he is."

I walk toward Sylvie and place my hand on her shoulder. Angrily, she shoves my hand away, and swipes at the table with her arm, sending a milk jug of violets crashing to the floor. "Get that slut out of here! This is a private matter," Sylvie screams irately.

"Go for a walk," I instruct Isabella, "and come back in about an hour."

Isabella is trembling as she disappears into the bedroom. Within fifteen minutes, she has dressed and packed her suitcase. I stop her at the door and try to obstruct her way. "What are you doing?" I ask.

"I shouldn't be here anymore," she answers, as she opens the door and begins to descend the spiral staircase.

"Where will you go? You must come back!" I shout, as I

watch her leave. She doesn't look back or answer me. When I return inside, Sylvie is examining my apartment with the precision of a detective at a crime scene. She barges into the bedroom and sniffs the bed sheets.

"This pillow smells like *eau de rose*. The slut must be sleeping here!" she exclaims disgustedly.

"I give up. This is unnecessary. But do whatever you like," I say.

She begins to open my armoires and searches through my drawers, pulling out silk ties, underwear, and socks. She then returns to the living room and starts opening up all my desk drawers. Irately, she throws brushes and tubes of oils paints on the floor. I'm terrified she's going to find my journals. She stops looking when she finds a pile of receipts. My wife begins to read each one aloud, naming the cafés I had gone to, the dates, and the amounts I had spent. For a moment she is calmer, until she discovers that on the back of each bill is a sketch the size of a cameo pin. Each receipt has a picture of a different woman's face.

"Who are all these women? How many are you fucking?" Sylvie grills me.

"They're strangers of no importance. I'm always drawing something or someone. There's nobody in my life but you," I sincerely avow.

"I need a strong drink for you to convince me of that. What do you have in this stinking place? I don't know how you can breathe in here," she says coughing and fanning herself with her hands.

I run to the kitchen to fetch her some booze. Before I get to the liquor cabinet, I stop to open the window. Wistfully, I stare out at the cobblestone courtyard of place Saint-Sulpice; the surrounding benches are empty. Isabella is nowhere to be seen.

"I don't think this is good for you," I say, handing her a Pernod bottle and a glass.

Sylvie grabs the bottle and glass out of my hand. "If it's good for you, it's good for me too."

"You didn't have to behave like that. Isabella's a sweet, innocent girl. She's been like a sister to me. I only let her stay here so she won't have to be out on the streets. She doesn't deserve to be treated with contempt."

"I don't give a shit about that tramp. What's more important to you, our family or her?"

"You and the baby of course."

Sylvie winces and says, "I don't feel well." I help her stretch out on the settee. She takes my hand in hers and whispers, "I'm scared something terrible is going to happen."

"Hush, sweetheart." I kiss her forehead. "Everything is going to be fine. You've just had a baby. I hope it wasn't too painful. You must be exhausted. Please rest."

She calls one of the servant girls over and says, "I want you to go back to my apartment. Here's the key. On your way, you'll need to do some marketing. Here is the list. Please don't forget some fresh fish for my cat. When you get to the apartment, I want you to unpack me and prepare dinner for my husband and me. Paulette will stay here with me and the baby." Sylvie hands the girl money.

"How long are you staying in Paris?" I ask Sylvie.

She refuses to answer my question. Then she seems to calm down.

"I didn't mean to get angry and frighten your model. But how do you think this looks?" She then sighs softly. "I wanted to surprise you with the baby, rather than write to you about the birth. I wish you had been there. I didn't want to disturb your work. I'm happy to be with you again. Let me rest here a while," she says, closing her eyes. Almost instantly, she falls asleep, before taking a sip of her drink.

I glance over at Paulette, who also looks exhausted. Her eyes are closing as she is rocking the baby in her arms. The tired nurse looks back at me, and doesn't say a word as I leave the apartment.

Frantically, I search place Saint-Sulpice for Isabella. I walk up and down boulevard Saint-Michel, checking all the cafés and bookstores, but she's nowhere to be found. I even force myself to look inside several churches, hoping that she may be hiding in a pew or confessional. Alas, after an hour of futile searching, I solemnly return to the studio. As I open the door, Sylvie greets me. She is awake and extremely irritable.

"Where the hell have you you been?" she asks angrily.

"Out." I rush over to the nanny who is holding up our son.

"He's so adorable. Can I hold him?" I ask Paulette.

Sylvie walks over to Paulette and grabs the baby from her. "You answer only to me," she says to her. "You can't hold him now," she tells me. "I have to feed him. Will you be joining me at home for dinner this evening?"

"Yes, of course. I'd be happy to."

Sylvie takes the baby and closes the door to the bedroom. She won't let me in. Once she is finished, I leave with her and the nurse. Wishing Isabella will return, I don't lock the studio. That night, after dinner, I try to comfort Sylvie with kisses and professions of my adoration and devotion.

"Let me pose for you," she suggests.

This is her excuse to avoid reciprocating my affection, to test me. She looks elegant and beautiful, dressed in her long silver peignoire, as folds of satin material drape over the antique sofa where she lounges with her loyal Burmese cat. Clouds of smoke from her Chinese jade pipe float up in the air. Yet something is wrong with the picture. Perhaps it is just me. There is nothing daring or provocative in her sedate pose. My right arm, hand, and shoulder are exhausted. I concede, only to placate her. As a result, I can barely hold up a charcoal. The sketch is rushed and superficial, but she'll never know. She smiles wryly and asks, "Am I still your favorite model?"

The following morning, René calls to tell me he needs me to rush more paintings for another group show, as there are buyers waiting. There is no time for a leisurely breakfast with Sylvie or to visit with my son. Gulping down a cup of coffee, I kiss her quickly and the baby, before leaving for the studio. Once I arrive, I see that nothing has changed. Everything is the way I left it yesterday. Isabella has not returned. Disheartened, I collapse on a pine dining room chair, burying my face in my sweating palms. Never can I let go of this charming studio. It's the first place I had in Paris; my adult life began here. My roommate, Guy, moved out before I married. This space is all mine; no one can interfere with my thoughts here, except Isabella.

I try to begin the triptych I was planning, but I find it un-bearable to remain indoors. Once again, I begin roaming the cafés, hoping to find her at a table, eating alone, or to catch her crossing a street. As I write, I ask what is happening to me. The pen usually has all the answers. It tells me nothing. My wife and son are in Paris, and I do want to spend time with them. Yet I can't stop worrying about this benevolent Spanish Communist. Has she already left to fight? The visions she gave me are fading. Without her, I cannot recapture them.

PARIS, MAY 1937

Sylvie continues to stay in Paris to keep an eye on me, watch-ing my every move and gesture. Not once does she speak of returning to Loire. She constantly asks if I'm working with models. The truth is, this time, I've chosen to stay away from people by only painting Surrealistic cityscapes of Paris, Ma-drid, Barcelona, and New York. When I return late at night, Sylvie becomes hysterical. I explain to her that René keeps demanding paintings. And if I'm late turning them in, he comes to collect unfinished ones, which enrages me.

Sylvie often shows up at my studio, claiming she wants to see my latest work. More than that, she likes to distract me and search my place. Watching me work is her way of feeling in control. She is only content when she models for me. I can't tell her that I'm dissatisfied with my inspiration. Painting after painting of her ends up turning the same murky green color.

One day, I paint a gargantuan emerald sea nymph with Syl-vie's face. It pleases me. Part Medusa and Siren, this bare-breasted sea creature with a fin for legs rises out of the Seine, reaching over the pont des Arts. She is larger than a boat sailing past. In her left hand, she holds up a decapitated head and the ripped-out heart of her lover. Her right hand raises up Neptune's trident. Lately when Sylvie models for me, the aura around her continues to be opaque. Her presence used to shim-mer the sparkling platinum-silver of constellations; now she reflects the shade of an industrial river. Like the mermaid, she wants to possess me, subjugate and compartmentalize me, dis-sect me, slice me apart and carve out my heart for a treasure.

ELEVEN

Djuna Cortez

PARIS AND LOIRE, NOVEMBER 1985

I awakened in a cold room at the American hospital in Paris. As I opened my eyes, I saw Jean-Auguste sitting attentively beside me. Leaning over the front of his chair, he jumped to his feet when my eyes opened and asked, "How are you feeling? I couldn't believe it when I saw you all over the news. I was so frightened for you and called all the hospitals. Fortunately, I was in town so I could get here quickly. How are you feeling? Are you in any pain or discomfort? Can I get you something? What can I do?"

"Please relax. I think I'm all right. Could I please have some water?" I asked.

He hurried to fetch me a cup.

"Are you sure you're not in any pain?" he asked worriedly.

"I don't think so. I'm just feeling a bit dizzy and nauseated. How long have I been asleep?"

"You've been out for a day." He gingerly touched my forehead, where there were some stitches.

"Those must hurt. You're really lucky," he told me.

It took a moment before I felt the heaviness of a cast on my left arm. Before he could say another word, a stern-faced doctor entered the room. The physician appeared to be in her early thirties. When she cleared her throat, Jean-Auguste understood the message to leave. After he had politely excused himself, she took my blood pressure and listened to my heart with a cold stethoscope.

"I'm sorry this happened to you. How are you feeling?" she asked.

"Not too well. The room is spinning."

"Your CT scan showed only a mild contusion and you probably have some injury to your inner ear. That will cause some balance disturbances. You also fainted. Have you ever fainted before?" she asked.

"Not that I can recall."

"We sedated you for the CT scan. I felt it was best with all the stress you've been under. You slept through the casting of your arm."

"Is it badly broken?" I asked.

"It is factured, but the break should heal just fine. Your pulse is still elevated. That's to be expected, considering the trauma you've endured. Could you please stand up and walk around the room?"

Slowly, I eased myself out of bed. I tried to walk, but it was impossible to maintain my equilibrium.

"Vertigo is an extremely difficult symptom to treat, and is common for your type of head injury. I recommend these medications," the doctor said, as she began to write out some prescriptions.

"How long will the cast have to stay on?" I asked, while gripping a chair.

"Please sit down," she said taking my hand. "I don't want you to fall. The cast should remain on about six to eight weeks. The laceration on your forehead required a few stitches. Those can come out in two weeks. You should be grateful that your injuries are minor. There were many who lost their lives in this disaster. Anyway, in time, and with adequate rest, you will recover. Please try to have someone stay with you over the next week. I don't expect there to be any complications, however, it's better to be prudent. The most important thing for you to do right now is to take it easy. You've endured a terrible ordeal. The stress from this incident will be the most difficult to overcome. For a brief time, I want you to take these medications as directed. The Antivert should help with your vertigo. Xanax is an antianxiety medication that will help you remain calm and relaxed. Motrin is for your pain. I've prescribed some antibiotic ointment. Here is a note to allow you a respite from your responsibilities be they work or school. Please try to eliminate the stress in your life. Consider yourself fortunate that you survived this atrocity. You may leave here tomorrow, only if you promise to rest for as long as you can."

"I will. Thank you," I said.

The doctor nodded and then exited the room. Jean-Auguste quickly returned. "She told me you could leave tommorrow, as long as I stay with you. Let me help you out of here," he offered.

"It's really nice of you to do this. I'd be completely alone if you weren't here."

"I want to help. I'm only sorry you're inconvenienced. Will you want me to take you back to your apartment?"

"Yes. But just to collect some things. I don't want to stay in Paris."

"Where do you want to go?"

"If it's possible, I want to spend more time with you in Loire."

"I think that's a wonderful idea. My offer still holds," he said.

"What are you offering?"

"I want to look after you. I want to help you," he said.

We arrived at the Château Hélianthe d'Or the next evening. Jean-Auguste stayed with me for five consecutive nights. In the late afternoons, after he had surveyed his vineyards and mine, we established a ritual of watching the approach of nightfall from the balcony of my bedroom. Together, we sipped refreshing glasses of *menthe à l'eau* with fresh garden mint leaves floating on the top of each glass. We toasted with our glowing emerald drinks while admiring the view of the Loire Valley and its vibrant shades of jade. It was as if our apéritifs had spilled out of the crystal stemware and painted the landscape. Outstretched before us were the hectares of chartreuse-golden vines, the dense virgin forests filled with the aromas of pine trees and nettle, the winding Vienne River laced with moss, and the pastures with grazing cattle. The second evening, he finally kissed me. His lips were cool and quivering. After one kiss, I knew I belonged with him in the countryside. I was earth, the ground below us, the soil that helped to nurture the plump cabernet-franc grapes, jasmine, oranges, apricots, plums, and almonds in the spring and summer months.

Was he my soul mate? He was everything I desired. He had a rock-solid foundation, a silent and serene quality. Jean-Auguste absorbed warmth and secrets like the white limestone of an *abbaye* where monks pray and procure superior liqueurs and lavender-blossom honey. Which elements are stronger? Earth or rock? One can dig into the soil of a garden and form a wad of dirt in their hands, and it will fall apart and gather together again. But stone, once cracked, cannot be repaired. Even so, I was feeling too vulnerable to test the sincerity of his affections. Rarely have I trusted anyone. Yet, I needed him to be my sole strength. Therefore, I clung to him with all my raging insecurities. During lovemaking, I wrapped my legs tightly around him like the clinging wisteria that covered the stone exterior of this medieval fortress. His grasp was fragile, but the pleasure he gave immense. Never could I have told him that I had become terrified to be alone, and to remain in crowds of people. Freedom had been robbed from me, a peace of mind that money could never buy. For now, only the splendors of the country helped relieve some of my overwhelming anxiety.

The last night we spent together, I felt such gratitude that someone was with me during an electrical storm. Thunder detonated like the sounds of war missiles; my body began to tremble as I replayed the horror of the Champs-Elysées bombing in my mind. He patiently held me in his arms as gallons of rain cascaded down the leaded glass windows. Hail was bouncing off the turrets, tap dancing on the slated roof, and pinging in the chimneys. The branches of lilac and willow trees were knocking against the wood shutters, sounding like angry temperamental ghosts.

I was envious that he always slept deeply and tranquilly. Most nights, since my accident, I would toss and turn. As I lay awake, the room spun. I watched him sleep naked, unguarded, and exposed to the world. I had to have the protection of silk pajamas and be covered in down blankets, even during the summer months. I touched his solid shoulder. His skin was scorching. As he slept, tiny beads of perspiration collected on his upper lip. A tear ran down his tanned chiseled cheekbone. I kissed him, feeling the warmth of his flesh and tasting the tart saltiness from his skin.

Intrigued again by the view, I opened the balcony window. The storm had cleared, and only a few floating clouds remained. A gentle apricot hue of sunshine was beginning to warm the valley in roving shadows. I called downstairs to have my *petit déjeuner* sent up. And while sipping chrysanthemum tea, I heard the delicate footsteps of a shy doe walking on soggy winter leaves. In search of her favorite delicacy, she gracefully persevered across the calla lily garden to get to the greenhouse. She could sneak inside if the door wasn't closed properly. When this happened, the deer would devour each blooming rose petal, leaving only the naked stems.

As I inhaled the crisp morning air, the scent of wood-burning fireplaces and sweet rain lingered from the previous night. I heard my lover sigh and yawn. He was beginning to rouse. Walking back to the bed, I was tempted to ask him a few questions. What did he dream of? Where were his thoughts? Did he love me? Then I found myself unable to intrude into his mind, his privacy.

"Coffee or tea," I asked formally.

"Coffee with milk and sugar please," he answered stretching and groaning.

Adoringly, my passion for him intensifying, I prepared his hot beverage, handing him a brimming ceramic blue bowl.

"Thank you," he said, carefully sitting up. "You're so sweet. I enjoyed last night. How are you feeling this morning?"

"Not too bad. The vertigo is always better in the mornings," I answered.

"You know, I've been meaning to have a costume wine-tasting fête. What do you think?" he asked.

"I remember you speaking about it," I said offering him a chocolate brioche.

"I think I want to have the party for Christmas. It's such a festive time. There will be a lot of planning to do. It may keep me quite busy. If I do this, I may not be able to see you this week. Will you be all right with that?" he asked.

"I'll be fine. Will there be many people at this event?" I asked hesitantly.

"Not that many. I'd like to keep it under a hundred and fifty."

I gasped. My heart began to flutter; my pulse raced. Suddenly the room began spinning. Already I was fearing the large gathering. The sensation from the bombing, of bodies crushing me, and the smell of death returned. This was embarrassing, if not idiotic, that the thought of going to a party was too much to handle. Smiling politely, I tried to hide my anxiety from Jean-Auguste, as I didn't want him to take it personally. I excused myself and left for the bathroom. In privacy, I quickly swallowed my anxiety medication, hoping it would work immediately. By the time I was feeling better and had returned to the bedroom, he had collected his clothing and vanished. I would miss him. A week would seem like an eternity to be apart. A note was resting on his pillow. As I reached for the piece of paper, I could feel that the bed was still warm from his imprint, the sheets fragrant with his lime and musk cologne. The note pleased me. Instead of writing any romantic words, which also could have been endearing, he had drawn a picture of two entwined hearts.

Goddesses, Wine, Dead Artists, & Chocolate

The Journals of Joaquím Carlos Cortez

PARIS, JULY 1938

To liven Sylvie's spirits we decide to move to an elaborate penthouse on avenue Foch. Sylvie has purchased the apartment in my name, not hers.

"This is my gift to you," she professes. "You must own something of your own."

For three months, decorating the apartment occupies all of her time. I cannot argue with Sylvie's impeccable taste. Every room is adorned with the finest French Empire antiques with fabrics of purple-red, emerald-green, and aquamarine. What is most appealing are the Egyptian and Roman influences in the furniture, discovering sphinxes and lion's heads carved in the deep mahogany wood.

In addition to the decadent furnishings, Sylvie continues to purchase a collection of modern paintings. Some of them are my contemporaries, whom I know personally. I probably could get her a far better deal. Stubbornly she insists on selecting them herself. Unlike most husbands, I don't have much of a say in her lavish spending. After all, it's her fortune. When I sell a painting, I spend it faster than I can earn it.

Even though the new apartment has an art studio built under the roof, I leave every morning to paint in the Latin Quarter. It's imperative that I spend time away from my despondent wife. Since the move, she refuses to ask about the status of my work and resents that I must leave. I offer for her to come with me and model, but she adamantly refuses and instead complains about her chronic exhaustion.

Now that the apartment is finished, she rarely leaves our enormous canopy bed, except when she does the banking or goes to the coiffeur. Motherhood doesn't thrill or interest her either. Most of the time she wants nothing to do with precious Emile and allows the nanny to care for his every whim.

Emile is a sensitive and often irritable infant. There is little doubt he has Sylvie's mercurial temperament. Otherwise, he is already the spitting image of me and has my dark penetrating gaze and the cleft in my chin. I'm certain his hair will eventually darken to a deep black. When he cries at night, Sylvie thinks he is manipulating us for attention. His gut-wrenching wail rips me apart. Unlike Sylvie, I want to indulge him. When I work a full day and return late in the night, Emile is asleep. My need to see him is often ignored. It seems that a father's demands rarely matter in child-rearing. But I don't care about decorum and disobey the nanny and Sylvie. Incidentally, it is at those times—in the middle of the night, when my son and I laugh together—that I feel the sincerity of his unconditional affection for me. Kicking his feet up in the air and waving his chubby little arms, he's elated to see me and to be fed another bottle, changed, and cuddled. He especially loves kisses on his round Buddha belly. For hours, Emile and I can entertain each other. During those moments, there is nothing more powerful than the love of this innocent baby.

Sometimes, that is all I need to carry me through the coldness of the rest of my days. The following morning, Sylvie refuses to speak to me. Her reproach can last for weeks, only because she feels I've discredited her advice and domain.

Paris, September 1938

Emile gets stronger and more vivacious. Consequently, Sylvie somehow grows weaker. She's abandoned all her responsibilities in Loire and has given me the bills to pay. Mundane work bores me. At any rate, once a week, I'm forced to travel alone to survey the winery and pay the staff. If I had my way, I'd shut down the business. At any cost, Sylvie wants to maintain her reputation. Thus far, it's impossible to give up the profits that keep pouring in.

Instead of being pleased about her wine sales and my success in the art world, she spends her days whimpering and mumbling under her breath. Now that Emile is sleeping at night, she is up, pacing the long halls of the apartment. To cheer her mood, I often return from a long working day with two-dozen white roses. Every time I bring her flowers, she reacts in the same fashion. She thanks me by giving me a quick kiss on the cheek. Then she grabs the flowers, sniffs a few buds, and walks to the terrace. From there, she dramatically tosses the entire bouquet off the balcony. I should stop trying to please her, as I always regret giving in, hoping that she'll react differently.

One evening, I finally get up the courage to ask, "Why do you do that? Why do you hate everything I give you?"

She responds without flinching, and says in a detached manner, "It has nothing to do with you. It's just too painful to watch beauty fade, wither, and die."

"Can't you enjoy it temporarily?"

"No," she says adamantly, storming away from me.

Nothing I do pleases her. Finally, I have given up trying. There are days when she is distrustful of everyone. When we converse, she repeats ominous phrases: "Something terrible is going to happen, something inconceivable. Life is too harsh. That's why I don't care to go out, because people are brutal. Paris isn't safe."

"That's ludicrous. Paris couldn't be more vibrant and alive. Nothing will happen here. This is the greatest city in the world. Sylvie, darling, you can't live your life locked up in this apartment. Why don't we go back to Loire? It will make you feel better. You were happy in the country. Or, maybe we should throw a party or go to one of the festive Parisian balls. Perhaps we could assemble a group of scintillating people. Would you like that?"

"You know I don't give a damn about stupid parties or balls," she retorts. "I'd rather be left alone."

Other days, her mind is lost in a placid and illusory world— a place I cannot reach. By her bedside she keeps the first volume of *À La Recherche du Temps Perdu* by Marcel Proust, a pink silk-covered journal, and her tin of wine labels that she's been collecting all these years. Sometimes I hear her speak about needing to write about her life and regrets. Alas, when I peek in her journal, the pages are blank. It's out of complete frustration that I invade her privacy, wishing only that she would talk to me about her disillusionment. Clearly, the formality of our conjugal union remains impossible to pierce; she has her secrets, and I have mine. Since we've married, I have never told her that I often write before beginning to paint. Writing helps clear my thoughts, unblock my inhibitions. The only secret I've kept are these journals. Instead of indulging in a mistress, I surrender my abandoned desires, divulging all my fears and improprieties to the forbidden white page. Words have replaced carnality, a comforting embrace. The sins of truth I keep locked away in my desk, hidden from view.

The doctors are perplexed by Sylvie's behavior. All I can do is obey her wishes. She is fragile like the branch of young tree: the slightest rainstorm would cause her to break off completely. I try to buffer her from any harshness that may distress her. Therefore, I have taken on more responsibilities as I educate myself about the wine business. I hope that she will write about her hermetic feelings and find herself again. I want to understand.

Every morning when I approach my studio at place Saint-Sulpice, I think about sweet Isabella, and imagine her waiting for me by the fountain steps. Nobody knows but me that my paintings have lost their impact since Isabella left in body and Sylvie in spirit. My vision is muddled. Sometimes, instead of painting, I'll drink a glass of Napoléon brandy. With every sip, I hope to taste the ardor of the emperor—his fierceness and courage. Instead, I feel something dislodging within me. My own island is floating away while the ground quavers beneath my feet. I'm in a constant state of treading water. Once I manage to paint, colors explode, mirroring my inner conflicts. All the same, I can't hide the truth that surrounds my brushes. I long for passion, a live model, a provocative beguiling female. The paintbrush feels lifeless in my arm, like a molted python skin left hanging on a branch. Blood oranges and strawberries are my favorite fruits, yet I don't care to eat them; so I smear their red juicy pulp onto the blinding glare of a canvas. I want to bring back the sweetness to my painting, to my somber existence. I used to taste a refreshing nectar in Sylvie's kisses, but now, when I manage to steal a disgruntled kiss, she tastes like rancid lemons.

Another diversion has consumed me. When I walk back from René's gallery, after having sold a collection of paintings, I enter a pet shop on rue Mazarine. I replace the sadness of letting go of my paintings with exotic birds. A painting for a parrot is more redeemable than a fuck for a franc. However, since my marriage, contrary to Sylvie's belief, I haven't strayed.

Here I am, writing this as the birds are flying wildly about my art studio. Parrots have become my models and most loyal companions. Mirroring some romantic entanglements, peace between these creatures can be difficult to attain. I assumed with birds, I could escape possessiveness. Typically, my parrots are prone to fits of jealousy and rage, especially when I favor one over the other. It has become evident to me that every living creature needs attention and affection. There have been little dramas and crises. The cockatoos have bitten me nearly to the bone and clawed my skin, leaving striated scars. Some of the parrots have also chewed each other's beaks, feet, and wings. On one occasion, I returned in time to rush a bleed-

ing bird to the veterinary hospital. It has become clear to me
that the level of intelligence in an animal equates with its
capacity for jealousy.

I preferred when Sylvie was suspicious, rather than her current indifference. At least when she was distrusting of me, I
knew she cared. Even so, I can only guess what she must be
thinking, assuming I continue to paint cheap whores and pu-
erile models.

PARIS, NOVEMBER 1938

Throughout the months, my wife and I continue to be cordial
to one another. Ultimately, our exchange is superficial and
completely unsatisfying. Why doesn't she ask me to leave?
I'm the weaker one who doesn't want to let go, clinging to
the memories of our jubilant times and to the image of the
glamorous and scintillating woman I had once passionately
adored. Pathetically, I remain her merciful servant, unable to
relinquish her, hoping that one day, she'll bounce back with
renewed fervor. We haven't made love or held each other in
months. Now the tables have turned: I'm the one overwrought
with suspicion and plaguing thoughts of her infidelity.

Once a week, she makes herself up to look beautiful and
leaves the apartment. Never will she dress up for me. Whenever I want some diversion and suggest going to a club or
bistro, she's suddenly too exhausted to leave, and will quickly
retreat to her bedroom. Meanwhile, I am forced to assume the
worst-possible scenario.

TWELVE

Djuna Cortez

The evening of Jean-Auguste's Christmas costume ball and wine-tasting event began with a procession of expensive cars, entering the endless curving driveway to his château. I was chauffeured by Jacques, who dropped me off in front of the grandiose Briard estate. For the first time, the Château de Triomphe stood before me in its splendor of French Renaissance architecture and opulence, reminding me of the palace of Versailles. In the gardens were sculpted fruit trees, stone balustrades, manicured hedges in mazes of geometric patterns, fountains of mythological deities, and enormous reflective pools shaped like gilded mirrors. On display were *Son et Lumière:* a colored lights exhibition, which was choreographed to classical music, giving the illusion the basins were filled with glowing amber and the fountains overflowing with sapphires.

A crowd was gathering in the front courtyard. It was reassuring to find that those invited had also gone to painstaking efforts for their costumes. Some ladies, I swore must have gone to the same local dressmaker that I had. I was told my dress was a copy of a Madame de Pompadour gown, made out of a rich lemon-gold satin with a fitted bodice and corseted waist. The gown also had lace and pearl trimmings, layers of flounces, and a three-foot train. It was the most expensive item of clothing I had ever purchased, and I saw several copies of the design. At least I didn't see anyone wearing the same color.

More guests arrived dressed in outlandish outfits: men in curled bouffant wigs, silk suits, ruffled shirts, bows, white-stockinged legs, and fur capes. Many women had powdered Marie Antionette faces, penciled-in beauty marks, and breasts that spilled out of their ornate gowns. Even those with ample figures wore bustles and corsets that seemed uncomfortable and impossible to breathe in. The celebrants pretended to be royalty; therefore, the attitude of the evening was to remain aloof and temporarily forget about the Revolution—and the lower classes that had once suffered. On this night of ostentation, fine jewelry was taken out of safety deposit boxes and a husband's wealth was measured by the size of the diamond necklace his wife wore.

A group of juggling court jesters in harlequin costumes welcomed me as I approached the front entrance of the château. Merging with the crowd, I entered the *grande salon*. The enormous room was illuminated by candles set in crystal chandeliers to reenact historical times. To light more rooms, men dressed in gold suits were posed as statues, raising burning torches above their heads. The spacious rooms had marble floors, elaborate gilded moldings and mirrors, frescoes, and wall-length tapestries. An orchestra of mandolins, guitars, lutes, violins, violas, and a harpsichord played symphonies by Beethoven and Mozart. Each guest held a foaming glass of champagne. As soon as their glasses emptied, liveried servants rushed over with magnums of Dom Pérignon and Perrier-Jouët. Silver platters of smoked salmon appetizers, hot canapés, caviar and pâté were served. I accepted everything that was offered to me. Eventually, remaining in a crowd of strangers began to make me feel anxious, especially as more people flooded in. There appeared to be at least two hundred visitors. Before panicking, I wandered upstairs and found a wood-paneled library with thousands of volumes of encased leather-bound books in every language and topic. Alone in the room, I could take in a deep breath, and hope my glass of Perrier-

Jouët would eventually calm me. The library was tastefully decorated in red satin walls and curtains, a black marble fireplace, comfortable embroidered chairs, and tables with draped fabrics. Looking up, I noticed a hand-painted ceiling, depicting impish-faced lovers cuddling on a garden swing.

"I see you've found one of my favorite rooms," Jean-Auguste announced, as he stood in the doorway.

"Goodness, you startled me!" I exclaimed.

"May I join you?" he asked.

"Please."

He entered the library, wearing a costume of the French revolutionary army with gold epaulettes, brass buttons, and gold medals. Tipping his navy blue hat toward me and extending a white gloved hand, he reminded me of what I imagined Napoléon to look like, except Jean-Auguste was a much larger man.

"You look ravishing this evening. I've missed you so," he said.

"I can't believe I'm here. This place is magnificent. I wondered for a long time what your home was like. But I never imagined it to be like this."

He made himself comfortable in a chair. "Please sit down with me. How are you?" he asked, pointing to my left arm.

"I'm counting the days before my cast can be removed." As a slave to vanity, I had tried to camouflage the cast by tying a gold scarf around it, hoping that the scarf would blend in with the tones in my dress.

"You do look wonderful," he said. "It's been maddening getting things ready for the party. I've hardly slept in days. I'm very sorry that I haven't been able to see you as often."

"I understand. The party looks like a great success," I commented enthusiastically.

"I hope it will be. I'm glad you like this room. This ceiling was painted by Fragonard. We have several other rooms painted by him. My mother especially likes his work."

Once again, I gazed up at the ceiling, this time leaning back in my chair and resting my head on a soft cushion. "The painting is exceptional," I agreed. Before I had a chance to feel dizzy, I looked at Jean-Auguste and asked, "What was it like growing up here surrounded by all of this history?"

"If I answer, will you promise not to tell anyone?"

"I won't. What's the big secret?"

"For one, I used to climb all over the place and roller-skate on these marble floors. My cousins and I had a great time playing hide-and-seek in the dumbwaiters and scaring the wits out of the servants. We were never bored and restless like most children when it rained. There were always plenty of rooms to hide in and ghosts to invent."

"You sound like you were a little demon."

"That I was. Although, my mother thought I was a perfect angel, so I don't want you to ruin her image of me. Anyway, we shouldn't stay up here much longer. I want you to meet *Maman.*"

"What if she doesn't like me?"

"Since we met, I've only been talking about you. She already likes you," he affirmed.

"Now I have even more to worry about. God knows what you've said about me," I teased.

"I've only told her how enraptured I am with you," he said with gushing flattery.

Wraping his arm around my shoulder, he led me downstairs, returning to the *grande salon.* At one banquet table a line gathered for pheasant, venison, and trimmings. Jean-Auguste guided me to a separate oblong table prepared only for the vintages.

"That's *Maman,*" he whispered, before we approached.

He directed my attention to a woman who stood as poised as a Grecian statue, while serving red wine to her guests. Madame de Briard was tall and slender with impeccably straight posture, undoubtedly resulting from years of finishing school and ballet training. Obviously, she had mastered the art of social refinement and grace. I found Madame de Briard fascinating, yet daunting; there was an impalpable and paradoxical air about her. She seemed both detached as well as keenly interested in her surroundings. The resemblance between mother and son was remarkable. Like her son, when her features were analyzed separately, her nose seemed too long, its bump apparent, and her chin came to a sharp, angular point. However, when viewed in a complete package, she was dramatically alluring, which resulted in part from her exquisite bone structure, and the manner in which she carried herself. She reminded me of a stately lioness. One of the main differences between her and Jean-Auguste was that she carefully avoided the sun, maintaining a pale, almost ghostly white complexion. For a woman in her late fifties, she had few wrinkles, and those she did have only added a strength and texture to her face. Every detail of Madame de Briard's appearance was cared for with impeccable taste and scrutiny, which included her perfectly coiffed platinum mane piled into a pompadour, and her extravagant silver Renaissance gown made of glowing satin and tulle. In addition to her costume, she wore one of the largest diamond necklaces of all the guests. During our introduction, the sparkling white pavé diamonds distracted me from her piercing steel-gray eyes.

"Djuna, this is my mother," he announced with complete reverence.

"*Joyeux Nöel!* Merry Christmas! It's so nice to finally meet you. I've heard such lovely things about you from my son," she said, pouring us two glasses of wine.

"*Enchanté.* I'm also pleased to meet you, Madame de Briard. You have an incredible château. It's a pleasure to be here. Thank you for inviting me."

"Please call me Patrice. Madame makes me sound much too old. How do you like our Bourgueil?" she asked, pouring me a full glass.

Taking a sip, I answered, "It's very rich, supple, and aromatic."

Our conversation was interrupted when another crowd of thirsty guests swarmed the wine table. Patrice insisted on serving them and carefully listened to everyone's comments.

Guiding me away from the wine table, Jean-Auguste politely asked, "So, what do you think of *Maman?*"

"I thought you were going to ask me about the wine."

"No. I heard your answer. It was perfect. I wasn't aware you knew anything about wine tasting."

"I've been doing my homework," I answered.

"Then you don't need me anymore," he teased.

"Yes I do," I said reaching for his arm.

"I'll have to arrange a quiet dinner for the three of us."

"Your mother seems charming and is certainly a gracious hostess. Do you have any idea what she thought of me?"

"It's really too early to tell. I'm almost certain she'll adore you," he whispered, kissing my right hand.

"Now I must make an announcement," he said, as he tapped a knife to his glass and raised the glass above his head. "Excuse me, everyone, if I may ask for a moment of your time. First, I must thank you for attending our Christmas soirée. My mother and I wish all of you a *Joyeux Nöel*. We feel very fortunate to have such loyal friends and patrons. We're thrilled to celebrate Christmas with you and our latest wines of this year. There is one more topic I would like to address. This evening, I must share with all of you a very special moment, as I propose to the beautiful lady beside me." He turned to look at me.

I began to tremble. The attention of the entire room was focused on us. Kneeling down on one knee, he retrieved a black velvet box from his coat pocket.

"Djuna, will you take my hand in marriage?" he asked beseechingly. Gasps and loud exclamations of surprise were heard from the crowd when he opened the box, thereby revealing a fifteen-karat canary-yellow marquis diamond. Then with trembling hands, he carefully removed the ring, sliding it onto the wedding finger of my right hand. The ring fit perfectly. I didn't object to his mistake.

"The ring goes beautifully with your dress. Are we a match? What do you say? Will you marry me?" he asked in a softer voice.

I could feel my cheeks flush. The room fell silent. Strangers' heads turned to look at me, craning their necks, as they waited for my response.

"I never expected this. But, yes, of course, I'll marry you," I enthusiastically replied. After my answer, he jubilantly picked me up and lifted me in the air, twirling me around in a circle. Our audience cheered and applauded.

"Please stop! You're making me dizzy," I gently admonished him.

"*Zut!* I'm so sorry. I forgot about that problem."

Gingerly, he set me down and kissed my lips.

Patrice raised her glass, and in a cracking voice said; "It's time for another important toast. I always thought if my son ever got disheartened with the wine business, there's always the Comédie Française. Indeed, this is a most wonderful surprise. I wish you both sublime happiness."

The clinking of glasses began and then the classical music recommenced.

"Merci, Maman," he said, bowing to her.

Whispering to me, Jean-Auguste said, "I can't believe her sarcastic remark, after all I do for her. I work myself to the bone for our family business, and she makes a flippant statement like that. Let's get out of here."

He led me outside. We passed some tables that were set up underneath heaters. Alone in the garden, he spoke more candidly, explaining: "You would think my mother would be thrilled for us, since she's the ultimate romantic. She even had this part of the garden designed to represent four types of love."

"What are the four?" I asked.

"Tender, passionate, adulterous, and tragic," he calmly explained.

We sat down on a wide stone ledge of a lily pond.

"Why only four types of love? I would think there would be more," I mused.

"I don't know why she chose only four. Romance is a common theme in château gardens. Which one describes your affection best?" he asked.

"Isn't that for you to discover?" I answered coquettishly, kicking up one leg and then crossing it at the knee.

"I can't wait to find out," he said, standing up and facing me.

"I'm sure your mother is happy for you. She was probably just surprised, as I am. I imagine it must be difficult for her to let you go."

"That's her problem. I'm all yours now. Are you pleased?" he asked, holding up my right hand with the sparkling diamond.

"Thrilled. This evening doesn't seem real. I couldn't even dream up something like this," I answered.

He raised the hem of my gown and began caressing one ankle.

"You have such beautiful legs. I wish we could make love here," he said breathlessly.

"We might offend the fish swimming in the pond," I said, giggling.

His hands continued to glide up my left leg, until he found the end of my lace stocking, and the top of my garter.

"I want you," he intoned.

"Hello. Hello!" a voice called to us from behind a sculpted orange tree. Footsteps crunched loudly on the graveled path. Immediately, Jean-Auguste pulled back his hands, and announced, "Look, there's Xavier."

I quickly smoothed down the flounces of my dress. A dandified Xavier costumed as Louis XIV walked toward us.

"You remember Xavier, my accountant," Jean-Auguste announced.

"Yes, it's nice to see you again," I answered.

"It's a pleasure to see you. And don't you look stunning this evening," Xavier commented.

Moments later, Naravine came trailing behind him.

"I thought I lost you back there," she says breathlessly to Xavier. "Well, look who's here. We're not the only crazy ones to be outside."

Naravine was dressed for the occasion in a full-skirted crimson velvet gown with her ample cleavage exposed. That evening she had captured a classic elegance: her hair was piled high in a chignon, and her voluptuous lips were painted red to match her dress. Even her jewelry was tastefully chosen, a garnet choker, along with dangling ruby earrings that hung from her delicately shaped earlobes.

"Don't you look captivating *ce soir*," Jean-Auguste commented to her.

"She certainly does," Xavier affirmed, grabbing hold of her narrow waist.

"Why, thank you. I believe Djuna looks lovely too," she artfully added. "What an extravagant place you have here. More importantly, I just can't believe the brilliant news!" Turning to me she said, "It was so romantic the way he proposed. Let me see that rock—my gosh, it's absolutely huge!

I'm so envious," she said, taking hold of my hand.

"Hello out there," Patrice said, suddenly standing behind us. "We're serving dessert and coffee inside, if anyone is interested. There's also dancing."

"We should probably all go in," Jean-Auguste suggested.

"Are you enjoying your evening?" Patrice asked, approaching me.

"Yes, tremendously. It's a wonderful party. Thank you," I answered.

The four of us began to walk back with Patrice to the *grande salon.*

"This is a splendid affair!" Xavier said.

"Everyone will be taking about this soirée for a long time to come," Naravine interjected.

Once we were all inside, Naravine and Xavier left to mingle in the crowd. Madame de Briard turned to me and said, "I was sorry to hear about your tragic accident. Jean-Auguste told me all about it. How are you doing?"

"I have good and bad days. The worst part has been the vertigo. There are days when the spells are rather debilitating, making it difficult to walk."

"That is terrible! What can you do for it?" she asked with concern.

"I wish there was something. Usually nothing helps, not even the medication. During these bouts, I just have to lie down, sometimes for an entire day."

"I'm truly sorry to hear that." Turning to her son, she said, "Why don't you run along. Djuna and I haven't had a chance to converse. I need to get acquainted with my future *belle-fille.*"

"That's a good idea, *Maman,*" he answered. "I'll be waiting for you beside the dessert table," he informed me.

"You and I should have lunch sometime," Madame de Briard said sweetly, as she guided me to an empty black-and-gold striped banquette.

As soon as we sat down, the placid expression on her face altered to a mordant grin, which made her pencil-thin lips almost vanish. She looked as though she were all eyes and enormous white teeth like a skull. Her voice toughened as she asked, "How did you do it?"

"Do what exactly?" I asked.

"Trap a good man like my son. I want to know about your secret ploy," she demanded.

"I didn't do anything. This comes as a surprise to me as well."

"Come on now, you can tell me," she forcefully insisted, as her mocking sneer was widening.

"There wasn't any manipulation involved. Everything between us has been very romantic," I calmly explained.

"Then you must know what everybody will be saying."

"I'm not aware of what others think. Perhaps it is best that I don't know," I calmly retorted.

"You should be aware that my son is one of the most eligible bachelors around."

"Yes. I am most fortunate," I answered.

"You may think that if you want to. Frankly, I'm disappointed he's settled for an American, especially someone as nouveau riche as yourself."

I tried to speak up, but my throat closed, not even a murmur came out. Swallowing several times, I felt parched, as if I had been walking in a desert for days. I pretended that her comments had not disturbed me and folded my hands neatly in my lap. She couldn't see that I was clenching my fists so tightly that my fingernails were cutting into my palms.

Patrice continued. "Most people will assume that for this engagement to have happened so suddenly you must be expecting. Are you pregnant?" she asked bluntly with her reptilian eyes glued on mine.

"No. Absolutely not!" I protested.

"Maybe it's all that lying around you've been doing. May I suggest then that you watch your waistline? Please don't fault me if I'm wrong. It may just be that dress you chose. Whatever is your problem, I suggest you don't bring it here. My son would never have a wife that is less than ravishing. But maybe you won't care if Jean-Auguste has mistresses. It could be that you won't care either that you'll be the laughingstock of our social circles. However, I could be all wrong about you. Perhaps you are indifferent to what others think. In that case, well, just disregard my opinion," she concluded with her cavalier demeanor.

"Excuse me, but I better go to your son," I announced abruptly.

"You should do that. And really you must be my guest for lunch sometime," she offered, with her arrogant smile.

The room was beginning to spin when I reached the dessert table. Jean-Auguste had fixed me a plate and was anxious to feed me.

"What's wrong?" he asked, holding up a spoon. "It's chocolate mousse. I thought that was your favorite."

"I'm not in the mood for dessert tonight," I politely refused.

"Then we'll dance instead," he offered.

"I'm sorry, I'm not feeling well," I said.

"I understand. I keep forgetting about your *vertige*. It would be rude if I didn't dance with some of our guests. Please sit down and rest. I'll be back as soon as I can," he explained.

I moved toward an open French door. The cold air temporarily helped me regain my composure. While leaning against the frame, I noticed blood dripping from my right hand. I wanted to go home, but was afraid of disappointing Jean-Auguste. Even when he danced, he would occasionally glance over in my direction and politely wink. I nodded my head, as he danced with another female guest. Candlelight gave everyone on the dance floor a flawless complexion. All the women's gowns appeared iridescent, as the rich materials flowed and billowed with the music. I tried to suppress a pang of jealousy as I watched my new fiancé waltz with Naravine. Never could I compare with her exotic and provocative beauty. I tried to think of something else to distract my attention from the other attractive women who had asked Jean-Auguste to dance. But, for the rest of the evening, Madame de Briard's comments continued to haunt me.

Patrice de Briard disappeared before the party finally ended. It was a relief not to have to see her again. And before I had a chance to leave with the other guests, Jean-Auguste insisted I visit his suite in the left wing of the château. Inside his large childhood bedroom were sketches of Italian sports cars framed on the walls and collections of toy cars and trains displayed in glass cabinets.

"Please be seated," he said, pointing to one of his single beds, which was decorated with an airplane bedspread.

Instead of joining me, he removed a book from his bedside table. Standing up, as if preaching from a pulpit, he read me one of his favorite poems by Jacques Prévert. While he recited the words, I couldn't have cared less about the poet's broken heart. All I could think about was if my fiancé desired me, if I could make him happy, and if I was special to him. I hoped he would drop his book and ravish me. Instead, he continued with his dramatic performance. For the first time, I made a bold advance and kissed his smooth neck. Gently, he pushed me away.

"I can't stop thinking about her. I thought the poem would help distract me," he said.

"Who are you talking about?"

"*Maman*. Can you believe the snide comment she made about me and the theater?"

"Oh! I think she was only joking. Although, I must agree with her. You are perfectly suited for the stage. I'm sure you would be a wonderful actor."

"I don't know about that. Anyway, that's not the issue. The point is, she wants to control everything about me, even my marriage. This time, I won't let her. Can you believe how insensitive she can be? That moment I proposed to you was one of the most thrilling events of my life, which she had to ruin by openly criticizing me before all our guests."

I twirled my hair in my fingers and contemplated telling him what his mother had said. Instead I asked, "Do you think for some reason she doesn't approve of me?"

"That's impossible. You're so sweet and sincere. I wouldn't worry about that. Anyway, she has no choice in the matter. There is one simple solution to all of this."

"What?" I asked.

"Let's get married next month, just after the new year, and take a long luxurious honeymoon. If we wait to get married, *Maman* will insist on planning our wedding for a year, driving us both mad in the process. Let's just do it and not tell her," he said hurriedly.

"I don't know. Eloping may make her even more angry."

"I don't care. She can't rule my life anymore. And I won't let her destroy yours and our future. This way we can be completely independent. You won't have to bother your father either."

"I hadn't thought about that. It would be quite awkward contacting him, as we haven't spoken since our last argument."

"I don't want you to worry about the financial aspects. I'll take care of all that," he said.

"I don't know if that's fair. You shouldn't have all of the burden."

"With everything you've been through, you don't need to be encumbered with planning a wedding. It's my duty, as your future husband, to relieve as much pressure from you as I can. You still need to recuperate and get better. More stress won't help you recover. Please let me take care of this. I want to help you. You must allow me to do this for us," he insisted.

"I don't think I can argue. You're so persuasive when you want to be."

He set down his book and knelt before me, reaching his solid arms toward mine.

"I want you desperately, but not here, not under her roof. Let me take you home," he offered.

"Jacques is waiting for me with a car. If you want, he can drive us both back. Will you stay with me tonight? I asked.

"Of course I will," he said, kissing my hand with the ring.

Fortunately, he didn't notice the dried blood on the inside of my palm.

Goddesses, Wine, Dead Artists & Chocolate

The Journals of Joaquím Carlos Cortez

PARIS, JANUARY 1939

The flames of our passion have turned to dying embers. I rush in like William Blake's enthusiastic chimney sweepers to clean and start up our fire, but get covered in soot. It's impossible to recognize the woman I once loved. Sylvie spends most of her time in her bedroom, adorned in satin nightgowns, bright garish makeup, and diamonds to hide her ghostliness. The servants detest catering to her every whim and are quick to point out to me her indulgences: bottles of whiskey and boxes of chocolates that are hidden under her bed. I never mention to Sylvie what the servants say or show me.

For months now, the doctors continue to be perplexed by her melancholia, which has been with her since the birth of Emile. Every time I touch her, she continues to brush away my advances. In her own way, I know she must be pleased about my success, yet she wants to punish me with her lassitude. She is only able to give affection to her cat, who sleeps beside her day and night.

Everyone has failed to point out the obvious; I have been a stupid, naïve fool. While I am working, she has been having a torrid affair, giving her both pleasure and remorse. All this time, I have blamed my arduous profession for the personality changes in Sylvie and her withdrawal from work and society. Now I know her true love was never me, but a simple flower—the poppy—that often grows wild in bold shades of orange or vermillion. And so, in her cherished Chinese jade pipe, she inhales her confidante, her Casanova, the ultimate seducer and devotee that alights and quells all of her voluptuary senses. A lover whose intoxication I could never compare with—opium, her tamed god of the underworld.

One afternoon, Sylvie calls me over to her bedside. Holding up a hand mirror and glancing at her reflection, she says, "I look like a blow fish."

"You shouldn't be concerned about that," I say, comfortingly.

"I took my appearance for granted. Mitya was right. Beauty only lasts in paint. I want to look at my portraits. Do you know where they are?"

"They're in the art studio upstairs. I told you that when we moved into this place."

"I'm sorry. It slipped my mind. Can you fetch my paintings and hang them in the bedroom for me?"

"I'd be happy to."

She bursts into tears and says, sobbing, "I'm a wretched person. I deserve all suffering that will come to me."

"What are you talking about? That's the most ridiculous thing I've ever heard." I sit next to her on the bed and take her soft hand in mine.

"Money always had its advantages. I'm being punished for it," she declares.

"Don't be ridiculous," I answer.

"I was mean and I treated people badly. My wealth is useless now. I can't buy my health back."

"The doctor says there's nothing wrong with you. He suggests you go to Montacatinni, Italy, and take the water cures. Why not give it a try?"

"It won't help. I'd rather spend my money on something more useful. Did you ever see that model again after my outburst?"

Her eyes are holding back her jealousy and are fixed on mine for a response. I refuse to show her any emotional reaction, so I shake my head.

"You must find her. She inspired some wonderful paintings. René can't stop talking about them. Do whatever it takes to find her again."

"Since when do you talk to René?"

"He often calls to speak to me. He's a sincere man. I've always been fond of him. Anyway, he misses your alluring women. Nobody paints nudes like you do, Carlos. Is this my fault? Have I damaged your muse?"

"I don't know. It's—"

She interrupts. "Try to find that model. But first, I need you to also find someone for me."

"Who?"

"The last I knew of her she lived here."

Sylvie writes down a name and address. Eliane, 8 rue de Lourmel.

"Rue de Lourmel is mostly a commercial street. It should be easy to find. You've been in the fifteenth arrondissement before."

"Yes. Who is this woman? Why do you want to see her?" I ask.

Sylvie doesn't answer and gives me her hand. I begin to kiss her smooth fingers. "Why do you always blame yourself? All I want to know is how you feel about me. What has happened to us? Did I fail you?" I ask.

"Neither of us listened to what we truly wanted. I told you never to worship me, because I knew one day I would fall off the pedestal you put me on. Furthermore, I never wanted to believe that your art would consume you. In time, I thought I could adjust to the models and our separations. Meanwhile, I hoped that Emile would be our magnet. Your success only made everything worse. Our natures are different. I know you love our son. Unlike you, I can't express my affection. Every day, my blood feels like it's being drained from me, like there's a leech attached, sucking away at my life force. I wish I could be a good mother. The truth is, I'm always exhausted, impatient, and completely overwhelmed."

Sylvie picks up the hand mirror again. Her hands are shaking. I grab it from her.

"You need to rest," I gently instruct.

"Do you remember when I modeled for you in Versailles?" she asks.

"That was such a special day. You were so . . ." I stop before saying the complimentary word I had intended.

"I remember when you called me your white dove. I so wanted to be your docile dove. Look at me. No, don't look at me. I'm so ugly. I belong in a circus act. Are you repulsed by me?" Sylvie looks at herself and slams the mirror down on the bed and screams, "I can't stand the way you look at me!"

"You almost broke the mirror."

"Why should I care about bad luck? I don't give a damn about anything," she rants.

"I'm sorry."

"Don't apologize. It's not your fault. It's mine," she admits remorsefully.

"I should let you rest," I propose, standing up.

"Where are you going?" she asks.

"To search for your friend. Isn't that what you want me to do?"

Sylvie nods her head in approval and pleads, "You have to find her. It's extremely important!"

PART THREE

A TRAMPLED ROSE

THIRTEEN

Djuna Cortez

I dressed alone on my wedding day. Jean-Auguste and I were staying at the elite and secluded Hôtel du Cap in Eden Roc, which resembled a remote palace more than a resort. The window of my room overlooked the ocean and pine forest gardens, almost the exact location where Joaquím Carlos had proposed to Sylvie. I tried to imagine which tree they had stood beside, perhaps carving their initials in the bark. This entrancing panorama was timeless, suspending me in their world of the past, a past that was now becoming deeply entrenched with mine, connecting their memories to my own. Carlos and Sylvie, the lovers whom I met posthumously in a memoir, felt more real to me than my own living relatives and friends.

That morning, I missed not having a calming maternal influence to safely guide me through this matrimonial passage. Naravine had promised to show me some makeup techniques. Then, at the last minute she decided to have a massage in the privacy of her room. As a result, I faced my future in solitude. Nobody was there to give me their approval, advice, or encouragement. Oddly enough, I missed my father. Would he have been proud? Was it a huge mistake that I hadn't contacted him? Maybe, on this optimistic occasion, we could have set aside our anger and resentments.

Our wedding was planned for noon. At eleven-thirty, I carefully slipped into my champagne satin Renaissance bridal gown. It was a pleasure to be free of my cast and wear long sleeves again. The dress, which I had purchased this time from a bridal designer in Paris, had a plunging neckline and was decorated with pearl beading, lace, satin roses, and delicately tied bows sewn into the three-foot bridal train. As I began applying a shade of rose lipstick, a screeching fire alarm sounded off in my room and through the hotel hallway. Before the incident, my anxiety was barely containable. The noise unfortunately sent me over the threshold. My knees began buckling, and my hands trembled. Frantic, I bolted out of the room to see what had happened. Simultaneously all the doors in the hallway opened, as curious guests were poking their heads out. Across the hall from me, in full view, stood Jean-Auguste, handsomely dressed in his black Armani tuxedo. I hoped he wouldn't look in my direction, but he did, and he gave me a flirtatious wink.

"Oh, no! You're not supposed to see me," I cried out.

"False alarm. False alarm," I heard people shouting down the halls, as doors began slamming.

Within seconds, I furiously returned to the room, shutting myself in. Bad luck was said to follow a marriage if the groom saw the bride before the wedding. Bad luck. Bad luck. Those words kept running through my head like a lousy fortune cookie message printed in red ink. At the same time, I scolded myself for thinking negatively. Who wrote fortune cookies anyway? What type of training do these writers have? Who started these marital old wives' tales? If one can't name the source, why should I believe them? As for our marriage, we chose to abandon traditions, making our own rules. Essentially, it was an elopement. He never informed his mother or any other members of his family. Even so, it was still my fairy-tale wedding, one I had dreamed about since I was a young girl.

Noon was approaching. All tension left me when I applied a crown of pearls, allowing the delicate gossamer veil to gently cover my face and flow behind me like a billowy cloud.

That afternoon, I didn't walk. Instead, I glided into the mar-
e lobby, where I met Naravine, who handed me a fresh bou-
uet of white roses tied together with pink satin ribbon. She
so looked like a bride, wearing a Grecian style golden-beige
lk and mousseline Chanel gown that wrapped tightly like a
ga around her bodice but flaired at the bottom with a fluid
alloped hemline. Setting the tone for the ceremony, Naravine
entured into the gardens before me, indiscriminately scatter-
g a trail of rose petals along the graveled path.

I chose to give myself away, and walked alone through the
rounds, where I calmly joined Jean-Auguste and the wedding
arty. Everyone stood on the verdant lawn shaded beneath the
verflowing palm trees. Xavier stood to the groom's right.
aravine was on my left. A minister stood in the center. For-
nately, that day, the sun was shining brightly, unobstructed
y clouds; the temperature was mild. Framed before us was a
rystal-clear view of the Mediterranean coast, the sky blending
 with the sea in deep azure tones. Halfway through our vows
e burst into laughter when a mynah bird in a cage near us
imicked our words. "Honor and obey, honor and obey," the
ird parroted.

"Do you take this man to be your husband?" the minister
ontinued, ignoring the vocal bird.

Saying no crossed my mind for a split second. Was I ready
or this? I was to become a wife. What is a wife? Am I no
onger a woman, a lover, a friend? Suddenly, I am domesti-
ated through a common word. Yet, he remains the same, a
an, is a man, is a man. But I become his woman—his *femme*.

"I do," I answered.

"Man and wife. Kiss the bride." The bird repeated the min-
ter's last words.

Gently, Jean-Auguste kissed my lips, holding back his in-
nse passion. Nonetheless, I was certain, in time, I could draw
ut more of his ripening emotions. At lunch, we feasted on
resh lobsters and Beluga caviar. Over and over again, we
asted with Perrier-Jouët. For dessert, a white chocolate
ousse cake was made especially for us. The top tier was
overed in sugar-coated grapes. While cake was being passed
ut (we shared it with all the guests in the restaurant), Nara-
ine took me aside.

"Are you feeling better with all your health problems?" she asked.

While I was answering, her attention wasn't focused on me. Instead, the entire time, her eyes were watching Jean-Auguste who seemed engrossed in a conversation with Xavier.

"What a pity you're still having difficulties. When you're feeling better, you must come visit me in Venice. I hope to be there by spring," she said dispassionately, as if her statement was tediously rehearsed.

"That is most generous of you. But I wouldn't want to impose," I answered.

"What are you two talking about?" Jean-Auguste interrupted, moving between us.

Naravine quickly resumed the conversation. "I was telling your wife about Venice. It would be my pleasure to have you as my guests."

"That does sound tempting. Thank you for offering. Now I'm afraid we must leave," he said urgently.

"Where are we going?" I asked.

"You'll see. I have a surprise planned."

Jean-Auguste took me by the hand as we exited the restaurant. Our guests were also curious as to where he was taking me, and followed behind us. At a brisk pace, he led me through the gardens and down a path until we reached the sunbathing deck and bay. Swimmers could dive into the sea or in a luxurious salt-water pool, depending on which way they turned.

"There it is," he said pointing toward the tree-lined peninsula.

A sleek blue fiberglass speedboat was approaching. Its loud engines soon muffled all conversation. Once the boat met the dock, Jean-Auguste yelled, "That's our ride. Jump on. It's only for the two of us."

"Will we be gone long? What about our luggage?" I asked.

"Don't worry. That is being taken care of."

He jumped on first and then helped me onto the boat.

"Wait!" Naravine shouted. "Your bouquet."

"My God! I forgot," I said, tossing it to her. Unfortunately, the bouquet flew past her and landed in the middle of the pool.

Horrified, we watched it float and then sink to the bottom of the deep end.

"It's time to go," Jean-Auguste announced to the driver.

As the boat took off, I kept saying, "Poor Naravine. It really looked like she wanted to catch it. She must be so disappointed."

"She'll be just fine," Jean-Auguste answered sharply. "I don't think she wants to marry. She's certainly not the type."

"I think a part of her does. That may be why she's been peculiar lately. It's hard to feel close to her. Naravine may have convinced herself that marriage is wrong for her. However, what I think she ultimately needs is emotional security, perhaps even children."

Jean-Auguste snickered, "Please! Sometimes you sound more old-fashioned and traditional than I do. Naravine is a party girl, that's all. I wouldn't read more into her. But we should take her up on her invitation. She'll show us a terrific time in Venice. Show me her power," he shouted to the captain.

The driver shifted two silver throttles forward, causing the engines to roar like angry lions. As we picked up speed, the hull of the boat repeatedly rose out of the water and then came crashing down, smacking harder against the rising waves, splashing our clothes with cool sea water. Occasionally, my attention drifted from admiring my new husband to the vastness of ocean surrounding us. We were not alone. Quick flashes of shimmering silver caught my attention. A school of flying fish followed our boat, diving in and out of the water. It didn't take long before the motion of the boat made me feel ill. Jean-Auguste insisted I lie down on my back, resting my head on his lap.

"I should have guessed you'd be quite sensitive to motion sickness after your accident. I promise for the next boat trip, I'll have medication for you. Try to rest," he said comfortingly, as he gently stroked my forehead.

"Do you mean there will be more boat rides after this one?"

"I have a lot planned. I want this to be a honeymoon you'll never forget."

⌒

The boat slowed down as we pulled up to the Carlton Hotel pier in Cannes. Attendants helped us off the boat, greeting us with their placid, but jaded expressions. These young and middle-aged beach boys had seen guests arrive in every indulgent manner possible. There was probably nothing exceptional about us. To them we were part of a wealthy class that provided their mocking entertainment, which I was certain they gregariously discussed behind our backs. I would have liked to have had a photograph of us, arriving on the empty beach in all the pomp of our wedding attire. That moment I realized Jean-Auguste had forgotten to hire a photographer. Before I had the time to say anything, a tanned servant handed us each a white terry-cloth robe with a small monogrammed insignia of a golden crown, the trademark of the hotel. The tide appeared to be absent that day. Tourism season had ended; all the lounge chairs and tables were folded away. Even the popular thatched-roof beachfront restaurant was closed.

On route to the hotel, as we traversed the sand, the weather began changing; a cloud layer was forming. At the same time, a strong wind was kicking up. I stopped shivering after Jean-Auguste gave me his jacket to wear over my gown. He wore one of the robes. We must have looked quite eccentric as we headed up a stairway that led us to the palm tree–lined Croisette. Across the wide street, the Carlton Hotel loomed before us—a landmark famous for its white palatial architecture and silver cylinder towers that are recognizable in every Côte d'Azur picture postcard.

Once we had passed through the revolving doors, a staff greeted us with the warmth of their semitropical sun and the gregariousness of their Italian neighbors. Even the French they spoke had a softer, more melodic and welcoming tone.

"You'll love Cannes. The people here are very friendly," Jean-Auguste said, generously tipping the bell captain as we entered our suite. Then he walked toward the balcony and opened the doors. Looking out, he said, "Maybe tonight for dinner I'll take you to one of my favorite restaurants near Le

Suquet. We can walk there, if it doesn't rain. It's very close. The owner, Claude, always prepares a quail egg appetizer for me that you'll just adore. The *loup* is also excellent."

"You eat wolf!" I said horrified.

"Oh, no! Of course not. Same word, different meaning. It's a local fish. And tomorrow, maybe we'll go to Biot to see the glassblowers and visit a collection of Miró's work, or we can go to Saint-Tropez. There's so much I want to show you. But first I've been wanting to do this."

He walked toward me and removed his jacket that was covering my wedding gown. He eased himself behind me and began gently taking down the pins from my hair, which I had tied up in a French twist for the wedding. While he took out each pin, he slowly combed my hair with his sturdy hands, letting the long ringlets glide through his open fingers and fall naturally below the center of my back. As if in an Argentinean tango, I turned to face him. Our eyes met for a brief instant. Timidly, I glanced away, yet stood motionless, waiting for his next move, while he continued to observe me with incredulous adoration.

"You look like a doll, too precious to touch," he voiced endearingly.

Taking hold of his left hand, I pressed his palm over my breast, allowing him to feel my rapidly beating heart as I rubbed my thumb against his solid gold wedding band.

"I'm very much alive. You can touch me. I won't break," I seductively replied.

He eased in closer to me and in one swift motion, lifted me in his arms, carrying me across the vast room, setting me down on the white cotton and down-quilted bed. My head fell into soft feather pillows.

"You rest here for a short while. I'll be back soon," he said.

"But where are you going?" I asked.

"I'll be back. It's a surprise." And without directly answering my question, he quickly left our suite, gently closing the door behind him. A heaviness came over me when I shut my eyes. Exhausted, I eventually dozed off, until I was later startled awake by a loud knocking. Thinking it was Jean-Auguste, my heart began racing in anticipation. Hurriedly, I rushed to get the door and almost tripped over the long train of my dress as I got there. I was terribly disappointed to see that it wasn't him. The moment I opened the door, a group of ten liveried bellboys marched into the suite, each one carrying a vase filled with a dozen roses. In a manner of poised servitude, they set down each vase wherever they could find a flat surface or empty tabletop. Although all the flowers were beautiful, my eyes focused on a bouquet of violet-gray roses. They had been set on a desk beside the balcony, where I had a view of swaying palm trees and the seashore. This was not a moment I had wanted to spend alone. The sun was setting, and the waxed-looking buds were turning a shade of sterling-silver. Whoever had sent all these lavish flowers hadn't even bothered to enclose a card. It was five in the evening and two hours had passed since he had left. Where had he gone?

I soon learned how concern for a loved one could quickly escalate into panic and hysteria. With the absence of Jean-Auguste, I began to imagine all sorts of disastrous things that might have happened to him. He could have taken a stroll on the beach and then been robbed and beaten unconscious by a band of Gypsies, or he could have been hit by a car and was bleeding to death in a hospital. I phoned the concierge and asked if they had seen him or if they had received any messages. But they hadn't any information. I hated myself for calling room service and ordering a pack of cigarettes. Soon I was pacing the room and becoming more worried and anxious by the second. I couldn't stand the thought of being without him. Then there was a knock on the door. I ran to answer it, thinking it was room service. Finally it was Jean-Auguste, who entered carrying an enormous picnic basket, followed by more bellboys bringing in our luggage from the Eden Roc hotel.

"Thank God you're alive! Where have you been all this time? I've been worried sick!" I said irritably.

"I'm sorry to have upset you. But I was getting you all this," he said, gesturing to the vases surrounding the room. There was another knock at the door. I let him answer. A waiter arrived with a table, wheeling in a bucket of iced champagne, caviar, a basket of fruit, and my pack of Rothmans cigarettes. Jean-Auguste signed for the bill and tipped all the hotel employees with his usual extravagance.

"As you can see, *chérie*, I bought out a florist on the rue d'Antibes. I want this evening to be very special, like nothing you've ever experienced before. Are you not pleased with the flowers? Aren't they your favorite?" he asked anxiously.

"Yes. They're stunning. But I was just so worried about you. I'm glad to see you're alive. I couldn't stand the thought of never seeing you again!"

"I'm right here. I'm perfectly well. In fact, better than ever," he said, popping off the cork of a Perrier-Jouët bottle. Carefully, he poured us each a foaming glass. Lifting his glass, he said "*Pour l'amour*. I'm very fortunate to have met someone as precious as you."

Our glasses met and chimed. He insisted on entwining our arms in a second toast. After taking several sips of pink champagne, I began to feel giddy and less agitated.

Playfully, he began tickling me around my waist.

"Please stop," I said, laughing. "I'm going to spill my drink all over my dress."

"I'll do anything you want," he said, withdrawing his hands. Right away he walked over to the table and began peeling a bunch of grapes. Holding them in his curled open palm like newly found sparrow eggs, he beckoned me to him.

"Madame de Briard, would you like to taste these?"

Gingerly, he placed a plump red grape in my mouth.

"Do you want more, madame?"

"Please. But you don't have to peel them for me."

"I want to. How do you like your new name?"

"It sounds so mature. I'm not used to it yet, especially the madame part."

"It's very becoming," he said.

"I agree."

"Shall we move into the bedroom?" he suggested.

Collecting the picnic basket, the glasses, the fruit bowl, and bottle of champagne, we entered the bedroom. It was an elegant room painted an eggshell pallor with high crown molding ceilings. I set down the glasses, the bottle of champagne, and the fruit on an antique mahogany dresser. Jean-Auguste opened the picnic basket, which was filled with fresh rose petals in every color imaginable. Next, he emptied its contents, sprinkling the entire bed and sheets with mounds of soft flowing petals. This intensified the perfume of a blooming rose garden—a scent that was sweet, soothing, and tranquil. He reached for my hand. The moment the tips of our fingers touched, I felt an electrical surge of energy, as if all the cells in my body had just awakened. Then with some difficulty, I began to unfasten my dress.

"Can I help?" he asked.

"Thank you."

He moved behind me and assisted with the zipper, until the gown dropped to the floor, and I gracefully stepped out of it. Once again, I turned to face him. In his penetrating blue eyes, I saw minuscule reflections of my beaming face. He smiled proudly in return, while glancing at me from head to toe. The act of disrobing, baring our nude bodies, our weaknesses to one another, was still quite novel to us. As I stood in my wedding lingerie, all white satin and lace, I tried to mask my bashfulness by drinking another glass of champagne. He was patient with my initial hesitance, as he probably understood that in time our inhibitions would vanish; doors would no longer be closed. I was also embarrassed watching him undress, but this time stopped myself from turning away as he removed his clothing with confidence and flair. There was nothing hesitant or timid in his gestures. Quickly, his nimble fingers unbuttoned his white tuxedo shirt, removed his wine bottle cuff links, and unzipped his trousers. At a leisurely pace, he folded all of his items, neatly draping them on a chair. My knees began trembling when he sauntered toward me. At first, I couldn't resist pressing my face against the hardness of his smooth torso; closing my eyes, I could have rested beside his chest for hours, just inhaling the clean fragrance of his skin that was ever so intoxicating. Gently, he patted and stroked my head as if I were a child. The consummation of our marriage was slowly beginning. He wanted this night to meet all my expectations. Therefore, he was afraid to make a bolder overture. One of Joaquím Carlos's paintings had best described us. My new husband was like the cool dense forests, often found beside the castles scattered on the outskirts of Paris. He was filled with shady patches, tree branches covered with verdant moss, delicate leaves, running streams, and fathomless lakes. In contrast, I was an exposed desert, burning in the sun, shifting golden-red sand, hot, thirsty.

"They shall never meet," the artist had written on the back of his painting, describing the characteristics of two women he had loved. Even so, types like us had indeed met and didn't want to remain apart. Sometimes we weren't that dissimilar. That evening his shyness dominated his emotions. Although I found this charming, it was also a challenge to find his source of passion. I had to delve deeper into the darker recesses of his nature, a place that compelled me because of his mysterious intensity.

He separated from me and walked over to the bed, propping himself on the edge, balancing most of his weight in his strong arms, as his legs dangled over the side. His soulful eyes stared pensively out the open window, where the sky had darkened, soon to give us the freedom of diminished light and the abandonment known to evening lovers. I stood away from him, admiring his anatomically perfect physique that was the ancient Grecian ideal of leanness with defined musculature. The perfection of his contemplative pose would have been a compelling painting accentuated by the regal masculinity of his strong features, his tousled mane of thick blue-black hair, his chiseled cheekbones, which had now flushed a healthy glow. I was timid about approaching him. Yet I could sense his imploding lust buried deep inside him, needing me to draw him out. Before more time lapsed, I cautiously approached. Standing up, he wrapped his arms around me. Meanwhile several of his cool tears fell onto my shoulders. Then he slowly leaned back on the bed, taking me with him. The soft rose petals lay beneath us, caressing our skin. He urged me to seduce him, to take complete control over our lovemaking, which made me feel powerful. For the first time, I dominated him, continuing to draw out his fierce ardor, melting away his precarious reserve. We found our harmonious balance that only opposites can attract. Where he found solace in my intensifying infernal warmth, I found replenishment and completion. On our first conjugal evening, in our unspoken silence, we communicated in a primal cadence which the uninhibiting darkness of the room allowed. The only light came from the motorboats at sea and the dim street lamps. All physical boundaries between us dissolved when I held him as tightly as possible, hearing only his gentle breathing, his beating heart, and his soft moaning. We returned again and again to this instinctual communion, our bodies rising and falling together like our background serenade of falling rain. Our wedding night was dramatically different from all other times. For us, the union became sacred, every touch a resurrection, sending us each time to greater heights of ecstasy and spiritual awareness. At the same time, I was treated like a delicate possession, shielded in his arms of steel. Never again would I have to face this harsh world alone. And finally, I would come to understand the vast dimensions of romantic love.

The week we spent in the Carlton hotel, maids in black-and-white uniforms catered to our every whim. Like angels that do not disturb, they always left fresh towels, soaps, and shampoo in our suite. Furthermore, Jean-Auguste left me little to be concerned about. With him, every day, our itinerary was carefully planned, all the details taken care of. My anxiety attacks were slowly fading away. He made me feel safe and protected. Each night, after a full day of sightseeing, we returned to our pristine room with our bed turned down, our pillows plumped with a Swiss chocolate set on top. I slept well in our hotel room, sharing the same bed. Often we would fall asleep holding hands.

One morning, while were having breakfast on our terrace, Jean-Auguste stood up and pointed toward the beach and the blue stretch of coastline.

"What do you have planned for today?" I asked.

"Do you see that sleek yacht docked out there?" he said, pointing to an enormous white boat anchored in the bay.

"Yes. It's impressive. Who does it belong to?"

He didn't answer. Smiling, he paced before me and cinched in the waist of his white robe.

"What do you find amusing?" I asked.

"That yacht is ours. It's your wedding gift."

"What? *Tu es fou!* Have you lost your mind? It must cost a fortune!"

"Yes. But together we can afford it."

"It seems too extravagant a purchase, and completely unnecessary," I protested.

Kissing my hand, he said, "Please don't be afraid of getting more enjoyment out of life. Why should we deprive ourselves, if we don't have to? I paid for half of the boat, but I'll need you to put in the rest. Please, just give me a chance to show you how exhilarating yachting can be."

"I don't know. I usually get seasick."

"Please, just come and take a look at the boat."

"I'm enjoying it here."

"I know. But please come. We won't have to stay long, just have a fast tour. The boat will return to the port in half an hour. That should give you enough time to get dressed," he said, quickly kissing my lips.

"You are persuasive when you want to be. Do you always get your way?"

"Usually," he answered, grinning.

"All right. I'll get ready," I conceded.

A taxi drove us to Port Canto, also known as the new port. When the car pulled up to the opened gates, a security guard blocked our entry. As soon as Jean-Auguste gave him our names, we were issued inside. The yacht had been returned to its tight berth and was docked at the far end of a long quay. Since this was not the tourist or film festival season, the port, like the beach was almost empty of people and cars. Only a few inquisitive pedestrians had entered from the Croisette and were walking along a stone ledge that faced the yachts. Once they saw us about to get on the boat, we became the focus of their attention. I carefully followed Jean-Auguste up the gangplank to the hundred-foot yacht. Lined on deck, waiting for us, was a crew of six men, each one dressed in a spotless navy-and-white uniform.

"Let me give you the grand tour," Jean-Auguste said eagerly, "but first you must remove your shoes. The decks are brand new, and all the wood railings have been varnished. As you can see, everything on this boat is in tiptop condition. Few boats are made like her. Her maker, Esterelle, originally designed these boats for the French navy. But this yacht was build especially for luxury and cruising at high speeds. Don't you just love her crisp nautical smell?" he said, inhaling the air, while gliding his hand over the smooth mahogany railings.

The yacht had a sun deck, three sitting rooms, and two dining rooms: one formal, the other informal. There were five guest and four crew cabins, seven bathrooms, a sauna, and a large galley with built-in freezers, stoves, and ovens.

After the tour, he asked, "So tell me, what do you think? I hope to take many trips with you. And when your château takes off, we'll be able to hire another *négociant* to look over both wineries. Like you, I've always wanted to travel. We could see the world with this boat." He opened a map of Europe and instructed, "Close your eyes and pick a place. The Mediterranean is at your fingertips."

Following his instructions, I closed my eyes and pointed.

"C'est beau la vie. Corsica! It's one of my favorite places. You must see it. The beaches are spectacular, as well as the food. We could sail in a few days. What do you say? Please say yes," he implored.

"How much money is needed to own the boat?" I asked.

He pulled out wads of papers from his jacket pockets. Before showing them to me, he said, "Why don't we order an aperitif? They have everything on board. What would you like?" he asked.

Since I had been staying at the Carlton, I noticed that every afternoon, on the hotel terrace, glamorous visitors lounged on the black-and-tan wicker chairs, sipping their colorful mixed cocktails, as they chatted, people-watched, or played endless sets of backgammon. As a result, I had a craving to taste something different.

We were seated on an outdoor banquette, and to call an attendant, Jean-Auguste rang a buzzer on the wall behind him. "Campari and soda," I ordered.

"That sounds refreshing. I'll get the same," he told the steward. Before our drinks arrived, he spread out a stack of folded papers, scattering them on the table. "I hate paperwork. Thank God I have Xavier to do most of it for me. Okay, now let's see. You should look at this. Xavier forwarded these to my attention."

I began reading the papers, but had some difficulty understanding some of the technicalities in French. "Is this an insurance policy?" I asked.

"Yes. I want you to feel secure, in case anything should ever happen to me. And this one is for the boat."

"I understand."

"There's that paper I was looking for."

"These look like important papers. You really should be more organized," I suggested.

"I know. Maybe you can help me with that. Here's the rest of the amount owed on the boat," he said, handing me the bill.

I gasped. "That's a huge sum. It's probably about as much as I have liquid in my bank account."

"Don't worry. With the future success of our wineries, I promise that we'll make back the money, and much more. This yacht is perfect for entertaining clients. And we can write off a portion for our business expenses. Xavier has that already worked out."

"I'm going to need money if I put everything into this boat," I informed him.

"We'll have a joint banking account. You'll have access to money whenever you need it."

"Yes, that makes sense."

Eventually, I knew this time would come, and we'd have to discuss practical matters. Planning my future was something I preferred not doing. Having money allowed me that luxury. Since my injuries, I had left many bills unpaid. I needed help and didn't know where to turn. This was also my opportunity to ask Jean-Auguste for more assistance.

A selection of appetizers arrived with our drinks. After nibbling on a stuffed shrimp, I said feebly, "Talking about money makes me feel completely overwhelmed. Since I've come to Paris, I keep seeing my money dwindling away. As you know, I've had difficulty taking care of things since my accident. I don't know what to say to you about this boat. All I know is the winery has to generate an income for me to keep up with this lifestyle with or without this added expense."

"I know that. I promise your winery will be a success. I don't want you to worry about finances anymore. We're a team now. I know you have bills and probably all sorts of taxes to pay. You shouldn't be bogged down with all that mundane work anymore. Xavier can do the accounting for both of us. He'll even advise you on proper investments. I'm here to make life simpler for you."

"That will be helpful."

"Xavier can explain all your accounts. Please don't worry anymore. I'll do anything to make you happy. What do you think? Do you want to get this boat?"

"It would be nice to travel more. Okay, I'll call my bank and confirm the funds."

"Thank you. You won't regret this. Are you feeling all right?" he inquired.

"Yes," I lied. My nervousness and anxiety were returning. The boat was still, yet I swore it was swaying to the point of making me ill.

"You're such a sweet girl. What did I do to deserve you?"

"Obviously, some very good things," I remarked.

"We're going to take some wonderful trips. To our future, it's nice to know we can enjoy these luxuries. There's a French expression I've always cherished: *Les amoureux existent sur leur amour et l'eau fraîche*. In truth: all we really need to live on is our love and fresh water. This is all superfluous," he said, raising his glass for a toast.

"You don't really believe that, do you?" I asked.

"Maybe I do. There's a lot about me you still don't know."

Goddesses, Wine, Dead Artists & Chocolate

The Journals of Joaquím Carlos Cortez

PARIS, JANUARY 1939

The provision shops are open and bustling with activity as I walk along the commerce street of rue de Lourmel. While I pass quickly by, I inhale the pungent aromas of cheese shops, cooked delicacies from charcuteries, fresh pastries, and breads. Merchants beckon me to sample a piece of fruit, a slice of country pâté, or a taste of a ripened Camembert. My stomach begins rumbling loudly. That morning I'd forgotten to eat breakfast.

It is past lunchtime when I approach a dilapidated green gate that matches the address Sylvie gave me. Finding the gate unlocked, I pass through a brick entrance to find the residences situated at the far end of the courtyard. Hesitantly, but nevertheless persistently, I knock on an apartment door. A man with a disheveled appearance answers with a cigarette butt dangling from his lips. Standing in a coffee-stained undershirt and worn gray slacks, he skeptically stares at me with tired, bloodshot eyes. On his face and shoulders are striated claw marks from what looks to me like damage done by women's fingernails.

"I'm sorry to have disturbed you. I'm looking for Eliane. Do you know where I can find her?" I ask politely.

"She doesn't live here anymore. Go away," the man says gruffly, with breath that reeks of pastis.

As he begins to close the door, I exclaim, "This is an urgent matter!"

"Are you police?" he asks.

"No, I swear I'm not. A friend of Eliane's is very ill. Actually, she's my wife; and I'll do anything to please her. Please, you must believe me! I don't mean any harm to anyone. Do you know where Eliane can be found?" I plead.

The man debates answering me, scratching his unshaved chin. Finally, he says, "All right then. You seem honest enough. She's moved near the *bois.*" He disappears for a moment inside and quickly returns with a piece of paper.

"You'll find her at this address," he says abruptly.

"Thank you. Thank you very much," I answer.

He slams the door before I have a chance to say anything else. I race down the stairs.

The address he gave me is for an Art Nouveau building located only a few blocks from our apartment. This time, I don't hesitate and immediately ring the corresponding number. Much to my surprise, the door is automatically released, even before I'm identified. Since it is freezing outside, to get warmer, I bolt up the stairs. It's a steep upward climb to the apartment, which is located on the top floor. As I approach, the door begins to open. Standing before me is a dark-skinned woman wearing a maid's uniform.

"You must be the masseur for madame. Please come in," she says, stepping aside, so I can enter.

Trying to regain my breath I blurt out, "No, I'm looking to meet someone by the name of Eliane."

"Who are you?" she asks skeptically.

"My name is Joaquím Carlos. I'm the husband of Sylvie Goldstein."

"I'm Eliane. I don't have time to speak with you," she snaps.

"Sylvie has specifically asked to see you. You're the only person she's asked for. She hasn't been well."

"I don't care. I have work to do. I'm extremely busy. Please leave," she orders. Suddenly a young girl runs to her and begins tugging on Eliane's apron.

"I'm hungry. I want cookies," the girl whines.

"You know the rules. Your mother doesn't want me to give you any, so you're going to have to wait until dinner," Eliane patiently answers the child.

"You're mean and ugly!" the girl shouts running away.

"I beg you to help me. Please let me take you to my wife. We don't live far from here."

"I don't care. Didn't you hear me? Are you deaf or something? Now go!" She begins to close the door, and I force myself between the door and the jamb.

"I assume you were once friends. Please, Sylvie is extremely despondent."

She opens her mouth wide like a mocking raven, exposing several gold teeth. "You really don't know anything. Friends? What a joke. Friends! How dare she call me that!" she scoffs.

"Madame, I agree with you. I can sometimes be an ignorant fool. But if you've ever been in love, then you may understand this vulnerable human condition. I'm at a complete loss at trying to please my wife."

"That doesn't surprise me," Eliane sneers.

A woman's voice calls from down the hall. "Is that the masseur? Send him in, already. I've been waiting!"

"No, madame. I'm sorry. The person is here for me."

I continue. "Our marriage has deteriorated. Sometimes I lock myself away in my studio and wish I never had to come out."

"Studio? What kind of studio?" Eliane asks with sudden interest.

"Art," I answer meekly.

"Do you know that I rarely get a chance to visit the museums of Paris? Whenever I get time off, they're always closed," Eliane tells me.

"That is a pity. If I had more time, I would introduce you

to the Louvre. Please forgive me for troubling you."

The woman's voice calls again from another room.

"Where's the masseur?"

"I don't know, madame."

"Make me some tea and biscuits. Now!" the woman shouts. Eliane sighs.

"She sounds dreadful. I bet you could use a break. I'm terribly hungry and need to get something to eat. May I invite you to join me? It's obvious you're an intelligent woman. A good meal and stimulating conversation can often be hard to come by. You can pick any brasserie or restaurant of your choice."

"It would be nice to get away from here. Let me ask permission."

The door is closed in my face. As I wait on the outside steps, I'm terrified that she's shut me out for good. My nerves are agitated; I'm getting hungrier by the second, ravenous. To pass the time, I can't stop tapping my foot against the wood banister. This annoys a nosy drunken concierge who keep coming out of her apartment to see what is happening. I have to keep apologizing to her, when all she really wants to know is if I'm having some scandalous affair with someone in the building. One couldn't have any privacy with an insipid *poule* like that around. And as I thought, just as Eliane opens the door, the concierge hovers around the corridor to watch us.

Much to my surprise, Eliane has changed, presenting herself in a worn rust-colored dress that gathers in folds around her hips. Over the dress, she's wearing a rabbit coat that has missing fur, like her own partially balding scalp. However, to appear more glamorous, she has covered her head with a black fedora, which also matches her dramatic eyeliner. She tries to appear chic and composed as she descends the stairs. But it's apparent by her wobbling ankles and her overly cautious steps, that she isn't used to wearing high heels.

"Your concierge reminds me of a woman I once met at Miró's studio. She lived in his building and was always spying on him."

"You know Miró! He's my most favorite artist," she exclaimed. "What's he like?"

"He's very modest, conservative in appearance, and rather shy. I met him at a café in Montparnasse. Later, he invited me

over to his studio, where we painted and conversed all through
the night. I owe a lot to him. He taught me the importance of
organizing paintbrushes and every aspect of my working environment."

"Can you take me to the café where you met Miró?" she
asks.

"I'd be happy to."

"How do you know my wife?" I casually ask.

"I'll explain later," she says irritably.

After a fast Métro ride, we arrive in the Latin Quarter. Even
on this blustery day, the cafés and restaurants are teeming with
clients.

"I used to come here with Sylvie. We had our first date in
Montparnasse," I say reflectively.

"I'm sorry she has hurt you so much."

"How do you know this?"

"I may be just a maid, but I'm an excellent observer of
people, especially men," she says with a sudden confidence in
her voice.

When we reach La Rotonde, to be gallant, I open the door for
her. Once we enter, since we stand unattended, the attention of
the café is blatantly focused on us, primarily Eliane. Eventually
one of the owners recognizes me and comes up to us.

"Monsieur Cortez, it's so good to see you again. It's been
quite a while. Would you like a booth? I can seat you at that
one in the corner."

"But that's the back of the restaurant. I don't want that one.
I want my usual table."

"I'm sorry. It's the best I can do today," he says, without
acknowledging my guest.

Whatever excitement Eliane had about going out, is quickly
fading. Her face has turned solemn, and her demeanor begins
to wilt, causing her shoulders and head to slump forward. I
quickly brace my arm around one shoulder, bolstering her up;
she feels as though she'll slip away like a paper doll caught
in a sudden gust of wind.

"It's fine. We'll take it," I say to placate Eliane.

Since the positive aspect of this secluded booth allows us a voyeuristic view of the café, once seated, I subtly point out the clientele. Orating in a soft voice, I say. "At that table, the man wearing the striped suit and black trilby hat is Henry Miller, the provocative American writer. I believe he's seated with Anaïs Nin, the delicate-boned lady in the red cloche hat. That attractively dressed woman with the large nose is Violette Leduc, a talented French fashion writer. On some nights at that table would be Simone de Beauvoir. Over there, in that booth is where a group of Surrealists meet: Giacometti, Camus, Brancusi, and Soutine. In that corner is my friend Princess Mitya. She must be with her baron suitor. I hope they didn't notice us when we walked in. He's such a fop. He'll talk our ears off about nonsense. There's a place for everyone in this city. You should be openly welcomed."

"Maybe. But I can't change the way I look. And I don't have any redeeming talents. I'm not special in any way."

"You shouldn't sell yourself short. All I see that you're lacking, my dear, is a bolder attitude. You need to create some sort of mystique about you, then people will become interested."

Eliane orders a Kir royale. When the drink arrives, she takes a sip, and confesses, "There are few people that I trust. I was hurt once, very badly. It's hard to forget."

"Who hurt you?" I ask.

"Mostly, the human condition."

"Do you mean love?"

Refusing to answer, she opens her cluttered purse and pulls out a blue pack of cigarettes. She offers me one first and then helps herself. As she raises up a Gitane, I quickly strike a match, lighting it for her. After her first deep inhale, she muses, "I left Morocco when I was fifteen. I thought I'd have a better life in Paris, more freedom. But I quickly learned that women with my skin tone are often reduced to menial work. I was hired for the job as Sylvie's personal *bonne*. Then her parents moved me to the château in Loire. Sylvie and I practically grew up together. We were like sisters. Coincidentally, our birthdays fall on the same day. Except she's five years older than I. After a few years, I was appointed the head of the staff of housekeepers."

"Why do you dislike my wife?"

"I don't dislike her. I loathe her," she says with deep resentment in her voice.

I call the waiter over and place our order. Then I say, "You don't have to tell me."

"I want to. I like talking to you. You make me feel validated, not like a ghost. I like everything about you. Especially your . . ." She hesitates for a moment and blurts out. "Eyes. You have understanding eyes."

"How do you know men so well?" I ask.

Ignoring my questions, she says, "Everything changed after the tragic death of Sylvie's family. Afterward she became the *patronne*. She was *sauvage* and had wild parties all the time and drank excessively."

"How did this bother you?"

Eliane coughed several times and took several sips of water. "Stupidly, I fell for a man. Believe me, I know how love can hurt. He was an aristocrat, white, and a friend in Sylvie's circles. You must know the type—a professional houseguest. They know when to make a fast exit if a situation gets unpleasant. He was extremely charming and seduced me."

"Sylvie never mentioned anyone like that."

"I wouldn't expect her to. I became pregnant by him."

"That's quite an entanglement!"

"When I told him I wanted to have his child, he burst out laughing. I was completely humiliated. He ran to Sylvie and told her. I became part of their amusement, another diversion, another game. They both found my situation hysterical and opened a bottle of champagne for the occasion. I'll never forget what that *salope* said to me."

"What did she say?"

"She said, 'How dare you whore around in my house? I never want to see your ugly black face again. Get lost!'"

"How could she have been that malicious? I can't believe she would say that."

"I assure you, it's true. Over and over again, I have asked myself that same question. I begged her to let me stay. I had nowhere to go. And I wanted this child that was growing inside me. I remember her words as clearly as if they happened yesterday. Sylvie chided, 'You're disgusting! Get out before I have to throw your black ass out myself.'"

"I can't believe she could have been that heartless. What happened after that?" I ask.

"I packed up my meager belongings. Sylvie and my lover were completely intoxicated and roaring with laughter when I left. To spite me, she started kissing him in front of me. He didn't pull away from her either. I felt like an animal that had been hunted and disemboweled, and they were amusing themselves with my entrails. Every ounce of blood felt drained from me. I could hardly walk.

"When I arrived in town, I was running a high fever, and collapsed in the street. The wrong person found me and led me into a vicious cycle. I was forced to sell my body to sustain my body."

"What happened with the child?"

"I miscarried," she says tearfully. "I've always wanted to be a mother. Now, I'm again a *bonne*. I look after rich people's spoiled brats. I live in envy, as I'm always watching others have all the amusement. I do the dirty work that the wealthy won't dare touch. My reward, like their dogs, is to eat gourmet leftovers, pick at their poultry carcasses, or chew the meat left on their steak bones."

"I'm very sorry."

"It's better than sex with drunken strangers. And it's less painful then catching syphillis." She bows her head, empties the bread basket into her purse, and throws in a bowl of sugar cubes. I call the waiter over for more bread. Immediately, he brings another full basket. Then she polishes off a plate of rabbit stew and soaks up the remnants of her sauce, using the entire loaf of bread.

"Are you still hungry?" I inquire.

She nods. "I'm especially ravenous today. Do you mind if I order a *plateau de fromages* and then dessert?"

"Not at all. Eat as much as you need to."

"I imagine you must bring out all sorts of appetites in women?"

"One cannot always be entirely aware of how we influence others. That's the mystery we all share. I think you may also provoke something in me," I comment, removing my Basque beret.

"What do you mean? Nobody has ever taken an interest in me without ulterior motives," she says.

"Well, I do hope you'll consider visiting my wife. But regardless of that, you have an intriguing, multifaceted look."

"What does that mean? I'm not beautiful. I know that, so don't lie to me," she says reproachfully.

"Beauty is in the eye of the beholder. To quote my friend Breton, 'beauty is convulsive.' Recently, I've been feeling the need to paint average women, those who give and constantly nurture, be they mothers, wives, or servants. Some may be perfectly fulfilled in this role. Yet I want to reveal what is behind their personal sacrifices. Is it truly their natures? Are women kinder then men? Do you know? How do you feel caring for others?"

"I don't have a choice. To eat and sleep in a bed, I must serve. It could be different if I worked for people I respected. For now, my kindness is a pretense, and bitterness is my only friend."

After we finish dessert, a pear tart and several cups of coffee, she insists on visiting my studio. I'm getting worried that I've left Sylvie alone for too long. Yet I comply with her wishes. Being with this woman is encouraging. Possibly, through Eliane, I hope to better comprehend my wife's bewildering character.

When Eliane enters the studio, she gingerly removes her coat like it had once belonged to Catherine the Great and gasps as the birds flutter about the room.

"I've never seen anything like this. Their feathers are outstanding," she says with her eyes following the birds.

"If you're afraid, I can put them in their cages."

"I like them. I'm fine." She walks around the room and studies my canvases. "You seem to like painting nudes. Do you always work with live models?"

"My life would be simpler if I didn't need them. But, I often need to work with models."

"What sort of artist do you call yourself?"

"You can call me an Expressionist or a Surrealist, or a combination of both."

She nods her head and asks, "Where do your models pose for you?"

"Anywhere in this room, depending on the light."

As I move toward my easel, she awkwardly begins to pose with her dress on. "How do you usually ask a model to stand?" she questions.

"Anyway that she is most comfortable. It's better if she is lounging or seated." Leaving her, I return with two glasses of cognac.

"Would you like one?" I ask.

Her black eyes sparkle when she sees the amber liquid.

"I was feeling a touch of *grippe*. Thank you. I think this will help."

"It always works for me," I confess.

I begin to play a record of *The Three Gymnopédies*. Mesmerized by the classical music, she closes her eyes and collapses into the red velvet divan. I announce: "Sylvie and I have a son."

She says nothing and is lost in the music until the symphony ends. After a moment of silence, her face contorts in anguish.

I comment, "You remind me of one of Picasso's women, especially in his blue period. You look so sad, Eliane. Is life really that tragic for you?"

"It's just that . . . that's the most beautiful piece of music I've ever heard," she says, wiping a few tears from her eyes.

"You really have been sheltered if you've never heard Erik Satie."

"Do you want me to remove everything?" she asks.

"What are you talking about?"

"I want to model for you," she explains.

"I must paint you, but not now. Sylvie is waiting."

"I need you to paint me now," she insists, the alcohol making her even bolder.

She begins to remove her dress and the rest of her undergarments. Hesitantly, I pick up a palette and begin mixing oils. I walk over to my easel and stare at a primed blank canvas. I touch the canvas lightly with my finger. The gesso has dried. My trained eyes scan her physique. Her earthly beauty is revealed through her nudity, with breasts that are larger than I imagined them to be. Bestowed with a curvaceous body, matronly hips, and wide shoulders, she has a hearty constitution. All of her vitality seems to be in her limbs: bulbous calf muscles, robust thighs, and muscular arms. Her black eyes are soft and gentle like a sea lion. They tell me she can be fiercely loyal, while bluish-gray circles under her eyes give away her many sleepless nights and sorrows. There is a sweet and bashful quality to the way she holds her head, often tilting it to one side. It seems the weight of life is sometimes too much for her. Yet she manages to hold herself up. As a model, she makes me think of Gauguin's island women, and the rich chocolate skin tones he captured in his Tahitian paintings. Eliane's mouth is large, expansive, and free to express emotions, which she conceals, as her profession has taught her to be stoic. Unfortunately, her plump lips are dried and cracked like her lost innocence.

Two hours pass, and I begin to learn more about her. She allows me to gently position her heavy arms. I imagine her on the top of a giant stone fortress. On canvas, Eliane becomes part woman and part dragon—fire spews out of her mouth, and severed rabbit hearts are wrapped around her clawed feet. She's an excellent model, and rarely moves to stretch or complain of muscle cramps.

"Will you pose for me again tomorrow?" I ask. "I'll be glad to pay you. You've done outstanding work."

"I would like that. This is much better than cleaning toilets and changing endless sets of diapers."

"It's getting dark. I need to get back to Sylvie. She's probably already worried. I didn't tell her that I'd be working today. Are you coming home with me?"

"I'll go. Give me a minute," Eliane answers irritably.

"I don't know what she wants to tell you. Honestly, I don't know what she wants from you. But she's been suffering for too long."

As Eliane dresses, her face looks gloomier. Turning her head, she catches a glimpse of her own reflection in a gilded standing mirror. She tries to style her short cropped hair with her chapped fingers, but quickly gives up and returns to covering her balding head with her hat.

"I had scarlet fever as a child. That's how I lost some of my hair. But, I'm strong as an ox now," she zestfully explains.

I warn her, "Please don't tell my wife you posed for me. Sylvie gets unnecessarily jealous of my models. The last thing I need is for something else to upset her."

Helping Eliane into a black Renault taxi, I treat her like the finest of ladies. During the ride, we sit together in the back. To me, her existence is certainly worth more than toilets and diapers. She's a woman blessed with wisdom, honesty, and depth who needs to feel cherished.

"I appreciate what you're doing for me," I say.

"You don't have to thank me. I should be thanking you for lunch and for letting me pose," she remarks.

Looking deeply into her eyes, I see compassion beyond the bitterness. I want to tell her more about my frustrations, confess to her about how my intuition has often failed me with my wife. Already I have burdened Eliane enough, so I keep my mouth shut. I don't want to make her more uncomfortable.

Eliane and I enter the avenue Foch apartment. As I knock on the bedroom door, Eliane stands silently beside me and is cowering again, like she did earlier. Knocking a second time, I don't get an answer. So, quietly, I let myself in. Sylvie is sleeping peacefully, surrounded by her satin and chintz pillows. Her cat is curled up beside her legs. Softly, I call to her, "I found Eliane, darling." Sylvie slowly stirs and opens her eyes.

I tell her again. "Eliane is here. Do you want to see her?"

Sylvie nods and sits upright. "Please send her in. First give her these," she says, removing a pair of Art Deco diamond and marcasite earrings that are hanging from her earlobes.

"What are you doing? Those are my favorite," I tell her.

Ignoring my comment, she hands the earrings to me.

"Also, get us both a glass of Cointreau," Sylvie orders.

"Whatever you want," I reply, slipping the jewelry into my pocket.

Obeying her, I fetch the bottle of crystal-clear liqueur, tucking it under my arm, as I carry out two tumblers. I hand Eliane both sifters and the diamond earrings.

Eliane snidely asks, "Are these real?"

"I believe they are. I think every item of jewelry that Sylvie owns is authentic. She wouldn't have anything fake. She wants you to have them. Would you mind taking these drinks in to her? She wants to be alone with you."

Eliane refuses to budge.

"Never mind. I didn't mean to treat you like a servant. Sylvie didn't ask for you to bring in the drinks. That's my fault. I'll take them in." Taking the glasses back, I carry them into the bedroom. Eliane shakes out her hands like she's touched something dirty and wipes them on her dress. When Eliane enters the room, the women stare grimly at each other without saying a word.

"I'll take that," Sylvie says as she reaches for one of the tumblers in my hand. Carefully, I set down the other glass on the marble top of her dressing table, next to some copies of *Gazette du Bon Ton* and her Elizabeth Arden face cream. Then, I try to innocuously tiptoe out of the room.

For several minutes, I'm frozen beside the door. I expect to hear screams, instead I listen to their soft muffled voices. Is Sylvie losing her mind? She gave away one of my favorite pairs of earrings. The earrings reminded me of the rare occasions we used to dress up for soirées. Sylvie was always one of the most elegant women in a restaurant. What am I to say? It is pointless for me to intervene. Before, I could never have afforded to buy her expensive jewelry. Since our marriage, I've become attached to beautiful possessions; it can be so difficult letting them go.

After an hour, I hear the bedroom door open. Eliane emerges holding a large suitcase in each hand.

"More cases are in the bedroom," she explains.

"I'll get them," I offer. Entering the room, I glance at the bed. Sylvie is sleeping again.

"I'll call a taxi for you. Let me help you downstairs with these."

Once we are outside the building, and just before the taxi door closes, I say to Eliane, "Thank you for coming. I hope it wasn't too unpleasant. Will I see you tomorrow at my studio?" I ask.

"I'll try to be there. But I'm not sure madame will let me leave after dinner."

When I return to the apartment, I check on Sylvie. She's so beautiful when she sleeps. I can almost remember what her body used to feel like beside me, the warmth she once gave. Her armoire doors are open and most of her wardrobe is gone.

Even her jewelry boxes are emptied from her vanity table. Gently, I sit next to her and softly stroke her hair. She wakes and sits upright in bed.

"I was so cruel to Eliane when she needed my help. God, I was stupid back then. Look at how she's suffered because of me. She lost her baby," Sylvie whimpers.

"I know. Do you feel better now?" I ask.

"A little," she says forcing a smile. "Bring me our sweet son."

I retrieve Emile from the nursery. He is sleeping and doesn't wake when I first pick him up and hand him to Sylvie. Warmly, she cradles him in her arms.

"He looks so much like you," she says, as she kisses his forehead and pinches his plump rosy cheeks.

"He's a sound sleeper like you are," I tell her.

"His skin is soft and he smells so sweet and fresh. I wish I could see him grow up," she says.

"What are you talking about? You will see him. I'm having the cook make us filet mignon tonight. You need to eat some meat for strength. Then I'm sure you'll feel stronger. Maybe tomorrow you'll feel like going out for dinner." I hold her hand and gently caress the inside of her palm. My other hand rests on Emile's plump knee.

"You're a good man, Joaquím Carlos. I only wish I deserved you."

PARIS, FEBRUARY 1939

The following morning after Eliane's visit, when I go in to wake Sylvie, her body is cold to my touch, much colder than it has ever been. It took me half the day to understand that my beautiful white dove had finally flown away.

Day after day, and now more than a month later, the shock remains. A human life is here today, gone the next. Who comes to claim our souls?

There was so much more I wanted to share with my Sylvie. The first week after she passed away, I felt her presence even more strongly than when she was alive. Every second, her spirit was with me, trapped in my fractured heart. Beyond the financial security that she left me, what I found most precious, the average eye could never see. Through all the darkness, I have remained pure, as a flame burns within me. Its source is coming from my heart, where a diamond lotus blossom is growing—the treasured gift of knowing love. I am empty, but also full, full of her impressions. Where has my dove flown to? When I feel angry, I try to remember to be grateful. Without her, the glamorous art world may have never been in my grasp.

Today, I'm at the Montmartre cemetery. Every time I visit, I relive her funeral, the worst day of my life, when Sylvie was returned to the silent earth. A part of me died with her. Throughout all my suffering, the most considerate person has become Eliane. She has quit her job and begun working for me. Every day, she comes to my studio and brings me a home-cooked meal. She is helping to ease my loneliness.

For a month, I've been unable to paint or write. I pasted a collage of Sylvie's collection of wine labels, and discovered her opium was stashed in that box, along with mounds of cash. Hundred-franc bills were neatly folded underneath the pressed wine labels. For some reason Sylvie, must have begun distrusting banks. With some of the money she left, I've also hidden more than a million francs in my paint drawers. But money doesn't bring comfort, not even painting, as my oils and supplies remind me of my painful loss. For hours, my eyes can stare unfocused at my canvases, reviewing all the lost memories, my disbelief of death.

Today, kneeling beside Sylvie's tombstone, I am able to read her journal for the first time. Miraculously, she had filled several pages just before her passing. As I begin to read her words, my remorse is released.

Sylvie's Journal
JANUARY 1939

Finally, my dear husband, I have given you something to feast your curious eyes on. During our marriage, I never wanted you to compromise your creativity because of me. The years you've known me, I feel I have dampened your adventurous spirit. You are optimistic, while I've become paranoid and distrusting. All this time, I have been strangling you, like clumps of seaweed weighing down a ship's anchor, not allowing a boat to sail for a long voyage.

My tastes are dangerous; they always have been. We

have that in common. Hence, through our years together, you have remained strong; whereas, I have fallen prey to intoxicating substances. By now, you must know that I indulge in opium. When I smoke, the most spectacular visions appear. Sometimes they are breathtaking, but lately those serene images have become fleeting. Now, whenever I smoke the same dream occurs. When I sleep and when I wake, this horrifying scene happens over and over again.

The two of us are running through a golden cornfield in the countryside of Provence. It's August and scorching hot. Friends of ours are feasting at a long picnic table. Bowls of grapes, pomegranates, peaches, plums, and slices of watermelon decorate a rectangular table draped in white linen. I feel serene, like I've stepped into a Renoir painting. Our friends are happily feasting on grilled white corn dripping with butter. You and I are standing away from the table. Suddenly, I notice that far in the distance the mountain ranges are black. Smoke is rising up toward the clear blue sky. Approaching us is a spinning ball of fire. I begin screaming for you to run. I grab your hand, but you won't move. You can't understand my words and look completely confused. Within seconds, wild flames ignite the cornfields; corn kernels are snapping. The angry fire avoids you and darts at me. I try to run, but my legs won't budge. Hot flames form a circle around us, but don't touch you. Fire lunges after me like lacerating red whips, and begins igniting my skirt. My skin is burning. Screaming out for help, I try to get the attention of our friends, but they don't hear me. They continue to feast on their meal, and are as oblivious as you are to my suffering.

Growing up, my duty was to be an obliging daughter. Therefore, I maintained the wine business, allowing it to take up all of my time. But that was my parents' dream, not mine. All my life, unlike you, I have lacked motivation, taking only what was given to me, and never wanting anything of my own until this child. The baby should have fulfilled me, I know. Yet I continued to feel that something was always missing. Besides, it is too late to regret that I have made nothing out of my talents, if I even have any. During our marriage, I hoped to become a devoted wife and mother. I thought duty would again restore me to a level of contentedness. Instead, I imagined you having affairs with sordid women. In addition, I envied your talent and resented your freedom as a man and as an artist. This made me feel completely helpless and even more stifled.

However, the more opium I smoke (as I am doing at this very moment), the calmer and the more sexless I become. Male or female, our roles no longer matter; my needs become completely superfluous. Dreams have all the importance, opening the doors to my imagination. Clandestine lovers, spiritual guides, and mythological figures now befriend me. I wish I could describe these vivid phantasmagorical adventures. Only now can I understand your clairvoyance, how you see through women, understanding their fears and desires. I should never have deprived you of painting a diversity of models. However, unlike the chiaroscuro captured so perfectly in your oils, my darkness and light constantly clash within me. Nevertheless, there is a predominating somberness, images of violence, bones, charred ashes. My savior is the pipe. Even though I know the risks of the beguiling poppy, it's impossible for me to stop this addiction, which becomes more demanding than any human being.

Please don't fall prey to it like I have. You must be there for Emile, as any time I could leave this callous world. When I go, please forgive me for disappointing you as a wife and mother. I have set things up so that you'll become a very wealthy man. You deserve everything I own. Please take over the winery, and care for it with your tender heart, as you have already so admirably done.

The ancient voices of saints and sages are speaking to me now. They say I need not fear death, only welcome its emancipation. I am told my time is approaching, that I should leave with them to another land without ignorance and bigotry. Oh no, I'm back in the burning field. Fire! Fire! Leave me alone! I can't breathe! Let me be. Help me, someone, please. I'm burning. No. No. No. It's too late. I'm plummeting into a bed of dancing red flames.

FOURTEEN

Djuna Cortez

Rain, rain—almost everyday there was a deluge in Loire through the winter months and the beginning of spring. This gave me the opportunity to remain indoors and read. One dreary afternoon, while I was reading the journals, several pages of Sylvie's diary slipped out, falling onto the floor. The pages had been inserted without any adhesive; therefore, I took it upon myself to glue in all the loose pages. Even when this happened, I kept my place, never reading out of sequence. Reading did occupy most of my time. Others must have thought I did very little every day. Mostly I spent them with the journals. Thus far, I never told anyone, not even my husband. It was a great privilege to learn about my family's personal turmoils and triumphs. In an odd way, I felt a need to protect them, before exposing their lives through publication. I especially enjoyed my solitude when I was reading, which was usually in the morning. Sometimes the hours would fly by and I wouldn't even realize that it was past lunchtime when I had stopped. However, that luxury was coming to an end. I was resolved to become an attentive wife. Surprisingly, or perhaps not so much, we both fell into rather traditional roles.

Jean-Auguste became consumed with the wineries and the pressures of earning profits, taking over all of our financial responsibilities. In order to keep up with a vigorous work schedule, he left near dawn and returned late in the evening. In the meantime, during his absence, I was determined not to become like Sylvie—spoiled, self-indulgent, and removed from the world, allowing the servants to care for all my needs. Ironically, I became more like Eliane (the woman Joaquím Carlos was currently painting), submissive, a nurturer, and caretaker.

As I remained in Loire, my health began to improve. Every morning, rain or shine, I would venture into the forests for a long jog. The air was especially invigorating. Exercise proved to be the best remedy for my vertigo. Each day, I would clock my time, trying to run faster. Rarely did I miss a day, not even when I attended a gourmet cooking school in town.

When I first started the class, I hadn't a clue how to roast a chicken or even a potato. Nevertheless, I was determined to learn and soon began taking on more complicated recipes and preparing lavish sauces. At the same time, I also learned how to prepare nouvelle cuisine, which I preferred to make, as the dishes were much lighter and healthier.

Most of all, in these beginning months of our marriage, I was enraptured with being in love, feeling that this powerful human emotion could transform and conquer all of my character weaknesses, even smoking; however, that became more difficult than I had anticipated.

Several times a week, I insisted on preparing dinner for Jean-Auguste, which would take me all day. I did my own shopping and prepared every aspect of the extravagant meal, including baking my own olive bread and making the dessert. In the beginning, this seemed to please and impress him. In addition, I always made sure there were fresh flower arrangements in the house and that all the meals were planned for the week. Mionne was rather laid-back, and I would have to oversee that she had collected the laundry, cleaned and properly pressed Jean-Auguste's shirts, and that the other housekeeper had cleaned all the rooms. I was completely bewildered by how fast a day could pass. I often didn't even have a moment to begin my artwork. Domesticity took up most of time, along with caring for my appearance. Rarely would I spend a day without wearing makeup, as I knew how much he preferred me to be all fixed up.

Jean-Auguste never expected anything of me, or placed any demands on me in the beginning of our marriage, except in the bedroom, which I will explain later. Our life was peaceful. Even the wave of terrorism had settled throughout Europe, making me feel safer about traveling again. One evening, the tranquility of our union suddenly changed. This happened when Madame de Briard unexpectedly showed up for dinner.

Jean-Auguste and I were settled into the downstairs sitting room by the fireplace. I was reading a new novel by Marguerite Duras and he was glancing at the newspaper when Mionne rushed in to tell us we had a visitor. Before we had time to get up, Patrice de Briard was walking toward us. I almost didn't recognize her out of costume; she seemed diminutive, wiry, and frail in a fitted black pants suit. She was carrying an enormous white box tied with gold ribbon. The box looked as though it weighed as much as she did and had holes perforated on each side.

Jean-Auguste jumped to his feet, taking the box out of her hands. "Please make yourself comfortable, *Maman,*" he said. "It's so nice to see you. What can we do for you?"

After she sat down next to me, she said, "I've been thinking that I've hardly had a chance to get to know your dear wife. This gift is long overdue."

Abruptly Madame de Briard stood up, reclaimed the box from her son, and handed the gift over to me. "Please open it. I feel bad that I never gave you a wedding present."

When I opened the box, two Italian greyhound pups leaped out. Each one was excitedly wagging its tail and covering me with kisses.

"How adorable!" I exclaimed.

"Thank you, *Maman,*" Jean-Auguste affirmed.

"They're the pick of the litter," she added. "A boy and a girl."

"What a wonderful gift! Thank you," I said, holding up each delicate puppy. They were trembling in my arms. "Do you think they're hungry?" I asked feeling their protruding ribs.

"Greyhounds always look hungry. *Maman* always feeds them well," Jean-Auguste informed me.

"You'll need to feed them several times a day. They're only three months old," Madame de Briard told us.

I couldn't get used to calling her Patrice, nor would I have ever dared address her informally. When we spoke French I always used *vous*, and she did the same.

"What sort of dog food do they eat?" I asked.

"Dog food!" Jean-Auguste scoffed. "These dogs don't eat food from a can."

Madame de Briard began to explain. "You will need to cook for them. They eat a variety of proteins. One day chicken, the next lean beef or calf's liver. In addition, I add an oat mixture that I get from the veterinarian. Then you can mix in some cooked organic carrots, celery, and spinach. Once a week, you should give them brown rice and a raw egg. Oh, and you mustn't forget to blend in a tablespoon of brewers yeast, some fresh boiled garlic cloves, and a teaspoon of flaxseed and cod liver oil."

"That shouldn't be a problem," Jean-Auguste said. "Djuna is an excellent cook. She's been taking lessons and is the best student in her class."

"Isn't that domestic. Certainly feeding dogs should be simple enough," Madame de Briard said in a condescending tone.

"Maybe you should write it all down," Jean-Auguste suggested to me.

"I think I'll remember," I answered.

Later on, I instructed Mionne to add another place setting for Jean-Auguste's mother. But nothing changed when we sat down at the table. Madame de Briard's attitude continued to be patronizing toward me. In fact, she privately scrutinized everything about me, from my style of clothing, to the selection of flowers on the dining room table, to our dinner menu. I was grateful I hadn't cooked that evening. Nevertheless, she ate quietly and said very little, until midway through dinner. Suddenly she made a bold announcement. "I'll be moving in with you."

For a moment, Jean-Auguste choked on a forkful of chicken crêpe. Finding the situation shocking, I tried to hold back an outburst of nervous laughter, which was difficult to do with a mouth full of water.

Calmly, Jean-Auguste asked her, "Is there something wrong, *Maman?*"

"Oh, no. I'm just renovating the Château de Triomphe. I can't stay there while its under construction because of my asthma."

"Of course," he answered. "Well, that shouldn't be a problem. We have plenty of guest rooms. Right, Djuna?"

I nodded. Evian was trapped in my mouth; I couldn't swallow. Without excusing myself, I got up from the table and rushed to the bathroom. After spitting out the water, I began to feel a sinking feeling in my stomach. Since our marriage, Patrice had never wanted to see me, nor I her. Jean-Auguste often met her for lunch while he was working. Now, it was impossible for me to imagine what it would be like having to live with her, not that I could have protested. Even so, we weren't asked if this would be an imposition. Trying to hide my indignation, I returned to the table, calmly taking my seat.

"Are you all right?" Jean-Auguste asked.

"Fine," I lied, while giving him a placating smile.

"I could teach your wife a lot about maintaining a winery and château," Madame de Briard impudently commented.

"Yes, anything you want to suggest I'm sure would be helpful to Djuna," he said, answering for me.

I refrained from getting defensive, although I wanted to know what I could possibly be doing wrong. Yet, I remained composed, continuing to eat, even having seconds, which I only did on rare occasions.

"My your wife has a healthy appetite!" Patrice de Briard exclaimed.

"She's usually very careful and disciplined with her diet," Jean-Auguste said, coming quickly to my defense.

"Yes, well, I think it's time you both started entertaining. It's important for the wine business," she interjected.

"You're right. The time is now, in the spring, when guests will want to visit the region," Jean-Auguste agreed.

"There's a lot I see that needs attention," she said. "Tomorrow, maybe Djuna will give me a tour of her winery and vineyards. Maybe I could make some suggestions."

"That would be nice," I said, as I tried to hide my dread.

All of a sudden, just before dessert, Jacques frantically ran into the dining room. "Madame, we don't know where to put all these things." Excusing myself, I followed him into the foyer. Racks and racks of clothes were being transported in, along with ten or more valises.

"Is she moving in?" he asked.

"I'm afraid so."

"For how long?" he asked.

"I haven't a clue," I answered bewilderedly. "She may need two guest rooms, but for now give her the yellow room."

Returning to the dining room, I said to Madame de Briard, "I've set you up in the largest guest suite. These are more modest accommodations than what you're used to. For the time being, I do hope you'll be comfortable and make yourself at home."

"These rooms are quite small. Despite that, I'm sure I'll be content," she said with her expansive grin.

Goddesses, Wine, Dead Artists & Chocolate.

The Journals of Joaquím Carlos Cortez

PARIS, APRIL 1939

It's been three months since my wife's passing. Every Sunday I visit Sylvie's grave in Montmartre, and speak to her as if she can hear me. I explain to her how I'm learning to care for a child alone, and that it's difficult, even with all the money she's left me. When I bring Emile to my studio, he steals my brushes and cans of turpentine. The moment I tell him not to touch something, he'll intentionally grab it, defying me. Then he'll collapse on the floor laughing. He's a mischievous toddler. I haven't a clue how to discipline him. He's beginning to speak and is enjoying the power of his voice. Often, he cries for his mother. I can't stop him or tell him that she's gone. I'm afraid once I do this I'll break his little spirit.

Kneeling on Sylvie's grave, I ask her to tell me how to explain her death to a two-year-old. Abandoning all my stubbornness, I hope that there is an afterlife, so that Sylvie can respond to me. I need her now more than ever.

Alas, I'm left with no answers on how to raise my son. What frightens me the most is how quickly I have forgotten the shape of her almond eyes, their shade of emerald green, the sound of her voice, and the curl of her lips when she smiled, even her inflections. I told René how I wished I had more paintings of her. He wants me to hire assistants and make stone-plate reproductions of my oils, but I refuse. I don't believe in duplication. There will never be anyone like Sylvie.

Every Thursday, Marcel and I meet for dinner. His romantic life is still at the mercy of this coquette stripper, Fifi de la Villette. Because of her, he never left to fight in Spain. Lately, he's been warning me of war approaching France. While we're eating, he reaches under the table and hands me a gas mask in its case. The case is the most original-looking one I've seen, as pasted on the outside are clippings of his favorite Apollinaire poems. Inside, beside the mask, is a section for a set of poker dice and a flask of brandy.

"I want you to have it. I got it for you. There's even your favorite cognac in the flask. Please take it," he orders.

"It's very nice of you to offer, but I can't accept," I reply.

"Why? I don't understand."

"I refuse to buy into this endemic paranoia. The Germans will never invade France. We're well protected."

Marcel points to the empty tables surrounding us.

"Most people don't agree with you. Look around you. This place used to always be mobbed. How do you explain this?"

"I think everyone has gone stark raving mad," I comment. "My life won't be ruled by fear. As an artist, I battle with fear every fucking day. When I wake, I fear that one day I won't be able to see. What will I then do with this life that is centered around my vision? Fear wants me to surrender. But never will I do that."

"Maybe that's why you're successful and I'm not. What do you think of our Surrealist group disbanding? Many have already left France. Some have gone as far as New York. Most are afraid."

"I think it's ridiculous. René fears I'll leave. I keep promising that I won't forsake him. I'm not about to abandon my adopted country because of rumors. René promises my work will be on permanent display in his gallery. For now, the only distance I'm going to travel is back to my apartment. I'm tired. Good night, Marcel."

Before going home to sleep, I stop by my studio. A few women have gathered in front of my building. Models are lining up to pose for me. Every lost girl thinks I am her savior. Word about me has traveled through the underground world of debauchery. I'm the artist with a ticket to absolution. Every young girl or used-up whore wants to get ahold of me. Often I can't leave a café without a couple women chasing after me. They grab me, clutching at my arms like starving Indian children. I want to help them, but cheap sex bores me. Frankly, I'm sick of harlots and paramours. In these women's eyes, I see only weakness and desperation. For weeks I've been sending girls away. Sadly, I'm aware that I've ruffled their dirty feathers. In single file, they march off like a cluster of tainted hens. Maybe the news will spread that I'm temperamental and they'll leave me alone. At this point in my career, I don't need anyone. If I want sex, my maidservant Eliane will comply. She will also pose for me and care for my son. She is loyal, jaded, and often bitter, but to me she is always caring. It impossible for me to love her, yet I would miss her dedication if she weren't around.

At the same time, I yearn for another woman to uproot me, shake my foundation. She must shock, perhaps evoke hatred in some people, even moral repugnance. Give me opposition, bring on more whores. I'll find the one who will inspire. No, I'm deluding myself. All harlots are created equal. Eventually all of them end up insane, or staggering drunk along the urine-soaked streets of Clichy. The next morning, they're found collapsed by the gutter, frozen to death. It always happens on the coldest of Parisian winter nights, when their charm and beauty fades, because on that night, nobody dared to lend them a warm bed or pay for their services. How many of these women have I already killed or will continue to hasten toward their death, by turning them away?

FIFTEEN

Djuna Cortez

Our lives were not the same once Madame de Briard moved in. I learned that she had an intolerance for many things, especially disorder, dust, and me, but not necessarily in that sequence. If I or Jean-Auguste accidentally left the morning newspapers crumpled or open, she would immediately have them folded, as she did with the cloth napkins after our meals. As for dust, she claimed she was terribly allergic, and if she was exposed, an asthma attack could be set off. She carried around a bronchial inhaler in a platinum case that was designed especially for her by her favorite jeweler. She usually had the inhaler on her when she was chasing after Mionne or her helper, showing them how the dust still lingered on the furniture, even after they had cleaned. Consequently, the château did look immaculate with her around.

As for myself, every second I felt her disconcerting glances, measuring me up to some fantasy she had of the ideal type of wife her son should have married. Madame de Briard would notice the flaws in every situation and was always quick to point them out. She criticized everything I did, especially my cooking, and loved to comment on a dish that I had painstakingly prepared, saying that it was either oversalted, or over-peppered, or too bland for her refined taste buds. I tried to be diplomatic with her, never showing her or my husband how much she irritated me. Eventually, Jean-Auguste began to mimic her critical behavior. Although my cooking, which I was tempted to abandon, didn't bother him as much, he would remark that I needed to wear more makeup, or that the color of the dress I had chosen was unbecoming. Often, when we were getting ready for dinner, I would ask him what he wanted me to wear. It could take me fifteen minutes or more to decide, when in a split second he could assemble an elegant outfit, that I had to admit was usually a good choice.

Almost everyone displeased Madame de Briard, except for her son; in her eyes, he was perfect, along with her dogs. My puppies, however, had "discipline problems." She felt that they were spoiled from being allowed to sleep in our bed. On the other hand, she had taken over the room I had set up as an art studio, converting it into a dog bedroom, as if dogs having their own bedroom wasn't an indulgence! All the guest rooms, except for one, were taken over by her, as she needed a separate room for her extensive wardrobe. We were left with one remaining spare room, and Jean-Auguste insisted that we needed it for guests more than my painting. Therefore, I had to wait until summer to set up my artwork outside.

Everything about Jean-Auguste's mother annoyed me. For one, she was always snooping around the château. Since she was asthmatic, I expected to hear her wheezing, but she rarely had attacks—or none that I had witnessed. There was no privacy having her around, as suddenly, from out of nowhere, she would appear in a room, without anyone even hearing the sound of her swift footsteps. Several times, she caught Jean-Auguste and me locked in an embrace. Soon she discovered that I smoked, and was quick to bring up this "vile habit" of mine whenever there was an opportunity.

When she moved in, it was not exactly clear what was expected of me. Inevitably, she became the mistress of the house, making sure the servants were always frantically busy when she was around, probably because she terrified them. Eventually, I learned what my role was to become.

One afternoon, I had returned early from my cooking class.

As I began to enter the study, from the hallway I overheard her arguing with her son.

"So, when is she going to get pregnant? Do you think there is something wrong? Maybe you both need to see a specialist?"

"No!" Jean-Auguste shouted. "Nothing is wrong. Everything is fine, normal. I'm sure it will happen soon."

"I certainly hope so. We haven't got all the time in the world!"

"I know, *Maman*. I know. I'll keep my promise."

Neither of them ever knew that I had overheard their conversation. My husband and I had never spoken about having a baby. It was a complicated subject for me that I avoided at all possible costs. Thus far, I wasn't able to bring myself to tell him that I was opposed to having children at this time in my life and that I was taking precautions to prevent any accidents. What promise had he made to his mother? All I could guess was that this could explain how his behavior in the bedroom had changed. There was now very little foreplay. He would pounce on me, and at the oddest times. He would begin by kissing me, usually when I was getting ready for dinner. The only part that I liked about this was that this made us late, and this would enrage his mother. She would be waiting for us at the dinner table, strumming her skeletal fingers on a wineglass.

As the months passed, Jean-Auguste became more and more demanding in the bedroom. He continued with a similar pattern of seduction, always upon his initiation. Usually he preferred me to be partially clothed, keeping my shirt and bra on. Sometimes when my back was turned he would grab me, scaring me to death. When I objected and I didn't want to continue, this seemed to excite him even more. While I was undressing one evening, he shouted, "Don't move from that position."

"Please, not tonight. I'm tired." My shirt was half on.

"My God! You look—" he stopped himself before he said more.

"Do I look bad?" I asked.

"You've lost more weight."

"I probably have. It must be the running," I answered.

"Come closer to me," he seductively intoned.

I obeyed, knowing that if I protested, it would have aroused him more. But it was too late. Pulling me closer to him he said, "For a second, when you were undressing, your body looked so different . . . so innocent, so much like . . ."

"Like who?" I asked.

Then surprisingly, he released me, letting his hands drop clumsily to his sides. Turning his head away, he refused to answer my question. My mind could have read so much into this. But I stayed with him, in the moment, in the dark room. A mystifying look of raging desire mixed with indifference clouded his eyes, as he walked across the bedroom to get to the crystal decanter of brandy. Standing nude beside the balcony, his face was distorted by the shadow of flickering candlelight. He looked like a complete stranger, someone I would never have wanted to marry—a man who had made concessions.

I didn't want to believe what I thought I had seen that night, sensing that I wasn't enough, that he desired more than what I could give him—someone else. I tried not to become jealous like Sylvie had, as I knew how this could destroy a relationship. Instead, for a long time, I continued to make excuses for his behavior. I thought that having his mother around made him more tense. He was always having to prove his dedication to his profession. I begged him to go away with me, leave everything for a while, and take a long vacation on our yacht. I even agreed to leave his mother in charge while we were away. Sometimes, he would talk about us going away to Greece and visiting some of the smaller islands. He promised to take me, as soon as the business settled down. Meanwhile, he continued to drive himself too hard, sleeping only five hours a night, often less. Even before the workday began, he would be in the library, sorting through bills and stacks of papers. I felt fortunate that he was taking care of the finances and looking over my vineyards. On the other hand, I wasn't certain if it was worth having him absent so much, as he kept a seven-day-a-week schedule. Every month the pressures continued to increase, rather than diminish. Again and again, our vacation plans had to be postponed. All I wanted was for his mother to leave, hoping that this would restore the romance to our marriage. I wanted to please him, yet that was the most difficult task of all. As much as I didn't want to admit it, like the union between Sylvie and Joaquím Carlos, we also had our insidious secrets.

Goddesses, Wine, Dead Artists & Chocolate

The Journals of Joaquím Carlos Cortez

PARIS, JULY 1939

On the rue de Seine, outside René Vouchon's gallery, a fine collection of Mercedes-Benz cars, black coupés, saloon, and white tourer convertibles are parking and stopping in the middle of the street. A cacophony of horns are blowing. Before the gallery exhibit is officially open, my art dealer is frantically checking each oil painting, making sure they're all properly aligned.

"These people look stinking rich. This is going to be another sold-out show. Looks like money is coming our way," René says, rubbing his hands together like a praying mantis.

Finally, with a surge of energy, he opens the glass doors. Ostentation is in the summer air, as an elegantly dressed crowd drifts in. Within minutes, the room is overflowing with people. The men look like penguins in their tuxedos and black ties. Accompanying them are fashionably bold women with fine-lined Bette Davis eyebrows, blood-red lips, tailored hats, backless Chanel gowns, embroidered Schiaparelli jackets, and for those who dare: clinging evening dresses that sculpt their innate goddess-made physiques.

The music playing is Bizet's *Carmen*. The theme of my show is Goddesses of Love and Destruction. I am trying to keep a low profile. It's rather impossible, since René wanted me to wear a pale citron matador's costume with gold epaulettes and a brocade bolero. In addition, a magenta and cardinal cape forms a flowing arabesque over my right shoulder. I watch the painted ladies standing before my artwork as they sip a glass of red wine and smoke their monogrammed cigarettes, while furtively whispering comments to their dates or husbands. Most of the guests are drinking my Bourgueil. Cases of Château Hélianthe d'Or are being emptied. Still, not a single person is pulling out their checkbooks. All we need is one purchase, which usually sets off a buying frenzy. René is sitting behind the wine table with a worried look on his face; his skin tone had turned sallow. Mitya sees me standing in a corner of the gallery and eases her way through the crowd. She is wearing a low-cut haute couture gown with silver and gold fishscale sequins that look as though they were applied directly to her body like plaster of Paris. All of her sleek curves are showing, as well as her cleavage and slim back.

"You look stunning, like a mermaid dipped in precious metals," I tell her. She points to the painting of the sea creature, rising out of the Seine. "I really love that one. "These people should be buying your work. It's marvelous. Who are these guests? Do you know them?" she asks.

"I haven't a clue who these people are. René must."

"The women are all wearing the latest couture, so certainly they can afford your paintings. Art makes this metropolis thrive. Most of these people are going on to the Opéra tonight. This is most peculiar. They seem to be enjoying your work and obviously appreciate the arts."

"Where are you going?" I ask.

"Baron Fritz and I are going to the Ritz Bar and then we're going to see Edith Piaf perform. And you?"

Before I can answer, I feel a light tap on my shoulder and a soft voice calls to me. As I turn around, I'm stunned to find Isabella: the nymphette Spanish Communist. With the passing years she has transformed into a striking woman. Her dark eyes and olive skin glow with an innocence and natural beauty that far surpasses all of the glamorous ladies in the room. I have never seen her dressed up before. She is wearing a black and rose Gypsy dress with Peruvian embroidered armlets. I bow and tip my hat to her.

"I can't believe it's you!"

"I just got back from Spain," she says.

"How did you hear about the show?" I ask.

"I saw a poster for the opening in place Pigalle. I feel honored that one of the paintings of me was chosen."

"Which painting is it?" I ask.

Mitya points to the oil of Isabella on the steps of Barcelona's burning cathedral. "That poster is all over town. Where have you been?" Mitya says.

"Inside painting. I've hardly been going out," I answer. Turning to Isabella, I say. "I had lost hope that I would ever see you again."

I introduce her to Mitya. Then I grab Isabella by her velvet armlet and say, "Let me also present you to René. He'll be thrilled to meet you."

René kisses her hand, and offers her a glass of wine.

"Carlos has told me a lot about you. You look as ravishing as in the paintings. It's a wonderful thing you did to help the children in Spain. Good luck to you, and if I can help you in any way, please let me know. Please promise me you'll model for him again. Some of his best work was when you posed for him."

"By now, you must have many other models," Isabella turns to me and comments.

"An artist has to keep working. But you have no idea how thrilled I am to see you again."

"If I had money, I'd buy every single painting," she enthusiastically declares.

I glance over at the refreshment table. As the last bottle of wine is being served, my heart sinks. Nothing has sold. I don't see Mitya or her baron.

René whispers nervously to me, "I keep hearing conversations about the German military expansion. I don't think they're focusing on your work."

I'm not so sure that's the problem. Maybe my most recent work is not as inspired, since Isabella left and Sylvie died. My attention drifts back to the room. It has gradually emptied. Isabella is the only guest remaining. Grabbing her hand, I say, "Come on. Let's get out of here. Let's go somewhere lively." René is too ashamed to say anything to me when we leave.

I take Isabella to Le Boeuf sur le Toit for dinner and dancing. Lately, when I have gone out, I only go to clubs where they play live music. I can't stand the somberness of cafés and restaurants. Dinner conversations of the café society have drastically changed since Isabella was last in Paris. Discussions used to revolve around dreams, the latest art exhibit, novels, films, and philosophy. All I hear now, is the same topic: the

Führer and what country he's invading next or, they rant on about Il Duce. I couldn't give a damn about that bastard Hitler, Mussolini, or their pact. I keep telling everyone not to worry. Our borders are guarded. Germany made a promise. France will be protected.

The current jazz sensation of Paris is Benny Goodman. We dance to a few swing tunes. I sense Isabella is removed from the high spirits around us. She must need to talk to me in a quiet atmosphere, so I suggest returning to my art studio. Willingly, she complies.

As I open the door to my studio, she shouts, *"Dios mio!"*

An encroachment of exotic birds are flying through the rooms. Tonight, the parrots are out; I hadn't a chance to put them to bed. My affectionate hyacinth macaw begins showing off his violet feathers, and the mischievous military macaw with red, yellow, and blue feathers swoops down on my shoulder. Already the white and pink cockatoos, who are separated in a large cage, are getting jealous. They are calling out to me and want to come out. The cockatoos are bobbing their heads up and down and shifting their weight on their perches. Even the peach-faced love birds are active tonight, singing at the top of their lungs.

"I can't believe what you've done to this place!"

I laugh. "It's a fucking zoo in here. But I rarely get lonely. Do you like them?"

"I adore birds. They must have cost a fortune!"

I did make several pet shop owners quite happy. Make yourself comfortable. I'll get us something to drink."

As she reclines on my red velvet divan, one of my hyacinth macaws jumps on her shoulder.

"If you're afraid I can put him back in his cage."

"A little. His claws are sharp."

"I know. That's Goya. He likes you."

After putting on thick gloves, I extend my arm, and Goya automatically jumps on me. Eventually, one by one, I carefully return the parrots to their cages. Lastly, I cover their cages with blankets; the birds drift off to sleep. The room becomes silent. I return to Isabella with two glasses filled with Eaux de Vie—a spirit perfectly named, the water of life. After taking several sips, she begins to recount her experiences in Spain.

"I wasn't aware what we were going to encounter over there. Hell can't be much worse. It was by pure chance that I survived. Your imagination cannot conceive the brutality I saw. You wouldn't believe how many orphaned children we helped feed. I wanted to adopt every one of them." Her eyes drifted away from me, as she reached for a Gitane cigarette.

Using all of my intuitive abilities, I try to see through her eyes again, feel her thoughts. With her evocative words and my imagination, I can visualize everything like the newsreels shown before a film: bombed villages, ruins, ashes, human remains, stray dogs, crying orphans, and all the innocent blood that poured daily into the streets. Shivers run through my spine; the hairs on my arms are standing on end.

"I'm so very sorry. The neighborhood where you grew up was completely destroyed, burned to the ground. I made inquiries and I think your parents were killed," she says.

She begins to weep. Comforting her, I cradle her head to next to my chest. "You're safe here. Don't be sad for me. I already assumed the worst. My parents never answered my letters. The sad truth is I lost touch with them when I moved to Paris. They never approved of my career. They have been dead to me for a long time." I am silent for a moment and try to picture my parents faces, but I can barely even do that. "How's your family?" I ask.

"They're fine. Carlos, you won't believe this, but you kept me going. I told myself I was crazy for caring about a married man. We were just friends, but you showed me such kindness. You helped me open my eyes to art and its importance. I can't thank you enough for that. We will need more writers and artists to document the brutality in Spain." She looks at me and then turns away, adding, "But perhaps that is best left to those who experience it first hand."

"How did it go with your mission?"

She begins to frown, as she recounts, "My comrades and I had such good intentions. Then everything backfired on us one day in Madrid." Isabella's voice begins to quiver.

"What happened? Can you tell me?"

"Our group had set up a station in the Buen Retiro Park to feed mothers and children. Everything was going fine, babies were being fed, until some crazy woman began accusing the

Young Communist League of poisoning the milk we were serving. People were spitting at us, saying how they hated and distrusted Communists, that we were evil. Before we knew it, a riot broke out. Everyone was kicking, punching, screaming, and clawing at each other. Bottles were thrown. The crowd went insane. The incident became a way to ventilate all of their anger and frustrations. In the process of trying to escape, I was trampled on and beaten. Several friends of mine . . ." Isabella inhales deeply and takes a long sip of her drink.

"It's okay," I say, wiping a tear from her cheekbone.

"No it's not! I lost them," she says with her voice, rising and falling in anger and then despair.

"My God! How terrible! Poor *querida*. Were you badly hurt?"

"I'm useless now," she says, covering her face with her hands.

"What do you mean?"

She lifts up her dress and shows me a scare that covers the width her abdomen. "The doctors say I can't have babies. Life is never fair. Now I want them more than ever. I'm ugly. You won't want a scarred model. Nobody will have any use for me."

"You're wrong. Isabella, you're exactly what I've been missing. I find you more captivating than ever before."

"Do you mean that? Please don't take me out of pity."

"I never forgot you, either. You deserve to be treated with all the kindness in the world. Please stay with me."

"What will your wife say?"

I abruptly gulp the last few drops of translucent liquor.

"I lost her. I mean, she passed away."

"I'm sorry, really I am."

"I worry about my son. He desperately needs a mother. But I won't bore you with my problems. I'm grateful you're back. Even though I don't need the money anymore, I really wanted this show to be a success. I feel like a failure," I confess.

"You don't have to feel that way. I won't let you. You're a great artist," she says, as she softly kisses my cheek.

I take her into my arms and hug her tightly. She then begins to remove her dress and stands in her lingerie. Kneeling below her, my finger traces the seam of her black silk stockings, beginning with her ankle and climbing up to the back of her thigh. At the same time, I'm letting her control the situation. She reclines on the sofa and reaches for my face. "I must need another shave. I'm sorry. I didn't have time today," I explain.

"It doesn't matter. I like it," she says, brushing her trimmed fingernails against my slight growth of beard.

I stay on the floor and kiss every millimeter of her scarred abdomen. After, she lifts my chin to her full crimson lips. Her kisses are delicate and timid. I find her irresistible.

"You're safe now. No harm can come to you here. I'll protect you," I tell her.

PARIS, AUGUST 1939

Several weeks have gone by. Isabella has been living in the art studio. But now, I want my space back. I must return to painting in solitude. At the same time, I don't want to lose her again. There is only one solution, and fortunately she agrees with my idea that she move into the avenue Foch apartment. Now I dread the first meeting of Eliane and Isabella. It will be a brutal welcoming for the two women, as neither of them knows about the other. In Eliane's eyes, I read that this is the first time a man has treated her as an equal; therefore, she idolizes me. I don't deserve her loyalty. She has taken over the role of a domestic wife and mother, and insists on preparing most of my meals. Sylvie never cared what I ate and loathed cooking. Eliane indulges me by modeling if I ask her, and always takes excellent care of Emile. The nanny hardly does any work anymore. Eliane even buys my art supplies. There is nothing I can't ask her to do. The woman is a saint and never stops serving me. Yet, even to this day, she continues to loathe Sylvie's memory. But, out of respect for me, she never discusses it.

I enter the apartment. Eliane has put Emile to sleep. Everything is quiet. I know I must tell her that Isabella is arriving and will be moving in with us, but for the moment I refrain. Eliane and I sit down and have dinner together, as we often do. Her insights are usually refreshing.

She laments: "I don't know why, with all your money, you choose to stay in Paris? Most people are leaving."

"I like it here. Paris will always be safe. We have the Maginot Line."

"I don't know about that. I'd rather be in Tahiti or Brazil, anyplace where the weather and the people are warmer. Please take me away from here, to a country where we can wear fewer clothes and everyone's skin is bronzed and beautiful. Even Spain sounds more liberating than this icy city. I'm tired of being called *une étrangére*. I hate Paris. Its gates are only open to beautiful white women. Can't they see I'm French too? I wear the same perfume and drink the same wine. I have the same *orgueil*, the same pride of birth. And I can be just as arrogant. But, as you know, actions speak louder than words. People continue to give me the worst tables in restaurants. Why do most men prefer women who are pure and white like their baguettes?"

"I don't. Only the simpleminded are that way. I'm sorry, Eliane. I've been treated as an outsider and I know how it hurts."

She wraps her arms around me and says, "I adore you, Joaquím Carlos. You don't have to care for me the same way, but I will always be grateful for the kindness and respect you've shown me."

"It's the least I can do."

She asks, "Is there anything more you need tonight? Would you like some dessert?"

"I do have a favor to ask of you," I say. Her eyes widen with curiosity. This is the first time I've needed something extra from her.

"What is it?" she asks.

"I must ask for your tolerance."

"What do you mean?"

The timing of the situation is staged like a theatrical play. The doorbell rings. Eliane rushes to answer. Enter stage left: Isabella. She is carrying her luggage as she timidly stands in the hall of the avenue Foch apartment. Silence. Neither woman says a word. I take her luggage. Isabella smiles bashfully.

"Stunning apartment," Isabella says, as she looks up at the stained glass domed ceiling.

Shock and jealousy are raging in both women's eyes, as they look each other over Eliane hasn't moved; her hands are hanging limply by her sides with her mouth wide open. Confidently, I reach for both their hands, and bring each woman to either side of me.

I explain, "You're both in my life now; this is a blessing that I owe only to you lovely women. What you both need to understand is that I will never marry again, nor select one mate. I care about both of you; my affections will be divided, and also will be open to other models, if they so happen to enter my life. This may sound selfish, cruel, and misogynistic, but I swear it's because I never want to hurt either of you. I refuse to make promises of fidelity. You can either accept or reject me. Never will I force you to care for me. Affections are simple and natural. If you can control them, then you may as well forget the person. Please make your own choices."

Both women are silenced by my comments. Isabella doesn't disappear out the door again, as I fear, nor does Eliane. On the contrary, Isabella finds her own way to the bathroom and Eliane vanishes into the kitchen.

"Would you care for dessert?" Eliane asks me. Her face is stern, but oddly enough she doesn't seem angry.

"No, thank you."

"Coffee?"

"Yes. That would be nice."

"What about Isabella?"

"She'll probably have some too."

"I'll fix her a slice of tart," Eliane says.

"We'll take our coffee in the study. Please join us," I say to Eliane. Both women seat themselves on chairs, one on my right, the other on my left. I am sitting alone on a banquette. They continue to ignore one another and focus their attention on me. Tension is in the air: that monster of jealousy is rearing its ugly head again. The women are like two panthers protecting their territory, which is me. I dread what will follow, especially our sleeping arrangements. What have I done? I should have kept Isabella in the studio. Getting these passionate women to like each other will be a complicated and arduous task.

SIXTEEN

Djuna Cortez

It took me an entire week to shop and prepare for Jean-Auguste's birthday. I must have spent over five thousand francs in gifts alone, getting him several ties, a Limoges box for his stamps, a leather organizer, a silver money clip, and several shirts. I also decided to cater the dinner party myself. Hoping this would only be an intimate affair, I invited Naravine, Xavier, and Pascal to join us. Unfortunately, nobody could attend. Therefore, much to my dismay, his mother turned the occasion into a business opportunity, inviting several wine merchants. Madame de Briard had also gone out that week to shop for her son, but I hadn't a clue what she got him. It would have been nice if she had offered to help with some of the preparations. Coincidentally, that week, she had chosen to have frequent meetings with her interior decorator, as once again, the schedule to finish the renovations on her château was delayed.

For the last few weeks, I hardly even saw Jean-Auguste, except when he went to sleep. Meanwhile, our vacation plans were again put off because of an increase in his workload. However, several hours before the party, he unexpectedly appeared in the kitchen, startling Mionne.

She was the first to notice him silently standing by the swinging doors. Before saying anything, she rushed up to Jean-Auguste, and tried to block his view of a vanilla cream cake covered in fresh fruit.

"What can I do for you, monsieur?" she politely asked.

"I just want to see what's going on in my kitchen," he said. I turned to look at him.

"Your wife wants everything to be a surprise. She's been working very hard."

Instead of complying, he pushed Mionne aside and began peaking into the pots on the stove.

"This looks like coq au vin," he said.

"It is," I announced proudly, wiping my hands on the apron I was wearing.

Mionne chimed in. "It took madame and I three hours last night just to peal the pearl onions before marinating the chicken in wine and cognac."

His face was expressionless as he observed us in silence. Mionne continued to ramble on in her usual way: "In the morning the chicken had turned bright purple. Can you believe it! What a sight. But it's going to be delicious. What can I get you, monsieur?" she asked enthusiastically.

Without answering her, he returned to the stove, lifted up another lid and then slammed it down on top of the pot.

"I'm sick of chicken! In fact, I'm beginning to hate the ugly bird. What's wrong with having duck, quail, or even rabbit? We eat like poor folk. Yet, we spend a bloody fortune every month on food so that the servants can stuff their fat faces."

I dropped the wooden spoon I was using and turned to look at Mionne. She was on the verge of tears. After having spent hours in the kitchen together, I had grown fond of her, and I also knew how sensitive she was.

"I'm sorry this wasn't what you were expecting. I thought coq au vin was your favorite dish, that's why I prepared it. I'm very sorry it displeases you," I answered, trying to keep my own tears, as well as my anger in check.

He moved beside the cake and began pacing back and forth, flaring his nostrils. I stood as immobile as a statue, while Mionne vanished into the laundry room. Something began burning in the oven, and smoke was threatening to engulf the kitchen.

"What's burning?" he asked.

"Oh, no, the rosemary loaves!" I rushed to take them out, when the pot holder slipped, and I burned the side of my right hand.

Jean-Auguste continued to rant, while I held my hand under a cold faucet.

"It's your own fault. I never asked you to bother with all this cooking business."

"I'm aware of that! But, what has gotten in to you?" I asked.

Exhaustively, he collapsed in a chair, burying his face in his hands.

"I don't know. I'm sorry. Maybe you're right and I do need a break from all this. Is cooking what you really want to do? Does this make you happy?" he asked.

"I thought it pleased you," I answered.

"Wouldn't you rather travel?" he asked.

"Yes, you know I want that more than anything."

"So do I. What are we doing staying here? This has gone too far; I hate to see you working so hard in the kitchen, when we pay all this money for a cook. Incidentally, I probably should have told you this earlier. I think you should be aware that your couple, Mionne and Jacques, have been stealing from us."

"How do you know this?" I asked skeptically.

Before he could explain, Mionne and Jacques returned to the kitchen. As they approached us, Jean-Auguste turned to both of them and said: "I want you both to pack up your things and leave the premises. As of tonight, you're both fired."

"I don't understand. What have we done?" Mionne pleaded, bursting into tears.

"For one, you're both lazy. *Maman* has to always keep after you. And I've been adding up the accounts, so I know you been pocketing a lot of extra cash."

"Please, Jean-Auguste! We need to discuss this first," I said firmly.

"There's nothing to discuss. We're running a business here. Everything has been out of control. You haven't been the one studying the accounts, so you don't know what's been going on. Plus, you've become too chummy with all the staff. A mistress of the house never does that."

"I don't know why you had to bring this up tonight of all nights," I said angrily.

Displaying a hidden temper, Jacques turned to me and yelled, "You were a nice lady, until you married that evil brute. This estate should go up in a blaze, and if it does, I hope all of your rotten family burns with it. Monsieur Cortez would have never treated us the way you both have. Go to hell!" he exclaimed, spitting at Jean-Auguste's shoes.

Our attention was diverted for a moment, as Madame de Briard glided into the kitchen. She sparkled in diamonds and was wearing a long black tulle evening gown. Patrice announced, "Some of the guests have arrived. We need a bottle of Sauternes and our finest red, and some hot hors d'oeuvres."

"You can take care of them, *Maman*," Jean-Auguste answered, "you know where the wine cellar is. Come on, Djuna, were going to get away from here."

"But what about the guests?" I asked.

"The food is on the stove, *Maman*. Please take care of them," he answered. Turning to me he said, "Run upstairs and pack enough things for a week or two."

"Should we bring the dogs?" I asked.

"No. We need to have our freedom to travel. I'm sure *Maman* will take good care of them."

As I reached the bedroom, I heard scuffling footsteps coming from behind me. It was Jacques, whose face was inflamed with rage and his veins were bulging in his temples. I clung tightly to the banister, hoping he wouldn't get too close. As I feared, my personal space was encroached upon. He was nearly stepping on my shoes, and soon remnants of his saliva would splatter my clothes. Before he could say a volatile word, Jean-Auguste came bounding up the stairs, quickly grabbing hold of me.

"Please leave my wife alone. You've been given orders. I suggest you obey, or I'll call the police," Jean-Auguste sternly reprimanded.

His neck craning forward, Jacques's hardened face was now turning as red as a lobster. His fingers were constricted and raised toward Jean-Auguste, looking like sharp claws that would at any moment grab hold of him.

"My wife and I have a right to be here for at least two weeks. You owe us severance pay and a pension," he protested.

"We don't owe you anything. My orders are for you to leave in twenty-four hours. Is that understood?" Jean-Auguste shouted.

Jacques answered in a berating manner, "I know people like you; corruption is in your spoiled blue blood. Your family were always traitors. I bet hundreds of years ago, your ancestors blamed the Jews for poisoning the wells in the village. You probably don't care about all the innocent lives that were taken on account of your ancestors aristocratic ruthlessness. I bet your father probably collaborated with the Germans. You cheat, you lie, and you steal. We deserve this château, not you or your American whore. If I set fire to this place, justice would finally be done," he shouted.

Jean-Auguste grabbed my hand and led me into the bedroom, shutting and locking the door behind us.

"What is he going on about?" I asked.

"He's completely lost his mind."

"Do you think we should take his threats seriously?"

"Possibly," he answered, taking out a suitcase and beginning to fold some of his belongings.

"Should we call the police?" I asked.

"They won't do anything until he actually does something violent toward us, or something destructive to the property. Threats mean nothing."

"Do you think he's serious?" I asked again.

Taking me in his arms, he said, "I don't really know. He's probably all bark and no bite. I'm sure nothing will happen. You know I'll always protect you. We'll drive in to Paris tonight and spend some time in the city. We both need to get away. Then maybe we should think about selling this château and being free of all this."

"Could we?" I asked.

"We can do anything you want," he said.

"Are we really going to leave your mother here alone?" I asked.

"*Maman* will be fine. She'll probably bring some servants over from her place. You must trust me; everything will be well protected with her presence around."

When we walked downstairs with our packed suitcases, Madame de Briard was placidly entertaining her four guests. All of them were dining tranquilly, as if nothing had happened. Patrice was of course seated at the head of the table, which was Jean-Auguste's place setting. Already, a new maid, dressed in uniform, had arrived. The young woman was carefully serving the guests my coq au vin.

"How did she find someone so quickly?" I whispered to Jean-Auguste.

"She keeps four maids on staff in the Château de Triomphe. Believe me, they come when she calls them. I told you not to worry about her. She'll be fine."

However, not long after we had settled into Paris we learned that Jean-Auguste had made some misjudgments, even about his mother.

SEVENTEEN

Djuna Cortez

After a few days in Paris, we started to get distressing phone calls from Patrice in Loire. Apparently, Jacques had continued to return to the property, often entering the château, and verbally accosting Madame de Briard. Repeatedly, she had called the police and they would then cart the angry servant away. But this was only a temporary solution, as a few days later, he trespassed onto the property, toting a hunting rifle over his shoulder, and threatening all over again to burn down the château and the vineyards. Patrice was terribly upset by this, and whenever she called, I could hear her wheezing breath, as the situation had aggravated her asthma. She would then abruptly demand to speak to her son, and would never even have a conversation with me. When Jean-Auguste took her calls, he would have to console her for over an hour.

The timing of this couldn't have been worse. That week, we had booked a trip to Venice. The night before our scheduled flight we received another distressing phone call from Madame de Briard. After their talk, Jean-Auguste finally conceded to return to Loire.

"I've got to get back to *Maman*. This has upset her so much. I'm really worried about her asthma. But you should go on to

Venice without me," he said, taking out a suitcase from the master bedroom closet.

"It doesn't matter. I'll go back with you."

"Please. You must go. Maybe you should think about contacting Naravine. I think she may still be there. If you like, I can call her. Maybe you can stay with her," he suggested.

"I just don't know if I should go without you. It doesn't seem right for you to have to take care of my problems."

"I want you to go. They're our problems. I promise as soon as I can get things settled, and when my mother is better, I'll join you."

"I should go back with you and put the château on the market. It's been more trouble than its worth," I lamented.

"It may not be safe for you to go back. I think *Maman* is right to be afraid of Jacques. He's obviously a complete lunatic. At anytime he may go through with his threats. I've got to get her out. I just hope her asthma stabilizes, so maybe she can move back into her own place, even if they're still doing work. This isn't the time to put the château on the market. We need to wait until everything is under control. In the meantime, I'll try to find some dependable caretakers to keep a watch over everything."

"I hate to leave you. You shouldn't have to do all this work," I said.

"I want to help you. Anyway, I'll join you in Venice as soon as everything is under control. It's beautiful there. I know you'll like it. Please go on and try to enjoy yourself. I may also have to return to the city and check out some employment agencies. Would you mind leaving me the keys to the apartment?" he asked.

"Not at all. Maybe you can also find a trustworthy person to clean here. It's filthy," I said, running my finger over a desk that was covered in dust. "I've really neglected keeping this place up."

"I know. I'll look into finding a good *bonne*. But, as you know, servants can be so temperamental. It's sad to see all those dead lemon and orange trees on the terrace. They must have looked exquisite at one time," he said.

"Yes. When should I leave for the airport tomorrow?" I asked.

"The flight leaves at eleven in the morning. I'll drive you. We should leave around nine. All you have to do now is pack. I'll do that for you," he offered.

"You don't have to."

"I'm a terrific packer. You should let me help. I know you're tired," he said, as he began taking some of my dresses and a Fendi garment bag out of the closet.

"I don't know how you do it. Your clothes are always so perfectly neat and folded. I admire your organization."

"It just makes it easier to pack," he stated.

"My drawers are always such a mess. It's embarrassing," I confessed.

"You don't have to feel that way with me. I'm packing you for warm weather. It can get very hot in Venice during the summer. I'll give you the traveling iron and the blow dryer," he said putting them into the suitcase.

I rushed to empty my lingerie drawer, as I didn't want him to see the state of disorder it was in.

"I wish you were coming. I'll miss you," I admitted.

He didn't answer me at first. Turning his head away, he pensively glanced at a Modigliani oil painting that I had moved to the bedroom wall; it was an Expressionist portrait of a melancholic woman painted with the artist's exaggerated elongation of her torso, neck, and face. The model's eyes looked empty, and forlorn, as they were without pupils. Then he said in a stern, yet quivering voice, "I know. I'll miss you, too."

VENICE, JULY 1986

I spent two days alone in a quaint hotel overlooking the Grand Canal. It was a good time for me to catch up on my reading. However, by the third day, I was getting restless, so I contacted Naravine. This time, she was pleased to hear from me and insisted I stay with her. We arranged to meet the following morning at the Café Florian.

Naravine and I sheltered ourselves under an umbrella, at Café Florian in the Piazza San Marco. Venice's pulse was in the piazza, where all classes of people, from the wealthy to the downtrodden congregated. Rarely was there a quiet moment in the square. Flocks of gluttonous pigeons cooed and swarmed around tables of food and hovered near children eating rich gelato cones. Even in the late morning, musicians hit up each table for collections, as did portrait artists and magicians. Fortunately, they avoided our table, since I was sketching and looked deep in concentration.

A scorching summer sun was hitting our backs. Every minute the temperature was climbing, soon to reach one hundred degrees. When we first arrived, the sun had a delicate warmth that felt like two gentle hands resting on my shoulders. Two hours later, it felt like a scalding iron. Naravine was the center of my sketch; half of her face was in shadow. The roof of Saint Mark's was in the background with its golden lions, angels, saints, and horses reaching up toward the blue sky. Impressively, Naravine remained inert most of time I was drawing. Part of her secret was that she fixed her self-assured glances on a single point or object. Her winsome eyes that had seen hundreds of Venetian moons meditated on a lonesome white pigeon. The bird rested in an ashtray on its own table. Nobody dared disturb him, not even the other birds. The only time Naravine became distracted was when a fly flitted about her. She frantically waved her hands, shooing away the buzzing insect. When she did this, her manicure almost blinded me. She wore tapered fourteen-karat-gold fingernails.

As we observed the day unfolding feathers and grayish white bird droppings littered the square. This added to the ambiance, along with the ringing bells of Saint Mark's cathedral. Every second, my vision was tantalized with colors and textures. Parading before us was a fashion show from a local costume shop. People were disguised behind decorative masks and flowing capes as they danced through the hundreds of arches of Doge's Palace. A few of the masks had pointed red bird's beaks for noses.

"Those are rather frightening," I commented.

"They're supposed to be. That face was made to ward off disease during the plague."

An hour later, an aroma of fresh basil and garlic was wafting toward us from a nearby restaurant.

"I hope you're almost finished sketching. I'm getting rather hungry," Naravine announced.

"I'm never finished. But that's okay. I'll stop."

"Let's have lunch at my place. I went shopping yesterday. There's plenty of food."

"But it's so nice here. I hate to leave."

"We'll come back tonight. I can't wait for you to see the villa. I know you'll adore it."

After Naravine paid our bill, she began to stretch and shake her arms above her head. "My body goes completely numb when I model. Come on. We've got to move. Can you manage with your suitcases?" she asked.

"I'll be fine."

I followed her to the water's edge by Doge's Palace. Confidently, she placed her gold fingernails in her mouth and whistled loudly for a taxi boat. In a matter of seconds, a mahogany Riva speedboat arrived. Immediately, the captain took my luggage and piled the pieces into a storage cabinet. Within seconds he helped us both jump aboard.

We headed down the Grand Canal, for a scenic tour. As we passed under each bridge, Naravine called out some of their names.

"The bridge we're going under now is the Ponte de Diavolo, also known as the Bridge of Temptation. It has a history of scandalous affairs dating back from the sixteenth century. From my understanding, during those times, those who were caught in an act of sin were locked up in cages and put on public display at the Campanile."

"How barbaric! It's hard to imagine a daily existence here, even in present times. This city seems completely surreal."

"That it is. But, God, I love it, superstitions and all."

At that moment, we passed a funeral gondola, painted in ebony lacquer with gilded ornamentation. Haunted-looking vultures with enormous wing spans were carved on each end of the boat, and resting under a black canopy was the coffin, draped with a dark cloth.

"Why are you trembling?" Naravine asked.

"I'm not feeling well. I think it's just the heat and some seasickness."

"Do you want to get off the boat?" she asked.

"No. I'll be fine."

"That's the Rialto bridge." When I turned my head to look, I saw the Rialto's market. Stalls of oversized eggplants and *fungi* the size of pizzas, zucchini flowers in shades of bright orange, jars of ripe olives, and crates of ripe tomatoes were on display. I leaned back in my seat and inhaled the salty air, which was also spiced with cloves from open vats of mulled wine.

"You and Jean-Auguste should be here for Ascension Day, when Venice is wedded back to the sea in the most opulent ceremony. They do it every year. You shouldn't miss it. Gondoliers are out in period costumes. Music is playing from every bridge. You'll be serenaded wherever you go. It's simply glorious!"

"It certainly does seem enchanting here. I would love to see some of the festivals." I marveled as we continued around the main port of Venice and headed out to Lido island.

"Keep going past Lido Beach. Then you'll see an alcove. The villa will be on your far left side," Naravine instructed the captain.

Once we exited the Grand Canal, the water was more choppy. But the boat and my stomach fared well as we passed a long stretch of empty golden beaches that reminded me of the bathing scenes from the film *Death in Venice.*

"There on your left. Pull into that bay," Naravine ordered.

As soon as the boat approached the dock, the driver quickly tied a sailor's knot, unloaded my suitcases, and demanded his payment. Seconds after Naravine paid him, he untied the knot, revved up the engines, and took off in a fury, nearly hitting another Riva tied to the dock. We were left stranded on the beach with my three pieces of designer luggage.

Naravine explained, "Most taxi-boat drivers do this. Believe me, I'm used to it. It's because they don't want to walk up all those steps." She pointed to the top of the cliff, where a house was perched on the precipice.

"It's quite a challenging climb. But don't worry about the valises. Our guests will help us."

"What guests? I didn't think there would be anyone else but us," I said hesitantly.

"I wanted this to be a surprise. My friends came by that boat." She pointed to a small white motor boat tied to the jetty. They'll be able to take us back to the piazza later."

Naravine and I began to ascend the hundreds of narrow stone steps, which were a deterrent to any laborer. This was another passageway to paint, as purple bougainvillea and wisteria lined the walls. With each step, my heart had to pump harder, the heat intensifying the steep incline. During the climb, chameleons distracted and amused me. They would suddenly freeze at our approach and then go scurrying off. If I had been alone, my childlike fascination with nature would have made me stop and try to catch one, or at least take a closer look at their colors, perhaps even talk to one. However, if I had done this, Naravine would probably have thought I was insane. Finally, the moment arrived and we reached the summit—both of us grasping for breath. I felt a tremendous sense of relief and knew immediately that I liked my surroundings. The sun was baking down on us, as we paused for a moment on a slate veranda. Looking ahead, I saw the faded salmon-colored villa framed with olive, fig, plum, and lemon trees; its terra-cotta tiled roof was reflecting the afternoon light. Birds were eating a few of the ripe fruits that had fallen on the ground. The setting was blissfully quiet, only chirpings could be heard, and the delicate rustling of leaves that were gently brushing against the arched windowsills of the villa. Walking closer to the villa, we passed rows of lavender, mint, and rosemary plants, their fragrance permeating the air. The moment we reached the wooden front door, Naravine stopped and said, "Look behind you and take it all in. Isn't it lovely!"

I turned and inhaled the heavy, but unrestrained sea air; the ocean was below us, and from the hilltop the water appeared to be a deep shade of turquoise. As Naravine opened the door, a man walked toward us.

"Giovanni!" Naravine shouted. Giovanni was tall and spindly and appeared to be in his early thirties. He was dressed in khaki shorts, tan loafers, and a white Lacoste shirt. Following behind him was a younger and shorter man.

"I hope you haven't been waiting long?" Naravine asked.

"No problem. It's beautiful here. I've been waiting an eternity to see Nara again. What's an hour or two more?" Giovanni said boisterously.

Naravine enthusiastically added, "I want you to meet an American friend of mine. This is Djuna."

"I love Americans. Nice to meet you," Giovanni said, extending his hand.

"Is she staying over?" he asked.

"Yes. Her luggage is on the beach."

Turning around, he pointed to the man standing behind him. "That's my baby brother, Angelo. He's quite shy, but very strong. We'll help you with the luggage."

The brothers hardly resembled each other, except for their clothing, which was almost identical. Angelo was blond, and he was five inches shorter. Giovanni was dark skinned with brown hair, and had an aquiline nose and delicate lips. His dark-brown eyes were wide-set and large with thick black eyelashes. Angelo's hazel eyes appeared sad and slanted downward; they were almost the same color as the Venice canals. Angelo moved slowly, preferring to keep his hands in his pockets. His brother, on the other hand, gregariously gestured when he spoke.

Giggling, Naravine grabbed hold of Giovanni's arm, and said, "You've become even more handsome since the last time I saw you. What am I going to do with you?"

"I'm certain you can think of something," Giovanni said smiling and kissing her hand.

"How long are you here for?" I asked Angelo.

"Only one week. Soon my freedom will be all over," Angelo answered solemnly.

"What do you mean?"

"I start military service. Then I don't know when they'll let me take pictures. You see, I want to be a photographer," he said, pulling out a compact camera from his pocket. "Taking pictures is all I think about."

"He brought about five cameras with him. He was hoping to take some photographs of Naravine. Would you mind?" Giovanni asked her.

"Not at all. I'm used to it. Even Djuna is making me work. You should see her sketches," she answered.

"I'd like to. But we should get the luggage first," Giovanni said politely.

After the men left, Naravine gave me a quick tour of the villa and then excused herself to change. When I returned to the living room, she had made herself comfortable on the couch. Although the rooms in the villa had a rustic feeling with natural stone floors, faux-finished walls, and wood-beamed ceilings, most of the furnishings were ultra modern. Wearing a pearl-colored silk robe, with a white bikini underneath, Naravine's presence was unmistakable especially as she lay ensconced on a white leather sofa. The men returned with my luggage, setting the bags in my room for me. Giovanni disappeared into the kitchen. Angelo, on the other hand, sat down in a armchair facing Naravine and didn't move; his eyes were transfixed on her smooth ebony legs. I pulled up a director's chair beside him. Both of us were watching Naravine, who languidly raised her hand, lifting up a carefully rolled joint. Immediately, Angelo sprung to his feet, lighting it for her. Calling to us from the kitchen, Giovanni said, "I think I can prepare lunch in about thirty minutes."

"I understand your brother is a great chef," Naravine commented.

Angelo answered, "If my parents didn't offer him such a high-paying job running their factory, I'm certain he would have opened his own restaurant."

"What type of factory does your family have?" I asked.

"Clothing," Naravine answered for him. "One of the finest in Milan. Please have some. Take a hit," she said passing the joint to Angelo. "It's pure hash from Tunis. Beware, this stash can really blow your mind."

Angelo carefully took the joint, holding it between his fingers and began inhaling with his eyes closed. "It is good," he said, nodding his head.

"I'll go help the chef," I anxiously interjected.

Upon entering the kitchen, Giovanni fired instructions at me. Together, we quickly prepared a simple Italian summer lunch. Giovanni seemed impressed that I knew how to prepare gourmet meals. It took us a little longer than anticipated. But when we finished, both of us carried out platters of regional cuisine, placing them on the glass dining room table. Angelo and Naravine quickly joined us.

"Bravo," Naravine said, clapping her hands. "This looks marvelous. I simply adore men who cook."

"I can't take full credit. I had some help," Giovanni added.

We prepared some prosciutto di Parma and cantaloupe for an appetizer. Then we served a pasta putanesca with extra virgin olive oil and fresh Parmigiano-Reggiano. There were also grilled primavera vegetables in a balsamic sauce, and a porcini, rock shrimp, and roasted eggplant salad in a lemon, basil, and garlic dressing. And for dessert, the plan was to serve a pear and rose sorbet, which was already prepared.

"I hope you like everything. *Buono appetito,*" Giovanni said, as he began serving the melon.

"It smells wonderful," Naravine said.

"Have you ladies thought about what you want to do later?" Giovanni asked, as he was serving the pasta.

Naravine interjected, "I would like to take a Jacuzzi and a sonellino after lunch."

"What type of drug is that?" I asked.

Everyone laughed. Naravine explained, "She needs some help with her Italian. I don't know if it is the same for all of you, but summers in Venice make me feel incredibly lazy. I love taking a long nap after lunch. Later, when it gets cooler, I would like to go for a gondola ride, and then check out the scene at Harry's Bar."

"That sounds *perfetto,*" Giovanni added.

Angelo smiled and said, "It is so peaceful here. It's nice to not have to hear the sounds of cars. I remember the last time we were in Venice, I slept like a baby."

"That's because you are a big *bambino,*" Giovanni said jokingly, as he reached over and pinched his brother's cherubic face.

Angelo answered irritably, "If I am, it's you and our parents' fault for spoiling me."

Naravine interrupted. "It sounds good to me. I'd like to be constantly indulged. I don't see anything wrong with a little pampering. Consider yourself lucky, Angelo, baby."

"What do I have to do to spoil you?" Giovanni asked Naravine.

"Everything! But first, please pour me some more Grappa," she answered.

"It would be my pleasure," Giovanni replied.

"Do you ever come to Milan?" Angelo asked me.

"Actually, I may have an excuse for my horrible Italian. This is my first time in Italy."

"That's incredible!" Giovanni said. "That calls for an important toast."

Everyone raised their garnet Venetian goblets filled with Grappa, and Naravine said jovially, "First Djuna conquered Paris, then Loire, the South of France, and now Venice. She already has a dynamic husband, an apartment in Paris overlooking the Champs-Elysées, a château in the country, and a winery. I'm hoping some of her good fortune will rub off on me."

"If you ever come to Milan, you must contact me. I promise to give you the best price on leather clothing," Giovanni said.

The phone began ringing. Naravine got up from the table and rushed to answer it. The moment she recognized the person on the line, her face turned solemn. "Yes. Yes," she kept saying. Before she left the room, she asked Giovanni to hang up the receiver. Then she dropped the phone and raced into her bedroom.

"It must be an important call," Angelo said.

"How did you meet Naravine?" I asked Giovanni.

"For several years I saw her at the Paris collections, but we never spoke. Then, of all places, I ran into her at the Marbella Club in Spain. The night we finally got together, we must have danced until dawn. I always have such a wonderful time with her; it's a never-ending party."

"How often do you get to see each other?"

"We have a seasonal arrangement. Every summer we try to meet. The last two years it has been in Venice."

Naravine had finished her conversation and returned to join us. Once again, she lit up a joint. After inhaling deeply, she passed it to Giovanni.

"Who was that on the phone? Was that your winter boyfriend or your spring lover?" Giovanni asked.

"He gets so jealous. We said we weren't going to talk about that," she playfully warned.

The phone rang for a second time. Naravine got up again to answer it. This time she smiled and flamboyantly exclaimed, "Oh, Jean-Auguste, it's so nice to hear from you. I'm fine. Here she is. Let me have you talk to her. It's your husband. You can take it in your bedroom, if you prefer."

While I was walking down the hallway, I saw the door to Naravine's bedroom was wide open, so I quickly took the call in her room. Jean-Auguste went on about his mother, her asthma, our undisciplined but sweet dogs, Jacques's threats, and more of our same problems. Nothing had changed much, except for his determination to move his mother out of our home and hire a new staff.

"I do have some good news," he said. "Your grapes have ripened. I tasted one. It was very sweet. I was right all along."

"That's nice. Does this change anything?" I asked sadly.

"That is up to you."

Before I hung up, he reminded me that he had packed my seasick pills and suggested I take them on the boat rides. As I hung up the receiver, I noticed a pad of paper by the bed. Some bold doodling in black ink caught my attention. Several times the same figure was written. 100,000. Dollar signs were written beside it. The rest of the page was filled with crosses. I didn't think much of it and returned to the living room.

Giovanni took several hits of the joint and then passed it to me. I refused. This time, however, refusing to smoke made little difference. Just from being around them, I was inhaling the plants intoxicating effects, and a deep relaxation overpowered me. My critical eye and judgmental nature began to diminish. Perhaps this was the perfect state of consciousness for an artist. I was reminded of something, Bernard, at the Beaux-Arts, had said about observing with the innocence of a child.

Stretching like a panther, Naravine stealthily got up and commented, "It's a beautiful day out. I'm going to take my nap. I'll meet all of you at the beach in about two hours."

The rest of us retired to our separate bedrooms. Once I was inside my room, I opened up all the windows and drapes, letting the fresh sea air circulate through the room. The wind billowed the white veil of mosquito net shrouding my bed. I unpacked and took out my sketchbook. It was impossible for me not to begin looking over all the work I had done, beginning in Paris and ending in Venice. I needed others' opinions about my work; however, I felt shy about asking for it, or maybe I was just afraid.

There was a soft knock at the door.

"Who is it?" I asked.

"It's me, Angelo. We're leaving early for the beach. Do you want to come along?"

"Sure. I'll be there in about ten minutes. I just have to change," I answered.

A swim would be refreshing and invigorating. The two men were waiting for me outside. When we got to the beach, Angelo ran ahead of us and began wading through the shore.

Giovanni and I spread out a towel and sat down in the sand.

"The medusas are out! The medusas are out!" Angelo exclaimed.

"What is he talking about?" I asked Giovanni.

"Jellyfish, as you say in English. Today is a bad day for swimming. The water is filled with schools of them."

This didn't deter Angelo, who remained wading in the water, as he pulled out a pink starfish and a sea urchin.

"Sea urchins are especially delicious," Angelo asserted, as he turned its black prickly body upside down and pointed to an underbelly of orange flesh.

Giovanni added, "Angelo likes to eat them raw. Frankly, it makes me ill thinking about it. I think you'll do just fine in the military, as long as they keep you close to shore. Then I'll know you'll never go hungry."

"Well look who's arrived," Angelo said.

Giovanni and I turned around.

"Let's get the show on the road," Naravine announced, prancing onto the beach. This time she was wearing a leopard bikini.

"*Pronto,*" Giovanni said, jumping to his feet, and then dusting sand off his shorts.

Giovanni and Angelo gallantly helped us on to the boat. Giovanni drove. Angelo and I sat behind him. Naravine stretched out on a section for sunbathing and kept shouting, "Go faster! Faster!"

"I'll try. You're such a speed queen," Giovanni yelled back at her.

Feeling the effects of the motion, I realized I had forgotten to take the pills before leaving. As our knots continued to increase, the boat smacked against the waves.

"I love it. Isn't this fun!" Naravine shouted over the loud noise of the engines.

"Play some music," Naravine instructed Giovianni.

The current music craze that had hit France had also reached Italy. As soon as Giovianni turned on the stereo, Naravine sang along with Sadé. "Smooth Operator," she crooned, as she moved up front, slithering between Angelo and me.

"Hurry, Giovanni, she said, "I want to get on a gondola before sunset."

The sun was beginning to wane as we approached the labyrinth of canals. The pink sky was highlighting the Baroque white domes of Santa Maria della Salute, and the faded pastel residences of the floating city. A Canaletto oil painting was in every view.

"Come on, Djuna, stand up and dance with me. You've got to take more risks to have fun," she said. Before I could answer, Angelo stood up, balancing himself carefully against the side of the boat.

"Don't move," he said to Naravine.

"Get back down. You need to fetch me my dress. It's down below," Naravine instructed Angelo.

He didn't listen and began moving and crouching about the boat, snapping photographs of the windblown model.

"Come on, Djuna. You must stand up and dance. I need my dress, Angelo," Naravine ordered.

Just as I was about to stand up, suddenly Giovanni spun his wheel, tilting the boat completely to one side. I automatically sat right back down and so did Naravine.

"What the hell?" she shouted.

Next everything seemed to happen in slow motion, at the same time, in a split second, we realized that Angelo had lost his balance and was thrown into the water.

"Holy Mother of God!" Giovanni exclaimed.

"You bloody idiot!" Naravine shouted.

Giovanni slowed down the boat, leveling his wheel. The

boats behind and ahead of us killed their engines. Endlessly, we circled over the same section of ocean, searching for Angelo, along with the authorities, when they arrived. Stupefied, we stared into the Adriatic Sea, which was reflecting the rich sienna colors of the Venetian sunset. However, all we saw was the polluted and tainted vision of accidental death—a haunting abyss that had swallowed up poor Angelo.

"O Dio! Non è possibile!" Giovanni kept shouting, as he vomited and trembled. We felt so helpless. There was nothing more we could do. Angelo was gone. The *polizia* forced us to give up our search, and promised to telephone us if his body or any articles of clothing resurfaced.

My legs felt as if they were made of steel as we climbed the stairs to the villa. Giovanni could barely move. Naravine and I grabbed hold of his arms and dragged him up the steps. My shoulder felt as though it was dislocating in the process; he was heavier than we anticipated.

Once inside the house, Giovanni called his parents in Milan. For hours he sobbed over the phone, while Naravine and I sank like preserved mummies into the sofa, unable to move or talk. After his conversation ended, the three of us smoked a joint and polished off another bottle of Grappa. I wanted to forget this day had ever happened. Tormenting me, and certainly all of us, was the memory of our empty voices calling out for Angelo as we stared into the Adriatic, only to see the zigzagging patterns of our boat's wake and a rainbow stream of gasoline mirroring our petrified faces.

Giovanni mumbled, "Since he was a baby, he swam like a dolphin. He loved the sea. I can't believe he's gone. I just can't. Maybe he's safe. I have to believe that."

In my inebriated state, I kept repeating the same words. "How could this have happened? Why? Why?"

During most of the evening, Naravine sat on the couch, hunched over, with her face buried in her hands. It seemed that the grueling night would never end, along with Giovanni's hysterical cries of disbelief. Unable to take hours more of this tragic event, I stumbled to my bedroom, collapsing on the white feather bed. A reprieve came in the form of a drunken slumber; but this was only temporary. I woke several hours later, when the reality of the accident returned to haunt me, leaving a sour feeling in the pit of my stomach. It was too late to call Jean-Auguste. I wished I was with him in Loire or in Paris. Without turning on the light, I removed my clothes. An ominous feeling came over me; it felt like someone was in the room, a voyeur. Was it Angelo's spirit? Shivering, I slid inside the cool sheets. Turning on my left side, I stretched out one leg. Something stirred on the other side of the bed. My body stiffened. Before I could scream, a hand reached out and grazed my neck. A familiar voice said, "I won't hurt you. Please let me comfort you."

I wanted to run away, yet was unable to move. In the darkness, I was prey, a lost beetle; a black widow had me, and would soon be carrying me back to her web. Strong hands began massaging the arches of my feet, my aching calves, and legs, moving up to my back and shoulders. Shifting motions of fingers strummed over my entire body. Then lean, muscular legs wrapped around me. Simultaneously, hot lavender-blossom honey and whiskey was poured over my back allowing me to feel warmth, which I desperately needed. Scalding flesh was penetrating through my icy pores. Soft lips found my shoulders, my neck and ears, finding erogenous zones that I never knew before existed. Kisses of devotion blended in with my salty tears of fear and dismay.

"You need to have a child. You must become a mother," the voice said.

My body was weakening as my emotions were exposed. I didn't have the strength to fight. I was tired of being alone. The stranger in my bed continued to empower me with forsaken pleasures.

"I care for you deeply. More than you'll ever know. You must listen to me and do as I say," the voice said.

Finally, just when I was about to turn over, to completely surrender myself to this wild abandonment, I felt a wave of frigid air blow over me. Once again, the bed was empty and cold. With my legs and arms, I searched the sheets for that seductive warm body, for those comforting and gentle hands. Vanished. The moment was gone, as dead as poor, sweet Angelo. A rancid fate.

The following morning, when I awoke, I questioned whether last night had simply been a baffling chimera, a figment of my imagination. My head began pounding. The wine and the hash hadn't agreed with me. I hoped a hot shower would make me feel better. Then, as I got out of bed, I accidentally knocked over a bottle of whiskey on my beside table. I gasped, as the sad truth lodged itself in my heart along with an overwhelming guilt for having accepted another lover. How could I forgive myself? More than anything else, I now wanted to go home. Staying in this villa was suffocating me. I had to leave—at once!

Without disturbing the others, I quietly carried my luggage out of the house and down the long passageway. Luck was in my favor, as the moment I arrived on the beach, a water taxi was driving past. Frantically, I began shouting and waving my hands. Within minutes, the boat approached the dock. The driver collected my luggage and I jumped on. I turned briefly to look back at the hilltop. Naravine was standing on the veranda, waving to me. Ignoring her, I turned my head away, and faced the direction of the inviting morning sun.

"Please drive fast. *Rapido!* I must get to Marco Polo airport," I shouted.

"Subito! Si Signorina," the taxi driver replied, moving the silver throttles forward. Since it was early in the morning, the water was still, unperturbed by other boats' wakes. My return ticket was set for another two weeks. It didn't matter. I couldn't wait. I had to catch the next flight to Paris, no matter the cost. The Riva quickly picked up speed. Closing my eyes, I held on tightly to the railings, as the boat levitated off the surface of the water like a hydrofoil.

Goddesses, Wine, Dead Artists & Chocolate

The Journals of Joaquím Carlos Cortez

PARIS, DECEMBER 1939, NEW YEAR'S EVE

Our living situation has become more comfortable, as each woman has found her purpose. One plays the role of a domestic wife and mother and the other a mistress. Isabella has been studying Russian literature at the Sorbonne. Sweet Eliane spends most of her time caring for my son, taking him for long strolls along the Champs-Elysées. Even Bijoux, Sylvie's Burmese cat adores her, following Eliane all around the apartment. Everybody has forgotten Sylvie, (who could never fit into any category), except for me. I never tell either of the women that Sylvie is formost on my mind. She is who I think about when I fall asleep at night and when I first wake in the morning. I miss her more since she is gone. It's not fair of me to make comparisons among all these women, as they are completely different types of people with varying backgrounds. But Isabella and Eliane have bourgeois tastes. They can't discuss the museums of the world with me, or even the great masters. Nor do I have the time (between painting and traveling to survey the winery) to educate them. Only once was I able to show Eliane the Louvre, and the endless rooms of Greco-Roman sculptures only seemed to tire her. Neither of them have traveled extensively or know how to recommend the finest wine at a restaurant. How did I take my wife so much for granted?

It seems that Eliane and Isabella both accept the limitations of this arrangement. Marcel likes to tease me about it when we meet.

"How can you love two women? Tell me what it's like? Is it complicated?" he asks, in his poetically musing way.

"It's rather simple," I tell him.

"Do you love both of them equally?" he asks.

"I don't love them at all," I say without any emotion.

"That is really disgusting and cruel!" he exclaims.

"I don't know what love is anymore. All I know is that I believe in lust—pure physical attraction. I also respect honest friendships and for me these have been mutually exclusive. I will never love anyone again. This may be unfair to Isabella and Eliane. The sad truth is, I can only give them portions of my affection, scraps from my decaying heart."

"I don't know whether to envy or condemn you," Marcel answers.

"Just pity me," I tell him.

Both women have accepted that I alternate spending evenings with them and sharing their beds. On the nights I spend with Eliane and my son, Isabella often goes out with students. I try to divide my time evenly between them. However, my lust for Isabella sometimes wins. I am mesmerized at how her beauty brightens before me, as each day, she grows more confident and passionate. Sometimes, I can't wait to be alone with her. We set a date to spend New Year's Eve together in my studio with the birds. Eliane agrees to stay in the other apartment with Emile.

That evening, Isabella becomes extremely amorous. Throwing her arms around me, she says, "I adore you. You're so good to me. It's almost a new year. It's time you stop this nonsense and marry me. I know you love me more than Eliane. You only feel sorry for her," she boldly states.

I become cataleptic, unable to move. I count to ten so I don't say something I'll later regret. "I never want to marry again. I've done it once before. I don't believe that it's right for me. It means nothing."

"Not to me," she answers irritably, as she struts over to the divan.

"Don't I make you happy? I pay for all your classes, books, and clothes. Is there anything I'm depriving you of?" I ask.

"Yes. I'm sick of sharing you. And when I go to the cafés in Saint-Germain-des-Prés, I hear whispers."

"What do they say?"

"At the Deux Magots, a group of women will point at me and say in their loud whispering voices, 'That's one of Joaquím Carlos's mistress models. She's not as beautiful as how he paints her.'

"The next time I go to the Lipp instead. Yet, there I find another group of women who say 'There's one of Joaquím Carlos's prostitues. Did you know he often selects them off the streets? I heard he has so many women that he locks some of them up in his château. God knows what he does to them! It is rumored that he makes the Marquis de Sade look like a saint.' "

I burst out laughing. "What? That's absolutely ludicrous. I should be so lucky. I couldn't work at getting such a notorious reputation, even if I wanted to."

"Don't you care? Doesn't it bother you that people think you're a sexual deviant?"

"Let them gossip. You shouldn't be bothered about what café society thinks. I don't care what those bitches say about me, as long as I'm still a topic of conversation and people buy my paintings. Princess Mitya taught me that. The day people stop talking about me is the day I'll start worrying."

She places her hands on her hips and reprimands, "You're a selfish and arrogant bastard!"

"I know. I can't argue with that. Then leave me."

Shaking her head, she says, "I can't. You've captured my heart. But I hate having so little control over my life. I wish I was like your first wife and had my own money."

"Please don't ever bring Sylvie into this. That's not fair," I warn.

"I'm sorry."

"Nobody appreciates what they have. Every woman I've known, from high society ladies to the street urchin girls, wants something else. Either it's a different hair color, a different body, more money, less money, more men, or less men. Whatever it is, women especially want to change their fate. I can't help you. I wish I could."

"What about men? I don't think that women are the only culprits. What do you want that you can't have?" she asks me.

"I would like to have more respect as a painter without having to die. And I would like another sold-out show."

"I need respect too. I hate being in the same category as prostitutes, just because I'm associated with you."

"You must know I couldn't admire any woman more than I do you. Your professors take you seriously at the Sorbonne. You must forget about these inane strangers. They don't know anything."

"I'm also praised by my comrades."

"I thought you stopped going to those Communist meetings."

"My political beliefs haven't changed. I don't care that you can't see that Communism will cure this mess in our society. We have to fight Fascism, organize more unions, create an egalitarian society for men and women of all races. What is wrong with these ideals?" she asks.

"Nothing. It's just that you mention the word 'fight.' That bothers me. I want peaceful solutions with absolute nonviolence."

"That's impossible! I think the truth is you don't want to give up your capitalistic ways."

"Wait a minute, señorita. I never claimed to be a capitalist."

"You love beautiful things and that takes money," she declares.

"We always end up in the same tangle. You're such a feisty thing. I won't change you, so don't try to convert me."

"Fine. Come here, *Carlosito.* I'll forgive your arrogance if you'll forgive my politics." She puts on a tango record.

"Let's dance," she announces.

The fireplace is ablaze with flickering amber flames. We tango as the parrots fly through the room, chirping and vocalizing their tropical love calls. Outside, it is freezing. The windows fog, and the shape of the crescent moon is distorted into an eclipse. Unable to withhold my desire any longer, I tear off my shirt, and pull my mistress toward me. Freely, she removes her long Gypsy dress. In that instant, no woman matters more to me than my precious Isabella. She becomes my solid foundation—mother earth—pure womanhood. Twirling around, we then laugh and collapse on the floor, breathless and hot. She has fallen under me. As I ease myself on top of her, her face beams like a smoky topaz. Her beauty is like a rare gemstone found in the jungles of South America. I want to treasure her in a jewelry box all to myself. Miraculously, somehow I hope to fill her with my power, bestow life in her barren womb, as I know this is what she ultimately craves.

EIGHTEEN

Djuna Cortez

It was midafternoon when I quietly, almost surreptitiously, let myself into the château. The front door was of course unlocked. This wasn't uncommon, because the staff was usually distracted by Madame de Briard's meticulousness. She would tend to an omnipresence of gathered dust, rather than to the importance of security. It was no wonder that Jacques had repeatedly trespassed. As I walked inside, I hoped he wasn't hiding somewhere, waiting to accost me. In fact, it was rather daunting entering the silent hall, not even any of the dogs had barked. As I stood for several minutes in the foyer, a new maid rushed in, carrying two gray feather dusters. She was probably the same age as myself, and was dressed in a black-and-white uniform with a frilly lace apron.

"The bell didn't ring. I didn't know anyone was here. I'll be right back," she said when she noticed me.

She quickly returned, having discarded the feather dusters, and instead was carrying a gift bag decorated with blue ribbons and tissue papers. Before I had time to introduce myself, she handed me the gift. Inside was a box of Swiss chocolates and a rare bottle of Château Hélianthe d'Or, one of the most valuable, bottled in the sixties. The label was one of Joaquím

Carlos's first oil paintings of Sylvie lounging in the gardens of Versailles.

"Monsieur de Briard would like to welcome you to the château. He would like you to enjoy these gifts and hopes you will have a pleasant and relaxing stay here. If there's anything you need, please feel free to let me know or anyone else working on staff. We are at your service," the demure maid said politely.

"That's very nice of you. However, I live here. I'm Monsieur de Briard's wife," I casually informed her, hiding my irritation at this display of ostentation and generosity on my husband's part.

"Oh, my! I didn't even know he was married. I thought there was only one Madame de Briard. I'm so sorry," the maid said, bowing her head and then running off toward the kitchen. The practicalities of the matter were that she had completely ignored that I was standing in the entrance hall with my luggage, and that I needed assistance. But I wasn't about to make a fuss, so I left the valises and ran upstairs to our bedroom, hoping to find Jean-Auguste and our dogs. Then halfway up the stairs, I smelled cigar smoke and heard conversation and jubilant cries coming from the upstairs library. As I approached the room, the laughing grew louder and the smoke more noxious. Without knocking, I barged in and found my husband seated on a winged-back embroidered chair, puffing away on a fat cigar as he chatted with a group of men who were seated in a circle surrounding him.

"Djuna!" Jean-Auguste exclaimed, extinguishing his Havana and jumping to his feet. "I didn't expect to see you . . . home, so soon, that is. I was going to join you in Venice next week. Is everything all right?" he asked.

"Not really. What's going on here? Who are these men? Why are all of you such a mess?" I asked. His boots and clothing were caked in mud, there were red and purple stains on his pants, and sections of his clothing looked splattered in blood. All of the men's clothes were as filthy as Jean-Auguste's. He gently guided me outside the library and said, "These men are very important for business. You won't believe everything I've accomplished in the short amount of time you were away. It's all worked out so well. What a thrill it is to see you," he said, lightly touching the side of my face. I tried to embrace him, but he stepped back.

"I don't want you to get your clothes dirty. We'll have plenty of time to catch up on that later," he said.

"This is so unlike you. I've never seen you in such a state. What is that dreadful odor on your clothes?" I asked.

"We were gallivanting in the forest. You should get out there when you have a chance. The blackberries are in season and are deliciously sweet. We brought back lots of delicacies for dinner. It's a big surprise. You'll see. Now I must return to the guests. I promised to give them a tour of the château de Triomphe and both wineries. Some are staying over there, as well as here. We'll probably get cleaned up at the other château, before they see *Maman.*"

"Where is she?" I asked, hiding my dread.

"She's moved back."

"How is she feeling?"

"Her asthma is much better."

"Are the renovations completed?" I asked.

"Some workers are still doing some finishing touches."

"Where are our dogs? Did they miss me?"

"They're with *Maman.* She's been taking excellent care of them. You need not worry. Did you meet some of our new staff?" he asked.

"Yes. I was surprised how you hired them so quickly. The maid that greeted me didn't even know you were married," I said.

"That must be *Maman's* fault. She hired everyone. After I had fired Jacques and Mionne, she got the name of a couple who had worked for some friends of hers. The three maids were sent over from her place. Now we have five new people, a cook, butler, and three housekeepers. Did you notice how everything is sparkling around here?"

I nodded, not admitting that I hadn't paid any attention to the housekeeping.

"The cook is incredible. She's Cordon Bleu, and I'm sure she could teach you a lot of things. Fanette is her name. Even her name sounds like a dessert, doesn't it? Anyway, I think her last cooking school was the Ritz-Escoffier. You'll be amazed at what she can do. She's preparing an incredible dinner party for us tonight."

"Tonight! I was hoping we could be alone together."

"I'm sorry. Let me at least walk you to the bedroom," he said.

When we entered the room, I immediately took off my shoes and sat down on the bed. He stood beside me.

"Where is your luggage?"

"Downstairs."

"I'll have someone bring it right up," he said, turning to walk out.

"Please just stay a little longer," I pleaded.

"I'm afraid I must go. I don't think you're aware that the men you saw are entrepreneurs from all over Europe. Most are wine merchants and distributors. They're all very important in the industry. In fact, a few may even be interested in purchasing this property. This is an opportunity we can't miss out on. Anyway, as *Maman* had mentioned, we're way overdue this year as far as entertaining is concerned. It is important that you get yourself looking stunning for dinner tonight. Do you understand?"

"Yes, but I don't think I'll be able to . . ." I wanted to throw myself in his arms and sob in an emotional outburst. Yet I knew it would be better to hold myself back and try to maintain my reason.

My voice trembled as I said, "I really need to talk to you. Can you stay with me for a while?"

"I wish I could, but I can't keep them waiting much longer. We'll have plenty of time to catch up later. Just get some rest. You do look tired. Please be ready by seven for dinner."

"I've missed you," I said. Maybe I should have spoken louder, as he continued to walk away, closing the door behind him without responding to me.

My luggage soon arrived. Once I began unpacking, my head started spinning. I hoped the vertigo wasn't coming back. It had to have been that I was feeling completely overwrought, plus my hangover lingered. At the same time, I couldn't stop thinking about everything that had happened in Venice. However, not wanting to give in to my exhaustion, as I was afraid it would overtake me if I let it, I forced myself to get some fresh air.

After retrieving some art supplies from my bedroom closet, I decided to hike above the winery. Occassionally, a few field workers interupted my view, but other than those disturbances, it was a perfect day for painting. The skies were clear; summer had brightened the landscape, as everywhere wildflowers were in bloom, coloring the hectares of land in patches of lavender and golden yellow. And finally, above the vineyards, the sunflowers had started to open their bold faces, making the hills look like they were frosted in liquid gold, thereby revealing the reason for the given name of the château. I tried to mix into my oils some colors that appeared warmer, transforming them into crisp earth tones that sizzled with the high temperatures. As I struggled with blending the exact shades, I began feeling regretful and wished I hadn't so quickly abandoned my art studies. Being self-taught was more challenging than I had anticipated. I needed patience, which I often lacked, not to mention the rigorous discipline needed to work everyday. Each time I sketched or painted, I kept forgetting what I had briefly learned; even my vision seemed to be narrowing, as I was feeling further distanced from the zealous inspiration I had first discovered when I arrived in France. It was perplexing that I couldn't figure out what was missing in my artwork. Perhaps only the right teacher could pinpoint that. Furthermore, painting alone, I feared always remaining at this novice level. Nevertheless, I kept working. To study more details of the valley, I glanced through a pair of binoculars. Then something unexpected clouded my vision. A sleek, red Aston Martin convertible pulled into the driveway. My heart began racing, as I saw Naravine stepping out of the car. She was carrying an overnight bag.

My timing was bad, as I had returned to the château at the same moment Jean-Auguste and his guests were coming back from the wineries. The second my husband saw me, he latched onto me and without any warning, began introducing me to some of his guests. Then he led everyone into the main living room, where we found Naravine and Xavier, both of them lounging on a sofa. Naravine was attached to Xavier like an octobus, her arms tightly wrapped around him, and her lips kissing his neck. Jean-Auguste cleared his throat, watching Naravine disentangle herself. However, he refused to speak to them or introduce either of them to his guests. As I stood there, I gave Xavier and Naravine a brief acknowledgment. Naravine smiled audaciously at me in return. Perturbed and irritated, Jean-Auguste took hold of my arm and led me back to the foyer, where we stood by the staircase, away from everyone.

"I didn't expect to see her. Did you invite her?" he asked.

"No. I had no idea she'd be here."

"Xavier must have asked her without my permission," he complained.

This was the time I needed to play it cool, stay calm and composed. I couldn't have imagined that he knew anything. I would just have to pretend that nothing had happened in Venice, and try to forget about the death that horrified all of us who had witnessed it. That evening, I told myself that I would have to forget everything, including my infidelity. It would be better for all of us if I could begin at that very moment and put on a fake, placating smile, like Patrice de Briard usually did, as I greeted the guests.

"How can we get rid of her?" he asked me.

"What do you mean? She's our friend."

"From now on, we need to be around more sophisticated people. She's completely wrong for this type of crowd. Can you make up something and tell her to leave?" he asked me.

"I don't think I can do that. It wouldn't be polite. I was after all her guest in Venice. It's only fair that we reciprocate."

"I find her so tiresome sometimes, and she's so wrapped up in herself. God, I hope she doesn't go on again about her confiscated monkey story or how she had sex with some voodoo witch doctor in South America."

"I believe it was in Africa."

"Yes, well, can't you tell her that we don't have any rooms left?" he said.

"I don't feel comfortable saying that."

"Never mind then. Let her stay. I'll go tell the servants to add another place setting," he said irritably.

Before he left, two of the guests came toward us, and Jean-Auguste immediately changed his disposition, putting on a warm grin.

"Is this your lovely wife?" an older man inquired.

"Yes, Monsieur Dalmassot, this is my little *femme,*" he said, patting my rear as if I were a well-bred sow.

Monsieur Dalmassot, who was a stout, balding man, scrutinized me with rather bulbous eyes that must have been caused by a thyroid abnormality. Then he turned to a servant passing by and asked, "Could you bring us more wine and cigars?"

"Please do that right away," Jean-Auguste told the butler.

I was beginning to feel like a goldfish in a glass bowl who was being eyed by some hungry felines.

"This is Monsieur Henri Beville. He owns an outstanding winery in Burgundy. Please excuse the way my *petite femme* is dressed," Jean-Auguste said, pointing to the loose blue smock that I wore over my shorts. "You see she wants to be a painter. She's been out in the country pretending to be Van Gogh."

"Fortunately, I haven't lost my mind," I quickly retorted.

"It's a beautiful place you have here," Monsieur Beville said animatedly. His voice was high-pitched and flamboyant with a distinctive whining tone.

The butler promptly returned with the cigars and began serving everyone wine. Other guests came out of the living room and began to approach us, including Naravine and Xavier.

"I'd love to try a tasty handmade La Planta," Xavier said, greedily reaching for the silver tray of cigars.

"I'd love a Cuban too. Will Djuna have one?" Naravine asked Jean-Auguste.

He answered for me. "I find cigar smoking on most women to be quite vulgar. Djuna certainly isn't the type." He turned to me and said, "It's time you get yourself looking absolutely gorgeous for dinner. She doesn't always look this Bohemian," he apologized again to the guests.

"I can't tonight. I'm sorry I won't be joining all of you," I answered, selecting a wrapped cigar and swiftly placing it in the front pocket of my smock.

"I would like to speak to you in private," Jean-Auguste whispered in my ear. "Please excuse us," he said, smiling to his guests, as he angrily grabbed hold of my wrist, dragging me into another sitting room. His grip was intensifying.

"That's the wrist I broke. You're hurting me," I squealed.

"And you're doing the same to me, behaving in this childish way. What is wrong with you? I don't understand. You must be feeling better, since you were outside painting."

At that moment, I didn't know what had come over me. Perhaps I had misspoken when I said that I hadn't lost my sanity like Van Gogh, as I was quickly losing it. The thought of becoming like Patrice de Briard suddenly revolted me. Then, like a fine rubber band stretched too thinly, something inside me snapped. I couldn't pretend any longer that we had this perfect marriage. I was tired of being the giving and accommodating wife who nobody appreciated. I decided instead to play another challenging role.

"I've been upset the entire time I've been back. However, you haven't paid much attention to me to notice. All I've been wanting is to spend some time alone with you. But that seems to be too much to ask for. Naravine and I saw somebody tragically drown in Venice. A young man lost his life. You may not care, but I do. This has been upsetting me so much that I had to come home early."

"You say Naravine also saw this."

"Yes, and the man's brother. It was terrible." I felt myself shudder at the recollection of the incident.

"I am sorry. But Naravine seems just fine to me and is out there socializing. Maybe it's not so bad that's she here. After all, she certainly knows how to carry on an interesting conversation. The guests are utterly entertained. Why can't you be more like her?"

"How could you say that! Five minutes ago you insulted her. Are you asking me not to have feelings?" I shouted angrily.

"No, I'm telling you to grow up. I don't have time for your feminine wailings. You have a responsibility to me and as an owner of this château. We're both entertaining tonight and

you're expected to be present. There are no excuses. I want
you dressed by seven. Is that understood?" he impatiently
asked.

I turned my head away from him and refused to respond.

"I don't have time for this. There's a lot of work I must do.
I have to supervise the new cook and oversee the table set-
tings. I don't want to burden you with all that. All I'm asking
is for you to show up. Get a grip on yourself. You look a
mess. You should wear your black Dior dress or the Valentino
with some pearls. Please don't disappoint me," he warned.

Storming out of the sitting room, he slammed the hand-
painted door behind him. Before I had a chance to leave, Naravine sauntered into the paneled room.

"It's obvious that he makes you unhappy. You must feel
powerless," she observed.

"You're more insightful than I thought. However, this isn't
any concern of yours," I answered irritably.

Two servants entered the room. One handed us each a glass
of red wine, while another passed a platter of hors d'oeuvres.
Our conversation was silenced until Naravine had made her
selection and the servers left. I reclined on a Second Empire
divan and took several sips of wine, hoping that the rich Bourgueil would soon relieve my agitation.

Naravine got up from a chair across from me and then sat
down at the opposite end of the same divan. Coquettishly, she
slowly leaned toward me, as she held out a napkin covered
with several miniature quiche Lorraines.

"Let me feed you. You look like you're in dire need of
some nourishment," she said, in a comforting tone.

"No, thank you. I'm not hungry," I adamantly protested.

She quickly pulled back without flinching from my rebuff.
"You deserve much better than him," she said, finishing all
the appetizers that were on her napkin.

"You once told me I was so lucky to be married to him."

"I was mistaken. You should ask yourself, is he worth putting up with?"

"Maybe you're right. I do deserve someone better," I said
reflectively.

Naravine's dark eyes began to sparkle with animation, until
I replied, "There has to be a man out there who is caring and

sensitive, more understanding of a woman's feelings."

Naravine chuckled and said, "That would be a miracle! I've never known any men to be like that. Did you tell him about Venice?" she asked.

"Only about the loss of Angelo. But I would appreciate—"

She interrupted me. "I know. Don't worry. Everything between us is private. Anything you tell me, I'll make sure to keep in confidence."

"Thank you."

"I wish you luck if you stick with the marriage. Jean-Auguste is . . . well, I shouldn't tell you this . . . no, no, never mind. Anyway, I don't know if I could take having to constantly deal with the reputation of his family and all those stuffy business engagements. As you know, I like to speak my mind. It would be very difficult for me. And that mother! Isn't she a cow?"

"She isn't the easiest person to get along with," I admitted. "I better get ready for dinner," I said, standing up.

Naravine reached for my hand and clasped my fingers, which were splattered in oil paint. "Don't rationalize things too much, luv. You'll be better off if you leave him."

Before I reached the stairs, Jean-Auguste was obstructing my way. He was standing surrounded by his entourage of winegrowers. Another side of his personality came out while he spoke to the men; it was less taciturn, more boastful, and full of machismo, so much so that it turned my stomach. For the first time, to my knowledge, he bragged, "That was quite a killing. What a thrill it is, after all that struggle, when that baby finally hits the ground." He turned to me and said, "It will be quite a meal tonight. We caught some young venison, several rabbits, and an elk."

Trying to hide my shock and revulsion, I quickly ran upstairs without answering him. After I had entered our bedroom, I marched into our walk-in cedar closet. As usual, all of his shirts and suits were perfectly organized in sections by his color-coding system. His sweaters and T-shirts were folded in neat piles, arranged by the four seasons. Nothing was out of place, which drastically differed from my side of the closet, where everything was thrown together. Following his instructions, I selected the black Dior dress. Next I searched for some accessories, but I couldn't find what I was looking for. When I was searching for a new package of nylons, I quickly looked inside Jean-Auguste's underwear drawer, thinking that maybe a maid had accidently misplaced it there. Something struck me as odd. All of his briefs were tousled in a large mound, instead of being lined in symmetrical rows like they usually were. The tip of something bright was sticking out of the pile. Removing the briefs, I discovered a folded picture postcard. My curiosity got the best of me. Looking more closely, I saw it was a color photograph of an exotic beach. I turned the postcard over and read the explanation in English. It was Mykonos, one of the Greek islands. The card was sent to Jean-Auguste. It read:

Having a wonderful time. Great weather and food. You should be here. I can't wait for us to be together soon!

Love, moi.

I read the card several times, trying to interpret the sender's incomplete sentences. It was hard to tell if this was a romantic postcard or just a platonic one. The penmanship was composed in concise bold capitals, without any distinctive flair. The writing didn't look at all familiar. Who was *moi?* This had to be intimate. Who else would feel comfortable writing *me* instead of their name. Was it Naravine? Was that why she was encouraging me to leave him, so that she could take my place? It was all so confusing. Dinner hour was fast approaching. Hurriedly, I put the postcard back the way I had found it and left the closet. Furiously, I tore off my clothes, tossing them across the room. At that moment, I couldn't care less about tidiness.

As I walked to the bathroom, I stepped over my smock and noticed the cigar had fallen out of the front pocket. Instead of leaving it there, I picked it up and set it down on my bathroom vanity. I hoped a shower would invigorate me. Instead, the longer I remained under the hot water, the more irate I became, deeply resenting Jean-Auguste's controlling and secretive disposition. When I got out, the telephone intercom was ringing.

The phone was set on a mirrored counter, which was beside my collection of perfume bottles.

Jean-Auguste's voice resonated loudly: "Hello, *chérie*, how's it going?"

"How's what going?" I asked abruptly.

"When do you think you'll be ready?" he inquired. This time there was a sugar-coated tone to his voice.

"I just got out of the shower," I answered, out of breath.

"How much longer will you be?"

"I don't know."

"Don't be late. I'll send a maid in to help you."

"No! I don't need any help. I'm going as fast as I can," I impatiently shouted.

"Some new guests are downstairs and they're anxious to meet you. I thought you could come down sooner."

"I'm not ready," I stated angrily.

"Well, hurry up. I better get back to them," he said.

My hands were trembling as I hung up the telephone. As I began applying makeup, eyeliner and mascara smeared under my eyes and above my right eyebrow, where a thin scar remained from my stitches. When I began applying lipstick, resentful thoughts began to bubble to the surface. I became aware that from the beginning of our marriage, I had resented changing my last name and always playing by his rules. All this time, all he wanted was a replica of his mother, a wife to wear a mask of charm, to be affable, and to always reflect his impeccable taste. In truth, I would never be able to satisfy him, as in his eyes his beloved *Maman* was always perfect and no woman could ever compare; therefore, I was to become the adornment, an object, a decoration, a doormat, not a person.

"I don't want this. This isn't right," I shrieked.

Acting out my indignation, in a sudden frenzy, I covered my face with red lipstick, until I looked like a pathetic circus clown. Then I forcefully swung my arms, sending all my perfume bottles crashing to the gray-veined marble floors. Several oversized Chanel bottles of Coco and Cristal shattered. Exhaling a sigh of relief, I tried not to think of the hundreds of wasted francs.

All the rooms in the château were vast, with high ceilings

and solid limestone walls. Events change, yet people's sorrows remain the same. When Sylvie was raped, no one heard her screams, nor did anyone hear mine. My breathing quieted: glass fragments settled in the amber and gold liquid. Staring at me in the mirror was an unrecognizable woman; her face looked like a tropical fish with hollow, stained black eyes, ruby lips, and cheeks.

Perhaps, I was as much to blame, allowing his mystery to remain attractive. Meanwhile, a wall was growing between us. I realized too late that the top of the wall was covered with electric coils of barbed wire. Moreover, the reality was that I had fallen for a selfish man—someone who gave affection as miserly as my father had. Did I need more patience? Maybe if I could hold on, I might be able to change Jean-Auguste. My hope would be that I could get an important message through to him. Tonight would be the night for me to try.

I walked over to the bar of our bedroom suite and pulled out a crystal carafe of Napoléon brandy. The smooth liquid warmed my throat and vocal chords. I could breathe again, gather courage, and venture forward. Outside my window, I smoked a Rothmans cigarette and watched a cluster of candy-colored balloons drift across the sky, sailing south. After finishing the snifter, my problems felt as if they had departed my body and were floating away like the lost helium balloons. I felt sorry for the owner; a disheartened child must be crying.

Once more, I returned to the bathroom. The phone was ringing, but I didn't answer. It was time I surrendered to the responsibilities of the evening and clean myself up. I opened a bar of Provençal lavender soap and lathered my hands, washing away my clown mask.

A naked face stared back at me in the mirror. Like my bottles of perfume, I felt shattered—broken. What I detested in others, I was becoming, as I could not see beyond my own selfish concerns. Instead of being the complacent and charming wife, tonight I needed to provoke, rebel.

Deciding to be comfortable, I pulled out a pair of blue jeans and a white blouse from my closet. This was my home after all, and I could dress the way I wanted. There was no time to blow dry my hair, so I let it dry naturally in long ringlets.

Jean-Auguste preferred it straight or pinned-up.

Barefoot and casually dressed, I entered the living room and lit up the cigar. All the guests were in formal attire, including my husband, who was wearing a new tuxedo. My clothes may have worked for a party in Malibu, but not at this event. I stood out in contrast. Jean-Auguste was dumbfounded when he saw me and couldn't speak.

A servant offered me a glass of champagne and passed a tray of salmon mousse. Before I could help myself to the appetizer, Jean-Auguste calmly sauntered toward me, grabbing hold of my left arm. "I'd like to see you in private," he whispered in a commanding tone. Then without letting go of me, he led me into the kitchen. Servants were milling about preparing hors d'oeuvres and pouring glasses of wine and champagne. I never expected what was to follow. After I blew a cloud of smoke in his face, he grabbed the cigar from my mouth and threw it across the kitchen. A servant rushed to pick it up. Suddenly he struck me with his open palm. My heart felt as if it had been crushed the moment his hand imprinted the side of my face.

"How dare you humiliate me like this!" he shouted.

I bit my lip to keep from acknowledging the stinging sensation on my cheek, and instead of crying I began laughing nervously. This enraged him even more and he threw me against the granite counters, pinning down my shoulders. I shouted: "I don't know who you are anymore. I'm not a doll who you can dress up and take out to play with. And I'm not your cold-ass mother, either! I have feelings and needs that you so blatantly choose to ignore. I don't want you running this place anymore. I'm selling it and that's final! From now on, I refuse to follow more rules unless I make them."

"How dare you speak to me this way. After all I've been doing for you!"

I knew he wanted to slap me again. But I didn't care. I especially enjoyed humiliating him in front of the new servants. "I don't think I matter to you at all," I said. I almost brought up the postcard, but I held my tongue.

"Who do you think I'm doing all of this for? This is all for you," he said, pointing to the busy staff.

"I don't believe you. I think this is all for your mother."

Jean-Auguste turned to the staff and ordered: "We'll be eating promptly at eight. You don't have to come," he said without looking at me, as he began strutting out of the kitchen.

He had no sooner left the kitchen when Naravine rushed in to see me.

"The bastard," she said, coming toward me. "Get her some ice," Naravine instructed a servant.

"How could he do that? How do you feel?" she asked.

"I'm fine," I answered politely. "You don't need to be here. I can take care of myself. Please go back to the party."

"I want to help," Naravine insisted. The cook quickly brought us an ice pack. "Does that hurt?" Naravine asked, as she applied the cold compress to my cheek.

"A little." I groaned, downplaying the pain.

"That should stop some of the bruising and swelling. I've been through it a few times myself. You should also take a couple of aspirins. Come on, luv, I'll help you upstairs."

We walked up the servants' stairway, beside a dumbwaiter, as this way we wouldn't run into Jean-Auguste or any of the guests.

"Where do you keep aspirin?" she asked, as we entered the bedroom.

"In the bathroom medicine cabinet."

"I'll get it for you," she offered.

"That's not necessary. I can get it," I said entering my bathroom. She had followed me and quickly glanced at the broken perfume bottles without making a comment.

"Let's see if some makeup won't help cover up that nasty bruise," Naravine said.

The intercom rang. I declined to answer. This time the volume seemed louder. "Are you all right?" Jean-Auguste asked in a businesslike manner.

Naravine answered for me. "She's fine. What do you want?"

"Nothing. I just want to see how she is. I feel terrible about what happened."

"Well, you should," Naravine reprimanded.

"Is she there?" he asked.

"Yes, but she doesn't want to talk to you."

"I understand. I want her to know that I'm very sorry. I

don't know what came over me. I do hope she'll forgive me," he said apologetically.

I refused to respond and so did Naravine.

"I know Djuna must be terribly angry right now. And I don't blame her. Please tell her that she doesn't have to come down to dinner. A meal will be sent up to her. Also, *Maman* has arrived and would like to bring up the dogs."

I shook my head.

Naravine answered for me. "Now isn't a good time."

"Then maybe later," he said, before ending the phone call.

"God, she's the last person I need to see," I admitted.

"What are you doing?" Naravine asked, as I was fetching my black dress and makeup brushes.

"I'm getting ready for the dinner party."

"But, you don't have to."

"I know, that's why I'm going," I replied.

"Then let me try to cover up that bruise," she suggested.

"Don't bother. I want everyone to notice."

~

Naravine and I showed up in time for the main entrée: elk Stroganoff, roast venison, and rabbit in a Provençal sauce. I refused to eat the meats. During dinner, Jean-Auguste mercilessly flirted with me by smiling and winking and occasionally touching my shoulder. He pretended our fight had never happened. I imagined he must have made up a story for the guests that I had slipped in the shower. Nobody asked me about my disastrous-looking face. Throughout the party, the guests continued to praise the wine and culinary arts. Patrice droned on for hours about winemaking and how diligently her son worked at his profession.

"The venison and elk are absolutely delicious. Most women aren't hunters, but if they were in touch with their primal nature, they would be. My son is quite a hunter to take down an elk. How did you do it exactly? Could you explain it to everyone?" Patrice de Briard asked.

"My Remmington carabine and scope helped a great deal. I can also run quite fast. There's always a risk, if the target is wrong, that an animal of that size will charge at you. However, in this case my shot was precise; I aimed for the heart. It was almost an instant death," Jean-Auguste gleefully recounted.

I was cringing as he explained this. Mother and son were beaming. Everyone else seemed enthralled, except for Naravine who was only watching my reactions.

"I've also hunted tigers and elephants in Africa," Jean-Auguste announced.

"Elephants!" Xavier exclaimed.

"Naravine was born in Africa and has visited many regions. Can you tell us about your travels?" I asked her, hoping she would tell the story that Jean-Auguste disliked. However, before Naravine could respond Madame de Briard turned to her and said, "I'll have to show you my ivory jewelry collection. They're gorgeous pieces. I had one of Paris's finest designers work on them."

"Isn't poaching elephants against the law?" I said.

"Anything worthwhile is either illegal, immoral, or fattening. Right?" Jean-Auguste added, looking at Naravine, as he waited for laughter from the guests.

"I couldn't agree with you more." Xavier joined in as he raised his goblet for a toast.

Jean-Auguste took over and said, "Let us drink to the earth, the rich soil that has given us these sweet grapes and our fine wines, to my adoring wife, my amazing and vivacious mother, and to my charming guests. I thank you all for being here and sharing this splendid evening with us. Next year, I hope you will visit again and share with us a new vintage produced from the Château Hélianthe d'Or, a rosé."

After a round of applause, he lit Naravine's cigar and then Xavier's before lighting his own.

It was one in the morning when we retired to our bedroom. The dogs were waiting for us on the bed. While I was petting them, Jean-Auguste said, "Wasn't that a fantastic dinner? I already have orders for my wines and for yours that will keep us busy until next year."

"I'm happy for you," I said dryly.

"What do you mean happy for me? You don't seem the

least bit enthusiastic. What's wrong with you? One of the maids told me you broke all your perfume bottles."

"It was an accident," I said, kissing one of the dogs.

"I know it was wrong of me to lose my temper. I apologize. The stress of everything has been too much," he admitted.

"Why haven't you told your mother that I want to sell this property? It sounded to me like you invited them back for next year."

"Maman arranged for this evening and made all contacts. I'll tell her when I get a chance."

"I think you're afraid of your mother," I retorted.

"Don't be ridiculous," he answered. "Can't you just let things be? We had a nice evening. The guests enjoyed themselves. Why do you have to ruin it?"

"Has anyone made an offer?"

"Not yet."

"It's rather evident that you care more about the guests than me. And I don't find it at all amusing to know that we were forced to eat animals that you slaughtered."

"I didn't slaughter anything. If you're so against killing animals then you're a fucking hypocrite. You're not a vegetarian and you certainly didn't refuse the fur coats I bought you. Frankly, I find your kind of pedantic attitude more repugnant than a man who likes to hunt. At least I live by my word."

"You're right. I can't argue with that."

"I really don't know what's wrong with you, Djuna. You need to stop acting like a spoiled brat. You live in your own dream world, painting and reading God knows what. Where will that take you? Without me you would have completely lost your grasp on reality, and this place would have fallen apart, not to mention yourself!"

He removed his bow tie and placed it on a dresser.

"Do you know how many people dream to have what you've been given? I can't stand your ungrateful attitude. I'm sleeping in the library until you learn to appreciate me more. Good night!" he said, grabbing both of the dogs. He stormed out of the bedroom, slamming the door behind him.

There was some truth to his words. Alone, my eyes fixated on the decanter of brandy that was set on an Art Deco cocktail table. I needed solace. Impulsively, my body moved closer to the decanter, as I became hypnotized by the reflecting prisms on the cut crystal. At the same time, I reached out to touch the refractions of rainbows. Without even thinking, I poured myself a glass as I shivered from the coldness of Jean-Auguste's rebuke. Looking across the room, I caught my reflection in a hanging mirror.

With detachment, I viewed my image, like an artist studying a model: in the mirror was a face that reminded me of Joaquím Carlos's hardened prostitutes. The stranger staring back at me also could have been a German expressionist model from an Emil Nolde painting with black lingerie, garters, long disheveled hair, and mascara-stained eyes. The perils of tarnished love had altered her facial expressions; her jaw was clenched tightly, and she had dark circles under her eyes. Only an artist could help her. Joaquím Carlos would have been able to read beyond her sadness, find her soul, save her. I wanted to paint her, but my attraction turned to repulsion. What I needed was to alter my mood, which came in the form of a drink and a cigarette, instant companionship, warmth, hot smoke. In one of the drawers of the château, I had found Sylvie's Chinese jade pipe; I liked the way it felt between my fingers, the coldness of the stone, the security of holding on to something, a link to the past, anything, even an object, that may have belonged to her back in the thirties. Would I have been happier living in those times? Or were women even more powerless, and would I have become just like Sylvie, falling under the spell of opium? A vivid imagination was part of my makeup, as I happily lost myself in the journals and when I painted. Yet I didn't want to believe, as Jean-Auguste did, that this was a character flaw and a weakness. What was slipping from me now was a part of me I didn't want to lose. Feeling futile, I poured myself another sifter of cognac. By the second glass, I was floating in a jeweled amber sea of calm. Drifting to my walk-in cedar closet, I pulled out a full-length black mink coat. Jean-Auguste was right; wrapping myself in the soft mink, I felt like a hypocrite as I walked onto the balcony.

I didn't know if it was me, or if it was cold out. The air felt chilly for summer; I was freezing, even underneath the silk lining of my coat. The pool was below me. In the full moonlight, the cerulean-blue water glistened to a pale shade

of pewter. Gazing up at the constellations, I felt in complete
turmoil, not only was I alienated from my husband, but I was
a stranger to myself. Loud splashing coming from the pool
distracted me from my maudlin thoughts. Someone was swimming. After several laps, the swimmer emerged from the water. A lantern beside an oak tree outlined the lithe silhouette
of an adolescent boy, whose identity was completely unknown
to me.

When I returned inside, I was overcome by panic; my heart
began racing. All of my thoughts were dwelling on our decaying marriage, as our interlude of romance and enchantment
was abruptly ending, like the evolution in painting from Post-
impressionism into Cubism. Our relationship was distorted
with rough edges and jarring angles. Nobody could help us.
This was our own futile war. Our darker sides, our demons,
our imperfections, with all the dirt, the grime, and the blood
had been hidden from view, until now.

Was there a way back to our honest affections? What had
Naravine wanted to tell me about Jean-Auguste? It was foolish
of me not to have insisted. Should I have confronted him about
the postcard? I didn't know what to do. But as much as I
loathed being alone, I was terrified to remain with him. Like
the rumors that were once spread about Joaquím Carlos's mistresses, I felt imprisoned in this lush castle—a château of secrets and silent screams. Like spoiled grapes, Loire was
beginning to leave a rancid taste in my mouth. Nausea rose
up my throat; I rushed to the bathroom, where I purged myself
of all I had consumed that evening. After I washed my face
I felt a catharsis. The negativity of the evening was flushed
away. Robbed of makeup, I was recognizable again. What I
couldn't face was tomorrow. Could I keep this up, or would
I give in to his overbearing ways and return to being the ob-
sequious, demure wife? Nonetheless, I couldn't stand the
thought of spending another night in Loire, let alone a lifetime

PART FOUR
WAR AND RETRIBUTIONS

NINETEEN

Djuna Cortez

It was five in the morning when I opened my curtains. The sun was rising over the valley. The château and the gardens were completely silent. Everyone was sound asleep, including the staff. Another hangover was giving me a pounding headache. Once again, nothing stopped me from getting out of bed. After showering, I felt better and quickly dressed. Then I packed some belongings and jotted down a brief note, leaving it on my bedside table.

Jean-Auguste:

Our marriage isn't working out as I had planned. When I'm away from you, all I do is miss you. Yet, when we're together, we always end up fighting. I need a trial separation. During this time, you need to think about what's important to you, as I will do the same. I can't go on like this. I'll be in touch with you at a later date. Please don't try to contact me. I must be alone for a while.

Djuna

As quietly as possible, and trying not to wake anyone, I carried down two suitcases and left the château. It was fortunate that the dogs were sleeping with Jean-Auguste, otherwise they would have been whining for me. A taxi met me at the front door and drove me to the train station. On the train ride back to Paris, I tried to imagine how Jean-Auguste would react when he found my note. Would he become angry, sad, or relieved? I couldn't stay in Paris, as he would certainly find me there. There was another city, another county, I had to discover.

Once I arrived in Paris, a taxi drove me to Charles de Gaulle airport. And within thirty minutes, I had a plane ticket for a flight that was beginning to board.

"If you run you'll make it," the attendant told me. Never before had my legs performed with such speed and agility. I found my seat inside the plane and exhaled a loud sigh of relief. The person next to me must have thought I was a bit deranged. This time I didn't care. I closed my eyes as the jet took off, and the higher the plane climbed, the more liberated I felt, like an eagle gliding in a warm desert wind. Bright sunshine filled the cabin. Soon I would be in a Mediterranean city of diverse cultures. Barcelona, with its ardent sun and Moorish, Roman, and Gothic architecture. My visit would be a welcome respite. There I hoped to finish reading the journals and find a new perspective on how to handle my current problems.

My afternoons were spent exploring Barcelona with a detailed map folded in my pocket and one of Joaquím Carlos's journals tucked under my arm. And much to my surprise, near my hotel, I discovered dancers of the Sardana in the Plaça de la Seu. In the square, the sounds of Gypsy music, cathedral chimes, laughter, and the tapping of heels echoed through the narrow cobblestone streets of the Gothic Quarter. Even though I was merely an observer, I felt connected with another country of my heritage; the cells in my distilled Castilian blood were awakening.

The Spanish culture mystified and intrigued me. When I

crossed the Ramblas, men would shout from cars, *"Puta."* It seemed everywhere I wandered, whistles and screams of obscenities followed, regardless of how I was dressed; typically I wore simple clothing, such as a long blue cotton skirt, flat sandals, and a white blouse. Neither did it matter that I probably looked more Spanish than most of the women on the streets. At first the attention bothered me. Then I learned to ignore the comments, as I understood that existing in Spain were two conflicting codes of behavior: one of religious piety, and the other a complete lack of moral restraint, which suffused the Barcelona streets, especially at night, when the city awakened from a lazy afternoon slumber and the fiestas began with feasting past midnight and dancing until sunrise.

The ardor of the Spaniards fascinated me, as I yearned for a resurgence of passion in my life. There were times I would think about my husband and miss him. However, I kept busy, and this made it easier to forget about Jean-Auguste and France. One afternoon, I stumbled upon an immense library with a patio and café that overlooked a quiet park and ancient burial ground. From that day onward, I established a daily ritual. After a full day of sightseeing, I would stop at the library, browse through some books, and then sip a refreshing lemonade on the patio. It was on my sixth day in Barcelona when a woman in her seventies who was dressed in heavy black clothing walked past me and sat down at the table next to mine. Her face was full of character and distinction, with a long Roman nose, short silver hair, and wise, dark eyes. I begin to sketch her profile until she disdainfully glared at me. Setting my pencils down, I said to her in my limited high-school Spanish, "I'll stop if I'm bothering you."

The woman answered in heavily accented English, "I'm not part of a tourist display."

"I'm sorry. I didn't mean to offend you," I apologized.

The Spanish woman brushed the wrinkles out of her long skirt and shook her head.

"Who is buried there?" I asked her, pointing to the park.

She huffed and then answered bitterly, "Jews or Gypsies. I'm not sure. They should just burn it. This square is filled with beggars and licentious creatures. Barcelona was never like this when Franco ruled. Our streets were clean and safe.

Spain was once the richest country in the world. Before the war we had everything. Now, well, it's pitiful."

"What was the civil war like?" I inquired.

"It was bad enough that I won't discuss it. Listen, señorita, I don't talk to tourists. I can always detect one like the stench of death I learned too well from the war. Americans rob all the power from nations and only care about their own glory. You're a selfish people."

"I'm sorry to have disturbed you," I said, as I collected my things. Rejection was painful, even from a stranger. I stood up and tried to stand as rigidly as possible, but my legs were shaking. If only I could have said something about her rudeness, but I was caught so completley off guard, that all I could do was give in to her by leaving the café.

I returned to my room at the Hotel Colón. The Spanish loved to nap in the afternoon. Siesta time was strictly adhered to, and most shops closed down. I had quickly adjusted to this ritual, as my deepest sleep often came in the middle of the day. I had started to read, but eventually dozed off. Several hours later, I awoke confused and disoriented. It was dark outside, and I had forgotten where I was until the cathedral bells chimed nine times, bringing me back to Barcelona and the Gothic Quarter. Guitars and tambourines played below my window. The city was awakening for the evening. And as much as I wanted to join the festivities, hundreds of questions ran through my mind. It had been almost a week since I had been away. How long could I escape from my responsibilities? A part of me wanted to return home. At the same time, I didn't know where home was anymore. Impulsively, I picked up the telephone and began to call my father, but when the international operator came on the line, I cowardly hung up. I contemplated phoning my husband, just to let him him know that I was alive in case he was worried. But I also abandoned that idea. If at all possible, I didn't want our marriage to end in failure. Yet, I needed more time before speaking to him. Did he love me? Should I go back to him and try to work out our problems? Was I as much to blame for our disputes? My affection for him had not disappeared in a week. However, before calling him, I had to prepare myself for his reaction. Thinking positively, if he wanted to make amends, could I go back to being a docile wife, allowing him to make all the decisions? Could I forgive his temper and that postcard? Perhaps more importantly, I needed to know what I truly wanted.

Goddesses, Wine, Dead Artists & Chocolate

The Journals of Joaquím Carlos Cortez

PARIS, JUNE 1940

Everyone has a city that holds a key to their heart; for some, it is a mystical place that awakens them to an ancient past, a city that enlivens the senses, and refines one's tastes and perceptions. For me, it can only be Paris. The city ripens the aesthetic in all of us, the eyes of a painter, or the palate of a wine connoisseur. Paris will always be my first love. I fled to her during my youth, and like an experienced lover, she has taught me her language of art and passion. The city will always be feminine to me, even under siege. Alas, my heart is again broken, for Paris is declared an open city—a corrupted whore.

The newspapers have lied to us along with the government, telling us that the French army could keep the Nazis at bay. Meanwhile, the reports given to us were overly optimistic lies. I should have listened to Marcel. He kept saying: "You're insane to stay on. You don't know what the Nazis will do."

I have refused to flee with Marcel and a group of friends. Instead, I vow again to remain faithful to Paris, to the city that has blessed me with prosperity.

Paris has been invaded today. Hundreds of people have streamed into the city, while others just as quickly depart. Everyone looks tired and frightened, clinging to their few possessions. Many are escaping by foot and bicycles. Mothers are carrying their crying infants and pushing strollers filled with meager belongings. Leaving may be an intelligent decision for Marcel. However, I don't want to be another morose face loading up a car with a mattress for protection. I have to face the bullies—the pimps.

I have received some tragic news. Guy and Marcel's car was stopped on Route Nationale by a platoon of invading Wehrmacht soldiers. Most of the travelers were forced to return to Paris. Unfortunately, Marcel and his friends died by gunfire and enemy bombs.

Every day, at noon, hundreds of Wehrmacht tanks roll down our streets. German soldiers dressed in their gray-green uniforms and helmets parade down the Champs-Elysées. With binoculars, I can see them from my apartment terrace, as they arrogantly march, bang their drums, blow whistles, and triumphantly raise their flags, forcing us to endure Paris's rape and desecration. To show more of their control and domination, a swastika banner is wrapped around l'Arc de Triomphe. The chancellor has been given a key to the city. As a reward, he's driven around in a black convertible Mercedes. And like royalty, he waves to us as though we are his loyal subjects. I react like a mute observer, too terrified to cry out: "Stop this outrage! Do you think we're bloody fools?"

It's impossible not to watch. All my neighbors are also standing on their balconies. The weather is warm and the skies are giving us a clarity of vision we wish we didn't have. Everyone looks stupefied; their mouths are hanging open. We are the belligerent ones who never believed this could happen, so we stayed on. We were the stubborn optimists. Now our cowardly government has fled the capital and our newspapers have stopped printing. Should we stay imprisoned? I want to stop looking, turn my head, but I'm compelled, just as the other citizens are, to foolishly gape at this spectacle. The only voice of hope comes from our radios. Everyone is listening. It is the strong and cathartic French voice of General de Gaulle.

When night falls, we're forced to remain without electricity and to obey the curfew. My women and my son are with me in the avenue Foch apartment. We must be together, in case bombs are dropped. All of us are frightened by the darkness and huddle together in one large bed. All three of them are asleep. I hear their soft breathing. Emile is cradled between Isabella and Elaine. I'm relieved the women have made amends. My only separation from them now is that my insomnia has returned. I listen to every airplane that flies above us. It is my duty to stand vigil and to record this harrowing truth. I want to open myself up to the wounds of war and grieve for Paris, this precious, yet forsaken city. I write by candlelight and a quill pen. For weeks, all I can paint are black skulls and crosses, canvas after canvas of the same morbid monotony.

PARIS, AUGUST 1940

Every night, demons are rejoicing in Montmartre. All of Paris's cafés and nightclubs are packed with German soldiers and hungry local prostitutes. I don't care to go out anymore. The streets reek of impending death, wine, and urine. Below my window, I can hear a man being beaten to a pulp for being late at curfew by only one minute. I miss our vivacious, gay Paris. Every day, I find myself mixing more oils to capture the color that has tainted the city. It's the color of sin and lost innocence. I paint ten cityscapes of Paris at night and at twilight.

The lights have gone out in the city. At night, it's a forboding and tenebrous place. An enemy can be hidden anywhere, ready to slash your throat for a five-franc coin. Everyone is starving. Everyone has gone mad. Neighborhood cats are missing. There are thousands of excuses to extinguish a life. The catacombs are safer than the Latin Quarter. At least the rats won't kill you.

In my recent paintings, I refuse to acknowledge Paris's darkness; the Eiffel Tower, l'Arc de Triomphe, Notre-Dame, and the Sacré-Coeur shine in incandescent red. In each painting, the monuments glow in the dark, and the City of Light continues to sparkle in all of its brilliance, as it always has, like diamonds, rubies, and emeralds. I capture the wide panorama of Montmartre, or a more focused view from a *bâteau mouche*. Drifting on a dinner boat, I paint traces of glimmering light from the bridges across the Seine, rising up to the moonlit rooftops, and settling in the nocturnal waterfront restaurants and cafés.

Most of my friends are gone, except for Princess Mitya. I think she hasn't grasped the reality of the situation at all and is trying to continue to live in her glamorous nucleus. She calls me at my studio and says in her flamboyant voice: "Darling, please meet me at three o'clock in the Luxembourg gardens. You simply must come. And I won't take no for an answer." Then she hangs up the phone, without explaining what the occasion is, or how I should dress.

I wait for her by the Medici fountain. This is a black summer; ashes float in the air instead of butterflies. I recline on a bench and smoke several Gitanes. At first, I don't recognize the plain woman who carefully sits down beside me. She is dressed in oversized clothes that hide her figure: a long gray skirt, a vest, and a white blouse buttoned up to her neckline. Her platinum curls are tucked under a beret. She is without makeup, and her skin looks ghostly pale.

"Can I have a smoke?" she asks.

Recognizing her voice, I take a double take and hand her a Gitane.

"I know I don't look like myself," Mitya says, placing her hands on my shoulders. She then whispers, "Call me Notre-Dame. And I'll call you Étoile."

"Why did you need to see me?" I ask softly.

She looks around us before answering. "You're in a lot of trouble. But, don't worry, that's why I'm here."

"How can you help me?" I ask incredulously.

"Fritz has informants."

"Who?"

"My Fritz, the baron. He's working both sides. But his loyalty is to me and the Resistance."

"You're involved in the underground!"

"Yes. Please keep your voice down," she reprimands me. "Life is full of surprises. I would have never suspected you to get involved. Can you really trust a double agent? It's very dangerous."

She answers in a soft whisper. "I know, but so is everything now. I have to trust him. I love him. The Nazis have pillaged villages in Poland and in Russia—towns where I was born and raised. Like you, I have lost most of my family. Fritz is the only person left in this world I have to care about. My duty now is to help those who can still be saved. There are many innocent people who need our help. You happen to be one of them."

"I don't want you endangering yourself on my account."

"I won't be able to live with myself if I don't intervene. From what we can gather, the Nazis are planning to destroy some of the modern art galleries and seize paintings from museums. I don't know exactly when this will happen. But we do know that René Vouchon's gallery is on the list."

Before she can explain more, we are distracted by a hammering sound. Both of us turn toward the noise. Behind us, three SS soldiers are chiseling away at a statue of Bacchus. This goes on for some time, until they loosen the foundation. Right after, they clumsily try to cart it off; but art proves to be stronger than brutish force, as the stone god, drags behind them, scraping against the graveled path, making the sound of nails on a chalkboard. Shivers are traveling up my spine.

"Why take a statue?" I ask Mitya.

"Because they can. It's their property now."

I feel like screaming, but force myself to remain calm. My hands start to tremble. Suddenly, German airplanes fly above us; their humming BMW engines drown out the noise of the scraping statue and the gushing fountain. Looking up at the sky, I see the familiar swastika on the plane's tail as they tip their wings over the park. These planes are unlike any we've seen before. They're flying death machines and have black skulls painted beside an encased glass cockpit.

"Look at that piece of machinery," I exclaim to Mitya.

"They're just showing off to intimidate us."

Mitya helps me light a cigarette. My hands aren't steady enough.

"The enemies know everything about you. Because your wife was Jewish, you may be in grave danger. Circumstances are only going to get worse. If you want to save your life, and that of your son, you must get to an unoccupied zone."

"How do you propose getting me out?"

"We're still working on that. You have to trust us. We must work fast and first warn René. He has to abandon the gallery and remove all the paintings."

Mitya glances behind us. Another SS soldier in a dark coat is walking past. Immediately, she wraps her arms around me and kisses my mouth. She doesn't stop until the soldier is on the other side of the fountain.

"My, you do have nice lips and a wonderful strong jaw and chin. No wonder the ladies fall all over you. Look, I know how stubborn and dogmatic you can be at times. But you must do as I say," she instructs.

"Does that involve more kissing? If it does, I don't really mind."

She chuckles. "I'm afraid not. But we will have to pretend we're lovers and walk out arm in arm. Then we'll head on to the gallery."

After a quick Métro ride, we arrive on rue de Seine. A parade of German soldiers are marching down the street. Stockpiles of paintings are discarded on the sidewalks, some are being crushed under their stampede, others are being burned. Most of the paintings are of other respected contemporary artists: Picasso, Matisse, Kandinsky, Soutine and Miró, to name a few. When we arrive at René's gallery, the windows have been shattered; shards of glass cover the entrance and are scattered on the floor inside. The interior walls are vacant, except for swastikas and German graffiti that are painted with human blood. Mitya reads the words to me.

"Entartete Kunst. That means degenerate art."

Hesitantly, we enter the back office and find the floor flooded in blood. Mitya screams. "I don't know if I can take this!"

As we approach the main storage of paintings, we discover René collapsed on the floor. He is kneeling with his hands pressed together in a prayer. It appears he may have died pleading for his life. Machine-gun fire had pierced his chest and stomach.

"We've got to get you out of here," Mitya orders. She grabs

hold of my arm and drags me outside. The destructive procession is continuing along the street. Paintings are being slashed and thrown into bonfires. A woman shrieks, "No! No! You can't do this!" She is running toward the gallery as she grabs some of my smaller canvases from the sidewalk. She sounds and looks like Isabella. When she reaches us, I see that it is her. My Bella is completely out of breath and can barely speak, but manages to say in gasps. "I—won't let them—destroy your work!"

A German soldier with a loading belt link wrapped around his neck and an MP 43 assault rifle is watching her carefully. Grabbing hold of her arm, I try to quiet her. But she refuses to obey, breaking free of my grasp as she races off with my paintings. I call after her, but she continues running with the determination of a willful child.

"Bella, please! Give them up," I shout, chasing after her. Stubbornly, she continues to collect other paintings of mine that are scattered in the street. Without warning, the soldier aims his rife, opening rapid fire into Isabella's back. Mitya screams. My mistress's beautiful body hits the ground, falling like a hunted deer. A raucous guttural sound erupts from my vocal chords, akin to a rabid animal. I shove my way through the crowds of soldiers, and lie down on the ground beside her, cradling her head and torso in my arms. Isabella's skin is warm; her cheeks are flushed. But she's quickly losing consciousness, as her blood seeps into the crevices between the cobblestones. I close my eyes, wanting to be washed away in her warm blood. Her eyelids are fluttering rapidly and her breathing is tenuous. I don't want to look at her wounds. She must have at least a dozen pellets imbedded in her back. Blood continues to seep from her, covering my arms and chest. I don't care. "Take me with you, Isabella. Take me," I cry. Kissing her sweet lips, I feel her last gasp for air. And while holding her for what I know is the last time, all I can do is try to etch in my mind a permanent memory of her angelic face.

"Come on. We've got to get out of here," Mitya says tugging at my shirt sleeve.

"I can't just leave her in the street."

"You'll have to. We have to run for shelter."

Air raid sirens start their warning signals. The few people left in the street are running in haphazard directions.

"No. Don't move. It's too late. Just play dead," Mitya instructs. She runs back to the gallery and hides.

Another Nazi soldier approaches and stands over me. My eyes are closed. I'm collapsed over Isabella, trying not to move or breathe. Seconds later, he's stomping on my right hand with his heavy artillery boot.

"I should burn you along with these bad paintings," he roars.

I clench my teeth so as not to scream; all the bones in my right hand, along with my fingers are shattered. Over and over again in my mind, repeating like one of my parrot's voices, are his judgmental words: "bad, bad, bad!"

That is the one word I cannot tolerate. How can art be bad? Art is subjective and should be bypassed by moral judgement. Christ! The pain is making me delirious. That moment, I'm ready to admit that I'm corrupt; he had me. He took away my Bella, let him kill me. The wailing sirens start again. Between the pauses, I hear heavy footsteps approaching, more soldiers. One of them says, "They're dead."

Another one answers, "It doesn't matter. They're probably Jews. You can leave them. Come on, let's get out of here."

After I hear them running down the street, sensing that they're gone, I open my eyes. Mitya is already next to me removing the paintings from under Isabella's arm.

Before I can get up, bombers are swarming down on the burning street. From the air, the Junkers look as hideous as gigantic flying June bugs.

"Bombs! Run for shelter!" Mitya screams.

TWENTY

Djuna Cortez

It was the middle of the day when I set down the journals. I had just finished reading a most disturbing passage that I wanted to be fiction out of the sheer incredulity of the situation. But at that point, Joaquím Carlos's penmanship looked severely compromised. His words appeared to have been written by unsteady hands. Subsequently, my hands had started to shake as I had read about the destruction of the paintings and the brutality of the Nazis. My fingers began to ache just imagining the atrocity of having one's hand crushed.

What would I have done in his place? Would I have given up on painting because of my lack of coordination, or would I go on and struggle with my left hand? How terribly tragic that all those years of training for him were now obliterated. How did he overcome this? Looking more closely at his pained entry, I noticed that he still maintained a flair to his words, especially the way he curved his *y*s and *t*s. Then I wrote down the word *art* with my left hand. I continued writing whatever came into my mind, just to immediately experience what he had gone through. Surprisingly, I saw that it was also impossible for me to hide my own style, which showed even in my left hand. In addition, I noticed how similar our hand-writing was. We both printed, and our letters were perfectly symmetrical in size and could be easily read. I also curved many of my letters. In fact, when I wrote with my left hand our letters were almost identical, as if the sentences had been composed from a young child's hand, or a person writing on a boat that was out at sea. As a result of what I read, I found myself slowly writing some questions. Are the hands only an instrument to a vaster creative process—an indestructible desire for self-expression? Can the desire for expression transcend all physical boundaries and handicaps?

For the remaining afternoon, while I frequented the Café de l'Opera on the Ramblas, I sketched with my left hand. My subject was a performing mime, whose face and hands were disguised in silver body paint. As I began drawing with my left hand, I felt torn in half, completely divided. Working with my left hand made me feel like a child, while when I used the right, I was an adult. As a grown-up, I wanted to gently explain to this inexperienced girl that it didn't matter that her drawing was crooked, and that her efforts didn't have to be perfect. And above all else, that it was imperative to make plenty of mistakes. As my left hand continued to draw, I could see that one day, if the child was patient, all of her talents and abilities would shine through.

Goddesses, Wine, Dead Artists & Chocolate

The Journals of Joaquím Carlos Cortez

PARIS, SUMMER 1940

We run like bandits, rushing into the nearest shelter just before the bombs start to fall. Clinging to each other and to those silently whimpering around us, all we can do is hope our lives will be spared. Horrific images enter my mind. Will we be trapped in this shelter? Will we starve to death?

After two hours of darkness and constant bombardments, there is a break of silence. Then we hear digging. Our passageway is being cleared by the French police. Mitya and I find our way back to the rue de Seine. The light is glaring, even though the sun is masked by clouds. Around us, littering the street, are large pieces of rubble, shards of glass, and metal. We have to be careful where we step. Isabella's body is nowhere to be found. Instead, we see desecrated paintings and broken frames strewn about like scattered victims. For the time being, the Latin Quarter is empty of German soldiers and civilians.

Mitya and I rush back to my studio. I'm carrying two of my paintings under my left arm. She is carrying four.

"I don't know if it's worth risking our lives for these paintings," I tell her.

"How can you say that! Isabella did. We should honor her actions. To destroy art is to obliterate the human condition, the bonds we all share."

When we arrive at the square of Saint-Sulpice, I drop my paintings and run toward the gushing fountain. Unable to withstand the pain any longer, I soak my aching hand in the cold basin. There I see reflected in the currents of water Isabella's beaming face, and following her are my destroyed oil paintings. One by one, each colorful picture floats past me. As I glance across the basin, I notice between the two tiers of waterfalls, a fierce white stone lion. His mouth is open and he's baring all of his fangs. Instantly, I become him—ferocious. Blood rushes to my face along with a piqued fury. To calm myself, I dunk my head underwater, and with all my rage, I scream and roar, my voice only translating into silent bubbles. Mitya tugs at my shirt collar and then pulls my head out of the water. Like a drenched dog, I shake out my soaking hair.

"What are you doing? Let's not draw more attention to ourselves. That's enough!" she yells.

She drags me across the square. Below my studio, my favorite *librairie* and frame shop have been abandoned, their shutters permanently drawn. It is sad, as their exteriors were recently painted, one red, the other black. The Hôtel Récamier also appears empty. Looking up at my building, I see that every window is closed, the shutters rolled down. Nobody wants to admit to living in Paris anymore.

Eliane answers the door for us when we enter my studio.

"Where's Emile?" I ask her.

"He's sleeping in the bedroom. What happened to you?

Why are you all wet and covered in blood?" Eliane questions.

"They killed Isabella!" I bellow, collapsing on the divan.

"No! That can't be true," Eliane says, shaking her head and rushing to comfort me.

"I regret that it is. The Nazis shot her and also broke his right hand," Mitya interjects.

"Oh, no, the one you paint with," Eliane says, crouching on the floor beside my injured hand. "It looks terrible!"

"I need a doctor; I need painkillers," I demand.

"There isn't time for that. Did La Fourche call you?" Mitya asked Eliane.

"Yes. I did everything he instructed. But there wasn't enough time to remove the paintings from the other apartment. I also wanted to bring the cat, but I couldn't find her."

"Who's La Fourche?" I ask.

"That's Fritz's underground name. I'm not sure you'll be able to take the cat anyway. Please gather all the paintings in this room," Mitya instructs her.

"Can I have something for this pain?" I plead in agony.

"First go buy him some ice. And also some aspirin," Mitya orders.

"Yes, right away," Eliane answers obediently.

"Aspirin won't do anything. Get me a strong drink," I command.

Mitya fixes both of us a glass of Eau-de-Vie. After taking several gulps, I ask her, "So, when do we leave?"

"They are making arrangements as we speak. I'll be informed as things progress. What I do know is that a person from the Resistance will be arriving soon to take you to a free zone."

Fifteen minutes later, Eliane returns with a bottle of aspirin and cracked ice. After making me a compress and delicately applying it on my broken hand, she laments, "I knew something like this would happen. It was inevitable. I wanted to leave a long time ago."

At this point I have a short fuse. I shout angrily, "It's a little late for your asinine opinions. Isabella is dead and we can't bring her back! So shut up."

Eliane starts to weep. Never before have I spoken to her in such an abrupt manner. I feel badly, but I'm in too much pain to say or do anything. Mitya rushes to comfort her.

"Carlos, you don't need to be brutal. That's completely unnecessary. She's just scared like all of us. You're not the only one hurting. I'm sure Eliane is also upset about Isabella," Mitya reprimands me.

"I'm sorry, Eliane," I apologize.

The phone rings. Mitya rushes to answer. All she says is yes, and then she hangs up and explains, "I'm being informed on the progress of our strategy. Our final goal will be to get you back to Barcelona. The Galì Academy has an instructing position open for you. Apparently you studied there at one time."

"Yes, but I'm useless now," I moan. "The Nazis have destroyed me."

"I won't accept that, nor should you. You'll always be a great painter. Your talent is getting you out of this predicament," Mitya retorts.

I stare forlornly at my right hand. "I think all the bones have been broken! It won't stop throbbing, even with the ice. I may never be able to paint again!"

"I'm sorry about the pain," Mitya says.

I ask her, "What about you? How can you stay here? Won't you be in danger?"

"It's impossible to tell. But Fritz has to stay in Paris and I must be with him. I'm going to move into your apartment on avenue Foch and rent this place to a friend. The château will have to remain in the care of your servants. I suggest you sign all of your properties over to me. I don't want you to risk losing them. Whenever this war ends, and I do hope it will, then I'm sure you'll come back. And I'll return everything to you."

"How are we going to transport all of these paintings?" Eliane asks.

"I don't know yet. I'm still waiting for further instructions," Mitya answers.

"You're wonderful, Mitya. I don't know what I'd do without you. Could you please go to my paint drawers? Over there," I say, pointing to a tulipwood writing desk.

"What do you need?" she asks, walking over to the desk.

"Open the second and third drawers."

"All I see are notebooks."

"Please remove them and make sure to look at the bottom of the drawers."

"I don't believe this! These drawers are lined with money! What do you want me do with all these francs?"

"Take some cash, as much as you need, and leave the rest on top of the desk beside the jars of brushes. But first bring me all the journals. You can set them beside me. I have to take them with me," I instruct.

"I didn't know you wrote," Mitya inquisitively commented.

Changing the subject, I say, "I'll be in the bedroom. I know you'll respect my privacy and not peak at my writing."

"Yes, of course," Mitya says, as she looks at Eliane.

My son wakes as I open the door. I kiss him on top of his head and he brushes past me, running toward the kitchen, where Eliane is. She picks him up and rubs his round belly. "I'll go fix you a snack. You must be hungry," she says affectionately.

In the privacy of my bedroom, I lose all composure. Modeling peignoirs and scarfs are piled into a heap on the floor. There had been so many times that I had reprimanded Isabella for leaving them there. Now, all I can do is collapse into them and roll into a fetal position. Isabella's redolent scent lingers on the fabrics. Inhaling deeply and rubbing a red satin robe against my face, I become enraged by the loss of another lover. Death has again made me feel vapid and hollow. The pain in my broken hand cannot compare to the angst in my heart. Urgently, and with my left hand, I push open all the windows, not caring that the glass panes are slamming against the side of the building. My vision is clouded with tears, yet I notice the skyline of Paris is turning burnt orange, orchid pink, and amethyst, as if I had taken my paintbrush to the heavens. How terribly cruel it is for a city under siege to still be beautiful at twilight. The air is warm and inviting. What I must do next sends shivers up my spine.

As I approach the birdcages, the parrots and cockatoos begin screeching and bowing their heads to me. They think I'm going to give them some pistachios. Instead, I swing open their cage doors, and one at a time, I shoo them out the open window. Instinctively they fly toward the setting sun—a plethora of rainbow-colored feathers decorates the painted sky. At least they can be liberated. Perhaps they'll be reunited with Isabella and Sylvie.

There's a knock on the door.

"Who is it?" I ask.

"It's me. Can I come in?" Mitya says. She enters without my response.

"I don't know when he'll be here. Eliane is making us dinner," Mitya informs me.

"I'm not hungry," I answer sharply.

"I know. But you need to keep your strength up. What have you done?" she asks, staring incredulously at the empty birdcages.

I cannot answer, and continue gazing out the window, watching the sky darken.

"I would have kept the birds," she insists, sitting next to me on the bed.

"They're very demanding. I couldn't impose on you. You're doing enough for me already. You're one of the strongest and bravest women I've ever known," I reverently avow.

"That says a lot, since I think you've known every woman in this damn city."

"Known or slept with?"

"It's the same thing with you."

"Then I've never known you," I admit.

Mitya bursts into laughter. "Don't tell me I'm the only woman you know that you've never seduced."

"I can't give away all of my secrets either," I profess.

"I know I missed out. I can imagine you're quite a Casanova. However, you chose Sylvie over me. Remember?"

"Yes. But I couldn't have a better friend in you, Mitya. I hope one day I can reciprocate all the kindness you've shown me. Thank you."

I brush her cheek with my swollen and bruised knuckles.

"*Dios Mio!* As soon as I take this hand out of the ice, it's total agony."

"I've been informed by Fritz of some disturbing information about what's been happening throughout Europe. There's no question in my mind that we're making the right decision by getting you out," Mitya says.

"What information?"

"Wait! I hear something." She jumps toward the door.

Eliane knocks and says, "Someone is here. Should I answer?"

"No! Let me first see who it is," Mitya replies.

Mitya runs into the living room, leaving the bedroom door wide open.

"Who is it?" Mitya asks.

A man's voice responds, "Pigalle."

Mitya smiles and opens the door. A middle-aged French priest frocked in a flowing black robe and white collar enters. My knees begin to weaken. I feel my revulsion for the priesthood.

"He's in there," she says pointing toward the bedroom. "Have you brought all the papers?"

He pulls out some documents from his medical bag and hands them to her. Next they enter the bedroom. The priest approaches my bed and his familiar cloak brushes against my feet. I turn my head and cannot speak or look at him directly.

"Pigalle will explain the plan. You have to follow his instructions and do everything he says. Here are the ownership papers regarding your properties," she says handing them to me.

As I begin signing them with my left hand, my signature is completely different, but with some artistic skill, I'm able to make my name legible.

"Is he a real priest?" I ask Mitya, intending for him to hear. Pigalle answers for her. "I can't answer that. But I promise to get you out of occupied France." Then he hands Mitya two identity cards. She starts smirking and says, "This is going to be quite amusing."

"What happened to your hand?" Pigalle asks.

"What do you care?" I answer curtly.

"Maybe I can help. I have some medical supplies on me. And I may even have a splint in my car. I'll go check."

Once he's left the room, I protest. "If I have to obey that religious moron, then I would rather stay here and meet my death."

"What is wrong with you?" Mitya asks angrily. "You're really being a bastard. This man is putting his life on the line for you. You should at least treat him with some respect."

"How do you know I can trust him?"

"Because he's your only hope."

Mitya hands me some folded black clothing.

"You're going to need help getting dressed."

"I'll be fine," I answer.

"No, I don't think so," she says grinning.

"What is so damn funny?"

"Take off your pants."

"What?"

She unfolds the clothes and hands me my identity card and says, "Your name is Sister Maria-Pia Lucinda Ramos."

"You've got to be joking!"

"That's right, Carlos. Drop you pants and put this habit and padded bra on. I have some work to do on your face."

Pigalle returns with a splint and a roll of gauze. He hands Mitya a pair of spectacles and a pair of black shoes.

"Let me see your hand," he says in a monotone voice.

Snapping open a brown ostrich-skin doctor's bag, he walks over to my side of the bed and kneels beside me. Pathetically, I extend my black-and-purple hand.

"I'm going to first put some Mercurochrome on you."

"That burns like hell!"

"I know. I'm sorry. Your fingers look badly broken as well as your hand. It must be terribly painful."

"You can say that again!"

"You need a plaster cast. Right now this is all I have."

I grit my teeth as he begins setting my hand on the split, then wrapping it with gauze. "How does that feel? Is it too tight?"

"No. It's all right."

"Shouldn't he have dressed first before you bandaged him?" Mitya asks.

"Yes. That probably would have been better," Pigalle answers.

I hold up my hand to Mitya like the paw of a wounded animal. Without a moment's hesitation, she removes my shirt and fastens the bra around me.

"They're a bit small," I comment.

"We're not dressing you up to appeal to womanizers like yourself. You're a pious Catholic nun. You don't need to look as voluptuous as Mae West."

After Mitya places the flowing black cloak over my head, I begin to remove my pants. Once I'm changed, Pigalle finishes fastening butterfly clips to my bandage.

"Do you ever smile?" I ask him.

"Sometimes," he answers dryly.

"Does it offend you if I curse? Because I'm not going to change my language around you just because you're a God-damn priest."

"Swearing doesn't bother me," Pigalle says indifferently.

Mitya sits down on the bed beside me. Holding my face in her hands, she comments, "This is a handsome face for a man. But for a woman, it may be offensive. Fortunately, I have my makeup bag with me, a girl's best friend."

"A nun doesn't have to be beautiful," Pigalle remarks.

"Are you afraid that I may entice you," I say fetchingly to him.

"Stop toying with Pigalle. I swear he behaves like a child sometimes. I don't know how he can raise a son. Stay still. First, I need to clean up these Clark Gable eyebrows." She pulls a gold tweezer out of her bag.

"Hey, that hurts. I don't want to look like Dietrich."

"Don't worry. I would be completely envious if you shined up that well. I think a touch of blush, some shadow on your eyes, and some pale lipstick will do the trick. And you must make sure to always be clean shaven."

"You'll have to shave me," I tell her.

"We'll do that after your eyebrows," she says.

When we return from the bathroom, Pigalle places the eyeglasses on my face and a gold crucifix chain around my neck.

"I've seen uglier-looking woman," Pigalle comments.

I puff out my chest, wink, and blow Pigalle a seductive kiss. Mitya slaps my cheek.

"I don't want you behaving like a drag queen. Many people's lives depend on the credibility of this costume. Put your shoes on and come with me," she orders. Pigalle follows behind her.

"I can't see a damn thing," I curse, "and these shoes are too small. They're killing my feet!"

"What do we do?" Mitya asks Pigalle.

"He has to wear everything. Men's shoes will look conspicuous. These are the biggest we could find in a woman's size."

"You're going to have to endure some discomfort. Just feel fortunate you don't have to wear high heels," Mitya adds.

We enter the living room, where Eliane and my son are playing patty-cake on the floor. They are too involved to notice us at first. Mitya walks over to Eliane and interrupts their game. "Come see our man," she says to Eliane, taking her by the hand. Emile follows her. He is frightened of me and clings to Eliane's dress.

"Mon Dieu! I didn't recognize you," Eliane gasps as she approaches us.

"You're not supposed to. What do you think? Does he look like a nun?" Mitya asks.

"He looks completely different. I can't believe it's the same Carlos. Where are my clothes? What should I be wearing?" Eliane asks.

Mitya turns to Pigalle. He clears his throat and explains in a sullen voice, "We couldn't get any more identity papers. It is especially difficult getting something to fit mademoiselle's description. I'm very sorry."

"Carlos, can't you do something? I can be a nun too, or even a man. I don't understand. We can't be separated! We belong together as a family. You can't leave me!" Eliane exclaims.

"You should come work for me. I'll treat you well. We get plenty of good food from the black market. Now, darling, be brave. Joaquím Carlos is a very important person, who's in grave danger, much more then you are. Have you prepared all the paintings?"

"Yes," Eliane answers solemnly.

"It doesn't matter. We don't have enough time to properly hide them for our trip," Pigalle says.

I adjust my bra strap and crouch beside my son. My transformation still terrifies him. He begins crying to Eliane, *"Ma-*

man, Maman." She then lifts him up in her arms, showering his face with kisses.

I hold his little hand and say, "You have to come with me. I'm your father."

"No!" he screams, jerking his hand away and turning his head. Eliane then sets Emile down, and he drops to the floor and throws an enormous three-year-old tantrum, pounding his fists and legs into the herringbone flooring. I grab him by both arms and pull him to his feet. Angrily, he kicks me in the chins as he sticks out his tongue.

"I hate you," he rails.

"That is a terrible word! I don't know where you learned it. I'm your father. And whether you like it or not, you're coming with me," I order.

"I no want you. I want *Maman,*" he shouts, breaking free of me and running back to Eliane.

"She's not your mother. Your mother's dead. I'm your only parent. That's why you have to come with me."

Pigalle whispers something to Mitya.

"I don't know if drugging the child is advisable," Mitya answers back.

Eliane picks Emile up again, cradling him in her arms.

"We have some more dilemmas. The first is obviously your son's lack of cooperation with you. The second is that you won't be able to take any luggage, except for a small purse. You need to abide by the vows of poverty, chastity, and obedience," the priest explains.

"I can't be without my journals. I must take them, no matter the risks involved," I assert.

Pigalle adds, "Our car may be searched. That's why we can't transport anything out of the ordinary. Paintings, suitcases full of men's clothes, or even children's clothing could ruin our story. You need to know that Emile is an orphan according to his papers."

"Nuns can keep diaries," I say, "but I'm sure few read quite like mine."

"I suppose I could allow you to take them. We will be transporting medical and school supplies. We'll hide them with the French books. I've done this trip several times before without being searched. Let's hope that we'll be lucky. But you must hide your money."

"Here's my purse and a bag for your journals," Mitya says, as she dumps the contents of her purse on a coffee table.

"What concerns me the most is your son's behavior," Pigalle goes on to say. "I would advise sedating him. Emile could ruin everything for us if he throws another tantrum."

"I agree. What do you suggest giving him?" I ask.

Pigalle searches inside his medical bag.

Mitya interjects, "It's wrong to drug a child. Anyway, he's calmed down. I'll take care of your son and Eliane. They shouldn't be separated. She's his mother now. You don't have time to waste. Come back when the war is over. Don't worry. Emile will be safe with me. I'll treat him like my own."

I lose my patience and chide, "Eliane's not his mother. Neither are you. He's my son and he belongs with me."

Expeditiously, I remove the cash from the top of the desk and stuff most of it in my bra and underwear, putting a few bills in the purse Mitya gave me. The rest I hand to Eliane. She abruptly grabs the cash, clenching the bills with tight fists. Meanwhile, she refuses to respond or look at me. Her dark, expressive eyes cannot hide her shock and disappointment. After I have finished putting the journals in a shopping bag, I glance at my glass jars organized with paintbrushes, sponges, palette knifes, charcoals, and erasers. This accumulation of supplies has taken me years of careful selecting. I want to grab hold of a soft paintbrush; even my left hand feels empty without one.

"I'm sorry, you can't take anything else with you," Pigalle says. Just before leaving, he removes my son from Eliane's arms and carries him for me. Emile has finally settled down and is quietly sucking his thumb.

"We'll give him something later if he needs it," Pigalle whispers to me. As I'm collecting my two bags, Eliane is sobbing uncontrollably, and refuses to kiss me good-bye. Mitya escorts us downstairs and tells me, "I promise I'll try my best to hide the paintings and keep them safe. I'm very sorry about Eliane and the loss of Isabella. There was so much more I had wanted to explain to you about this war. I don't know when we'll be able to talk again. But before you leave,

I don't want you to forget one of De Gaulle's important messages. It has been helping me a great deal. You may have already heard it. Please forgive me if my memory isn't exact. I want you to always remember that 'Whatever happens, the flame of French resistance must not die and will not die!' "

"I couldn't agree with you more. I'll never forget those words or you," I say, hugging her.

The three of us enter a black Citroën with a Red Cross emblem. Mitya waves to us as we drive off. We drive past the Palais du Justice and the Santé prison where some of Isabella's comrades are imprisoned for being Communists. I glance at the iron prison gates that are protected by sentries. Tonight, the wind is carrying the inmates' sleepless voices. They are singing the "Marseillaise."

"Stop the car," I instruct Pigalle.

He obeys. I roll down the window and inhale their courageous song. As I listen carefully, Isabella feels more alive to me than ever. It is probable that if she had not died protecting my work, her fate would have been to end up behind these stone walls.

It seems like we'll never get out of Paris. Pigalle is hungry, so we stop for dinner in a brasserie in Clichy. By that time, the pain in my hand is so intense, I drink three cognacs and down a couple more aspirins. Pigalle offers to give me a more potent painkiller, but I refuse, as I had made a promise to my wife to care for my son and resist drugs. Emile is content in the restaurant, as he shares some of my croque-monsieur and drinks all of his milk, which I have laced with a touch of brandy.

"I wonder what people must think about a boozing nun," I say to Pigalle.

"Don't worry. Everybody here has another cover and is working for the underground," the priest explains.

This quickly becomes apparent when the radio plays another of De Gaulle's broadcasts and all the patrons cheer. De Gaulle is determined to fight and resist the enemy, just when I have finally resolved myself to escape.

We drive all night. At the Wehrmacht checks they study our identity papers and shine flashlights in our eyes. Each time, I hide my bandaged hand under the folds of my habit, while

Pigalle tells another version of our story. The most popular is with a Spanish accent, explaining that we work for the Red Cross in Spain as Catholic missionaries, bringing in medical supplies and books to orphanages. Our last stop, before going home, is at an orphanage in Toulon, where this boy is being transferred. Whenever they look at my son, I expect Emile to wake and start screaming, ruining our cover. Fortunately, he sleeps with his usual soundness through all of the check points. At one stop, they look into the box where my journals are hidden. A Gestapo agent even picks up a few schoolbooks, but quickly loses interest.

By morning, we reach the port of Toulon.

"Don't get excited. It's not over. It's still a very dangerous mission," Pigalle says. "You must again change hands and clothes."

We wait inside the fishing port. A whistling fisherman approaches. He is walking slowly, yet there is a bounce to his gait. Heavy fishing nets are draped over his shoulders; he seems oblivious to them.

"*Salut*, Pigalle. I'm Poissonnière," the man says, smiling and courteously extending his hand.

"*Salut*, Poissonnière. It's nice to meet you," Pigalle answers in his monotone voice.

"I've heard good things about you," Poissonnière says with great enthusiasm.

"I have as well."

I return to the car and try to lift my son out of the back seat, but have difficulty with one arm. Emile is awakened and asks in a groggy voice, "Papa, where are we?"

"In a fishing port. We're going to Spain. It's better that you try to walk with me."

His small hand clasps mine. As I help him out of the car, he asks, "What is Spain?"

"The country where I'm from. I know you'll like it."

Pigalle follows behind us, carrying the rest of my belongings. I am walking slowly so Emile can keep up. When we reach the boat, Pigalles asks the fisherman, "Do you have the clothes, identity papers, and the route planned out?"

"Yes. I have everything. I'll take it from here," Poissonnière says, tipping his black cap to Pigalle.

"He's your man now. Good luck!" the priest says.

"Where are you going now?" I ask Pigalle.

"I have to drop off some medical supplies to an orphanage."

"You mean that was real!" I exclaim.

"I have more people to take care of. May peace be with you," Pigalle says bowing.

"Whoever you are, thank you for helping us," I tell him before he walks away.

For the first time, a smile cracks Pigalle's stern lips as he proudly states, *"Vive l'art et l'amour."*

Pigalle's last words completely captivate me. This stranger, who I rarely spoke to, understood what I live for.

"Hey, Étoile," Poissonnière calls to me.

For a moment, I had completely forgotten my Métro stop name.

"Oh, yes," I answer, coming out of my trance.

"Here are your duds. Let's get both of you on board." He picks up Emile for me, before I climb on. The dilapidated fishing boat isn't much larger than my art studio.

"Are you sure this boat can hold up on such a long trip?" I say, jumping on the surface of the deck.

"She's may not be beautiful, but she's strong and reliable. Don't worry," the fisherman answers.

"The life vests are over there. Both of you should put them on. By the way, what happened to your hand?" Poissonnière asks.

"It's a long story."

"No problem. We'll have plenty of time to talk."

Kneeling down to Emile's level, I explain to him. "I know you like to sail boats in the bathtub and in the Tuileries. This is the real thing. We're going on an exciting voyage. I want you to be a really brave sailor for me. Are you up to the challenge? I think you are, because I know you're a big boy."

Emile nods and says, "Yes, I want to be sailor. I'm a big boy."

"There's some Camembert, fruit, bread, and coffee, if you're both hungry. I have enough food for three weeks. Eat up, because if you're not used to boats, you won't be hungry for long. Also, when you can, I suggest you get out of that bra and habit," Poissonnière says.

"You're right. I forgot how ridiculous I must look. I'll go change immediately."

As I walk across the boat, the wooden floorboards creak and shift. Salt crystals have worn away the boat's aquamarine paint, fading it to a pale shade of gray. I've been given a set of clean clothes belonging to another identity. This time I'm supposed to be a fisherman.

Weeks have gone by. We sail continuously. At night, I steer the boat while Emile and Poissonnière sleep. Emile has taken to the jolly Poissonnière. The fisherman is very patient with my son, explaining to him all about boats and fishing. Sometimes, he even allows the three-year-old to hold part of the wheel. During the day, when Poissonnière sails, I have to hide inside a small compartment of the fishing boat, sandwiched between nets full of decaying seafood. Often I hear my son laughing on the upper deck. Fortunately, Emile doesn't have to be locked up with these disgusting fish. The stench is horrific. It is dark inside the cabin. However, a crack in the door allows just enough light for me to see hundreds of dead fish eyes glaring at me. Octopus and squid tentacles stick to my arms and legs. When I eventually fall asleep, in my nightmares I am surrounded by the cold stares of Nazi spies.

During the time I spend alone, all I can do is reflect back on the life I had in Paris. I have left almost everything behind: my antiques, books, clothes, the priceless art collection, and my paintings. Furthermore, the two women that I have loved most have left this earth. Somehow, I can sense them near me. I envisage them dancing barefoot in flowing chiffon gowns. They move with the grace and fluidity that Isadora Duncan's choreography had. Above this boat, which is slowly crossing the vast Mediterranean, my sweet goddesses are dancing through the clouds.

Even in this freezing compartment, I refuse to call out or pray to God. What comforts me are a few Buddhist principles. Life is suffering; I am imperfect, but striving for wisdom and detachment. It may be impossible for me to attain these qualities and to quell my selfish desires. But I must try.

At night, the sea appears calm, but lurking just below the surface are submarines. I can only assume that Poissonnière must innocently wave to Nazi ships as he passes them. Poissonnière has enough charisma to charm entire fleets. I come up for air just as the sun sets. Poissonnière and I converse for an hour between shifts. When night falls, he pulls out his hidden radar and radio. Then he turns on a second engine. Our speed is doubled.

One night, Poissonnière explains: "I'm always at war and I'm always at peace. My *destin* is in the hands of this ocean. In French, the name of the sea is feminine, *la mer*. The ocean has become my mother, my lover, my only home. Every day, I rob her of food, making a profit off her abundance. But, at any time, she can take me. Inevitably I will become the sea kingdom's meal. The war with the sea, I can only win for a short time. In the end, she always wins, as one day, I won't be strong enough to pull up these heavy nets, or a tempest will flair up. I must sound like a fatalist. It's true, though. I know the risks; a gale can appear out of nowhere and capsize this boat in a matter of seconds. Ironically, I must continue to play at this game. The submarines don't scare me, nor do the navy ships. More or less, with this job, I can make my own rules. I enjoy talking to you, because my patience is not worn from noise and meaningless chatter. I can plunge to the core of a person, communicate from the heart. I have no tolerance for buffoons or drunkards. If I spot them in restaurants, I eat my meal quickly and leave. I don't spend a lot of time in cafés either. Rarely do I hear a conversation that's worth eavesdropping on."

"You're very different from me," I say.

"I know. I've also never married. Sometimes, I have regrets about not having a family. But I could never find a woman who would understand my need for solitude and open space. Every day I look out and direct this boat, I forget what's behind me, my past, my mistakes. Only the future lies ahead; my eyes cannot see the end of the horizon; therefore, my future is infinite. Follow my hand and look closely. Do you see that peninsula?"

"Yes."

"We've made it. That's the tip of Pamplona."

"I can't believe it! How long have we been out at sea?"

Poissonnière shrugs his shoulders. "I thought you were keeping track."

We refuel in Pamplona. To be safe, I return to my cramped quarters, the light of day hidden from me. I vow since we have entered Spain to relinquish my attachment to Paris. For now, I will have to forget about the masquerade balls, my favorite monuments and museums: place de la Concorde, the Panthéon, the Opéra and the Louvre. I'll also miss the chestnut and maple trees in the Luxembourg, the duck lake in the *bois*, and the nightlife, the Folies-Bergère, and Saint-Germain-des-Prés. I could go on. Enough! I'm returning home. I have to be grateful for Emile and my survival. Now I have thé opportunity to teach Emile about his Spanish heritage and the lifestyle in Barcelona, with bull fights, flamenco dancers, paella made with sweet saffron rice, dining at midnight, sangria, tapas, hot afternoons, lazy summers, and cathedral bells ringing all day and night in the *Barrio Gótico*. What will he think of the haunting and unfinished Sagrada Família? Perhaps he is still too young to form any opinions. This is the time for him to experience another culture. I'm looking forward to when he grows older, so we can communicate on the same level. As I close my eyes, I can already hear the Gypsy music on La Rambla. At the same time, the pain in my hand starts to throb with the rhythm. Christ! I want it to stop. But the pain won't leave. Oh, Barcelona, my Barcelona, what if you do capture me with your charm, but I may never again be able to paint you or your vivacious women.

TWENTY-ONE

Djuna Cortez

I was seated for dinner in the dining room of the Hotel Colón. Surrounding me were romantic couples holding hands and whispering. After I ordered my meal, a classical Spanish guitarist wandered from table to table performing for each couple. At the same time, a heavily made-up woman in a backless evening gown was selling long-stemmed red roses. Both knew to ignore me, which made me feel more awkward and conspicuous, being the only single person in the restaurant. A woman traveling alone in Spain is often treated graciously by servers, but furtively scorned by strangers. At this point in my journey, I was tired of being alone. Reading all the time wasn't enough. I longed for companionship, someone to communicate with and share all of these new experiences. Hypnotically, I stared into the votive candle that was flickering at my table.

The candle reminded me of earlier in the day, when I visited the basilica and isolated monastery of Montserrat. To get there, I rode in a tall bus that precariously wound its way up the side of the serrated mountain. As I looked down I could see hundreds of feet below into an agricultural community. Supposedly, the red clay soil of the region is extremely potent, producing an abundance of olives and nuts which are made into appetizing oils and liqueurs. One can also see hillsides decorated with butter-colored wildflowers that bloom year round. I was afraid that at any moment during the trip, the heavy bus could have tipped over. Yet, miraculously it safely made its way to the summit. The monastery resides just below the jagged, alienlike mountain peaks. And every day of the week, thousands of people flock to the region of Montserrat for its restorative powers. Fertility and healing are some of the promised effects of this spiritual community. Most importantly, cures and visions are said to come to those who pray to the twelfth-century Roman and Gothic style black virgin: a Madonna and child carved out of wild cherrywood, flax oil, mineral salts, and gold. Over the centuries, an unexplainable phenomenon occurred, causing the hands and faces of the icons to deepen to the tone of roasted chestnuts. The rest remained a brilliant gold.

Inside the basilica, I knelt before several rows of colored votive candles and lit one for my father. I hoped that one day I could set aside my anger. I realized that I still deeply cared for my only parent. If anything had happened to him during the time we had been apart, I wouldn't have been able to forgive myself.

The candle at my dinner table was flickering. Melted wax had built up and risen to a level that was slowly extinguishing the flame. All I had wanted was to run with that burning flame of passion which Paris had provoked, as I knew I wouldn't feel complete or be able to move on with my life until I could define love in the arms of a man. Thus, Jean-Auguste appeared to be the one I had imagined would transform me.

The waiter brought me another candle and a glass of champagne. "I didn't order this drink," I said politely.

"It's compliments of the gentleman over there," the waiter said, pointing to a dark-haired man who was seated alone. The man raised his glass to me in a toast. That moment, when we made eye contact, I knew I should have prayed to the black virgin's serene face. I should have respected her history and spiritual powers, as I didn't know that from this evening onward, I would desperately need divine intervention.

He walked to my table and stood perfectly still. I tried to speak; but my vocal chords refused to work. Only a squeal

came out of my throat. Patiently, he waited for me to acknow-
lege or reject him. In his sea-blue eyes, I saw what I wanted
to see, promises of devotion. My heart began to flutter with
the excitement of a first encounter. He extended his arms to
me. On his left hand was his solid gold wedding band. The
ring looked too tight for his finger. As usual, he was dressed
impeccably in a navy blazer with brass nautical buttons. His
neat trousers were blue-and-white pinstriped seersuckers, and
a white cotton shirt showed off the bronze tones of his Bain
de Soleil tan. I stared for a moment at his chest. His shirt was
unbuttoned to the beginning of his defined pectoral muscles,
exposing the smoothness of his youthful skin. Vivid memories
came back to me. He smiled and cleared his throat.

"Would you care to have this dance?" he asked.

I stood up and followed him. As I had remembered, his skin
smelled of fresh sandalwood soap. The blessing and curse between lovers is that all can be forgiven in one embrace. My
husband held me while we swayed to the music. Each song,
he moved nearer, pressing himself tightly against me, until the
space between us closed. Before the night ended, he was softly
whispering in my ear, "I'm sorry. I'm so very sorry for everything. I don't want to be without you. Please forgive me."

Goddesses, Wine, Dead Artists & Chocolate

The Journals of Joaquím Carlos Cortez

SPAIN, OCTOBER 1940

I have few worries in Barcelona. We don't have rations, so I
can eat as much chocolate and drink as much coffee as I want.
Spain has not betrayed me; after all, it was by painting my
country that I first attained celebrity. I should have been more
loyal, as my people have graciously taken me back. But even
here, my life is not free of pain. My right hand is deformed
and bent like a lobster claw; the bones never had a chance to
heal properly, which has caused arthritis to settle into the
joints. Now, when I attempt to hold a paintbrush in my right
hand, the pain is excruciating. Therefore, I am forced to work
with my left. At least with some practice, I have been able to

form legible words to write with, but painting is much more frustrating. The doctors want to break all my fingers and reset them. But I refuse to go through that again. Meanwhile, I try to keep busy to forget about myself and the discomfort. Teaching has proved to be a welcome distraction. Most of the time, I try not to think about poor Eliane, who I have left behind. I try not to think about France at all.

Emile and I are living well in a charming apartment in Barceloneta with a view of the entire port. Like Poissonnière, I have gravitated to staying near the ocean, even though I can't stand the thought of eating seafood again. Each morning, I study every fishing boat closely, hoping that Poissonnière will be stepping out of one. But he never does. Today, like all the other mornings, I inhale the misty sea air and watch the fishermen unloading their fresh catch. If I don't wake up in time for my classes, the seagulls get me up. While all this activity is happening, I rise slowly, as I need several hours of contemplation before starting my day. Only then do the nightmares of war begin to dissipate.

~

The days here are slow and indolent. In the late afternoons, after I finish teaching, I take a long siesta and drink far too many glasses of Manzanilla. As the sun begins to set, I awake feeling rejuvenated and so do the muchachas of the evening, my night goddesses and moon divas as I call them. The ladies appear at the same time in the evening when the sun casts an orange-and-red halo over the beach. Just like a pack of wolves, they parade up and down the streets with their bright, phosphorescent faces, decorated in colored skirts, resembling a lavish display of candied fruits. Clumsily, I work with my left hand, creating my own still-life. Their dances are well choreographed as they swing their hips and lift their skirts. Some are perfectly ripe like summer peaches and plums, while others are old and tired like prunes. Nevertheless, they are all appetizing, available, and wanton. Men yell out to them from the streets. Old widows curse them from their balconies. I relax and enjoy the show with eyes free of judgment and scorn. It is important that I remain a spectator, not a participant. For the time being, I must try to remain celibate, before I am the cause of another woman's demise. Yes, I must stay away from models—all sorts of women. I've captured and displayed too many on my walls like prize-winning exotic butterflies for all to admire. Without meaning to, I've crushed their wings. As a result, their colorful powder has stained my fingers.

BARCELONA, FEBRUARY 1944

Time continues to pass quickly. Meanwhile, I have let myself down. I haven't been able to stay away from the night goddesses. I am compelled to paint them, even with my left hand. Lately, my work has been looking more like Soutine's oils and some of Van Gogh's paintings in Saint Rémy. It's been easier for me to work with a palette knife, which gives my portraits distored angles and textured effects created with thick impasto work, instead of the smooth precision I used to give them. Even though it slows me down, I continue to write with my left hand. Like before, I set a sacrilegious routine that I follow religiously, from the moment I awaken in the morning, to when I close my eyes with a woman by my side. I've even gotten used to the shocked expressions on their faces when they witness my changed mood after sunrise. I know I made them feel like queens the night before. Most of them love to pose for me, as most men don't usually care about their pleasure. But as soon as the sobering light of day hits their eyes, they get sent back to where they came from.

I'm a different man at dawn when the seagulls begin screeching and hovering around the fishing nets. The moment I get up to make coffee, I usually find my son waiting for me in the kitchen. Those hours of the morning, when I see his sweet face and gentle eyes, I vow to never touch another whore again. Every time I'm around him, I try desperately to hide my bitter futility. Emile likes to help me toast and butter bread. Together we make his favorite breakfast of rice cereal and hot chocolate, before the nanny arrives to take him to school. Most often, we have breakfast on the balcony, while Emile sits on my lap. In unison we admire the boats, calling out their names. Eventually he follows me into the bathroom and watches me shave before I leave for work. I try to make a point of always having my morning meal with him.

BARCELONA, AUGUST 1944

When I first learned of the liberation of Paris, I was at one of the cafés on La Rambla. A newspaper boy passes by as he flashes the headline: "Paris falls to the Allies."

Immediately, I grab the newspaper from him and read every word. "This is fantastic." I stand up and shout, waving the paper above my head. "I lived in Paris. I lost those I loved. I lost loved ones in the war here, and now it's over. We're all free again."

Moments later, a group of excited people lead me to the square where we drink sangria and dance the Sardana—our unique Catalonian dance. Isabella would have been so happy to have known that Fascism is being conquered. Paris has finally been liberated by the courageous efforts of the free French and the Americans.

I write Mitya and soon receive a letter back.

SEPTEMBER, 1944
My Dearest Carlos,

It's so good hearing from you. I can't believe I survived it all. I watched over your properties and your art collection and they're yours to reclaim. I miss you. I do hope you will return to live in France. I have many important things to discuss. Paris is not the same without you. Please come back soon.

Your loyal friend,

Mitya

I was pleased to hear that it was safe to return and that Mitya was fine. However, I was surprised that she never mentioned Eliane. I hoped that Mitya had kept her promise to treat her well. As much as I was looking forward to seeing Mitya, it was Eliane that I really couldn't wait to be reunited with. It would be nice to live with her again, as nobody was ever as selfless or as devoted to my son and me as she was.

By April, I terminate my position at the Galì academy, and I leave Barcelona the beginning of May. Emile and I board the night train and arrive in Paris in the early morning. The moment we exit the Gare Saint-Lazare, the fragrance of fresh bread and coffee permeates the streets instead of gunsmoke. Alas, my son and I have returned to a city filled with emotionally scarred and bruised strangers who treat us as foreigners. Even at eight years old, Emile is too young to understand what could have happened to us if we had stayed on. The news came as quite a shock to me when I found out about the extermination camps. Images of stockpiles of bones will forever torment me. How can I tell my son that I may never recover from knowing how evil man can be? Still, parenting keeps me strong. These are Emile's most imaginative and impressionable years. I have to protect him, so that he can grow up with aspirations and dreams.

We spend our first several hours at Fouquets eating croissants, while I read all the local newspapers. Finally, Mussolini and Hitler have met their gruesome deaths! Maybe there is hope. After several *café crêmes,* I retrace the walk up the Champs-Elysées to avenue Foch.

We meet Mitya at the avenue Foch apartment. She has changed more than I expected her to. The whites of her eyes are now dull, almost yellowed. She looks emaciated and tired. We talk for hours. She's hopeful that the fashion industry will prosper again, but confesses to me about her nightmares. In her sleep, the war still exists. We weep together for our reunion, survival, and the atrocities that will never be erased from our memories.

"I will never be the happy person I used to be," Mitya says. "I don't think I will ever trust anyone again. Carlos, you must feel differently. I won't let your life be ruined like mine has been."

"I don't know what you're talking about. My life has already been destroyed." I show her my deformed hand.

"Can you paint?"

"Only a little with my broken hand. It's not the same with my left."

"How is Emile taking all this? He hasn't said a word to me. I would like to talk to him."

I call to my son who is playing in the corner of the room with his toy soldiers. "Emile, could you please come here and properly greet Princess Mitya?" Emile ignores me and continues to play.

I explain to Mitya, "He's too young to understand the realities of war. I haven't been able to take away the soldiers or the toy guns. I don't know how to explain this to him. He's a smart boy, gifted in arithmetic. Most of his free time is spent solving equations. I was never like that. I hated math."

Mitya gets up from the sofa and walks over to him.

"Are you happy to be back in France?" she asks him.

"No. Are you a whore?" he retorts.

Mitya and I both laugh nervously. Emile enjoys our shocked reactions. Then I get angry. "When you are asked a question by a grown-up, the polite thing is to answer nicely. Never do you insult an adult!"

Emile ignores my remark and walks over to Mitya's piano and begins banging on the keys.

"It's hopeless. He refuses to listen to anything I say. I don't know what's wrong with the child. Every day it's a constant battle of wills."

Mitya smiles and says politely, "He is a beautiful boy. I'm sure it's just a phase that he'll soon outgrow. You're very lucky to have him."

"I know."

"Where do you plan on staying? I can move out by the end of the week. You're both welcome to move in here, or go to your studio. My friend who was staying there moved out last week. You know, the neighborhood in the Latin Quarter has completely changed. The shopkeepers of your favorite bookshops and art supply stores are all gone, along with their families. Oh, Carlos, it was so tragic to see all the Jews of Paris being sent away."

"Please, Mitya, I don't want Emile to hear this." I call to Emile, "Go play in another room." He runs off. "I'm sorry. Please spare me some of the horrific details. I can't stand hearing about it."

"You must know that it was terrible here. So many were

betrayed by their closest friends. At that point the Resistance was completely helpless. I was certain we had lost the war. I wanted to quit. But my sweet baron wouldn't let me. Fritz believed we could make a difference." Her face grew solemn and her lip began to quiver.

"I think Sylvie had somehow predicted The Holocaust. At that time, I never wanted to believe in her pessimism."

"That's what I was trying to warn you about before you left. Fritz had information on what was going on," Mitya said.

"Where is Eliane?" I asked, changing the subject.

Mitya stands up from the sofa and walks over to the marble fireplace mantel.

"Three months after she came here, one morning, she packed up her belongings and left. She said she needed her independence. There was nothing I could do to convince her to stay. She's a good woman. We got along well. I really tried not to treat her as a servant. This is what confuses me the most." Mitya shows me a card. "Every year she sends me a birthday card. She doesn't enclose her return address."

"How odd. I wonder where she is?"

"I can understand one's need for independence. You had given her a lot of money. She didn't need to work for me. I probably would have done the same thing. You know, for a long time, I thought I was different from other women. My life was spent competing with men, trying to prove that I was as capable. My impudence caused me to cheat on my men. But the baron was the love of my life. He was such a good person. I was completely devoted to him and should have had his children. Instead, I have his ashes." She points to a silver urn on the mantel and picks up a photograph of him.

"He was so brave. *Les Doryphores,* as we learned to call them for stealing our potatoes, captured and tortured him. His loyalty was always to me and France. He refused to give names. That's how I was protected. I can't think about what they did to my Fritz." She covers her face in her hands and begins to sob.

I walk over to her and place my arm around her bony shoulders. "He was a hero and you should be proud of him. You should also commend yourself. You survived with your dignity intact," I tell her.

"I'm happy you've returned. We used to have such fun. Do you think we will again?" she asks, pointing to the first portrait I did of her. "I moved it here along with my piano. Don't worry. All your paintings are safe in the studio upstairs. Gosh, I was libertine in those days. I enjoyed keeping people guessing about me. I knew the moment they had me figured out, they wouldn't be fascinated with me anymore. I still have to keep up my provocative image. I'll be right back," she says.

As she leaves the room, sensuality remains in her movements; her slender hips swing gracefully as she walks. A fragrance of gardenia and patchouli clings to the air. Returning with a set of keys in her hand, she coquettishly, brushes her fingers against my beard and drops a set of keys in my lap.

"I like your new look. The beard suits you. Here are your keys. They're all there, this apartment, your studio, and the château in Loire. I haven't been to Loire. Here are the new property papers I made up for you. All you have to do is sign them and everything will be returned to you, even your cat. She is very old, but keeps going."

"Please keep the cat. It belonged to Sylvie and reminds me too much of her. I don't want to care for pets anymore. Emile is enough to look after. I can't thank you enough for everything you've done. How can I ever repay you?" I ask.

"You can begin by taking me to dinner," she says.

"I'll gladly buy you dinner for the rest of your life."

"Do you think we'll ever have fun again the way we used to?" she asks.

"I don't know, but I'm sure willing to try."

PARIS, AUGUST 1945

Mitya was right about Paris. The city had changed. Even after the passing months, most people are unable to hide their wartorn faces. My distress returned again. I cursed myself for celebrating the end of the war at the expense of all the innocents and the brave who have died. I wanted Paris to return to a city bursting with exuberant artists exchanging philosophies in cafés. But those days may never come again.

Emile and I spend most of our time in Loire. The vines have been severely neglected and the winery has to be restored to working order. Fortunately, my bank account has remained intact, only adding interest. However, during the war, the Gestapo had taken over the château. My servants were forced to cater to the enemies and to their wild parties. Most of the furniture, dishes, linens and draperies were destroyed. All of Sylvie's family's paintings and heirlooms have been stolen. Since I've been away, my tastes have changed. I prefer the walls bare, almost empty of decoration. Simplicity can be comforting. This is what I am learning to appreciate.

I thought Emile would thrive in the country with all the deer and wild rabbits. Yet nothing seems to satisfy him. He has terrible fits of rage when he ransacks his room and then refuses to clean it up. He needs more guidance and discipline than what I can provide. For the most part, living in the château is too lonely for him. He needs to interact with other children. Even though I will miss him terribly, I've sent him today to a boarding school in Switzerland. There he will be able to have an excellent education and hopefully continue to excel in mathematics and foreign languages. Already my son is fluent in Spanish and French. By the time he graduates, I hope he will learn English, Italian, and German.

SUMMER 1962

With the passing years, most of my energy is spent on the winery. I have begun producing some superior vintages. At the same time, painting continues to frustrate me, due to my arthritic hand. Often my brushwork is sloppy, the strokes uneven and jagged, lacking fluidity and smoothness. Why can't I transform my style? Monet painted the formidable water lilies when his vision was failing him. Am I too much of a perfectionist? It could be that my creative force is all gone—dried up. When I look at myself in the mirror, I see tired, drawn, and wrinkled eyes that stare back at me, eyes that lack the luster and intensity that used to entice women, lips that are colorless, dry, and hair that is turning white. Finally, regret has carved its way into my flesh.

It's impossible to stop this free association of thoughts onto paper. Writing saves my sanity. Drawers are now filled with these diaries. Will anyone really care to read them one day? Do I really think I can become immortal? Did I deserve to live while my loved ones died? I would like to have befriended more men of truth and imagination, men like Victor Hugo and Emile Zola. We could have become lifetime friends. They understood suffering. If Marcel were alive today, he would have laughed at writing for my own atonement. I wonder if he would have published. He was a lost artist, a victim of war, a voice that could have obtained poetic immortality like Rimbaud and Baudelaire.

The Beaux-Arts has asked me to teach, so I've agreed to go into the city once a month and also host lectures from my château. For the rest of my days, I will continue to challenge those who see me as a monster of forbidden desires. The pleasures of sin help me forget my pain. Therefore, let them slay me with their polished swords. I'll sacrifice my blood if it's to prevent art censorship. Let them dissect these words, analyze my paintings, and mock me, because I no longer care what the fickle public thinks. Likewise, I have removed myself from the puppets of this earth, as I am only searching for raw volcanic material. The misunderstood heart appeals to me most. The artist who is not afraid of finding his own path, without any guidance. There is no point in writing or painting if I can't peal apart the truth, layer by layer, like a fat purple onion until it stings the eyes. Sting me, sting me, onion, scorpion, or critic. *Je mens fou.* I laugh like a mocking black raven. Assassinate me. I have been stabbed many times in the heart. Let my blood splatter onto these words, and maybe then my heart will stop feeling like an open artery.

TWENTY-TWO

Djuna Cortez

After our slow dance, I left with him for the Barcelona harbor where the yacht was docked. Before stepping onto the boat, Jean-Auguste announced, "I've made some significant changes. The first of which you can see for yourself." He pointed under the gang plank to the white stern of the yacht. *Djuna* was written in bold silver letters.

"I don't know what to say. I'm flattered," I answered timidly. Soon I was at a complete loss for words. We were all silent as we walked on board. It was a breezy night: all the boat's flags were snapping in the wind, tarps and canvases rattling. The yacht gently swayed and rocked, causing the thick ropes attached to shore to stretch and tighten. The lulling motion made me sleepy. Jean-Auguste called for an attendant to take down the yacht's French flag. Two men arrived; both had my name printed on their white shirts. Without speaking, we watched the deckhands carefully remove the flag, folding it into an olivewood box.

"Please make yourself comfortable," my husband said, as he opened the sliding door to the upper deck salon.

Immediately upon entering the room, we were greeted by our two Italian greyhounds.

"I didn't expect them to be here," I said, bending down to the dogs' level. "It's so good to see them."

"They love the boat. I'm having sailor's uniforms made up for them."

"That will be amusing."

I was beginning to feel tense. The champagne had worn off. Rigidly, I sat down on the sofa. Jean-Auguste reclined opposite me on a stuffed chair. A glass-and-rattan cocktail table was separating us. The salon had been redecorated since I was last on board; a bright polished cotton fabric covered the upholstery on the chairs and couches. The color scheme was now forest green and gold with a pattern of sculpted lemon trees, instead of brown suede.

"How do you like the Valentino fabric I chose? The master cabin has also been decorated with same pattern. I do hope you like it," he said hesitantly.

"I do. It's elegant and cheerful."

Jean-Auguste rang the buzzer and ordered coffee and dessert.

"How did you find me?" I finally asked.

He cleared his throat and answered, "I know it was underhanded, but I was going crazy with worry. I contacted the credit card company. They traced your whereabouts for me."

"I see."

"I've been doing a lot of thinking lately," he said.

"So have I."

He leaned toward me in his chair, resting his hands on the glass table. "I'm really sorry about what happened between us. Honestly, I don't think we should discard our marriage because of a few squabbles. The pressure had been too much for me. I never meant to take it out on you. Finally, I'm taking a month off. I've hired someone to look after the wineries. When we get back, we can put your place on the market if you like. I do hope you'll give me another chance and travel with me."

I kept my composure and listened attentively. Both dogs were stretched out on my lap. I was petting them while he spoke. Still, I had no urge to respond.

"Please let me make it all up to you. Please talk to me, Djuna, tell me what you want. Tell me what's important to you. I do want to make you happy. What does your heart say?"

"I can't answer you yet."

"Then spend the night with me. You know how well you sleep on board. Please don't leave," he pleaded.

"I'm sorry, but I have to go back to my room. I must spend this night alone. I'll be able to give you an answer by morning," I said firmly.

"I can respect that. Will you have lunch with me tomorrow?" he asked.

"Yes, I think that's possible. What time?"

"Anytime you want. Just come over."

"Well, I'd better be going then," I said standing up.

"I'll call a cab," he politely offered.

After the taxi was confirmed, he walked toward me. Kissing my hand, he said, "You look more beautiful than I remembered. I especially missed your laugh. The dogs have also missed you."

Once again, my demeanor was reserved and guarded. Another power struggle ensued; I didn't want to give in to him right way. This made him more interested and intrigued. He refused to let go of my hand. At the same time, his pleading eyes looked worried and anxious. By morning, I would have to make a final decision. There was a possibility that he had lost me forever; both of us understood this. We were distracted by a steward who entered the salon announcing that the taxi had arrived.

"Good night," I said formally. He moved closer to kiss me on the lips, but I gave him my cheek.

"I'll be waiting for your answer."

Goddesses, Wine, Dead Artists & Chocolate

The Journals of Joaquím Carlos Cortez

LOIRE, JANUARY 1963

I am searching for a woman to inspire me. There has to be another beautiful and intelligent female who will make me want to paint again and forget my arthritic hand. Over a hundred people have arrived at my château this afternoon for an art lecture and wine tasting. Word has traveled that I'm searching for a model. Fifty of the guests are female art students; each nymph hopes she will be the exalted one.

My audience was captivated with my lecture on the expatriate artists of Paris during the 1930s. To get me to paint again, art dealers have offered me high-class prostitutes, which I politely decline. I don't find them as colorful anymore; the drugs they now take have turned them all gray like birdshit. Each lecture always ends in the same way; I never find anyone I want to use as a model. Anyway, I'm afraid of becoming attached, as every woman I've ever loved was taken from me.

The only living person I care for is my son, but when we're together we continually fight. Emile has completed his military service and graduated university with honors in foreign languages and international business. It's hard to believe my son is grown up and will soon be returning home for a visit with his new wife. In Emile's letters, he has refused to tell me anything about her. Every day, I wait in anticipation for their arrival. Thus far, they are a month late. My hope is that when they finally do arrive, they will decide to live here, and Emile will take an interest in the winery. One day, I would like to leave this place to him and rest in my old age. It is for Sylvie's memory that I continue to maintain this château. The only consistent progress in my life are my wines. They are purchased and distributed throughout Europe, giving me a steady and reliable income. A bottle a day keeps the doctor away. It has worked for me. My buyers also swear this is true. I wish life were really that simple. Fortunately, every year the wines improve in flavor, as I alter the recipe, sometimes adding sweet seasonal berries or ripe peaches to mellow the acidity of tannin and alcohol.

At last, my son has arrived. It's a beautiful day. The sun is out for a change and the air is refreshing. I am outside in the gardens facing the swimming pool and pond when Emile walks toward me. I'm seated alone at a table that is scattered with winemaking ingredients. He slaps me on the back. Sometimes he hits me too hard, but I don't say anything. Excitedly, I get up to hug his stiff body.

"It's good to see you. Happy New Year!" I say.

"You too," he answers.

I notice that tucked under his arm are books on World War II airplanes and combat weapons. Just seeing the graphic covers makes me cringe. He intentionally places the books near me. To be polite, I don't show my disdain for them. Sometimes, I am completely astonished at how Emile has turned out. Unlike me, he loves war memorabilia, books, and films. Everything I had tried to shelter him from, he now relishes in. All I tried to do was preserve his innocence so that he didn't have to grow up as abruptly as I had. Have I failed? All I want is for him to respect me. Yet that seems too much to ask for.

Emile eases himself onto a lounge chair and closes his eyes in the sun.

"Would you like to taste the Bourgueil?" I offer.

"God, no! It's probably poisonous," he shrieks.

"Don't be silly. So, tell me, how did you meet your wife?"

"At a café in Aix-en-Provence. It was near the school where she teaches English. It was completely unexpected. We just shared a table," he answers with some warmth in his deep voice.

"How long are you both planning to stay?" I ask.

"Only a week or two. Then we have to get back," he says, looking at his silver watch. "She should be coming outside anytime now. It was a long trip. She wanted to shower and change before seeing you."

"I'm looking forward to meeting her. You know you can stay as long as you like. Tell me though, whose idea was it not to invite me to your wedding?" I inquire.

"We didn't have one."

"I could have given you a lavish affair here. It would have been beautiful," I muse.

Emile raises his hands to block the sun and chides, "Since when are you the helpless romantic? Don't try to hide the fact from me that you're a misogamist. I've heard you condemn marriage many times. You prefer whores."

Before I can answer, a door from inside the château opens.

A woman walks slowly toward us. When she is close enough for me to see what she looks like, I'm stupefied. It is as if the clock had rolled back thirty years. She's the spitting image of Sylvie, except as a blonde. She even dresses like Sylvie did in floppy hats and long flowing skirts. I am too nervous to speak. Emile takes her hand and introduces us. "I would like to present to you my new wife."

I expect him to call her Sylvie, but he says Josephine.

"It's nice to meet you," she says with a slight American accent. Her wry smile is just like Sylvie's, a grin that is both innocent, intelligent, and mischievous.

Josephine is a classic American beauty of pilgrim stock. Her ancestors were some of the first British settlers in America. And just like Sylvie was to me, she is much older than Emile.

Emile says to me, "I've found my lady of liberty and I want to become an American. One day, we're going to live in the land of opportunity. I want to be free, not damned like you."

Again, I let his insults roll off my shoulders. I raise my glass and say in a toast, "Congratulations to the new couple. I wish you both loads of happiness."

As the days pass, each time I see Josephine, more memories of Sylvie return. Her almond eyes are the same emerald green. Even the scent of her skin reminds me of my wife; she smells like burnt sugar. I like that she speaks passionately about her ideas and opinions. One cannot help but admire her statuesque body and mellifluous voice, which is ripened by her preference for whiskey sours. Most of all, and what is so refreshing, is that finally someone appreciates my art and wines. However, since Josephine has arrived, I rarely sleep. At all hours of the night, I'm up, pacing in the winery—in the room I've set up as a studio. Never before have I been as terrified of my son or my lust.

I need to paint Josephine. She may be the answer to my stifled creativity. One morning, at the breakfast table, I ask for Emile's permission. His response is to tip over a platter of cheeses and then toss a bunch of grapes at me.

"You're a disgusting pervert! I'm getting the fuck away

from you. Everything has been taken from me. You killed my mother and took away a nanny I loved. You're not going to take my wife too," Emile shouts.

"You don't know anything about what happened with your mother. It's unfair of you to blame me!" I exclaim angrily.

. He grabs Josephine by her narrow waist. Gently, she pushes him away. "Why doesn't anyone ask me? I'm the subject matter here. Do you think I'm a doll that you own? I'm my own person, Emile, and it's not up to you. I can pose for whomever I want," Josephine says irritably.

Emile lets her go. "Yes, but not that *cochon*. Start packing, I won't have anymore of this."

Josephine intervenes again. "You're a brilliant young man, but when it comes to your father, you behave like a spoiled brat," she scolds. "Your father has been wanting to paint for years, but hasn't found the right model. I'm flattered that he thinks I can help him. I've never modeled before, and certainly the thought terrifies me, but your father's work has inspired many people. We must help him."

Emile grunts. "He's only interested in you because you're my wife."

Josephine's face flushes to a light crimson. Irately, she asks, "Are you insinuating my appeal can only extend to you?"

"No. I'm not saying that," Emile answers.

She takes Emile's hand and says pedantically, "Love is not about limitations. If you want to possess me then you'll need to put me in a cage, under lock and key. Is that what you want?"

He shakes his head and bashfully glances at his shoes.

"It's only fair that we should try to help your father," she adds.

Emile sighs and collapses into a chair beside the spilled food. "If you want to pose for him, then I won't stop you," he says begrudgingly.

〜

The following morning, Josephine poses for me. She stands beside the wine barrels. It's blissfully quiet in the winery as both of us are entombed in these stone walls. An intoxicating aroma permeates the damp air: the ripe and mellow fragrance of red wine and cork. Nobody can disturb us here. Nobody would dare. To warm the room, I light a fireplace, tossing in some pinecombs and extra brush logs. Afterwards, I begin to dip a paintbrush into some linseed oil. As I do this, electrical impulses travel through me; a warmth begins to spread like wildfire to my arms. Then the fingers in my right hand become limber and my joints relax. Because of her, a precious gift is bestowed upon me; I can paint with my right hand. Suddenly my clairvoyance returns. This woman is a temptress, a rebel, a sorceress, a saint. Squelched dreams are in her wistful eyes. Like Sylvie, she's a woman torn apart—wanting her independence, but clinging to a man for security. At the same time, her true passions frighten her the most.

Emile has agreed to extend their stay for a week more. During their visit, he has nothing else to do but hang around the vineyards and learn about winemaking from the staff. However, he prefers to spend most of his time drinking our product. Knowing that Josephine will soon leave makes me suffer in mind and in body. I remember reading an engraved passage by the Trocadéro fountains. Part of the inscription said that the act of creating for an artist engages all of his being. And the artist's pain fortifies him. Josephine helps me surrender to and accept my *angoisse*. Once again, my palette is provoked. Instead of dwelling on the imperfections in my work, I let the dynamic spirit of the model come through on canvas, which is stronger than my decrepit hand. Furthermore, the painting no longer becomes mine, only hers, and what she wants to reveal. Soon, I learn that it is more than I ever anticipated. When she changes, I discover that she can sing the blues like a chanteuse in the finest of Parisian nightclubs. For some reason, she asks me to promise never to tell Emile about her voice. That was the beginning of our first deception.

I start ten paintings the week Josephine poses for me and finish them several weeks later. My art dealer in Paris sells each one from a photograph. I really don't want to part with them, but I give in to get my name circulating again. Josephine has made me feel twenty years old. Every time I paint her, I am reminded of the splendor of the thirties in Paris.

⌐‿⌐

Now, I stare at my last portrait of Josephine. This painting is like none of the others I've done before. My artwork has finally blended with my winemaking. It took all this time to set most of the work aside, allowing the creative processs to mature and ripen like the wines. My oils appear vibrant, yet soothing to the eyes. As I stand before the center of this five-foot canvas, I see Josephine, dressed in a mint satin chinoiserie gown, and in the background are the verdant hills of Loire. But when I walk to the right of the painting, the colors are altered, and so is her face and clothing. The model becomes another person: the beguiling Sylvie, wearing a mecurial silver gown, as she stands before the sea at the Eden Roc hotel. And when I walk to the far left, the model transforms into sweet Isabella with her dark mane that glistens like an Arabian horse. Her gown is blood red and she's standing before the Sacré-Coeur in Montmartre.

At this moment, it's impossible to transcend the pain. The joints in my hand have stiffened and curled up again into an ugly claw. I miss Emile and Josephine. It's lonely here without them. Beside my bottle of brandy is the note Josephine was polite enough to leave me before their departure. I haven't been able to throw it away. She wrote: "I will always love you and admire your work."

As much as this pleases me, these are the exact words I have always wanted my son to say.

Alone and cold, all I can do is huddle by the fireplace and drink Napoléon brandy. The rains have aggravated my arthritis; I feel every crushed bone, like that haunting day in 1940. Bomb sirens go off in my brain. Airplane engines drone into my skull. I can hear the desecration of paintings—canvases ripping, frames cracking. Isabella is screaming. And there's the smell of bonfires and innocent blood. How can I forgive? How can I forget?

I receive a letter mailed without a return address. It was sent from the Provence.

> *Dear Joaquím Carlos,*
>
> *I never meant to separate you from your son. My intentions were only to help you, as I was flattered that you thought I would be an interesting model. Emile doesn't appreciate art in the same way as I do. You see, I came to France not just to teach English, as I have. Instead, I had really wanted to meet an eccentric artist. I had visions of singing in a club while he painted at night, and we would rendezvous during the day. Everything changed when I met your son. He was flattering and charming and so filled with practical ambition, that I decided to abandon my dream and settle down. I've always wanted to have children. Although I would prefer to raise my daughter in Europe, I must help Emile realize his ambitions and take him to America.*
>
> *One day, I may regret not pursuing my aspirations in France. But thanks to you, I got to know a painter. You are a special person. I never planned on us getting as intimate. Except, I knew you understood the impratical side of me, the fanciful dreamer. With you I could let her out. Now, I hope you will also understand my plea for you to not contact us. You see, a new life needs me now. During the time I was modeling for you, Emile refused to touch me or even share the same bed. He said he would again, as soon as we left. This was his way of punishing me for giving in to you. I don't hold it against him. However, this child can only be yours. She reminds me so much of you. I will never bring this up with Emile. He has forgotten about what happened in Loire and never discusses our visit. Therefore, I feel it is better that you don't communicate with us. Seeing you again would be very difficult for me. And I would never want to hurt my*

husband or jeopardize our marriage. The truth would certainly devastate him.

Emile is excited about raising his baby girl. I have named her Djuna. She is very smart and sweet. Most of the time, I try to speak French with her. Emile also does on occasion, but he mostly wants to emphasize English. I also want him to teach her Spanish. I wish for her to be like him and be able to converse fluently in several languages.

Please forgive me for demanding this of you. I do trust that you will keep away from us and be silent.

Much love,

Josephine

TWENTY-THREE

Djuna Cortez

The cathedral bells chimed twelve times. Furiously, I threw the journal across my hotel room, not caring that part of the binding came loose when it hit the wall, and several inserted letters slipped out. Anger and rage were overtaking me again. It was terrifing, as I felt out of control. This intricate web of lies was strangling me. Feeling clautrophobic, I had to break out of the room. I needed open space, fresh air. I had to breathe!

Rushing downstairs, I stood briefly outside the hotel. The evening was lit by a hot August moon that maintained most of its fullness from the night before. Hoping to release some of my frustration, I began running through the deserted and shadowy cobblestone streets of the Gothic Quarter. It didn't matter to me that it was dangerous being alone, nor that the sweltering temperature of the day still clung to the air. As I ran, the narrow Roman walls felt like they were caving in on me. Some sections were nauseating, as they reeked of urine and rotting garbage left in bins for the stray cats to raid. At night, this ancient neighboorhood breathed of mystery, reckless abandonment, and a history of violence engraved in stone. For a second, I stopped before a plaque describing a civil war

massacre. The streets had to be safer now. Yet it was foolish
to run alone at night. Most people gathered in *plaças,* so this
had to be where perpetrators hid. Even so, I continued running,
hoping to exhaust myself, to be numb, so I could no longer
feel the hurt. At the Plaça de Sant Just, I almost knocked over
an elderly person who was walking in the opposite direction.
When I slowed down to make certain I hadn't hurt them, I
saw that it was a woman. Suddenly she shouted angrily, "Die,
American whore. Die!" I immediately recognized her scratchy
voice; it was the hot-tempered woman from the café. The dim
light had contorted her face with shadows, making her look
like a gargoyle. Terrified, I began running. This time faster,
hoping I could find a way out of the maze of the Gothic Quarter. Miraculously, I was able to retrace my path and make it
back to Plaça de la Seu. Exhausted and completely breathless,
I found myself before the Gothic cathedral.

As I faced the intricately carved façade, the cathedral looked
like a fairy tale castle from Disneyland, illuminated in bright
gold-and-white lights. Hypnotically, I walked up the steps,
heading toward the center of the main archway. Desperately,
I tried to open the front door, but it was bolted shut. All I
wanted was to drown myself in cool holy water and then collapse beside an altar and pray. Perhaps I was cursed like the
fortune teller in Avignon had said. Frantically, I tried more
wooden doors, rattling the brass handles, which awakened
flocks of peculiar-looking birds with long beaks and red beady
eyes that were nesting in the two bell towers. The bells chimed
one time. An hour had passed. The birds began screeching
like bats while rapidly fluttering their wings. There had to be
a door that had been accidentally left unlocked. I ran a circle
around the cathedral, ending up again at the front steps. There
I collapsed underneath the central Gothic archway that was
engraved with patron saints. It was the exact same location
where Isabella lay in one of the civil war paintings. This time,
instead of the cathedral being on fire, it was me. I was burning
up—drenched in perspiration—too exhausted and emotionally
drained to move. Alone and huddled against the stone structure, I spent the night there weeping, falling asleep only for
two hours in the early morning between the bell chimes.

I awoke to the gentle hands of a priest, who helped me up,

and offered to take me inside to hear my confession. I thanked him and politely refused. It was now too late for prayers, wishes, and ruminations. What I needed was immediate courage more than a prolonged absolution. As I walked away from the cathedral, the morning activities were beginning. Crates of produce and flowers were being carried by hard-working men. Some people were rushing to work. Others were strolling at a more leisurely pace, as sunlight was melting away all the demons, evaporating the shadows of the night before. It was time that I face all the consequences of my actions and of those related to me. From this point onward, I refused to let bitterness corrupt me and become like that angry woman. Somehow, I had to find the sweetness in life, searching for beauty found in art. Perhaps I could give love another chance.

Once I returned to my hotel, I quickly showered and packed. That morning, I couldn't face looking at myself in a mirror, nor did I have the patience to fuss with my appearance. There were more important matters to tend to. Jean-Auguste would have to accept me completely unadorned.

It was close to noon when I boarded the yacht. As I set down my luggage, I inhaled the crisp nautical fragrance of wood varnish and sea salt. Unlike yesterday, this afternoon promised to be perfect. The winds had died down. It was a day that called for new beginnings. Jean-Auguste soon greeted me on the upper deck. He was dressed in nautical navy shorts and a white T-shirt with the boat's emblem. He appeared serene, as we sat down to be served lunch outside. From where we were both seated, we could view the perimeters of Barcelona.

"I've heard there are roads up there paved with glass," he said, pointing to an Andalusian castle built on a distant hilltop.

"Do you really believe that?"

"Possibly. Since you like Spain so much, why don't you come with me to Madrid? I would love to show you the Buen Retiro Park and the Crystal Palace."

"That would be lovely," I said.

Once again, my husband's demonstrativeness was expressed

in every detail of his lavish entertaining. Ivory table linens were brought out to the aft deck table, along with polished silverware. Next came a flower arrangement of white roses, cala lilies, and gladiolas that had to have been recently purchased from the Boqueria market. At one o'clock sharp, lunch was served. First, he insisted on pouring me three glasses of wine: a rich Bordeaux, a sweet Sauternes, and a Rosé d'Anjou. Once we began eating, the dogs appeared. Jean-Auguste had them sit on the banquette with us and between bites of our omelette, which was packed with chives and caviar, he handfed each dog.

"You're spoiling them," I commented.

"I know. But they have excellent taste. I would like to be able to do the same to you," he answered.

"Do you mean hand-feed me?" I asked.

"Why not? Taking the initiative, he carefully placed a forkful of shrimp salad in my mouth.

"You do that well," I affirmed.

"It's an art, one in which I have many hidden talents," he said flirtatiously. In a matter of seconds, as if perfectly timed, a steward arrived, presenting me with a gold foil–wrapped gift.

"Please, no more presents," I adamantly stated.

"It's nothing. Just open it."

While I unwrapped the gift, the dogs were anxiously poking their cold snouts under my arms, wanting to see what was in the box, and hoping it was some delicious treat.

"Books!" I exclaimed.

"I know how you enjoy reading. They're travel guides," he added.

"Thank you. That's very thoughtful."

"You'll see there's one on Madrid and one on the island of Gibraltar," he cheerfully explained.

"I've read so much about Madrid. I'd like to go. And I've always been curious about Gibraltar. I understand it's very close to here."

"That's where I'm planning to go first. I want to see the wild monkeys and speak English. It would also be nice to have tea and eat some savory shepherd's pie. If you come along, afterwards we can fly to Madrid. You haven't told me your answer yet. I promise I'll never hurt you again. Everything will be different without all the pressure. What do you say? Will you take me back? I see you've brought your luggage. Does that mean you'll come travel with me?" he asked in a boyish tone.

"Yes, but first there are some important things I would like to discuss with you," I said firmly, as I began picking the petals off a white rose, forming a pile by my glass of Bordeaux.

"Yes, of course. Let me first tell the captain to prepare for our trip," he said ringing the buzzer three times, signaling the captain's cue.

The French captain arrived and bowed. "We can be ready to leave at any time," he told us.

"How is the forcast?" my husband asked.

"It's supposed to be perfectly calm."

"Excellent! Let's go," Jean-Auguste announced clapping his hands.

"Yes, monsieur. Is there anything else?"

"No, just take her away."

After the captain left, he turned to me and said, "You may not even need to take any motion sickness pills. This will be a very smooth trip. I'm so pleased you're here. I've been a stupid fool to let you slip through my fingers," he said, stretching and yawning. He continued. "That lunch made me sleepy. How about you?"

"I'm fine."

He moved closer to me and began kissing my neck. His lips were cool, the lingering moisture on his mouth refreshing. At that point, I was eager to dive back into his promising ocean, float in his warm lapis sea, swim out to his private island, and do anything to remain with him.

"Not now," I said, gently pushing him away, "before we get started with all this. I must clarify a few things . . ."

The engines started rumbling, drowning out the rest of my sentence.

"Grab hold of the dogs. Sometimes they get scared when the engines are first turned on," he shouted.

Suddenly there was a frenzy of activity. Several men were running about the yacht, untying knots that were connected to the dock. Then a person on shore threw back the ropes and power cables that a crew member had to run and catch. After, two more deckhands rushed to push away the boats that were on each side of us, so we wouldn't collide as the yacht pulled out of the tight berth. And while all of this work was going on, Jean-Auguste and I, and the dogs, were still languidly seated on the banquette watching the performance. Next, the man who stood at the front of the boat, began shouting to a person in the galley, who was collecting and cleaning the anchor. He was warning the fellow below of seaweed and other entanglements that were on the anchor as it was being pulled up. As soon as that task was completed, the boat began to slowly traverse the enormous harbor. At a snail's pace, we watched Barcelona fade from view: the fishing boats in Barceloneta; the seaside restaurants painted orange, red, and green, where cases of fresh seafood were always on display before their entrances; and lastly Columbus's ancient galleon. My eyes were glued on the coastal city and its background of hills. I tried to recall all of the places I had visited. Soon, all I could see was the wide entrance of the port, and a stone lighthouse with opaline waves crashing against the rocks. Adieu, Barcelona. Farewell. Adios.

The boat picked up speed and cruised south, staying close to the shoreline where the water lightened in colors to aquamarine, as farther out it was a dark cobalt.

"Let's have dessert in our cabin and talk where it's quieter," he said, ringing the buzzer and then instructing the steward to continue the service downstairs.

The dogs were pleased we had reconciled; both were wagging their tails and kissing us as I was carrying them.

When we entered the attached salon of the master cabin, the dogs ran off to sleep on our bed. "Why don't you change and get comfortable? You may want to take a nap," Jean-Auguste suggested.

My suitcases were placed on a divan. I opened one, pulling out some white silk pajamas.

"Don't worry about the unpacking. I'll help you with that later," Jean-Auguste said.

After I had changed, I joined him on another sofa, which had the same lemon pattern as upstairs. A copy of *Town and Country* magazine rested on the coffee table.

"You're as beautiful and as rich as the women featured on their covers," he said.

"What difference does that make? Those things aren't that important. Perhaps now we can talk. You see my priorities are changing. It very important to me that—"

I was interrupted again. This time by the steward knocking on the door.

"Come in," Jean-Auguste answered.

The crew member entered, carrying a silver tray with a set of cobalt blue Christian Dior china.

Jean-Auguste boisterously asked, "How many sets have we gone through?"

"This is the third, monsieur."

Jean-Auguste said casually, "It's only money."

The steward poured the coffee and served us each a slice of *tart Tatin*.

"Will that be all, monsieur?"

"This is fine, thank you." Jean-Auguste followed the steward to the door and locked it behind him.

"How's the tart?" he asked.

"It's delicious."

"It's not as good as the one they make on the Tahiti beach in Saint Tropez. Now, that dessert is to die for. I'm sorry we never made it there on our honeymoon. You must try this *noisette* liqueur," he said, handing me a snifter. "So, what were you saying?"

"I've had a lot on my mind lately. If we're going to start over, I want us to be completely truthful with each other. I would like to get a few things out in the open."

"Like what?"

"Well, I'll begin with me first. A while ago, I overheard you and your mother discussing when I was going to get pregnant. I was meaning to eventually tell you that I don't want to have children for maybe a long time to come. You see, I've been taking the Pill to prevent that."

Without commenting, he strummed his fingers on the cocktail table.

"I feel even more strongly about this now. You see, just last night, I learned my father isn't my biological father; Joaquím Carlos was. Now, the last thing I want to do is continue a pattern of deceit in my relationships."

He poured himself more liqueur and silently listened as he swirled the drink around in his glass.

"Before I tell you more, I must ask you about a postcard that I accidently came across in one of your drawers."

"You went through my drawers!" he exploded, forcefully slamming down his drink. I was afraid he was going to break the glass.

"I didn't mean to. But I had run out of nylons and I was just looking to see if there were any hidden in another drawer. I'm just curious who sent you a postcard from Greece, signing it *moi*."

He stood up and inhaled deeply. His face was flushing.

"How dare you go through my things!" he scornfully reprimanded.

"I told you it was by mistake! I'm sorry. I didn't mean to read it, but the picture was so inviting. I had to look."

He began pacing the perimeter of the room. This awakened the dogs, who sat up on the bed, inquisitively watching him.

"Are you having an affair?" I boldly asked.

"Absolutely not!" he retorted. "Are you a having an affair?"

I sighed. "Not exactly."

"What in the hell does that mean?" he asked, lunging toward me and grabbing hold of my shoulders.

"Please let go. You're hurting me. You promised you wouldn't do that again," I reminded him.

"Have you been fucking around on me?" he railed, throwing me against a row of drawers.

"I will properly explain when you calm down."

"You little tramp," he berated.

"Please, it's nothing like that," I said.

He grabbed hold of my left arm, twisting it behind my back.

"Please, stop. That's the arm I broke. Please, Jean-Auguste, that's unfair."

"No!" he protested, "not until you tell me who you've been fucking around with."

Again, we started a battle of wills and instead of giving in to him, I was compelled to fight back, as I yelled, "Why should I answer? You still haven't explained the postcard. Why did you save it?"

Angrily he threw me onto the bed, pinning me down with all of his weight, which was almost twice mine. The dogs scampered off and began whimpering in the corner of the cabin. "Can't you see I'm much stronger than you? You should honor and obey me. Those were the words you promised in our wedding vows."

"What!" I began laughing.

All of a sudden he slapped my face with his open palm.

"You're a fucking bully," I chided.

He did it again. This time hitting me harder. I heard a crack in my nose. Blood ran down my lips and chin.

"So this is how you get your kicks. You're a disgusting sadist!" I yelled.

He guffawed. His face transforming into that of a bull who'd been taunted to madness in the ring and was ready to gore his matador. I was terrified, but I refused to show him my fear. On a boat, it was impossible to grab hold of a lamp, or some kind of blunt object, as everything was bolted down. All I could do to defend myself was to continue protesting against his aggression by biting, kicking, and clawing at him.

"You don't know anything. It's time you do things my way. I'll show you who's boss here," he commanded. Then he abruptly got up and yanked open a drawer. I heard the clanking of chains and the snapping of a whip. I closed my eyes and began frantically kicking. Then he leaped like a lizard, throwing himself on top of me. Next, I felt the prick of a needle pierce my thigh. Within minutes, I began rapidly weakening. He pulled out a vial of cocaine from his pocket and a tiny spoon and began inhaling deeply. Blood rushed to his cheeks; his nostrils flaired. All I saw next was a long purple whip. He began lashing me several times on my torso, tearing open my silk pajama top. Before I realized it, he tied a choke hold around my neck. The smooth leather was cutting my skin. My muscles were weakening as I felt a strong dose of tranquilizers course through me; all I had left to hold on to was my biting sarcasm.

"This must be what you wanted all along. Then do it. Kill me! You greedy bastard. Just make it quick!" I shouted.

The cabin was spinning. It was becoming impossible for my vision to focus, as Jean-Auguste looked like he had an extra eye in the middle of his forehead like the hunchback of Notre-Dame. This was the last I was able to communicate, as an overpowering exhaustion overtook me. Turning my head away from him, I refused to see what he was doing next. Instead, I stared through the porthole and tried to disassociate my mind and spirit from my tortured body. The open sea looked more foreboding than ever. Drowning, I tasted salt water in my mouth. My eyes were burning. The water was choking me; I could no longer breathe. I felt completely isolated on this luxurious yacht, sailing in the middle of the vast Mediterranean. Pain and disillusionment were sinking me deeper and deeper into the abyss of despair, as I was being dragged into its cold depths by the weight of Jean-Auguste, who was chained to me like a sack of stones.

TWENTY-FOUR

Djuna Cortez

TANGIER, MOROCCO, AUGUST 1986

I awakened alone, completely stripped of clothing and dignity. Flies swarmed around me like I was already a corpse. The room was stiflingly hot and felt over ninety degrees. It appeared to be midday; a glaring sun was shining brightly though the opaque window curtains, shedding light on unfamiliar surroundings. The room I was in had two twin beds set against terra cotta painted walls, where a gold hand of Fatima was posted between the beds. One of my suitcases was placed on the other bed. As I tried to moved, my stomach, shoulders, neck, and sides were in agony. The only way I didn't ache was if I remained curled up in a fetal position, and if I tried not to inhale too deeply. As I slowly eased myself out of bed, I saw that my arms and legs were covered in bruises. There also were lacerations around my rib cage and thighs. It was difficult to think clearly and shake off a lingering barbiturate fatigue. An acrid taste of bile rose up my dry throat; the bitterness made me shudder. Just as I was about to place my foot on the ground, I noticed a flash of movement, and realized, only in the nick of time, that a scorpion was scurrying under my feet. Reacting instinctively, I grabbed a goat-hide mat, hurling it across the floor, which temporarily covered and trapped the poisonous creature. I could only hope that there weren't more lurking under the beds. When I stood up, the pain intensified in my neck and around my ribs. Sluggishly, and completely hunched over, I dragged myself over to my suitcase. It was open. I panicked. My belongings were gone. Frantic, I searched all the side pockets, where all that was left was one journal, the last one I had been reading. Then I remembered this was the suitcase where I had split up the volumes, as I nearly forgot this one, when I had tossed it across the hotel room. Grabbing the journal, I glanced at the dresser. My purse was tipped over, the contents emptied. A lipstick, hairbrush, compact, my wallet, jewelry roll, and my American passport were beside it. When I inched my way over, I saw that all my jewelry was missing and the money in my wallet was gone, along with all my credit cards. Next, I began to open the drawers, and while looking down, I noticed something sparkling on the floor beside my feet. At first, I thought it was another scorpion, but as I got closer, I saw that it was a harmless diamond earring. With great difficulty, I bent over to collect it. More pain ricocheted through me, as I pulled open the top drawer.

Some of my clothes were precisely folded and put away, telling me that it could only have been the meticulous work of Jean-Auguste. All the items that I found were everything that I had packed in that suitcase. Suddenly, I heard heavy footsteps outside the room. A silhouette of a hooded figure walked past my window. My heart began to race; I knew I was in danger. Although I desperately needed to use the bathroom, I dressed as quickly as I could, only taking my most important belongings, which I stuffed in a pillowcase. There was a knock at the door. Should I ignore it? Should I hide? I refused to answer, and instead hid in the bathroom, leaving a crack in the door, so I could see who it was. A maid entered with a cleaning cart. When she turned her back to begin making the bed, I ran out of the room, stumbling into a dimly lit hallway. My plan was to flee as quickly as I could. Tiptoeing, I managed to sneak quietly past a man at the front desk who was busy rolling cigarettes. Because I was paying attention to my footing, I was able to step adroitly over a crate of sliced red figs that were placed to dry on the front steps. A busy street greeted me along with the glaring afternoon sunlight of a tropical warmth and intensity. I had to be somewhere near the Sahara Desert, as grains of red and gold sand covered the ground and fully cloaked figures moved in the market. Most of the noise from the street came from a bustling bazaar, which was crowded with haggling shoppers. I headed toward a colorful rug stall. For a moment, I glanced back at the hotel. A man wearing a white burnoose with his face and head disguised in the folds of material began walking up the steps. The outline of his turban resembled the figure I had seen earlier. He turned and faced the bazaar. Part of his face was exposed; his skin was dark, but much lighter than everyone around me. I ducked under a sheepskin rug. Just as I did this, he tripped over the crate of figs, causing a knife to drop from under his sleeve; the long blade reflected in the sun. Self-consciously, he looked around him to see if anyone had noticed the mishap before he picked up the weapon and proceeded inside the hotel. I sensed he was coming for me.

The air outside was humid and scented with incense, mint, fruits, spices, and roasted nuts. Buzzards flew above the souk, some perched on telephone poles. Could the birds smell death? Was I supposed to have been their next meal? As I entered the tented area, I found a bathroom at the entrance. It was barely large enough for one person. The toilet was a hole in the ground, which was teeming with cockroaches. That moment, I yearned for American conveniences. There was no soap or towels, only brown toilet paper that was as rough as newspaper. However, what was perhaps more frightening than the bathroom's poor sanitation, was my reflection in a wall mirror. At first, I dissociated myself from the bruised and battered face. In the past, I had thought of such women as pitiably weak, and since they were adults, that they deserved their miserable fate. I had taken psychology classes in college, and thought I knew better than to fall for an abusive man. But books couldn't teach me about the complexities of personal demons, the trappings of romantic love, or how to recognize those who wear a cunning mask of charm, pretending to be what they are not. These may be some of the practical teachings I had lacked from my upbringing. My grandmother had never warned me about men, only Satan. But in Jean-Auguste's case, they seemed to be one in the same.

It was humiliating to be seen this way. I tried to wash some of the caked blood from around my nose and upper lip. My lower lip was also split open. As soon as I acknowledged my pride, my ego presented itself, and my anger surfaced, turning into rage. I wanted justice. Revenge. An eye for an eye. When I left the bathroom, several men hissed at me, and Muslim women stared with ferocious curiosity. All I could see of them were dark penetrating eyes lined with kohl, as they carefully hid their faces and covered their hair. I watched the women as they selected their daily provisions. The only part of their anatomy they showed were henna-stained fingers and decorated palms. My own hands were smooth. Ironically, it was the only part of me that had remained unscathed. The Moslem women continued to stare at me in fascination and envy. For the first time, I understood how powerless they could feel. I was trapped in a country where most women didn't have a voice; I wished I could befriend one of them. We were equal in that we all understood what it was like to become a victim of male domination.

As I explored more of the souk, vendors with ocher baked skin and rotten teeth, shouted out their best prices in French as they sold fresh produce, ceramics, handwoven baskets, embroidery, painted boxes, jewelry, and live chickens. There was even a snake charmer who I carefully avoided. I approached a clothing merchant, and in exchange for some clothes in my pillowcase and the pair of Nikes I was wearing he gave me a black chador and a pair of sandals. The outfit was identical to what most of the Moslem women wore. Uninhibitedly, I changed behind some hanging rugs. Once my head and face were covered, the men stopped hissing and spitting. After I left the market, I walked through a whitewashed village. Tranquil harp music came from a rooftop garden. Looking through an aqua-blue painted archway, I discovered a temple where men were praying on their hands and knees. In other Moorish archways were groups of wailing women who were chanting as they prepared food served on the floor. There also were windows shaped like crescent moons and stars, and hanging wood partitions, instead of doors, that made a pleasant chiming sound as children and dogs ran through.

Beyond the village were empty beaches of soft pale sand that shimmered like mother of pearl and clear azure water. I continued walking in the direction of the beach until I found shade under a date palm tree. Around me were blooming jasmine and red hibiscus flowers. Bees hummed. Some buzzards had continued to follow me, hovering like sentinels in the palm tree. Crossing my path was a man in a long burlap caftan who walked past with several trotting baby goats. Even though I hurt all over, I stood up to pet them. Relishing in the attention, the young goats turned their necks and reared up on two legs. One tried to nibble at my new clothes as bells chimed on his neck, frightening away the buzzards. After my brief rest, my hunger and thirst were overwhelming. I found a quiet café overlooking the beach. There was only one patron sitting at a table next to mine. Boldly, I called to the waiter. *"J'ai eu de mauvaise fortune. S'il vous plaît, soyez gentil, et donnez moi quelque chose à manger."*

The waiter was obviously used to beggars and turned his back to me, walking away without flinching. I sighed. Too weak to move, I rested my chin in my hands and gazed at the glaring white sand. A group of teenage boys were playing soccer and three giggling girls were watching them. The girls were free of chadors and happily munched on sunflower seeds.

"Pardon me, do you speak English, French, or Spanish?" I asked, turning to the tourist.

"I speak English best. Why?" the man asked.

"I'm sorry to bother you."

He set down his pen and notebook. "But you are, so get on with it," he impatiently replied in a cockney accent. His hair was pure white. He was in his midsixties and had a ruddy complexion that was probably a combination of overexposure to the sun and drinking spirits, reminding me of pictures I had seen of an older Hemingway.

"My money and jewelry were stolen. Can you help direct me to the American embassy?"

He rubbed his thick beard with his fingers. His voice was gruff and abrupt. "Am I supposed to feel pity for you?"

"You can feel whatever you like."

He noticed me staring at his bread.

"You might as well sit down and have lunch with me. The lamb couscous is super, but then again, you can't get much of anything else around here, except for couscous and fish."

I gently eased my sore body into a chair at his table and pushed the chador off my head, shaking out my hair. It was a relief to let my face breathe again. "Thank you. I'm so hungry. Although I would give anything right now for a hamburger, French fries, and a milk shake. I guess I've been away from home too long."

"And where is that?" he asked.

"France."

"France! That menu doesn't sound very French to me," he exclaimed.

"Also, America."

"That's what I thought," he said. "So, what the hell happened to you? You look like something the cat dragged in," he commented, calling the waiter over with a snap of his fingers. "*Garçon,* give her what she wants; it's on me. Don't tell me. It involves a man," he said.

I nodded. "Where are we exactly?" I asked.

"You don't know? That is peculiar. You're in Tangier, Morocco."

"Are you from London?"

"Nottingham. I'm Lloyd Patrick Donsworth. My friends call me Pat," he said.

I didn't give him my name, nor did he ask for it.

When we were served lunch, it was impossible for me to eat slowly; I was ravenous.

"God, girl, when was the last time you ate?"

"I don't know. It's nice of you to do this."

"I try not to judge anyone by their appearance or manners. I'm not one for formalities. I've seen worse-looking birds, and at my age, I don't look that devastating anymore. At this point in my life, I don't give a shit what people think," he explained. Pat ordered another lager and smacked his lips on the last drop of froth in his glass.

"How long have you been in Morocco?" I asked.

"Two months. The hunting and fishing are endless. The climate is usually good. I like to take long walks on the beach and watch the pelicans. I can do whatever I like here. If I want to fish all day, I can bring back tons of tuna, especially, in the spring. And there's never any shortage of food. The citrus fruits grow wild and are always plentiful. But this isn't a place for a single woman. You should be careful."

"It's too late for that. I just need to find a way to get to the embassy."

"I think it's back in the center of town, across from the main souk. I'll get exact directions from the waiter."

The waiter drew a map for me. The embassy was close to where I had been staying.

"Would you like me to escort you there?" Pat kindly offered.

"I'll be fine. Most people won't recognize me dressed like this. I'd better be going before it closes. Thank you so much for lunch. I really appreciate it." I groaned as I stood up.

"I hope you never go back to that bloke of yours. And that he get what he deserves," Pat said.

I found the tall iron gates of the American embassy. An American flag flew above the building. Never before was I happier to see that flag. A uniformed guard stopped me at the gate and refused to let me enter until I flashed my passport. Then the gates and the front door were opened to me and I felt safe, as if I had found a temporary home.

When I removed my veil, the employees were aghast at the condition I was in. They offered to take me to a clinic. That was the last thing I had wanted to go through again, but I agreed. After several rounds of X rays, the doctors concluded I had a series of minor fractures. Three of my ribs were cracked, along with a hairline fracture in my nose and one in my collarbone. They also placed my neck in a brace, while antiseptics and bandages were applied to my lacerated wounds. I didn't need to be hospitalized, so I was released with painkillers and anti-inflammatory medication, as well as a report on my battered condition. Before I left the hospital, one of the ambassador's assistants came to collect me and took me back to the embassy. There I was allowed to make as many phone calls as I needed. First, I tried the phone number I always had memorized, my father's in Los Angeles. I was surprised and rather bewildered that I got a recording saying the number was no longer in service. Few options were left. I called Paris's directory assistance for Pascal's number. Fortunately, I was able to reach her. After I explained to her what had happened, she gave me her credit card number, and I was able to purchase a plane ticket back to Paris.

Goddesses, Wine, Dead Artists & Chocolate

The Journals of Joaquím Carlos Cortez

LOIRE, AUTUMN 1967

A letter arrives from Josephine in California. I save the return address.

Dear Joaquím Carlos,

Our daughter Djuna is a beautiful and good-natured girl. I am very happy to have her. I must inform you that your son has been fighting in Vietnam. I worry about him every day. I have been against this war from its inception, but your son wants to feel as American as he can. I begged him not to go, but he's done this without my consent.

It's lonely here as we've just moved into my mother's home in Beverly Hills. I don't understand this war. It's all so cruel. Since President Kennedy's assassination I have lost faith in my country. I want to return to France. I don't understand why men have to prove their bravery by fighting and women have to stay behind. Not that I would want to be there. Every night, I have nightmares. Djuna sleeps with me. I wonder if she hears me crying. I'm a pacifist like you. I don't do well confronting situations. I wish Emile were less zealous about killing Communists, as so many men are returning home in caskets. And so many are already missing in action. I can't help but wish that we stayed in France. Emile was seduced by this American dream. If he returns, I wonder if he'll still want to be an entrepreneur. Will his dreams be shattered

by the horrors over there? Will he still be the same hus-
band? I need him to help me believe in the good of this
country. I need his hope and enthusiasm; I need his love.

Please don't write to me. I don't know when he'll be
returning. Why don't you phone me to let me know you're
well? How is your hand? Are you painting? How is the
château and winery? Do you go to Paris often? I wish
we were back in Loire. I miss the ancient, rustic smell of
the oak wine barrels and the coolness of the limestone
walls. I miss the rain. I miss the fragrance of your oil
paints and your orange turpentine. It is so boring and
dull here. Everything is new, austere.

When you call, if Emile is home and safe I'll say, "You
have the wrong number, Jack Smith doesn't live here."
If he's not home, then we can talk. I want so much to
speak to you again, but I don't want my mother to suspect
anything. Please take care of yourself. It was wrong of
me to get between the two of you, but a beautiful child
was created. Everyday I spend with her, I think of you.

All my love,

Josephine

I phone her the moment I finish reading the letter.

"Is Josephine there?" I ask.

"Yes, speaking," she answers.

"It's me, Carlos, from Loire."

"I'm sorry, sir, but you have the wrong number. Jack Smith doesn't live here."

"Is he home? Is he safe? Does he have injuries? How are you? How's the little one?"

"Fine. You have the wrong number. I'm sorry."

After I hang up, I cannot move or breathe. This is an insane game, yet I have no choice but to play along. At least Emile is home and alive. It seems everything I tried to teach him, he has rebelled against. I'm a peacemonger, while he's become a warlord.

PARIS, SPRING 1975

I continue to wait for more letters from Josephine and receive nothing. I don't know if I will ever be able to forgive myself for our affair. I have acquired yet another scar on my tainted heart. I would have risked never painting again, never knowing the reprieve of the crippling pain in my hand, never admiring another enticing woman, or feeling the raptures of seduction, by taking a complete vow of celibacy, if it had meant not losing touch with my son. The truth is: I didn't seduce *la belle* Josephine; she willingly offered herself to me, beseeching me to tell her how she compared to the high society ladies of Paris, the models, the mistresses, even the whores. She wanted a man of innocence and one of experience and had us both wrapped around her delicate wedded finger. Furthermore, her healing touch, her subterranean desires, her soulful voice, and her lurid secrets, I wish I had never known. Cause and effect. The simple laws of the universe apply; I deserve this punishment and alienation. Loire has never been the same without them. I miss having a close family and wish I had more children and grandchildren to fill these rooms with laughter. Alas, I cannot stand the quiet—an empty, bitter silence.

TWENTY-FIVE

Djuna Cortez

It was past midnight when I arrived at Orly airport. Pascal was waiting for me by the gate. I didn't meet her immediately. At first I took a few precautions and hid behind a check-in counter as I surveyed the people around her, making certain Jean-Auguste wasn't there or any other potential conspiritor. I could no longer trust anyone. However, Pascal seemed sincere, while she anxiously watched every passenger who was stepping off the plane. She did look terribly concerned, constantly checking her watch and glancing down at a piece of paper. When I eventually approached her, she didn't recognize me, since I had kept on the chador.

"Don't be alarmed. It's just me," I said.

"My God! What have you become?"

While we walked out of the airport terminal, I continued to look behind us and over our shoulders, making sure no one was following us. Once we entered her car, I removed the chador from around my face.

"What has that bastard done to you!" Pascal exclaimed. She couldn't hide her shocked expression and had covered her mouth with her hands.

"I'm afraid to go back to the apartment. What if he's there?"

"You can't spend the rest of your life fearing him. We have to go to the police and report this."

"I have a report from the embassy. I'm too tired to go to the police tonight." ·

"Have you seen a doctor?"

"Yes."

"Well, if it will make you feel better, I'll stay with you," she offered.

"Thank you."

Neither of us ever anticipated the aggravation we would find when we arrived at the avenue Foch apartment. A new doorman stopped me at the door and said, "I'm sorry, but I cannot let you in."

"This is outrageous! This is my apartment. You have to let me in," I demanded.

He glanced down at a notebook. "No, I'm afraid not. I've been given strict orders not to let anyone in, except for Monsieur de Briard."

"I'm not anyone. I'm his wife. I own this apartment, not him."

"According to our papers, your husband claims to be the current owner," the doorman said.

"That's a lie! Let me see that," I shouted in English.

He refused to show me his notebook.

"How can Jean-Auguste live with himself?" Pascal turned to me and asked.

"I've been asking myself that same question."

"Don't worry. You can stay with me. Together we'll find out what's going on, even if I have to talk to the bastard myself."

"That won't do us any good. I don't know where he is. There's no answer at the château in Loire. And his mother won't take my calls."

"First, you're going to find a lawyer and file for a divorce. You have to put this marriage behind you. Everyone makes mistakes."

"This is quite a big one."

We got back in her car and she drove to her apartment.

After I settled into her living room, I said, "I haven't even had a chance to ask how you've been?"

"I'm doing very well. I have a book of poems coming out this spring. Can I make you some herbal tea?" she asked.

"Yes, thank you."

Pascal spoke to me from her kitchen. "Life can be full of surprises, as you've also experienced. As it turned out, Mitya left me an inheritance, so I bought an adorable pied-à-terre."

"Where?" I asked.

"New York City. Beginning in the fall, I'll be spending more time there."

"Why New York?"

"I feel so alive in Manhattan, more than I do here. And I adore Americans, especially the people on the East Coast."

"I've never been."

"You'll have to visit me. The city is completely exhilarating. There's nothing quite like it for me."

"That's what I've heard. I'm still thinking about Princess Mitya. She was such an interesting woman, but it was impossible for me to communicate with her. You must have earned her respect. That had to have been difficult."

"It was challenging and did take some time. She was in better shape when I was visiting her than when you saw her. It was wrong of me to go on vacation and force that on you. I of course never expected that she would include me in her will."

"I don't think you did anything wrong. Were you upset that Carlos hardly left you anything?" I asked.

Stopping for a moment, she said, "He did give me some money that wasn't included in his estate. Long before he died, he gave me this apartment."

"This must have been his art studio, of course."

"It was. I fixed it up a lot. No, I'm not upset, only that he's gone. He treated me very well. What I am most sorry about was that I couldn't be there when he needed me. I didn't know he was depressed. It was a shock when he took his own life. He was always so vital. Well, we should get some rest. I hope you don't mind the sofa."

"That will be fine. It feels very comfortable."

"It is. I've fallen asleep on it many times myself. How are you feeling?"

"I'm going to hurt for a while. The painkillers are wearing off. I better take my medications."

"I'll get you some water. You may need to follow up with another doctor tomorrow."

"I think I'll be all right. It just looks worse than it is," I answered.

"I have an idea what we'll do tomorrow. After we go to the police, we'll go back to your place. I think I still have an extra key somewhere. We have to get inside your apartment. You need to get some clean clothes. More importantly, you have millions of dollars' worth of art and should make sure everything is intact. All we need to do is get past the doormen." She went to a desk and fished through some drawers. "Viola! Here it is. I thought I had saved it. That's a relief. Now we can get some rest. Clean sheets, towels, and blankets are in that cupboard. There's an extra toothbrush in the bathroom. And let me give you a T-shirt to sleep in and a pillow. You can also borrow some clothes in the morning."

"That will be perfect. Thank you so much. I feel much safer being here."

The following morning, we visited the police station, which was a dreadful experience. I was photographed and finger-printed and treated gruffly as though I had committed the crime. And there seemed a tone of disbelief in the stern officer that was taking down my information.

"I can't stand the police sometimes. They have absolutely no sensitivity in these matters," Pascal said as we left.

"I need to get some money. I can't have you continuing to pay for everything," I told her.

"We can drop by a bank."

On our way to my apartment, we stopped at the nearest BNP. Pascal waited for me in a café next door. The moment I approached the bank teller, I got the usual response I had been getting when people saw my face. It's as if they don't really want to look at me, but then find themselves staring between diverted glances. I gave her my passport and explained that I had several accounts with them and needed to make a withdrawal. Then she feigned a smile and excused herself. After she left, the branch manager arrived.

"Do you need more information?" I asked.

"No. Your accounts have been closed."

"I don't understand. I never authorized this."

"Your husband transferred the funds into another bank. I'm sorry, but we cannot help you."

"This is outrageous! Which bank?"

"We cannot say."

"What about my credit card accounts? Can you give me cash from them or order new cards? My wallet was stolen."

She nodded and confirmed. "The credit cards have been frozen. I'm sorry, but we can't help you."

"Damn him! Can you at least tell me when the last withdrawal was made?"

"Please excuse me for a moment. I have to check if I can give you that information."

Impatiently, I drummed my fingers on the marble counter top. The manager returned to say, "We cannot assist you any further."

"How can he do this? These are my funds too!"

"I'm sorry about your problem. It happens to the best of people, but we can't assist you until you resolve your personal conflicts. Now, if you do not leave this bank, we'll have you removed," the manager said sternly.

"How dare you threaten me? I don't understand how you can be so rude. I'll never bring my business back here," I replied angrily.

The manager cleared her throat and tried to appear oblivious to my comments. The longer I remained in the bank the more irate I became. A security guard finally had to escort me outside.

"What took you so long?" Pascal asked, when I met her back at the café.

"They won't help me. I don't know what I'm going to do. I'm broke."

"I was afraid he'd get his hands on your money. All you have to do is sell one painting and all your financial troubles will be over for a while. I'll go call an art dealer I know and see if he can meet us at the apartment. He can usually appraise things very quickly. I'll be right back," she said, leaving to make her phone call.

Another stoic doorman awaited us at the front entrance of the building. Before Pascal reached the door, she ũnbuttoned her blouse, so the top of her breasts were exposed. Then before I could say a word, she slipped the doorman a two-hundred-franc bill, giving him a flirtatious smile and wink. The front door was graciously opened for us.

"I can't remember how long it's been since I've flirted with a man. Never underestimate the power of feminine wiles," Pascal said.

"You should flirt with men more often. You seem to get excellent results."

The elevator opened into the apartment. Upon entering, we felt compelled to whisper and walk softly. Pascal excused herself to begin opening all the shutters. I turned on the lights and began perusing the rooms for signs of disorder. Someone had recently been in the apartment and had emptied the mailbox. It must have been Jean-Auguste; he was the only person who had access to my keys. Stacks of mail were piled on top of the entrance hall console table. As I sorted through the bottom of the last stack, I let out a loud scream. Pascal came running in from the living room.

"What's wrong?" she asked.

"Look," I said pointing to what I had found.

"How revolting! A dead rat." she shrieked.

"I'll go clean it up," I stammered.

"No. I will," Pascal insisted.

Beside the rat was a hand-addressed letter with my name on it. *Personal* and *Confidential* were underlined in red ink. The letter was so tightly sealed that I cut my finger while opening it.

"Damn. I hate paper cuts," I complained, as I licked my finger. Inside the envelope was a handwritten letter to Naravine. I quickly recognized Jean-Auguste's shaky penmanship.

July 1986
Dear Naravine,

After our phone conversation, I've been having second thoughts. I stayed up half the night drinking. I tried to call the villa, but the line was engaged. Maybe we should delay our plan. I was hoping to make this look like a real marriage to business investors. I wanted Djuna to give me an heir. Maybe she can't get pregnant. But what if she can? I don't know how long we should wait. Bernard is anxious for his share of the estate. I guess if a good opportunity arises for an accident then you should proceed. I will be sending you the money, even if it doesn't happen yet. Keep me informed.

Sincerely,

Jean-Auguste

Pascal returned with a broom and wastebasket. I was leaning against the wall, nauseated and dizzy. Without saying a word, I handed her the letter.

After she read it, she set it down and said, "I'm so sorry. Your husband sounds like a complete sociopath. They must all be."

"The last time I saw Naravine she was trying to warn me about Jean-Auguste. I never thought she would want to harm me."

"I don't think she really does. Think about it. She must have sent you the letter."

"Yes, it had to have been her."

"The best thing to do is to show it to the police," Pascal recommended.

"They won't do anything. You saw how they were," I said.

"You're probably right. Do hold onto it and show it to your attorney. He or she may know what to do. I know of someone not too far from here. But now, we must tend to the art work."

Pascal began counting the paintings in addition to Joaquím Carlos's canvases that were upstairs. The collection included oils of Picasso, Soutine, Matisse, Léger, Modigliani, Dali, Kandinsky, Miró, La Tour, and Bonnard. Nothing had been removed.

"The art dealer should be here any minute. He'll help us move the collection and store them at his gallery. Do you have any jewelry that you might also want to sell?" she asked.

"It was all stolen in Morocco, except for one diamond earring."

"I should have guessed," Pascal responded.

"We'll need a ladder to get some of these down," Pascal said.

"There's one in the studio. I'll get it," I said.

"No, you're not going to do anything in your condition. I'll go." Pascal started rolling up her sleeves. Just then the telephone rang and she quickly answered.

"Yes, let him up. It's Didier Le Blanc," she said, turning to me.

The art dealer and an attendant arrived and helped Pascal take down the paintings, wrapping them with bubble wrap, tape, and brown paper. Afterwards, I showed them to the service elevator, where it proved relatively easy to remove them, as the service exit was unguarded. Within thirty minutes, the paintings were loaded into a truck and sent off to the gallery.

An hour later, Pascal and I arrived at Didier Le Blanc's gallery in Montparnasse. As we entered, we saw most of my collection being displayed in viewing rooms under professional lighting. Some of his staff were discussing them. The suave art dealer invited us into his cluttered office. Cubist artwork covered every spare inch of the walls in his office, and modern sculptures littered his desk, along with mounds of paperwork. The dealer sat down and leaned into his black leather reclining chair, and then gestured for us to be seated on a matching leather sofa.

"Can I offer you ladies something to drink?" he asked.

"Not for me, but thank you," I answered.

"We won't trouble you. Have you had a chance to appraise the paintings?" Pascal inquired.

"Yes. They show quite a contrast in value."

"What do you mean?" I asked.

Didier Le Blanc crossed his legs and then stretched his

clasped fingers forward, cracking his knuckles. "Obviously you are not aware, but you have some fakes," he said.

"That can't be! You must have made a mistake," Pascal shouted.

"That's impossible!" I argued.

Le Blanc laughed arrogantly. "This type of subterfuge is a lucrative business. I'm afraid I see this all too often, and in good families such as yours; however in order for me to remain in my profession, I can't afford to make errors in judgment."

Pascal refused to believe it. "Joaquím Carlos only had authentic art. There has to be some mistake. He told me that his wife purchased those paintings before the Second World War."

"That may be. However, I have been trained to detect forgeries. I know these originals like the back of my hand. Please don't discredit me, or I suggest you take your business elsewhere."

Turning to me, Pascal interjected, "Do you think your husband may have something to do with this?"

"I don't know. I certainly wouldn't put anything past him," I answered.

"Which ones are fake?" Pascal questioned the art dealer.

Le Blanc glanced down at his notes and said, "The Picasso, the Léger, and the Miró."

"What about the Dali oil?" I asked.

"This is one of my favorites," he said, pointing to the painting on display in his office. He stood up and turned on the viewing light. "The title is terribly crude, but that is Dali. It's pure Surrealism. But there is no mistaking this as an original. There is gold leaf mixed into the rich oil paints. It would be quite difficult for someone to copy. You can see the traces of gold leaf in the woman's blond hair, in the cala lily flower, in the insect, and on the phallus, which he has obviously made the central theme of the painting."

"Can you confirm which paintings are authentic?" I asked.

"The Bonnard, the La Tour, the Matisse, the Soutine, the Modigliani, and the Dali. All have outstanding values in today's market."

"What about the Kandinsky?" Pascal asked.

"I haven't looked at it closely enough. I need more time on

that one. Did Joaquím Carlos insure his art collection?" Le Blanc asked.

Pascal shook her head. "No, it was too expensive."

"Did you insure them?" he asked me.

"It never occurred to me. I never thought anything like this would happen," I said mournfully.

"What about the Cortez paintings? Are they real?" Pascal asked.

"Yes. What do you want for them?"

He picked up a Cortez painting that was resting on the floor and placed it under the viewing light beside the Dali. It was the one of Isabella on the Gothic cathedral's steps. "I love this one. I remember reading it was featured in the catalogue of one of his exhibits and posters were made," Le Blanc said.

"It's also one of my favorites," I added.

"I have a client in Japan who collects Surrealist art and will buy every Cortez painting by telephone, along with the Dali. What do you want for them?" he asked.

"I can't sell any of the Cortez paintings," I stated.

Pascal smiled and seemed pleased with my decision.

"What's the best offer you can give on the Dali?" I asked.

He wrote down an offer and handed it to me.

I smiled and showed the number to Pascal. She nodded.

"I accept," I said.

"When can she have the money?" Pascal asked.

He opened his drawer and pulled out a checkbook. "I'm giving it to her immediately. Whom do I made the check out to?"

"Djuna de Briard will be fine for now. But, as soon as I can, I'm changing back to my maiden name."

"Do you paint?" he informally asked me.

"I do. But I'm still an amateur."

"Djuna is going through a transition right now," Pascal explained. "We need to protect the paintings, and it would be best if we kept them in a safe place. Can you store them for her for a minimal monthly fee?"

"Yes, that won't be a problem. And if you need to sell any others just let me know."

I wondered what he had thought of me. My bruised face must have made me look terribly desperate, but he was polite enough not to comment on it. When we left the gallery, I knew there were a few more places I had to return to. We hailed a cab back to Saint-Germain-des-Prés, getting off on the rue de Seine.

"Where are we going?" Pascal asked.

"Just follow me," I told her.

We walked through the courtyard of the École des Beaux-Arts. Once we entered the main building, I asked directions to where we would find Bernard-Luis Valencourt. The attendant was kind enough to personally escort us to his studio, which was in the main lobby, at the end of the hall. The door was open, so Pascal and I started exploring the enormous studio. It was an ideal place to paint or sculpt, as natural light shone through tall arched windows. There were high ceilings, a second-story loft, and rows of shelves fixed along the walls, giving extra storage space, where miniature Grecian sculptures of nudes rested on the top shelf. The bottom floor, where we were standing, was lined with easels, wooden stools in different heights, and painted canvases. Looking at the artwork more closely, we saw they were studies of Morocco: beach scenes and whitewashed villages painted in white-and-blue accents with scattered palm trees and pink tropical flowers.

"These are quite good," Pascal said.

Suddenly I froze before one of the paintings. It was of a Moroccan man standing before a crowded bazaar. A white turban was wrapped around his head and a knife was in his hand.

"What's the matter?" Pascal asked.

"Let's get out of here," I said.

"Don't you want to wait for him?" she asked.

"No. I want to leave. Now," I said impatiently.

Then as quickly as my sore body would allow me to move, I raced out of the school, Pascal rushing behind me.

"What did you want to tell him?" Pascal asked me.

"I don't know. I just didn't want to believe he was also involved in all of this."

Goddesses, Wine, Dead Artists & Chocolate

The Journals of Joaquím Carlos Cortez

PARIS, SUMMER 1975

Mitya and I have changed with the passing years. Her philosophy has become to exploit what comes in her path, mine is to cherish. I have become more reclusive while she is more social. Plastic surgery seems to have erased her war memories as with each tuck and snip, a younger but a more vacant look appears on her face. Even the friends that Mitya consorts with all look the same to me. All they do is enjoy flaunting their money whereas I prefer to sneak into restaurants unnoticed and only dine in expensive places when I'm with the princess. My best meals have been in small, unpretentious family owned restaurants that I've stumbled into.

I will always be grateful to Mitya for saving my life and that of Emile. However, I can only take her in small doses. We meet every Friday for dinner at Les Ambassadeurs. One of their best tables is always reserved for us in advance. As we dine, we look out on place de la Concorde. Tonight, I tel her about a girl I've noticed in a café. She refuses to commen about it. Instead she says, "I'm going to attend a series of galas in the south of France. You should join me at the Croix Rouge in Monte Carlo."

"It's not my thing. I hate all that pomp and circumstance. I can see you now on the beach in Monte Carlo. You're sitting on your chaise longue and you flash your famous femme fatale smile at the hundreds of young gigolos who lay oiled on the rocks like lazy seals."

"Yes. So what? The younger the better. And don't tell me you disagree, because I know you're in love with that school girl."

"I don't know about that. But I can bet that all those gigolos will go flocking to you the moment they see that the precious stones on your fingers are larger that the rocks on the beach."

"The beach in Monte Carlo is all rocks—enormous ones," she answers.

For Mitya, life is a *grande soirée,* and why shouldn't it be? Without war, we should be celebrating every moment.

Mitya pats my shoulder and says, "Are you the embodiment of me in a man's body? I don't know why we never ended up together. It seemed we were forever searching for something else. To be honest, I think neither of us are capable of everlasting love."

I reply, "My problem is that I can't stop wanting to seduce. The pursuit is the most enjoyable part."

"I can't blame you. I prefer to look into the eyes of a young man and hope he can still see a beautiful woman. I feel young when his unblemished hand touches me."

I laugh and say, "How true it is. What a pathetic pair we are. When I was twenty, I lied and said I was thirty. I could never accept my age."

"As long as I can get away with it I'll continue to lie about my age, but in subtraction. I'll be at the Hôtel de Paris if you need me. I should be back in a few months."

"I could be dead by then."

"So could we all. Don't be ridiculous. You'll be very busy. You have a young nymphette to get into bed. Just make sure she's of legal age. I don't want to have to visit you in prison. Oh, by the way, I almost forgot to tell you."

"What?"

"Eliane dropped by to see me."

"Where is she? What has happened to her?"

"She seemed well. She works in a Catholic boys school near Neuilly."

"Can you give me the address? I would like to visit her. Did she ask about me?"

"Yes. I told her you had moved back to Paris. I can tell she's still in love with you."

I confess to Mitya, "I cared for her, but I never loved her. She was a simple woman, but extremely kind. But I would like to see her again."

⌒

I often dread spending my evenings alone. Another series of recurring dreams disturb me after Mitya's departure. I dream

of a gorgeous black angel waiting to take me. Am I dying
She floats in the sky with her arms stretched toward me. Sh
terrifies me, as I don't know if she's good or evil.

I go to visit Eliane. Unannounced, I enter the kitchen of th
boarding school. An elderly woman is hunched over a hug
pot of onions and potatoes. A young man is working besid
her. He notices me enter. She doesn't, as her back is facir
me. As I walk slowly toward them, I recognize the woman a
an older Eliane.

"Somebody is here," the young man announces.

She turns around and stares at me in horror.

"How did you find me?" she asks incredulously.

"Mitya told me."

"She promised me never to tell you. What do you want'
she asks with her voice weakening.

"Nothing. How are you? It's good to see you," I say.

The young man glares at me disapprovingly.

"I have work to do," she says, resuming peeling a batch «
potatoes.

"My mother's very busy," the young man interrupts. "Sh
doesn't have time for visitors."

Her handsome son is much lighter skinned, a beautif
color, reminding me of the rich *café crèmes* I used to order
the Deux Magots.

"Do I know you?" I say to him.

"You could never know me," he answers bitterly.

I turn to her and say, "I'm glad to see you made it throug
the war and had a child. I remember how much you loved ar
wanted children. Why is he so rude?" I ask.

She reaches for his face and pats his cheek.

"I hoped this day would have come much earlier," she say
worriedly.

"Why don't you come back and work for me? I need som
one to take care of me like you used to. You still look robu
and healthy."

She shakes her head and wipes her hands on her apron.

"I have a home here."

Her son interrupts, "My mother doesn't need your handouts
sympathy. You never bothered to inquire how she was be-
re. She could have used your help raising me. It was terribly
rd for her alone. The war was exceptionally cruel. But she
d too much dignity to come begging for your support."

"Why should I have helped raise him?"

"Bernard is your son," she says, as her lips curl into a smile
at is a combination of pride and sorrow. "He's also a gifted
tist. He studied at the Beaux-Arts."

"That's where I must have seen him. Have you been to my
ctures?" I asked.

He didn't respond.

"I don't know what to say. Why didn't you contact me?
itya would have told you how to have reached me. This is
onderful. This is better than I could have ever hoped for.
ere is so much for us to catch up on," I say, reaching to
t my arm around him.

Bernard pulls away, backing up towards the sink. He retorts,
)on't you ever touch me with your disgusting, philandering
nds. It's too late for the bliss of a happy family reunion.
ou used and abandoned my mother."

I protest, "That's not true."

"Bernard, please stop distorting everything. This man
esn't deserve to be insulted. He never meant any harm to
," Eliane says.

"You're wrong. I know his kind. They think because they
ve money they can buy and sell people like slaves. He can't
ol me. You probably never mattered much to him because
your color, which didn't mix in with his high-class life,"
angrily rants.

"That isn't true," I shout.

Eliane begins crying, her tears dripping into the bowl of
ced potatoes, and without speaking, she continues peeling.

"I'm sorry things happened this way. But I never intended
hurt you, Eliane. I never forgot you," I plead.

Bernard says ruefully, "I don't know why she's still in love
th an asshole like you. You left her behind like an old dog!"

"Elaine, can you forgive me for what I did? I didn't have
uch choice in the matter."

"You could have stayed!" Bernard snarls, pointing the ti
of a carving knife at my throat.

"Bernard, please stop this! It wasn't that bad. I know Joa
quím Carlos did everything he could," Eliane yells to her sor

Refusing to listen to her, he moves closer to me with th
knife. "You're too forgiving, *Maman*. But I'm not. This ma
deserves to be punished for what he's put you through. If yo
dare get near my mother again, I'll shred you apart like wha
you've done to us."

Carefully, I back away, while the knife stays in his trem
bling hand. His eyes look as though they are filled with venor
and Eliane's are red from weeping.

"If you ever want to forgive me, well, I hope I'll be aroun
that long," I say remorsefully to him.

Neither of them respond. I hear more chopping and let my
self out the back exit, stumbling into a garden overgrown wit
weeds; white laundry is drying outside on racks. The shee
brush against my cheek. I wonder if Eliane's gentle hands hav
touched them. I crave the warmth of a woman's arms. I wai
someone to care for me.

That summer, I quickly reestablish my daily rituals. For luncl
I frequent a brasserie across from Notre-Dame. There I se
many familiar faces, but I choose not to speak to anyone. Aft
lunch I usually visit my loquacious art dealer. He is youn
and eager to sell my work. Every day we have almost th
same conversation. He asks me to consider making stone pla
reproductions. I protest against lithographs. Sometimes, I ke
protesting just for the sake of arguing. It's important for m
to know that I still have the strength of will for a disagreemen

Our fights are resolved when I vow to paint more original
But the truth is, I don't care. I don't have to prove anythin,
And I don't need the money. What I need is another muse.

My wish is soon realized. I've become entranced with th
young woman I spoke to Mitya about. Every afternoon sh
frequents the same brasserie. The pretty brunette sits alone .
an outside table and writes in a notebook, as she drinks sever

ups of coffee. She looks about twenty, yet is so serious; her
row is always furrowed in concentration. I want to speak to
er, but for some reason I'm intimidated. Instead of challeng-
g my fears like I used to do, I write to her. It takes me a
w weeks and several glasses of Merlot before I write her a
ote. It says: "Follow your passion." Silently, I hand it to her.
he looks up at me and smiles, but doesn't speak.

The next day I'm pleased to see she's there when I arrive.
send her another note that asks: "What are your passions?"
This time she writes back: "Goddesses. What are yours?"
I write, "Goddesses and wine."
She writes, "Goddesses, wine, and dead artists."
I write, "Goddesses, wine, dead artists, and chocolate."
A magnificent correspondence begins. I'm inspired to use
ose words as the title for my body of writing. The young
oman sends me another note.

Goddesses, wine, dead artists, and chocolate:

*These are all fascinating subjects. I am intrigued with the
mythological goddesses: Athena, Gaia, Aphrodite, and
Persephone. Not all of the artists I admire are dead. I
like Picasso, Braque, Rivera, Léger, Kahlo, Lempika, and
O'Keeffe. I'm a student at the Sorbonne, but I don't care
much for the structure of my classes. I prefer writing
poems and stories. I've filled many books in this café.*

Sincerely,
Pascal E. Maron

Dear Pascal,
*I admire your taste in artists and goddesses. Why do you
spell your name like a man? Would you share your poems
with me?*

*I can't answer every question. I don't trust most people
to share my poems with.*

Pascal

The following day, it takes all morning for me to prepare fo
the afternoon. My white linen suit has to be cleaned an
pressed. Everything has to be perfect. I wait in the café, eaves
drop on conversations, doodle on napkins, and drink far to
many cups of coffee. I must be sober and alert for her. Finall
my young poetess arrives. I feel twenty again; my heart flu
ters. I'm compelled to send her another note.

Dear Pascal,

*I have wisdom to share. Stay exuberant, never lose your
enthusiasm and do not give away your heart until you
are certain that in return you will be given priceless
treasures. I don't mean trunks of jewels. I am referring
to a person with inner beauty. Lift up your chin and face
this city with pride. Will you let me sketch your profile?*

She reads the note and walks over to my table. Withou
asking she sits down in a chair across from mine and close
her notebook. Then she lifts her chin and I sketch her sever
times. Her skin is pale and luminous. Her hair, cut in a sho
pageboy, shines like the magnificence of black mink. Her dai
blue eyes remind me of lapis lazuli, and her small upturne
nose is decorated with tiny freckles. I ask myself, Who is th
nymph who poses so perfectly still? How can I befriend he
My vision returns. She seems to be a lonely iconoclast an
this torments her.

Dear Pascal,

*As you know by now I am infatuated with you. How do
you feel about me? Will you have dinner with me?*

Carlos

*My answer for dinner is yes, yes, yes. When? But how I
feel about you, I cannot reveal; I never disclose my feelings to strangers. If you have a good imagination, I'll let
you fill in the details.*

I leave her at the café and walk over to the *tabac* across the street to buy a pack of Gitanes. She doesn't move from the table and is seated in the same position when I return. Holding her hand out like a queen, yet bowing like a servant, she formally introduces herself to me. "I'm Pascal E. Maron."

"What does the E. stand for?"

"Eulalie. It means well spoken in Greek."

She lets me kiss her delicate hand. Her soft skin smells of rose water.

"Are you ready?" I ask.

"Yes," she answers.

We hail a taxi around the corner. In the car, she is transforming again into a bashful schoolgirl; she sits quietly in the backseat with her hands folded in her lap. I compliment her on her navy blue and white polka-dotted dress and she thanks me. This girl is a pastiche of all the women I have loved, only she's crafted to perfection like a screen idol. Her eyes have the capriciousness of Vivien Leigh. Her smile has the innocence and mystery of Garbo. We get out of the cab and I stop first at my favorite charcuterie to purchase our dinner.

"You live here?" she asks incredulously, looking at the frame shop in the square of Saint-Sulpice.

"I work upstairs. I don't live here though. I have other residences."

"I get it. You bring me here because you have a wife and this must be where you take your mistresses."

"I don't have a wife or even a mistress," I answer sharply.

"I don't believe you. Never?"

"I don't like to use that word."

We climb the stairs to the studio and when we enter, I lock the door behind us.

"Can I see some of your work?" she asks.

I point to the stacks of paintings on the floor. She begins sifting through them.

"I've seen your work before. Do you know what I would like?" she requests.

"What?"

"I would like your self-portrait. I'm going to write a poem about you, while you sketch or paint your image."

"But I want to paint you," I declare.

"That won't be possible."

"Never?" I ask.

"I don't like to use that word either," she responds.

"I've been avoiding a self-portrait for a long time. I hate looking at myself," I say retrieving a mirror.

"It's hard to examine oneself objectively withholding judgment. Why don't you first begin by telling me about yourself?" she asks, as she curls into the red velvet sofa like a domestic cat.

It takes all the courage I have, but I walk over to my desk and grab one of my journals. My hands are trembling as I hand it to her.

"I've been writing since I was twenty, but I'm terrified of publishing. You're a writer, maybe you can tell me what you think. But you can only read one page."

"Are you asking for my opinion?"

"Yes."

She carefully takes the notebook into her hands. "I'm honored you're sharing this with me."

"You'll be the first. But, remember, only one page."

"I'm flattered that you trust me enough to read this."

She begins reading, as I set up a standing mirror and an easel. I begin massaging my right hand and stretching my curled fingers, yet I'm uncertain if this hand will work for me.

Between viewing myself, I glance over at the nymph, who is much more appealing to look at than the white-haired geezer in the mirror. Rodin and Ingres would have loved her pale opalescent skin, long arms, legs, and neck. It's a pity she won't let me paint her.

"What are you hiding?" I ask.

"I don't understand what you mean," she says defensively, while looking up from her reading.

"I think you do. Sometimes, I can sense things about a person, especially a young woman," I explain.

She begins snickering. "You'll never know how I feel. I'm not exactly your typical girl," she says haughtily.

"I agree. Why did you run away from home?" I observe.

"How did you know?"

"It's just a feeling I'm getting from you, that you're hiding something about your past from me. Are you afraid of me?"

"No!"

"You can tell me anything. I'm a good listener. I know you've been feeling isolated," I say.

"I used to feel that way even more so than I do now. I was unhappy at home for many reasons. But now I live with my eccentric aunt in an apartment full of cats."

"What does she do?"

"She makes a decent living as an astrologer and does tarot card readings. She has a gift like you do at being able to read people. Her clients come from all over France."

"She sounds like an interesting woman. I would like to meet her sometime."

Can I have a smoke?" she asks.

"Be my guest," I say, tossing her a pack of Gitanes.

She inhales deeply and says while squinting, "I left home because I was tired of being the dutiful daughter who stays with her family until she gets married. My parents have too many rules. For one, I hate traditions, nor do I believe in the virtues of marriage."

"Neither do I."

I hand her a few sketches of myself. Her eyes sparkle with excitement.

"These are wonderful. May I keep them?"

I nod. "That's enough work for tonight. Let's eat," I command.

As I serve the food, Pascal asks, "Will you meet me again at the café tomorrow?"

"I'd be happy to," I answer.

Pascal has finally given in to modeling for me. Every afternoon, after her classes, she poses, sometimes in the studio at place Saint-Sulpice, and other times I take her to the avenue Foch apartment. She speaks freely with me now, often sharing the details of her day, which includes the demands of academia and her financial struggles. The subject of money is rarely mentioned again, when I begin leaving hundred-franc notes inside the pockets of the modeling peignoirs.

One afternoon, I am feeling quite strong and rather brazen.

While she is lounging on a sofa, I pick her up in my arms. Pascal begins kicking and screaming. "What the hell do you think you're doing? Put me down," she balks.

Gently, I set her down and say, "I want to take you to bed."

"I'm not one of your whores. And I don't care to be your lover, either. It's time you know that I'm quite different then you anticipated, than most women you know."

"I know that and that's why I adore you. Is it our age difference? Do you find me revolting?"

"No, Carlos, you're very appealing. It's just that I'm a lesbian."

Unable to answer her, I walk to an empty canvas and become hypnotized by the glaring white nothingness.

"I must disgust you. I better leave," she says.

I grab hold of her slender arm and notice the hurt in her eyes. I plead, "Please don't go. You make me so happy. Why don't you keep this apartment? Most of the time you can have this place to yourself. I'll come sometimes to work. But it will be yours. I'll sign the papers over to you. I adore your company and want to learn to accept your ways. I don't want to judge you or risk that you'll ever leave me."

Our contretemps is forgotten when she moves into the Saint-Sulpice studio. She has become my only confidante. During the day, she disappears to study in libraries, while I paint. When we go out, she pretends to be my mistress, and we relish in a game of spreading gossip. For hours, we laugh at our own frivolous behavior. The truth they would never understand.

My work is shown at several more exhibits. Pascal is written up in all the popular magazines as my muse, lover, and model. For once there's a chance for harmony between the sexes. We are united in a leitmotif of creative visions; she has a desire, like myself, to communicate her ideas, and I help make it possible. Pascal challenges my prejudices, forcing me to be selfless. My opinions matter to her, as when I speak, unlike

Emile, she always listens, especially when we're in an art museum. I give to her the knowledge I wanted to share with my children.

Two years pass. Pascal has written a novel and a book of poems. She spends more time away from home than with me. I suspect she has found a suitor. I think it's one of her professors. Even though our relationship is purely platonic, jealously torments me. The same expression of admiration that Pascal used to have for me, I imagine is devoted to her other companion. Often, she doesn't come home to the studio to sleep. This was bound to happen. Who was I fooling? I loathe imagining Pascal tilting her head to one side and listening with complete reverence to every word her lover must be saying. Once again I feel an emptiness returning.

Every night, before falling asleep, I think of my two sons and the daughter I never had the opportunity to meet. My sons have persecuted me like *les doryphores,* who called my art bad! The war was the culprit in corrupting the lives of those I loved. Even so, it was never my intention to be cruel to others. A sinner, I was, but my crimes were being a degenerate painter who needed women, depending on them as muses, as my eternal flames of passion, challenging me in love, as well as in the world of my imagination.

My only hope is Djuna. However, I cannot wait for her. Perhaps that is why I have cherished Pascal. At first, I wanted her as a mistress, but she needed a mentor. Her role was to become a daughter to me and help me realize that a woman has many dimensions, and does not have to love a man to feel complete. I've enjoyed watching her mature into a confident and talented writer. With the passing years, she no longer needs me. It is clear that my company has become a burden to her. That is why death seems as much of a temptation as seducing women had once been.

My hand hurts too often to paint. I loathe growing old alone.

There's nobody to share cups of hot chocolate with. Women no longer respond to me. A wink is taken as a perversion, a hello an insult. As an Existential thinker, I reserve my right to suicide if I so choose. I know it is the greatest sin against the Catholic church; yet, I refuse to obey. Even though a priest once saved my life, another destroyed my innocence. Only one person could possibly save me, but she doesn't even know I'm alive. By the time she'll learn about me, I will be united with my aunt Rosa, my parents, Isabella, Sylvie, Marcel, and my vocal birds.

Death has more wisdom than birth; the dying know more than the living when their time is near. I crave the end of this mental anguish. Unfortunately, we are all selfish, as we are born of separate bodies, that feel pleasure as well as pain. I cannot endure this horrible abyss of loneliness that is strangling me like an invisible boa constrictor. If only my heart could give out. But no, this corrupt body is strong; it is my mind that is weak. Without being surrounded by love, death is a terribly lonely affair. Instead, I choose to depart in nights filled with goddesses, wine, art, and chocolate, allowing my senses to be indulged, and my eyes to see only beguiling models.

The nymphs are dancing for me now. All of them are here to help me depart this earth. Red and orange flowing crêpe de Chine dresses are brushing again my cheeks. For hours I paint and cry, salty tears mixing in with my oils. Then we feast. These surfeits of mine will be engraved in everyone's memory. Let the public curse on my coffin and tell me I'm blasphemous. When I'm gone, they can shout at my funeral that they love or loathe my work. I won't care!

My paintings are also my precious children. In my oils and through my words, I remain alive. Bacchus, the god of wine and song, my life, will soon be freed. A bevy of whores, some so young they've barely touched men, dance before me. The celebration of the end has begun. I have stopped answering my phone and opening my mail. Each day, more alluring women appear. They dance for me in twirling long dresses with vivid colors like a Botticelli painting. I paint their figures only in smudges, as my hand is frozen stiff, but I don't care. Maybe the rich cadmium oils are finally driving me mad. I taste them and sip orange turpentine. Mostly, I consume bottles of Château Hélianthe d'Or, while my goddesses feed me stuffed pheasants and boxes of Lindt chocolates. There are no rules; day is night, morning is for sleeping, and moonlight is for rejoicing in bed.

I feel young again; money ignites lust. Breasts taste of milk chocolate, hips and thighs of sugar cane, and lips of caramel. Women are desserts. I want to die in ecstasy. These Bacchanalian days will continue, until I will hopefully depart, like De Gaulle, in the arms of a mistress.

Before I die, I want Djuna to understand who her real father is, and how it has hurt me that I was deprived of knowing her. Nonetheless, I will carry the remorse to my grave that I destroyed many families. It is true that I lost a son because of my concupiscence, and another because of fleeing the war, but the worst punishment has been never meeting my daughter. I hope she will forgive me. All my hope remains with her, that she will carry on my legacy by continuing the production of wines and publishing these journals. I need her to be brave and stand up for my words. During this lifetime, I thought I was a man without a soul, now I realize, it was there all along, waiting to be freed.

TWENTY-SIX

Djuna Cortez

PARIS, SEPTEMBER 1986

Joaquím Carlos was correct in assuming I would have cared for him. More than anything else, I regretted that we were never able to meet; nevertheless, I felt fortunate to have known him through his writing and art. The gift of insight I was given into the personalities of my relatives, and the secrets that have tormented our lives, is far more valuable than all the material wealth and possessions. Ironically, now I don't know anyone as intimately as I do my father.

When I finished reading the last page of his journals, a year had passed since I had arrived in France. Past, present, and future—my dreams and memories of Paris all synthesized when I closed the notebook. I would miss the characters, on another level, I had absorbed them; they were a part of me, my heritage, my blood. It was time for me to work on ending this cycle of resentments that had plagued my family for generations.

That afternoon, after I had mailed a brief letter to Emile, explaining to him about my upcoming visit to Los Angeles, I entered the building of a law firm on the Champs Elysées. Confidently, I walked into the legal office, finding my way to the front desk. It took a while for me to get the attention of a busy receptionist. The woman was intent on ignoring me and proceeded to make a series of phone calls. This didn't deter me, as I patiently loomed over her cluttered desk, waiting for her to eventually acknowledge my presence. When she finally hung up her last call, she said curtly, "Have you an appointment?"

"I'm afraid I don't. Is there anyone available to see me today? I need legal help," I said politely.

"That is quite obvious. But we don't just take anyone. Our attorneys only handle an exclusive up scale clientele. And you seem . . . well, you should probably go elsewhere," she impudently advised, as she gave me scrutinizing looks.

It was foolish of me not to have expected this. Pascal recommended that I call ahead, but I didn't want to squander any more time, as my mind was made up to settle this divorce, and I couldn't wait even a minute longer!

When the secretary became immersed in another phone call, taking the initiative, I boldly walked beyond her desk, entering the first open attorney's office. A man in his early forties looked up from behind his desk, and jerked his cup, spilling coffee on his tie.

Even though I was feeling stronger, bruises still covered my face, arms and neck. My appearance generally surprised people. Few were sympathetic to my marred face. Most found it offensive, preferring to rush me out of stores and cafes. I realized that I might have startled him. He cleared his throat and asked irritably, "Do you have an appointment?"

"I'm very sorry to intrude on you like this. But I don't have time to look for another legal office. I need to get a divorce immediately," I said, setting my briefcase down on an empty chair that was closest to the opened door.

The receptionist came running after me.

"I never told her she could see you," she breathlessly interrupted.

He glanced at a schedule on his desk and stated, "I'm very busy today. We only take appointments."

"Your receptionist already made that quite clear," I said, as I glanced briefly at the woman hovering in the doorway. "You see, my circumstances are rather unusual and complicated, because they involve a large inheritance and several properties. I'm sorry to have bothered you," I told him, collecting my briefcase.

"Wait a minute! Please have a seat," he said in a warmer voice. He quickly got out of his chair, walked to the door, and closed it in the secretary's bewildered face. Returning to his desk, he looked down at his daily planner and clarified, "I just remembered that my luncheon appointment was cancelled. My time is all yours." Next, he reached into a drawer and pulled out some documents.

"I'll begin by asking you some general questions. You seem quite young, so I assume you haven't been married long.

"That is correct. Around six months."

"Are there any children involved with this marriage?"

"None whatsoever."

"I don't mean to pry but are those bruises on your face and neck a result of domestic abuse?" he asked.

"Yes. But it gets far more complicated that that," I warned, as I opened my briefcase, handing him the letter Jean-Auguste had written to Naravine.

After he finished reading it, he asked, "Was an attempt on your life ever carried out?"

"I don't know what I can prove," I answered, handing him the medical examination reports from Morocco, the statement from the embassy, and the recent police report.

While he was reading, he opened a desk drawer and pulled out a package of chewing gum. "Please forgive me for chewing. I'm trying to give up smoking. I'd offer you one, but it's nicotine gum and it tastes dreadful."

"I'd like to quit myself, but haven't been successful."

"This is quite a conspiracy against you. Who exactly are these other people involved?"

"Bernard is my half brother, who introduced me to Naravine. Jean-Auguste is my husband, soon to be ex."

"How large is the inheritance you've been given? Do you know what your net worth is?" he inquired.

"It would have to be before the marriage, because I'm uncertain of what Jean-Auguste owns, as he is involved in his family's business."

"That's fine," he said, taking down the information.

"I haven't calculated the exact amount. Maybe you can do that for me," I said, pulling out a folder from my briefcase and handing it to him. "You'll find there the estimated value of my apartment, the château and winery in Loire, and the art collection that is being stored for me by a gallery. The owner can fax you the value of the paintings. Oh, and I have a few more dilemmas. Some of my paintings have been stolen and replaced with forgeries and all of my jewelry is gone. I know my husband took the jewelry. But I can't be certain about the paintings. They could have been taken when my grandfather, I mean, when Joaquím Carlos was alive. Nobody knows when the copies replaced the original paintings."

"Have you reported any of the thefts?

"No."

"These are all serious offenses. We will need to report your stolen paintings and jewelry. I can start that paperwork for you."

"That will be helpful."

"Where is your husband now?"

"I don't know. He may be on the yacht we purchased together, which means he could be floating anywhere on the Mediterranean. I'm sure you wish I had never barged in here."

"I like the challenges that my profession can present. Although I must say, I've never encountered a case quite as convoluted as yours. I will need to get in touch with your husband; however, before I speak to him, I must know what are the terms that you would like from this divorce?"

"I'll forgo taking anything from him. All I want is to keep what was mine to begin with, that includes my properties. At any cost, I must have the journals back that were left to me. Ideally, I also want the money returned that I put into the yacht."

"You know that if there is enough evidence, the authorities will want to prosecute him."

"I'm aware of that and agree that he should face the consequences of his actions. I'll try to find out where he is."

"In the meantime, let me begin the paper work. You need to be aware that these are my fees," he said, pulling out a form, which indicated his exorbitant hourly rate. You don't have to pay me now," he interjected. "If it's better for you, you can pay me when this is all over."

"That will be helpful, as I don't have a lot of cash at the moment. My husband seems to have taken my funds."

"I am very sorry this has happened to you. This is a terrible thing to have to go through, especially when someone is so young. I won't tell you that this won't be painful and probably the worst experience of your life. But, if I have your complete loyalty, I will fight as hard as I can for you, and make sure you come out the winner." He stood up, removed a business card from his desk and extended his hand to me as he said, "I haven't properly introduced myself. Lawrent-Michel Bruges, at your service. Please call me as soon as you have your husband's whereabouts. I also need a number where I can reach you. Whatever you do, don't speak to your husband. From now on, it is to your best advantage that he only communicate with me."

"I understand. Thank you again. It will be nice to put all of this behind me and have some sanity in my life again," I answered.

Lawrent-Michel shook his head and said, "That is one promise I will never make to a client when it comes to a divorce. Be prepared for a journey into hell."

"I'm not afraid," I said, "it can't be any worse than what I've already been through."

As I left his office, I pleasantly waved good-bye to the receptionist, who returned a rather fake yet supplicating smile.

Later that afternoon, Pascal drove me to Loire. When we entered my château, the starkness of the rooms shocked us. All the furnishings were gone, including clocks, books, vases, lamps, rugs, and even drapes. We shouted for the staff. There was no reply, except for the echo of our own voices. I ran though each room; almost everything was missing; even the porcelain hand-painted sinks and bathrooms fixtures were taken.

"Mon Dieu! Quelle culot! Le Salopard," Pascal exclaimed. "Let's go see that bitch. She has to know what's going on with her bastard son."

The sun was shining brightly when we arrived at the Château de Triomphe. Both of us were squinting in the glaring light, as we rang the front doorbell. After several minutes, a young maid answered. The girl was wearing a frilly white uniform that looked gargantuan on her small frame.

"Is madame in?" Pascal asked.

"Who may I say is calling?" the timid servant girl politely stuttered.

"Tell her I'm the mistress of her son," Pascal replied, before I had a chance to answer.

The shy maid left with a bewildered expression on her face.

"That should get the bitch's attention," Pascal added.

The maid returned and without questioning us further, she let us in, guiding us through the vast rooms. Everything looked the same. I couldn't detect any renovations that had taken place. The maid directed us into a greenhouse, a room constructed of opaque paneled glass that was overflowing with lush plants, giving the illusion of a dense tropical rainforest. There we found Madame de Briard potting a white orchid. She was seated at an antique drop-leaf table that was set for afternoon tea with bone china plates and a silver platter of miniature chocolate and coffee éclairs. Her company was four Italian greyhounds who gathered beside her legs, their eyes glued on the sumptuous pastries.

Pascal and I stood staring at Patrice for a few seconds. It was amusing that the dogs she chose to breed resembled her in appearance, except there was affection and warmth in the dogs eyes, and not in Madame de Briard's icy stare. Before any of us spoke, we listened to the trickling of a lion's head fountain that was set in back of the room. Madame de Briard took a sip of her tea and exclaimed bitterly, "How dare you trick me! I have nothing to say to either of you. Get out! You're both not welcome in my château."

Bravely, Pascal walked toward Madame de Briard and said, "Your son is a piece of slime who's rotten to the core. And you're not much better. How could you have let him do this to Djuna?"

Madame de Briard began smirking and clasped a gardening shear tightly in her tight hand, pointing its sharp tip in my direction. "My son has excellent judgment. She was stupid and didn't even know that the Cortez winery was always a major competitor of ours. Whatever he did, it was only to protect our family's reputation, before she ruined everything we've spent generations working for. Anyway, she never appreciated what was given to her. My son deserves her château and winery."

"I trusted you and your son," I said. "I thought you sincerely wanted to help me."

"Your son deserves to be punished. And I don't doubt for a second that you were aware of his true intentions," Pascal yelled.

Madame de Briard pointed her shears at me again, and said, "There's no proof of your accusations."

"Where is he?" Pascal forcefully asked.

Patrice shrugged her shoulders. "How should I have knowledge of his whereabouts? He's a grown man who makes his own decisions. He works hard all year and deserves to take time off."

Madame de Briard rang a silver bell. When the young girl quickly appeared, Madame ranted, "These women are never welcome here again. You should always tell me the names of the people who enter this house. How could you be so stupid? This is the last mistake you can make. What an idiot you are! Also, my tea is ice cold. How many times do I have to tell you that I like my tea served hot? Do you even know how to boil water?"

"Yes, madame. Right away, madame," the girl said with her voice breaking, as she dashed out of the room.

"Wait!" Madame de Briard shouted. "Don't forget to show these despicable creatures out."

The young maid nodded her head. "Yes, madame."

"Hurry. Get them out of my sight!"

There were many insulting comments I had wanted to say to Madame de Briard, but vindictiveness was not my style, nor would it solve my current dilemma. Accepting our defeat, we left, and followed the severely chastised maid back across the polished black-and-white marble floors. Once we reached the front door, I took the servant girl aside and asked her, "What is your name?"

She looked terribly frightened, as if I were going to bite her, and answered in a trembling voice, "I'm Nathalie. Why do you want to know?"

"Nathalie, I promise I won't hurt you. If you don't like the way madame treats you and you would like another job, I'll hire you. I believe in treating people respectfully. I promise never to scream at you, and give you two days off per week. I'll also double your pay, but don't tell madame I offered you a job. This needs to be kept private. If you're interested, take a taxi to this address across the Vienne." Next, I slipped my address and two hundred francs into the large front pocket of Nathalie's apron.

Bowing her head, she smiled and said, "Thank you," before closing the front door.

"You're more slick than I thought. That was a brilliant idea. She has to have some information on your husband," Pascal said.

Just before sundown, we returned to the silent and austere grounds of the Château Hélianthe d'Or. Once nightfall came, it would be depressing in the desolate château, with the few matresses left in the bedrooms, and little else.

"I'm starving. How about you?" Pascal asked, as we walked through the empty dining room. "Do you think there's anything to eat in your kitchen?"

"I haven't a clue. But, I'll go take a look. I can usually fix up something with even minimal ingredients."

"Wait! Did you hear that?" Pascal asked.

"Yes. It's only the ghosts," I teased.

"No, I think there's somebody at the front door."

"What if it's him?" I asked worriedly.

"I don't think he'd dare. I'll go see," Pascal offered.

I continued on my way to the kitchen. But, before I got there, I heard Pascal calling to me. "Everything is fine. Come see for yourself."

When I got to the front hall, I saw that it was Nathalie, the servant girl, who stood in that same oversized uniform with a suitcase beside her.

"I didn't even tell madame I was leaving. Do you have work for me?" she asked meekly.

"Yes. Absolutely. It's nice of you to come."

"Where's all the furniture?" Nathalie asked, looking around the room.

"Most of it was stolen, but that's a long story, like my frightening appearance."

Nathalie was polite enough not to ask any more questions.

"Why don't you give me a hand in the kitchen. Do you cook?" I asked her.

"Not really," she answered apprehensively.

"That's not a problem. I do."

The kitchen was the last room we still had to check out. And like the others, almost nothing was left. The cupboards were emptied as well as the refrigerators and freezers. All we found was a bottle of olive oil and a box of wheat crackers.

"I'm afraid I'm not that creative," I said, holding up the remaining items. "I'm sure there isn't even a bottle of wine left."

"Then let's go out for dinner and bring her along," Pascal suggested.

"Will you have dinner with us?" I asked Nathalie.

"Yes, I would like that," she answered firmly.

That evening, in a nearby village, we found a rustic restaurant that was attached to a farm. A husband-and-wife team ran the place, cooking regional dishes. The bubbly wife was the only server. The moment we sat down, she raved about her husband's cooking and proudly gave us suggestions on what to order. Apparently, the husband was terribly shy and always remained hidden in the kitchen.

"Please order whatever appeals to you," I said to Nathalie.

Once we were served, Nathalie ate heartily. "I've never been treated like this before. You are both so nice," she said reverently.

"We need your help," I told her.

"I need to work," Nathalie said, between mouthfuls of her roast pork in a prune sauce. "I have a little boy. He's only two and lives with my mother in Rennes. I need to send them money every month."

"I won't be staying in Loire for very long. But I do need

someone to reside in the château. Would you be comfortable being there on your own?" I asked.

"I think so," she said.

"I need to ask you, have you recently seen Madame de Briard's son?"

"No," she answered.

"Do you remember answering any telephone calls from him?" Pascal asked.

Nathalie took a sip of wine and said, "Yes. He called just yesterday. He phones her quite often."

Pascal leaned across the table and asked, "Do you remember where he was calling from?"

"It was long distance. The phone connection was full of static. But I did overhear madame say, "How is Mico Noste? Have you avoided the winds? Where is that?"

"It must be Mykonos. It's one of the Greek Isles," I answered.

PARIS, SEPTEMBER 1986

A week later, Lawrent-Michel Bruges stood up from behind his desk to greet me as I entered his office. He gestured for me to have a seat and then informed me, "Since your call, I have made a lot of progress. Your husband is indeed in Mykonos. I called the port and was immediately connected to his boat. At first he wasn't there, so I left a message. Much to my surprise, he returned my call an hour later."

"What did he say?" I asked anxiously, leaning forward in the chair.

"He'll agree to the divorce if he gets alimony and the château and the winery in Loire. He said he'd give up the apartment in Paris and all of the paintings."

"What! He's insane! How can he do that? What did you tell him?"

"I agreed."

I bolted up from my seat and shouted, "I don't want anything from him, nor do I want to give him anything! I told you that before. All I want is what belonged to me from the beginning, before this marriage. How can you do that without consulting with me? What kind of lawyer are you?"

"A smart one. Please calm down and listen to my plan of strategy. First of all, he doesn't know we have his letter. This will benefit us. I never mentioned your injuries or the medical and the police report. He doesn't think you'll press charges. In addition, someone is again trying to help you by sending me this," he said, patting a thick manila envelope that was resting on his glass desk.

"What's in the envelope?" I asked.

"I will explain in a moment. But first, I want to clarify my plan with you. We'll agree to his terms only as bait, so we can meet with him in person. Very few lawyers will do this. Attorneys can make more money exploiting your anger and dragging things out for years. Believe me, you'd end up with nothing if I did this. I don't want to use people, except when it works for my client. You'll save a lot of money in the long run if you'll agree to meet with him in my presence."

"I take it he is also willing to meet with us."

"He said he was."

"I don't want him to have anything."

"I understand that. We just want him to think he's getting what he wants. Then I can negotiate with him."

"Doesn't he have a lawyer?"

"He's defending himself. I also did some research on your husband. It's astounding what we found. He hasn't paid his income taxes in two years. It sounds like he thinks he's one of those people who are above the law. And you're going to have to brace yourself for the next one," he said handing me an Express Mail envelope. This was sent anonymously to me from Mykonos. It arrived this morning."

I pulled out three black-and-white snapshots. Each one was a photograph of Jean-Auguste. One was taken in a discotheque where he was dancing in a nightclub filled with men. Another picture was taken on a beach where he was rubbing suntan oil on a woman's nude back. But when I looked more closely at the photograph, I saw that it wasn't a female at all, but an adolescent boy. The next snapshot was of my husband kissing the boy's ear. As I set down the photographs, my head began to spin. To steady myself, I planted my feet firmly on the ground, resting my hands on my knees.

"Are you all right?"

"I don't know. Is it hot in here?" I said inhaling deeply, which caused my ribs to ache.

"Maybe I should get you some water," Lawrent offered.

He poured me a glass of cold Evian. Once I took several sips, I began to feel better.

"I had a feeling this would be devastating for you," he said. "I'm very sorry."

"I never quite expected anything like this."

"We may have some leverage with these photographs. You see, if he doesn't agree to your terms, I'll threaten to destroy his professional reputation in court. Drugs and prostitution could also be involved, not to mention that this boy looks underage. So, shall we say you are owed half of his income for the grief he has caused you, as we should take into consideration what he's stolen from you? Believe me, nothing will be left unturned by me. Are you feeling any better?"

"Yes, I think so," I answered, between sips of water.

"Your husband will be getting back to me in the next few days or sooner." As I got up to leave, the phone rang. Lawrent quickly answered. "That will be fine," he said.

"That was your husband on the phone. We have a date with him a week from today. He'll meet us in Cannes at the Port Canto. The yacht will be arriving sometime between noon and four in the afternoon that Friday. I suggest we fly down to Nice together."

"That's great work," I said enthusiastically.

"You haven't seen anything yet. Oh, don't worry about the arrangements. I'll take care of all that. We'll fly out on the airbus at eight in the morning. I'll send a car to pick you up at six."

"I'll be ready, I said in a serious, yet reflective voice.

It was close to seven when I left his office. I had promised to meet Pascal for dinner at her most frequented bistro, Le Cours Saint-Germain. She was waiting for me inside the crowded restaurant when I arrived. Since Pascal was a regular client, we were seated quickly and given one of the best window tables, which overlooked the animated boulevard Saint-Germain. For a moment, I watched some of the activity on the street, until a waiter called me. As I turned my head in his direction, he proudly displayed a silver platter with a freshly skinned dead rabbit. It looked like a fetus as it lay in a pool of its own blood.

"Please no!" I cried. "There are some customs I'll never get used to in France."

"I'm so sorry. Would you like some wine? I think you can order it by the glass," Pascal said.

My stomach also turned at the mention of wine, as it reminded me of my husband. "No, thank you. I'm fine with mineral water."

"How did it go with your lawyer?"

"Very well. We'll be meeting Jean-Auguste in a week."

"That's great. I hope he'll be cooperative. Have you thought about when you're going to publish the journals?"

"I may as well tell you now. I only have the last volume."

"No! What happened to them?"

"Jean-Auguste must have them with my other suitcase. I'm hoping they're safe and are still on the boat."

"Does he know their value?"

"I never spoke to him about them. I was planning to tell him when we were last reunited. Then everything, as you know, got out of hand."

"I would hate to have him get the money for them. What if he damages them? Did you make copies?"

"I'm afraid not. I know that was foolish of me, but I do want to publish them. However, even before that happens, I want to speak to my father, Emile. I want him to know about the journals before they're made public, as some passages do involve him."

"What if he objects? He may have a right to sue. I don't know how that works exactly."

"I don't know either. In any case, I can't expose Emile's life without his knowledge. I think it's the ethical thing to do. I've already punished Emile enough by not speaking to him for a year. You're mentioned as well."

She ignored my last comment for the moment and asked, "When are you going to talk to Emile?"

"I haven't been able to reach him by phone. I sent him a letter that I hope he receives before I arrive."

"When are you planning to leave?"

"As soon as everything is settled and my bruises heal. I'm looking forward to getting away for awhile."

"You know, you should also visit me in New York. If you come toward the end of October, you can see the changing of the leaves in Central Park. It's really stunning."

"I'd like that," I said.

"When you get the journals back—and I hope that you will—you should let my editor read the first hundred pages. I know if she likes the work, she will be able to convince her publisher to buy it. I'm sure a book could also be written about Joaquím Carlos's art. Included could be photographs of all the paintings you own and the ones I inherited from Mitya. I'd even like to write it myself."

"That sounds like a wonderful idea."

"How's your grilled salmon?" Pascal asked.

"Very good. As you can see, my appetite has returned. The food is excellent here. Although, I must confess, I make a better Béarnaise."

"You really like to cook. Have you thought about that as a profession?"

"I do enjoy it. But I'm still uncertain what I want to do. Right now, I just want to get through this divorce."

"That's understandable."

"I have an idea," I said, leaning forward in my chair, while I rested my elbows on the table.

"What is it?"

"Would you mind going with me to one more place this evening?"

"Where would you like to go?"

"All I can say is that it's someplace very special. You'll know when we get there."

A taxi dropped us off in front of the white domes of the Sacré-Coeur in Montmartre. Across the front lawn, groups of back-packing tourists were huddled together singing and playing guitars. Nothing mattered around me, except for the sparkling city below.

"This is such an ethereal place," I commented.

"It's sublime, but awfully windy at night," Pascal said, shivering. "Let's walk up the side stairway to the top of the basilica. The best view is from up there," she suggested.

"I'll follow you. You must know I'm Joaquím Carlos's daughter," I said, as we were climbing.

Pascal didn't say a word, until we reached the top. "I'm not surprised. Somehow, I always knew that you had to be. What about me? You must know about my lifestyle."

"You mean gay."

"That doesn't bother you?"

"He mentioned it in the journals. I hope you're okay with that."

"I have nothing to hide. I'm looking forward to reading them."

"You're a very nice person and you've been a great friend. Nothing about you is bothersome. As for being gay, I imagine it's a lot like being an artist. There are so many personal struggles involved. Society isn't always accepting of your lifestyle. It has to be difficult, especially growing up. It must take quite a strength of character to be true to yourself. I respect that."

"Thank you," Pascal answered.

I walked to the ledge and leaned against the white Château Landon balcony, instantly feeling part of the magic of the Sacre-Coeur; nothing evil would harm me. I hoped the legendary good fortune of the basilica was contagious, since it had miraculously escaped bombings during both world wars. On this hilltop, where Joaquím Carlos was buried, time was preserved. A piano bar played Edith Piaf's "La Vie en Rose." Prostitutes still lurked in the shadowy corners along rue Saint-Rustique and rue du Chevalier. Gathering at place du Tertre struggling artists continued to create the same portraits of tourists and sketches of the magnificent city. Nothing here had really changed since the days of Degas and Toulouse-Lautrec. Everywhere, I felt the artistic and mischievous spirit of Joaquím Carlos mysteriously reverberating in the nightclubs and cafés, as cries of laughter and music were carried in the wind. This was the end of my sojourn in France. I couldn't stay any longer and needed to move on. It was the night for me to bid farewell to Paris, the City of Light, which had ignited my passion, as well as my pain.

TWENTY-SEVEN

Djuna Cortez

A WEEK LATER, CANNES, SEPTEMBER 1986

Lawrent and I lounged on the crowded terrace of the Carlton Hotel. Occasionally, the mistral whipped up, which gave us some relief from the baking sun. The time passed slowly, as we sipped on chilled raspberry juice and nibbled on peanuts, olives, and salted crackers. We were equally bored as we flipped through magazines and took turns gazing out at the sea with binoculars, carefully watching the boats entering the Port Canto.

After several hours, Lawrent and I looked like permanent fixtures on the terrace, along with the black-and-tan wicker chairs. We even took out a backgammon set.

"The women only get more attractive in Cannes," he commented, while peering through the binoculars in the direction of the beach.

"That's because they're half-naked with perfect suntans. Are you looking for the boat, or just at the beautiful women?" I teased.

"Then let me give you the binoculars," he said, handing them to me.

"You know, I came here on my honeymoon," I said, while pointing to the balcony of our suite.

"I'm sorry. If I had known, I wouldn't have suggested coming here. It's just one of my favorite hotels. My family and I came here last year on vaction. The kids love to water-ski and windsurf. I don't remember it being this crowded. Are you going to be all right?"

"I'm fine, really. When do you think the boat will come in?"

"It has to be anytime now. It's almost four," he said, taking a sip of his icy drink.

"Do you really think he'll negotiate?"

"He will. Don't you worry. I have it all planned. He'll be in for quite a surprise. Just leave it to me to do all the talking. It's best that you don't intervene. Wait! Take a look with the binoculars. Can you tell if that's the boat?" Lawrent asked excitely.

I lifted up my binoculars and again gazed out at the shoreline.

"Yes, that must be it. Few yachts have the same sleek aesthetic design of French naval ships."

"Let's go," he said, grabbing his briefcase.

I quickly paid our tab, leaving a two-hundred-franc bill on the table. Then we both raced across the congested Croisette and hailed a taxi. The port was close enough for us to walk, but we wanted to get there faster. It took us a while to be ushered through the gates. When we did arrive at the end of the quay, the yacht was backing into its narrow berth. Patiently, Lawrent and I and a few inquisitive spectators watched a crew of four men in tight white shorts run frantically about the boat, preparing ropes and separating the yachts on either side of them. Once the engines were silenced, a bell went off, and the gangplank was electronically lowered for us.

I walked ahead first, removing my shoes as I stepped down on the deck. As soon as Lawrent and I were both on board, the spectacle began. The sliding door to the salon opened. Naravine emerged, dressed in a MicMac St. Tropez creation: a clinging navy-and-white nautical dress with a sailor's hat. Haughtily, she sashayed toward us and ensconced herself on a folding chair positioning her body like the Sphinx, with her neck elongated, chest arched, and an aloof feline gaze that refused to make eye contact with us. The door slid open again, and a group of scantily clad Gypsy boys spilled onto the deck. Giggling like grammar school girls, the adolescent boys divided evenly on both sides of the railings and lined up in rows like flocks of pigeons; their lost eyes were intently watching Lawrent and me.

The door slid open again and Jean-Auguste emerged on deck. As usual, he was impeccably dressed, wearing a tailored white linen suit without a single crease or wrinkle on it. Everything he wore looked brand new: a lavender silk shirt, white Gucci loafers, and a diamond and gold Rolex watch. When he had commanded everyone's attention, and all eyes were on him, he strutted like a king over to the empty banquette. Moments later, following behind him, was Xavier, who was dressed flamboyantly in white harem pants, a pink silk tunic, and his left arm covered in dangling bracelets. One of his ears was pierced, something I had never noticed before, and he was wearing the mate to my diamond stud earring. Walking over to Jean-Auguste, Xavier quickly kissed him on the cheek and then slithered beside him.

"I want champagne," Xavier childishly demanded.

"No, *belle fille,* you need to wait for later. I know we'll have a lot to celebrate," my husband answered.

Jean-Auguste cleared his throat and said, "I'm glad you've agreed to my terms." He turned to speak only to Lawrent. "Djuna doesn't have any knowledge or class when it comes to wines. She guzzles it like Coca-Cola. My expertise is winemaking. I have years in the business and know how to run things properly. I'm glad she realizes that I only have the best interests at heart for the château." Jean-Auguste rang the buzzer. Seconds later, the steward arrived and bowed to him.

"Fetch me my briefcase," he commanded. While waiting, he adjusted the collar on his silk shirt and said, "I've had my divorce papers prepared for her signature."

Lawrent interjected, "Before you give us your papers, we have to show you what we have."

The moment the attendant returned, he grabbed his briefcase, snapped it open, and pulled out his contract.

I handed Jean-Auguste the envelope with the photographs from Mykonos.

Lawrent continued speaking. "I think you should agree to

our terms, or I'll be happy to publish these in *Paris-Match,* or share them in a court of law. We have proof that your wife was battered in Tangier.

"You slimy son of a bitch! Who took these pictures?" Jean-Auguste asked irately, slamming the photographs down on the table. "You snakes. Which one of you set me up?" He yelled, searching the eyes of his audience.

Naravine boldly stood up and said, "I did. For a long time now, I've wanted to get out of this mess. So, I did what I felt was fair; I take full responsibility. Djuna's lawyer gave me all the information I needed when I took down his phone message."

Jean-Auguste shouted, "I should have known not to trust a stupid whore."

The boys surrounding us began snickering.

Lawrent interjected, "We have a letter stating your motives for wanting Djuna murdered and your desire to carry that out. So, I suggest you put all of these matters at rest, Monsieur de Briard, and sign the annulment papers that state Djuna's terms. The bank accounts should be returned to her, along with access to her apartment. Everything that she owned before the marriage is for her to reclaim. Before we get into a bloodier battle, I suggest you comply. She will forgo alimony and taking anything from you," Lawrent explained.

"What will happen if I don't sign these papers?" Jean-Auguste sarcastically questioned.

"For one, my brother is a journalist at *Paris-March.* This would make a sensational headline story. 'He stole a fortune from the daughter of a famous artist, tried to kill her in Morocco, and then ran off with a harem of underage prostitutes.' "

Naravine added, "You may even have Hollywood at your door, Jean-Auguste. But you might also be one of the most hated men in the world. Even though I know how much you love money, I think you should sign her papers. After all, I'm sure you don't want your mother to know everything."

"You leave my mother out of this!" he yelled.

"We'll be happy to also inform her how you haven't paid your taxes. And she's at risk of losing her château," Lawrent said.

"How dare you!" he said, lunging at Lawrent.

Naravine pulled me away and quickly took me inside the salon.

"I think we should let the men fight out the rest of this," she said, taking a seat on the sofa and ringing an indoor buzzer.

"I've never met anyone so afraid of his mother," I commented.

"You haven't met mine," Naravine said in a serious tone.

We were interrupted when a steward arrived. Naravine ordered for a taxi to be called and for her luggage to be sent up.

"Did you actually know Jean-Auguste before we met?" I asked.

"We had met a few times; however, Bernard put me up to it. This was all his idea to begin with. Look, I'm really sorry, Hav. I got in way over my head. Once you start playing games with big money, it's hard to stop, like a winning streak in gambling. Soon you think you're invincible, until you wake up and find yourself dangling from a hundred-foot tightrope with a swamp of crocodiles beneath you. Then all you can do is hold on for your dear life, in any crude way possible. When it comes to survival we're all selfish. I must say, it's impressive how well you're taking all this. I'm not asking for your forgiveness. I don't deserve it. But I think everything will turn out in your favor, as I had hoped for. I doubt we'll ever meet again. And that will be my loss, not yours. The path you'll be walking on will be way too high for me to ever climb."

A crew member started carrying out her suitcases to the deck. He made several trips, until six pieces of Louis Vuitton luggage were set beside the gangplank. I walked back outside with her. This time, when Naravine and I emerged on deck, Jean-Auguste pointed his Mont Blanc pen at her and shouted, "You two-faced bitch whore! How could you have betrayed me?"

Naravine glanced at the street and said in a detached cool voice, "It's time for me to leave. My taxi has arrived."

"We had a deal," Jean-Auguste shouted to her.

"The game just got too ugly for me, so I stopped playing by your sly rules and followed mine instead. I know you too well by now. In the end, you'd have cheated everyone involved," Naravine retorted.

The taxicab honked several times. A deckhand began trans
porting her valises to the trunk of the car.

Naravine smiled and winked at me, before she made he
final exit down the gangplank and then vanished into a whit
Mercedes-Benz.

"I also think you should sign the papers," Xavier goade
Jean-Auguste.

Begrudgingly, Jean-Auguste signed my annulment papers
When he set his pen down, he said, "We bought this yach
together, so I'm still an owner. Therefore, I demand that yo
both leave!"

"I don't think so," Lawrent said.

A few minutes later, five white police cars with flashin
blue lights drove toward the yacht.

"Police?" Jean-Auguste questioned.

In single file, six uniformed policemen ran up the gan
plank.

Lawrent stood up and explained, "You see, Naravine con
fessed to the police about the plot to exploit Djuna's wealt
and the stolen paintings. The list of charges against you an
your violations of the law are endless. It seems you'll be mee
ing up with your friend Bernard in jail. His apartment wa
searched and the authorities found evidence that he forge
some of the artwork. When he was interrogated, in order t
lessen his sentence, he confessed to your involvement as we
as his own."

A policeman approached Jean-Auguste. "Don't touch m
you pig. I'm not going anywhere," he protested, flailing hi
arms at the man. It took three policemen to tackle him to th
deck, throwing him onto his stomach. Two more officers strac
dled him, pinning down his legs and twisting his arms, so h
could be handcuffed. The adolescent boys looked terrified a
they watched the scene. Some were trembling and grippin
the railings of the boat. Once Xavier was arrested and hand
cuffed, the boys acquiesced. And in single file, they all pile
into the police cars. Jean-Auguste was the last to leave th
yacht, as five policemen had to drag him down the gangplan

"Vindictive bitch! I'll make you pay for this," he screame
at me, as the police shoved him into the back of a flashin
police car.

"He'll be going to jail for a long time," Lawrent said, exaling a sigh of relief.

"I do appreciate all that you've done," I said.

Lawrent looked at his watch. "It's my job. Before it gets ο late, I must call a sales agent who can begin to work on elling the boat for you. I hope I'm correct in assuming that's hat you want."

"Yes, that's it exactly. I don't want to have to go near this oat ever again. Could you please excuse me for a moment? must look for something," I said.

"Let me know when you're ready to leave. I promised my ife I'd be home tonight."

I held my breath when I entered our cabin. Empty cocaine als and bottles of wine were scattered on the cocktail table. he bed was unmade, the black satin sheets tousled. Activities at I didn't want to imagine must have gone on in this room. s I searched for the journals, I began opening the closets and cognized Xavier's wardrobe hanging where my clothes had ice been. Some of the contents of my suitcase, my designer esses, were stuffed in the back of the closet. I sorted through e drawers, emptying them and angrily throwing the belonggs across the room. One drawer was filled with women's gerie that belonged to someone else, a much larger person. didn't take long before my persistance paid off. I found the urnals hidden underneath the drawer of bondage accoutrents.

There was a knock at the door. "It's me, Lawrent."

"Come in."

"Did you find what you were looking for?"

"Yes. I'm so relieved," I said, while counting the volumes, d quickly glancing through the warn yellowed pages, seeing the letters and Sylvie's diary passages were still inside.

"The crew is leaving. Is there anything you want to say to em."

"Could you ask them where they stored our luggage? I need suitcase."

"No problem. I'll ask. Oh, by the way, I spoke with the les agent. She said it shouldn't be hard to sell the boat, as s in mint condition. You can call her at your own convennce."

"I will. Thank you again for all your help and excellen work," I told him.

"You're very welcome. I think it will be smooth sailing from now on."

After he left, I heard a scuffling sound coming from the bathroom. Hestitantly, I entered and found my trembling Italian greyhounds locked in the shower. Urgently, I slid open the door; they came bounding out, ecstatically jumping on my legs. I knelt to their level and they covered me with grateful kisses.

"You poor sweet things. Don't worry. I'll take good care of you from now on," I told them, as I cradled a dog under each arm.

TWENTY-EIGHT

Djuna Cortez

stood in the driveway of the home where I had spent most
 my childhood. Nothing had changed in Beverly Hills since
 ad been gone. Beverly Drive was decorated with short and
 ll palm trees: the thin variety towered over fifty feet, and
 anaged to withstand even the roughest of Santa Ana winds.
 ardeners were scattered down the block, mowing lawns, clip-
 ng trees, sweeping, and blowing leaves with noisy machines.
 ur garden continued to be well maintained with lush jaca-
 nda, citrus, and avocado trees. I could have stood there for
 urs; nobody would have cared. One rarely saw those who
 ed inside the mansions of Beverly Hills. Occasionally, nan-
 es dressed in white uniforms could be seen strolling with
 eir employers' infants. This was part of the controlled bliss
 the neighborhood, where people lived for their luxuries and
 ivacy.

The air was dry and warm. The Santa Ana winds had flared
 . I moved under the shade of a lime tree. Temperatures were
 ickly climbing to the mideighties; my eyes were burning
 om the smog. Pausing a few moments, I inhaled the fresh
 ent of a watered lawn. Then, cautiously, I approached the
 20s Spanish Revival–style home. The house had the same

hand-finished white stucco exterior, Moorish arches, and Mex ican tile accents, that I always remembered. Once I rang th bell, it took a few minutes before a maid answered.

"I'm here to see my . . . I mean, I would like to see Emil Cortez, please. I tried to call from the airport, but somethin continues to be wrong with the number. Is he in?" I aske politely.

The Hispanic woman looked perplexed and answered, "En ile Cortez doesn't live here anymore. John Riverton and h wife own this house."

"Do you know where I can find Emile Cortez? I have urge family business to discuss with him and have come all th way from France to see him."

"Please wait a minute," she said, closing the door.

My fatigue from jet lag and this unexpected problem almo made me break down in tears. The maid returned before completely lost my composure.

"You seem like a nice girl. This is where I send his mail she explained, handing me a piece of paper.

I thanked her profusely and staggered back to the palm tre lined street. Stranded with my luggage, I had to trek up Sunset Boulevard, rolling my cases behind me. I was gratef I had packed lightly. My oasis was the notorious pink-an green painted Beverly Hills Hotel, enshrouded in more pal trees and tall banana palms, which spread their leaves over t exterior of the building like gigantic fans. An Eagles song ra through my mind. I did not want to stay more than the wee end. All I desired was to be welcomed there. I was craving tossed cobb salad, an iced tea, and a dip in the Olympic-siz pool.

Memories returned as I walked up the permanent red carp that ran from the carport to the front entrance. Emile used take me to lunch there as a child. I remembered a midg bellboy dressed in a red uniform who stood not much tall than I at the time. He would always greet me. The midget h long since passed away and could never be replaced. Eve time I visit the hotel, I look beside the stone monkey statue where he often stood. I was now a stranger in the hotel; hov ever, it didn't matter. When I approached the concierge des I was treated exceptionally well, unlike some of my exper ences in Europe.

In less than ten minutes, I was given a bright room located near the Polo Lounge at the end of a long green corridor. The room overlooked the gardens and pink bungalows. My dogs would have enjoyed exploring the grounds. I missed them, but felt it best I leave them behind with Nathalie in Loire, who seemed pleased to have them as company. On one hand, this setback, gave me time to order room service, take a shower, and rest in air-conditioning before embarking on another search for Emile.

After lunch, a yellow taxicab drove me along Sunset Boulevard, passing the flashy Sunset Strip with its popular row of nightclubs: the Whiskey, the Roxy, and the Rainbow. I had forgotten about movies and the mystique of Hollywood. Billboards for the latest films and television shows animated the curving street. It didn't take long. We drove into a residential section, crossing Fountain Avenue, where the architecture was unique and varied from each building, ranging from Spanish with terra cotta tiled roofs and stone-paved courtyards, English Tudor, French castles with turrets, and Art Deco. Framed on my left were the Hollywood Hills that altered in color with the mild seasons. Homes were built into every angle of the hilltop, and through the dense smog, looked like a scattering of broken seashells. It must have been a dry month, as the hills were bleached to a faded amber. The taxi suddenly stopped short, throwing me back in my seat.

"This is it on Harper Avenue," the driver announced.

Several times, I checked the address the maid had given me. I was confused. The cab driver kept pointing to a dilapidated apartment building.

"My father couldn't possibly live in such a rundown place," I said to the driver.

"Do you want to get out or not? I don't have all day, miss," the driver said impatiently.

I paid him and got out of the taxi.

Venturing closer to the building, I noticed an apartment window that was covered with cardboard; bed sheets were also used instead of drapes. A foul stench seemed to come from an ivy hedge that lined the side of the building. On one apartment door a sign was painted in nail polish: Don't bother us. Baby sleeping. Keep quiet or else!

A stern-faced old man with a cane noticed me pondering the apartment numbers.

"Do you know if Emile Cortez lives here?" I asked.

He didn't answer me, but pointed his cane to the last apartment facing a Dumpster.

Boldly, I knocked on the door. Emile answered. He had gained some weight and was wearing a gray sweatsuit. I must have awakened him, as his hair was disheveled and his eyes swollen. We stared at one another for several minutes without speaking.

"I doubted you'd find me," he said gruffly as he scratched his temple.

"I went to the house. The housekeeper gave me this address. Did they forward my letter?"

"Yeah," he answered dryly.

"Could I please come in?" I asked.

He nodded and without answering, opened the door for me. I entered a dark, air-conditioned apartment with orange carpeting.

"Why are you living here? What has happened?" I asked.

"After you left, my wife pressured me into a risky franchise that collapsed. It was a bad decision and the partners ended up screwing me out of a lot of money. Before I knew it, Ellen files for divorce and gets a sleazy, ball-breaking Hollywood divorce lawyer. She and that crook of a lawyer took almost everything I had left," he said.

"I'm sorry to hear that. You don't look too well. Are you feeling all right?" I asked.

"After all this time, why should you care?"

"I've always cared, Dad." I swallowed several times after using the word "Dad." Then I seated myself on a butterscotch plaid sofa and said, "Indeed, a year has passed since we last saw each other or even spoke. But, I'd like for us to be able to look at things in a new light."

Emile sat down at the far end of the couch, making sure to keep enough distance between us, and reached for a pack of Benson & Hedges that was on the coffee table.

"When did you start smoking again?" I asked.

"When I lost the house."

"When did the divorce go through?"

"The final papers were signed last week."

"I'm sorry."

Emile replied bitterly, "What have *you* got to be sorry for? You won't have to worry about money for the rest of your life."

"I haven't been as fortunate as you may think. I'm also going through a divorce."

"I had no idea you were even married. You're way too young!" he exclaimed.

"I agree. It was a horrible mistake. I had wanted to invite you to our wedding, but I rationalized that you'd still be too angry. I'm sorry. Do you think you can forgive me?" I asked.

"So, what is this important business you want to talk to me about?" he inquired, as he avoided answering my question.

Before I could answer, he began coughing and said, "I'm just getting over a cold. The doctor tried to encourage me to quit smoking."

"You should."

"But you smoke too. I always knew, even though you hid it from me."

I opened my purse and pulled out a package of nicotine gum. "I haven't had a cigarette in a week. Why don't you take these? I have more," I offered. "I don't like seeing you in such bad shape," I said, placing my hand on his shoulder. He jerked away from me.

"Why should you care?" he asked.

"I've missed you. You're the only family I have."

Emile began coughing again and finally put out his cigarette. "What do you want to tell me?" he asked gruffly.

"Your father kept an extensive journal of his experiences from the age of twenty until he took his own life."

"I'm not interested!" Emile protested.

"He wrote a lot about you and his personal relationships. It would mean a lot to me if you would read them. My responsiblity is to honor his wishes. Joaquím Carlos wanted them published posthumously." I placed a copy of the first volume by his thigh. Abruptly, he pushed it away.

"I don't want to read that *merde!* He never cared about me. I'm sure he said terrible things."

"That's not true. He was devastated when your communication ended."

"Do you think anything matters anymore? The bastard's dead. I don't have a reputation left in business to tarnish anyway. I don't have anything, so I don't care what the fuck you publish. Does that answer your question?"

"I understand your anger. But it's important to me that you read them."

"I don't need to be reminded of his philandering, egomaniacal ways or his selfishness. Are you afraid I'll sue the publisher?" he asked.

"Do I have your consent?"

"I told you I don't give a damn, so go ahead. Now that you've got what you wanted, you can leave. You're just like your mother," he said scornfully.

"What would that be like?"

"You're selfish and self-centered."

I swallowed several times and answered calmly, "Those are the traits that I dislike most in myself and others. I hope to someday overcome them. But, I'm here now, withstanding your insults. I'm not running out that door, even though you're making this quite difficult. Please don't drive me away again."

"You're the one who stayed in Paris."

Emile maintained his guard. It was becoming increasingly difficult to break the wall of ice he had surrounded himself with. Admittedly, I was tempted to run out the door and leave in a huff, yet I persisted at trying to win him over.

"I understand you're hurt and angry. However, I can't accept that you aren't concerned about me or that you can just shut off your feelings. It wasn't fair that you chose to deceive me. I'm not blaming you anymore. What is most important now is that we stop this cycle of resentments that have torn our family apart for generations. I refuse to hold onto grudges for the rest of my life. It's apparent you made mistakes in raising me, so did your father in raising you. Both of you did the best you could. Nobody should be blamed. You would understand everything more if you read the journals. I can imagine it was terribly difficult time for you being a single parent so soon after returning from Vietnam. I would never want to have been in your place."

"You have no concept how difficult it was," Emile affirmed, while reaching for my hand. Holding my hand firmly in his, he forced back his private anguish.

That moment, I wanted him to finally speak about his war experience or how he felt when my mother left, yet he remained silent. It was foolish of me to think I could penetrate these delicate subjects, like the memories of his childhood, which continued to hit a raw nerve in him, being too painful for discussion.

"You give me so little of yourself," I said.

"I'm well aware of my weaknesses. But I am pleased you're here," he replied, with a sudden warmth to his voice.

"Me too," I added, while looking around the room. "How long have you been living here?"

"You mean in this dump? Much too long. I hate it. This building stinks like vomit. They never clean these filthy halls or repair anything. The landlord is known as the slumlord of West Hollywood. He gets hookers and drug addicts as tenants, so he can get free dope and sex. This place is a hellhole, but it's rent-controlled and the cheapest rent around without moving to Koreatown. If something died in those hedges we'd never know it," he commented, while pointing out the window. "Can I get you something to drink?"

"Coffee. Please."

"I have instant."

"Oh? Then instant will have to do."

"You must have gotten spoiled by the Paris cafés. The coffee over there is quite good. I'm sorry I no longer have an espresso machine. You can guess who has it."

Emile got up and walked over to his small kitchen and began boiling water in a sauce pan.

"How did you like France?"

"I love France, but I won't be living there anymore. I need to find another home."

"Where will you be going?" he asked, as he pensively turned his head away and looked out his kitchen window to a view of an overflowing garbage bin.

"I don't know yet. My first priority is to end this silence between us."

"You've already done that," he said, "So, how long are you in L.A. for?"

"Only a few days. It feels strange being back. I saw myself as this free-spirited expatriate living in France for the rest of my life. If I ever did come back, I wanted something to show for the time I spent away. I haven't accomplished anything of my own. I feel like a failure."

"I disagree. I'm impressed with how much you've grown up, matured."

The praise shocked me. He rarely said anything complimentary. "Really?" I asked standing up.

"I was wrong to call you selfish. You've become a caring person. Your husband's a fool for letting you go."

Walking toward him, I said, "The marriage was a bit more complicated than that. I don't want to go into it; however, I was the foolish one."

"Do you still take cream and two lumps of sugar in your coffee?"

"Yes, thank you."

He handed me a full mug.

"You know, I remember when you were the first person to wake up in the house on Sunday mornings. I would hear your slippers echo on the stairs and get so excited to get up with you. I'd watch you make your strong coffee and help you fry eggs. Those were the best egg sandwiches. I don't know what you did to them. Do you remember?" I asked.

"Yes, you were so cute. You still don't look so bad," Emile admitted, smiling endearingly at me.

Before either of us could say anything more, an aspiring rock musician began practicing his drums, which set off a baby who began wailing in a nearby apartment. Emile glanced at his watch.

"I should have guessed. It's after five and all the degenerates are home."

"Can I take you to dinner? We can go wherever you like. I think you could use a change of ambiance," I offered.

"Yes. You can say that again! Let me shower and change. I promise I'll hurry. I know how you hate to be kept waiting."

"It's okay. Please take all the time you need."

When Emile left for the bedroom, I looked around the sparse apartment. Most of the furnishings were outdated Salvation Army donations. The main colors were avocado green and bright orange. I remembered the beautiful Swedish furniture and collectibles he once had. Instead of American Impressionists on the walls, he now had dime-store paintings of clowns and flowers. I looked in his refrigerator. Inside were several six packs of beer, hot dogs, a dozen eggs, and some Velveeta cheese. He had one mug in his cabinet, one plate, and one bowl. Emile's conversion to American tastes astounded me, but I was more upset to see his level of poverty.

It hadn't taken Emile long to shower and change into a black suit and an olive tie.

"Shall I call somewhere to make a reservation?" I asked.

"We're going to Lawry's. We don't need one. I'll drive. I still have the old Mercedes."

"Is that where you really want to go?" I asked.

"I'm in the mood for some beef. It was your favorite restaurant when you were a kid. It's very close to here."

I didn't remind him that I preferred not eating red meat, so I refrained from voicing my opinion. Perhaps, two years ago, I would have adamantly protested. This time, I wanted to learn to be agreeable, and above all else, I needed to please him.

Emile's eyes became animated when the waitress carved a large portion of prime rib for him. He smiled at me and seemed grateful to be back in a restaurant he had once frequented.

"This is a fine meal. How's your meat?" he asked.

"Good," I lied.

"I think it's a lot of *merde* what they're telling us about red meat. We're carnivores by nature. We need this kind of protein. Would you select a nice red wine?"

"I don't want to drink."

"You must. Come on. I want to relax. They have some French wines here. Will you recommend one? You must have learned about some good wines."

"I'm not sure what they have here. Actually, California wines can be quite comparable. I've heard the Hess Collection's Cabernet Sauvignon is full bodied and mellow. As for French wines, a Cru would be nice, like a Beaujolais Saint Amour Red. It's still too early for a Beaujolais Nouveau, which is much lighter and fruitier."

Emile ordered the Hess Cabernet Sauvignon. I had thought about turning my glass upside down, but at the last minute, gave in to taste the rich bouquet.

"I'm impressed how you've learned quite a bit about wines. How's the business going?"

"Nothing is happening with the winery. There is so much to learn. I've been trying to read up on the business, but I'm still considering selling it," I explained.

"All of a sudden you look sad. What's wrong?" he asked.

"It was beautiful there."

"Yes," he agreed.

"All this talk about wines reminds me of my ex-husband," I said, forcing a smile, "I just want the pain and disappointment to end."

"You must have loved him very much."

"I was a terrible judge of character. I hate feeling so used and stupid."

"I feel the same way. That little bitch turned on me like a viper. I couldn't help but think she'd never loved me and had been waiting for the day to eat me alive. I've been feeling worthless ever since."

"You shouldn't punish yourself like that," I advised.

Emile looked down at the table and shook his head.

"I've sunk so far down, I feel as though I'm drowning in the La Brea Tarpits. I'm practically fossilized. It's too late. My life will be over soon."

"Dad, don't say that! It's never too late. There are too many good things you have going for you."

"Like what?"

"You're a fine businessman. You always had an eye for investing. I'll help you get back on your feet. You have to start over again."

He reached for my hand and grasped my palm tightly.

"I don't think I can. I'm sick of the investment business

and the stock market fluctuations. It's nice of you to say that. You've turned out so well. I must have done something right."

I smiled and bashfully lowered my head.

Emile continued, "I should have set you free earlier. You would have learned even more on your own. You're much stronger than me."

"I am not!"

"Why don't you stay with me? You won't have to pay for a hotel. I'll take the couch," he suggested.

"I appreciate your offer, but I'm all settled in my room. It's very comfortable."

The truth was, I didn't want him to know that I was still recovering from injuries and needed extra rest. My bruises had healed, but the fractures were taking longer.

After dinner, Emile drove me back to the Beverly Hills Hotel. When I got out, he stood by his car door and glanced back at me with a tender expression I hadn't seen since early childhood.

"Please keep in touch," he said.

"I promise I will. Please give me a minute. I have something in my room I have to give you."

"I'll come with you," he offered.

He waited outside my room. I didn't want to be long and quickly returned.

"These are the rest of the copies I've made of the journals. The manuscript weighs more than ten pounds," I said, straining while I handed him the heavy box. My ribs were beginning to ache. It had been easier rolling them in my suitcase.

Emile didn't comment, but took what I gave him and wished me a good night. A surprise was waiting for him if he decided to open the box. On the top he would find an envelope which contained a check that was made out to him in the amount of five thousand dollars. I only hoped he would be tempted to read the journals and not discard them.

I stayed on a few days in the hotel to catch up on rest. Every morning, I woke to a room flooded with sunshine. Finally, on my third day, I was determined to take a swim. As I traversed the gardens to get to the pool, the air was warm and fragrant with honeysuckle; hummingbirds were happily feeding on flowers. I couldn't swim more than one lap without pain, so I got out and returned to my room. After a hot shower, I ordered room service. While I was having breakfast on my terrace, the phone began to ring. At first, I panicked and I feared it could be Jean-Auguste who had somehow tracked me down. That was one voice I hoped never to hear again. The reality was only a few people knew where I was staying in Los Angeles and all of them were harmless. I got up slowly and answered on the fifth ring.

"It's me, Pascal. I have great news," she announced.

"What is it?"

"I promised you I'd take good care of the journals while you're away, so I took it upon myself to show them to my editor. I hope you're not upset with me."

"I guess not."

"The good news is, my publisher wants to make an offer. You need to come back to Paris as soon as possible. They want to meet with you in person. There is room to negotiate the deal. We'll talk more about it when you get back.

"That's great news," I said.

"That's not all. I told my editor about my idea for the art book and she's very interested. Is everything going well with Emile? Do you think the publication will pose a problem for him?"

"Everything is fine. He's cooperating nicely. I'll try to fly out as soon as I can."

"I can collect you at the airport."

"You don't have to. I'll just call you when I get back into the city."

I saw Emile again before my departure. He insisted on driving me to LAX and waiting with me in the ambassadors' club. We sat side by side on a sofa, facing a window where we could watch the planes taking off and landing. It was noisy in the lounge. A bartender was blending cocktails. We spoke between the pauses of drink orders, airport announcements, rumbling airplane engines, and screeching brakes.

"I read some of the journals. Do you need them back?" he asked.

"They're your copies. I made them for you. Please keep them."

He reached for my hand and commented, "Isn't it strange how you think you know someone, but you haven't a clue as to what their dreams and sentiments are?"

"Yes, I know exactly what you mean." I paused for a moment and then continued, "This may be the wrong question for me to ask. No, forget it."

"What is it?" he asked, moving closer.

"I liked to know if . . . well, what I mean is . . . it doesn't matter."

"I'm sure it does, otherwise you wouldn't bring it up. Please go on. Don't be afraid. I want to know what's on your mind," he insisted.

"Do you know what happened to my mother?"

His voice weakened as he answered, "Three days after she left, her white Thunderbird convertible was found in the Moave desert. The contents of her purse, which included her wallet, driver's license, a scarf, and a pair of sunglasses were found in the car. Her body was never recovered. All these years, I haven't wanted to face the possibility that she could be alive. The hard part is I'm so angry with her that I'd rather she be dead."

"How devastating that must have been for you!"

"Don't kid yourself, it was terrible for you too. A death may have been easier, more final. It was wrong of me not to talk about it. Anyway, this is something I think she may have left for you." He handed me a present wrapped in brown paper.

I clung to the package. "Should I open it now?"

"I would give it some time, if you can. Maybe wait until you settle into your new home."

"Thank you."

My Air France flight was announced. There was more he wanted to say, but some mysteries will always remain in our family, along with the scars that may never heal. It didn't seem important to tell Emile that we had a half brother, Bernard, who was incarcerated, or for me to clarify that I was his sibling and not his daughter. It was impossible to erase the years we spent together, nor would I now want to. I will always know Emile as my father, the man who raised me as best as he could. If he had read Josephine's letters, then he knew of the deception. Perhaps he had known all along. Glancing at him, I swore I could read the bittersweet truth his eyes, but it didn't matter. I hugged him tightly before leaving.

"I love you, *petite poupée*. You'll always be my little girl. I'm proud of you," he said.

"I love you too, Dad."

TWENTY-NINE

Djuna Cortez

I had returned to Paris after my brief visit in Los Angeles. Within three months, I sold the apartment and the yacht. Inheriting a great deal of wealth at an early age taught me that money has little value unless it can be shared. That is why Joaquím Carlos's paintings are now hanging in the Georges Pompidou Center for a spring and summer exhibition, which is timed with the publication of the journals and the art book written by Pascal. In the fall, the exhibition will begin traveling throughout Europe and the United States for two more years. Despite the will, Emile and I both share ownership of the Château Hélianthe d'Or and the winery. For almost a year now, Emile has been residing in Loire. Returning to live in the château came at a perfect time for him, just before his depression became severe. I visit him every few months. The last time I saw him, I was astounded by the changes in him and the property. His mood had completely transformed, leaving him cheerful and affectionate, with a renewed sense of optimism and vitality. Every morning, he began his day with a jog through the vineyards. His diet had changed, as he maintained an emphatic dedication to eating only organically grown fruits, vegetables, and farm-fed animals. In fact, he's foreseeing a return to organic products and produce as a lucrative market, and has begun making some investments. The month I spent with him, I had never seen Emile as enterprising, spending hours surveying the vineyards and the wine production. He completely dedicated himself to the purity of not using pesticides or any chemicals on the grapes. In addition, he had his hands in several other endeavors. The job that he seemed to thrive the most on was completely his own concept: the château was converted into a bed and breakfast.

As a result of the events that had transpired in the last year, the Château Hélianthe d'Or had become quite famous in its own right. Jean-Auguste helped make this happen, not only through some of the clients he had procured, but also through his trial and that of Bernard's, which became one of the most popular in France. Every day, the progress of the case made the newspapers and returned the public's interest and curiosity to Joaquím Carlos's art work and the Château Hélianthe d'Or. The Château de Triomphe is still one of our competitors and occasionally Emile or I will accidently run into Madame de Briard when we're out shopping in the village. When we do, we are of course met by her cold and vicious stare. In addition to our disdain for her, most of the town seems to be in accordance with us. From what I understand, her wine sales have been plummeting. And nobody wants to attend her parties anymore.

On the other hand, our business continues to flourish. The profits are better than ever. Furthermore, to attract more people to the château, I decided to set up an art museum inside the winery. Therefore, while every stage of the winemaking process is taking place, a beautiful display of the art collection I've inherited can be viewed. Visitors can taste the wines and enjoy the paintings at the same time. Once the traveling exhibition of Joaquím Carlos's work is completed, his paintings will return to be on permanent display in the museum, which is dedicated to and named after him.

Tourists now flock daily to stay in the château or just view the art and taste the wines. The rooms are already booked solid from April through October. Business is lucrative; in the winery gift shop, we are constantly selling cases of wine, posters, art memorabilia, the published journals, and Pascal's fiction poetry, and art book. A kind and efficient staff works under Emile, including Nathalie and her mother. Emile also seems to enjoy Nathalie's little boy, who likes to follow him around the vineyards.

⌒

Looking back now, it's hard to believe I no longer live in Europe. There was a time when I thought I would spend the rest of my life in France. I try not to think about Jean-Auguste and Bernard rotting away in prison. Today I'm able to arrest my anger and forgive them for their greed and selfishness. In my opinion, hatred only impedes creativity.

The day I moved into my new apartment, I decided it was time to celebrate a new beginning in my life and open the gift my father had given me. Eagerly, I ripped apart the plain brown wrapping. The present included two books. One was *The Feminine Mystique* and the other *The Second Sex*. Women's issues had never interested me before. Yet, when I held these heavy books in my hand, intuitively, I knew they were meant for me. At the same time, I felt that my mother was indeed alive. Perhaps, one day, I would meet her again.

I can't regret that I hardly knew her, or all of the guidance I had lacked, as all of my experiences have made me into what I am today. After my divorce, I never thought I would find a place to call home, but I have. It's nice to set down roots, at least for a while.

Although I stand alone, I'm not lonely. Another metropolis has captivated me. I must be a city person at heart. I never imagined myself living where I do now. I had foreseen myself residing in Madrid or Barcelona. However, this move, like my one to Paris, was completely unexpected. It happened when I took Pascal up on her invitation. New York City has become my permanent residence.

From the terrace of my Manhattan apartment, I hear activity: the blowing and spinning of the air-conditioning fans on the rooftops of buildings, speeding cars, aggressive honking, sirens, and airplanes flying overhead. The energy is contagious, constantly bubbling, erupting, and transforming. This city

makes me feel effervescent, boldly alive, and alert, even on a
Monday morning. The Hot and Crusty bakery downstairs is
baking breakfast pastries; the sweet fragrance of apple turn-
overs is wafting all the way up to the eighteenth floor of my
apartment on West Sixty-third Street.

It's the middle of July, the morning air is fresh and invit-
ingly warm. There is a gentle breeze, but it's not invasive.
This morning, like most of the others, I couldn't wait to rise
at dawn so I could watch the sun begin highlighting the tops
of the tallest skyscrapers, while the energy of the city begins
to percolate. Pascal lives across the street. I find myself content
in New York, in my two-bedroom penthouse, where one bright
room is set up as an art studio. Joaquím Carlos was unique
because of his vision and obsessive determination to paint
women. I may never become a professional artist or even find
a subject that captures me to such a degree, yet I can honestly
say I'm content with painting for myself, never having to show
my work to anyone if I so choose. In the meantime, I'm taking
a variety of classes: Renaissance painting, a Martha Graham
dance class, beginning Italian, and Buddhist philosophy. These
centers and schools are all within walking distance of my
apartment. Finally, I am allowing myself to be an amateur, a
novice, to relax and not have to prove anything, to make
plenty of mistakes, and most of all to enjoy the learning process, not knowing where it will eventually take me. Every
situation I had taken on in the past, especially, when I was
devoted to my marriage, I tried always to please others and
within me created an expectation of perfection. Most of all
living in Paris had become my education in art, which continues to be an integral part of my life. Each day, I try to remind
myself to abandon judgment and remember something Joaquím Carlos wrote, which I agree with: "Art is as important
as having air to breathe, and colors will never betray me."

In New York City, I enjoy the spontaneity of every day.
European influences are all around me, from the museums and
art galleries to the restaurants. In my neighborhood alone there
are five French bistros. Like Paris, human contact is everywhere and cannot be avoided. For now, I have no desire to
live anywhere else.

All my experiences in Europe and my ultimate purpose became clear to me one afternoon in Greenwich Village. I was wandering through a weekend street fair in Washington Square Park, where tables were set up with everything I could possibly imagine. After browsing through sections with books, clothing, jewelry, and crafts, I gravitated to a table filled with colorful oil paintings. In this informal and friendly atmosphere, it was easy to enter into a conversation with someone selling their work or someone admiring the same items. Two empty chairs sat behind the table with the artwork. The artist must have temporarily stepped away. While I was carefully admiring the miniature landscapes, I felt a light tap on my shoulder and turned around. A man with long strawberry-blond hair and a rather Bohemian style of dress said, "Hi, Djuna. Remember me? Rudi Lasalle, from your art class."

"I don't believe it! What are you doing here?"

"I live here. And you?"

"So do I. How are you?"

Before he could answer, a man in his late twenties, returned to the table and sat down in one of the chairs.

"Let me introduce you. Alessandro, this is Djuna. We knew each other briefly in Paris. How long has it been?"

"Two years," I answered.

"You look great, exactly the same," Rudi said. He glanced at his watch. "My God, I'm going to have to get going in a few minutes."

"Is this your work?" I asked.

Alessandro confidently answered for him, "It's mine. Rudi works on a much grander scale."

"I'm glad you're still painting," I said.

"Oh, yes, all the time, but never in the way I would have thought. If I'm not doing commissions, I usually work on Broadway painting sets. In fact, that's where I have to be in thirty minutes." He quickly handed me his card. "Please call me and we'll have dinner. I don't live far from the park. It was really nice running into you again. I always wondered what had happened to you."

I waved to Rudi as he rushed off and then turned back to look at Alessandro's art work. Each piece was only five inches tall and was painted on a cutting from a brown paper bag.

"These are really good. They remind me of the South of France," I remarked.

"Actually, they're Palma. I spent a lot of time on the island of Mallorca," he said with a faint Swedish accent.

"Where are you from?" I asked.

"I was born in Argentina, but mostly raised in Stockholm. I was in Spain two summers ago. That's when I painted these."

"I was also in Spain two years ago," I said picking up one painting. "Why are you painting on grocery store bags?" I asked.

He swallowed and politely answered, "My funds are limited. I live in a very small studio, where I don't have much space."

As we spoke, it began to rain. It was a humid summer rainstorm, that erupted out of nowhere. I offered to help him put away his work.

"Can I buy you a cup of coffee?" I asked.

"I'd like that," Alessandro answered.

After we put his collection into a black leather portfolio, we rushed into a nearby café before we were completely drenched. The interior of the place had a Moroccan theme and was playing belly-dancing music. We found a table by the window and ordered two coffees.

"You're very talented," I told him. "Please don't think I'm rude, but how do you survive as a painter?"

"What do you mean? There are different levels of survival. There's spiritual, emotional, intellectual, and financial," he answered.

"Let's start with the financial," I asked.

"Are you not interested in the others?" he questioned.

"I am interested in everything you have to say," I replied.

"To answer your question, I have to take odd jobs to pay my rent. I walk pampered uptown dogs and give Tango lessons to lonely women."

"That certainly sounds like an industrious way to earn a living," I commented.

"I'd like to finish answering your question," he responded in a serious, reflective tone. "My life's priority is to try to exist on a purely spiritual level. That's where I find inspiration. I study Eastern philosophy: Zen Buddhism, Taoism, Yoga,

Hinduism, and just about anything I can read on mysticism. When I do this the art just flows out of me."

"You would like Los Angeles," I said.

"I've been to L.A. The weather is beautiful there, but it's too slow-paced for me. I prefer the excitement of New York. I also like to have a vast selection of museums and galleries I can walk to. I don't feel isolated here, even though I live alone with my frogs."

"You have pet frogs!"

"My tree frog and Australian water frogs can be quite entertaining. You should see them sometime. My tree frog likes to sit on the bed with me and watch soap operas."

I laughed. "Getting back to what I want to discuss with you, I envision your landscapes on large canvases," I said fervently, reaching for his portfolio, which he opened up for me and begain taking out drawings I hadn't seen before.

"In your landscapes, I see an eccletic, Impressionist influence from Les Nabis, which is a combination of Vuillard, Bonnard, and Gauguin's work. However, in your figure paintings, I see a more contempory Neo-Expressionist appeal, similar to Francesco Clemente."

"I admire Clemente's work a great deal. His paintings are very popular. Do you really see that in my work?" he asked.

"I think you have the potential to be very successful," I enthusiastically affirmed. "I'm sure your work would be well received by the public, commanding high prices if you painted on canvas, especially large ones. I'd like to also see you paint on wood, maybe some triptych panels for your landscapes."

"I can barely afford what I'm doing now," he said, his voice dropping and losing all animation.

Leaning forward in my chair, I asked, "Do you know of a center where you can take free art lessons and paint with all your materials provided? There would also be art history lectures, poetry and fiction readings with music—sort of a return to the Renaissance."

"I don't think a place like that exists around here. There's the Dia Art Foundation, but I'm not sure they have everything you've mentioned. That would be wonderful. I've been wanting to take classes. I never had the opportunity to attend art school. Are you an art dealer?" he asked.

"Yes," I answered, surprising myself. "I think we might have a bright future together. I need to get working on this immediately, so please excuse me."

"It's still raining out," Alessandro warned.

"It doesn't matter. I have a lot to do. It was very nice meeting you. Please give me your phone number, so I can contact you soon."

"It was a pleasure meeting you," he said appreciatively, while writing down his number.

Once I was outside, I knew exactly where I needed to go. I tried to hail a cab, but was unsuccessful, as the taxis were changing shifts. Giving up, in the pouring rain, with my umbrella flipping inside out, I walked to West Twenty-second Street. I had gone to the Dia, a month ago, and remembered seeing some lease signs for vacant warehouses nearby. I walked past the museum and found a warehouse for rent at the end of the block. Taking the chance that I might get lucky, I wrote down the phone number. Unfortunately, the museum didn't have a public phone, so I had to race back up the block in the rain. I was able to use a phone in a Chinese restaurant. An hour later, I met the landlord back at the building.

A wave of inspiration came to me, as I entered the vacant six-story warehouse. The top floor was available for rent and had ten colossal rooms filled with tall windows, some from floor to ceiling. The main room was the length of my yacht with doors that opened onto the roof, which was nearly the size of an athletic field. The landlord left me alone outside. The sky was clearing and there was a view of the sparkling Hudson River and New Jersey. My vision for this warehouse became clearer. These rooms needed to be filled with dedicated and talented artists, teachers, historians, and lecturers. There would be art shows and charity benefits. However, the emphasis would be for artists without funds, like Alessandro, to be able to study and display their work.

"What do you think?" the landlord asked, returning outside.

"I'll take it. Let me give you a deposit. I assume the rent is what we discussed on the telephone."

"Gosh, miss, I thought you were fooling me. You look too young to have that kind of money."

I smiled and pulled my checkbook from my purse. As I

wrote out the check, I didn't feel nervous, like I usually do when I write a check for an enormous amount. Instead, I felt invincible, protected—as though there was some sort of positive force behind my will, stronger than myself, pushing me to do this. I didn't have a single doubt or reservation about investing my time and financial resources into this creative center.

That night, I dreamed about Paris. Quite often, my dreams are in French and usually in black and white. However, this last one was in soft, muted colors, as if filmed through an oiled gauze. I was seated in a café on boulevard Saint-Germain. There was a mahogany bar built into the length of the room. Bottles of Pernod were decorating a glass shelf. I sat alone at a table beside a window, waiting for someone, I didn't know who. All I knew was that it was an important rendezvous, possibly romantic, but I was uncertain. As I waited, I anxiously stirred a teaspoon in my café au lait. When I looked up, standing at the door was a dramatically handsome man. He was tall and slender with coal-black hair and dark, vivacious eyes. I knew that he had to be the Surrealist painter Joaquím Carlos Cortez—my father—and he was everything I had imagined him to be, and more. He glided toward me. When he approached my table, he took hold of a chair, turning it around so that he could straddle it and rest his elbows on the back. His movements were flexible, suave, confident. In the dream, he looked to be around thirty-five years old, a time when youth and maturity are perfectly blended in one's features. For a few minutes, we didn't say anything. Our focus was on the deluge outside, shimmering water droplets running down the glass window. The entire café was silent; not even the waiters were making noise. I reached out to touch him; he was transparent, just like the image of ghosts portrayed in films. My hand moved through his arm, unable to grasp hold of him. He began speaking and said in a deep soothing voice: "My greatest love will always be Paris. I was young and impressionable like you when I first came to the City of Light. For me, it was an education beyond all comparison, far surpassing what one can learn from books. I learned about art, love, and transformation. Lovers will come and go. Paintings I've also had to part with. What is this human condition that we all share. Perhaps everything is in the mind—everything becoming memory, as at each moment time passes, becoming our history. Close your eyes, my dear child, and listen, listen to your remembrances of Paris. There will always be the delicate sound of the wind rustling through the chestnut and maple trees in the Luxembourg gardens. Try to recollect your favorite mythological statues from the parks and the Louvre, or recall the fragrance of rain soaking the cobblestone streets of Montmartre and the lingering taste of a refreshing pastis on a hot summer afternoon. Learn to treasure your impressions. These memories will bring you revelations of everlasting tranquility, as they've done for me. You can find beauty and grace in the simplicity of daily existence: plums positioned in a fruit bowl, a burnished leaf floating in a sudden gust of wind, or a Siamese cat sleeping in a lighted windowsill. You may find it in silence, in absolute stillness, the harmony of your breath. Art is about perception more than form or color. Find your own vision, even if you never paint. You will discover that once you've lived in Paris, your potential is infinite; the passion remains for Paris never leaves you."